The noise came again, this time with a feeble cry. That was no fox! That was a human being. She tensed. Whoever was there, they could go away. She wasn't drawing the bolt at the dead of night to a mortal soul.

The sound persisted; a hand was struggling with the heavy iron knocker, accompanied by desperate thumpings on the wood as the cry rose to a heart-rending wail. Kate jerked awake, alert, tumbling out of bed when the feeble cry became stronger.

'*Gran! GRAN!*'

The old woman stumbled across the room, snatched at the bolt and caught Sarah as she fell across the threshold. One glance was enough. The torn and earth-stained clothes, the half-stripped body, the signs of brutality — all told their damnable story.

Rona Randall hails from Cheshire, where, as a schoolgirl, she won a three-year art scholarship. A family move to London prevented her from taking this up. Submitting to a secretarial training, she battled her way into the theatre, with minimal success, but helping a renowned actress to edit a theatre magazine led to a job on a prominent monthly. She became a highly successful journalist, short-story writer, non-fiction author and novelist. *The Tower Room* is her fourth novel set in the Potteries. She has one son and two grown-up grand-children and lives in Kent.

By Rona Randall

Non-fiction
Jordan and the Holy land (*Foreword by
King Hussein of Jordan*)
The Model Wife, Nineteenth-century Style
Writing Popular Fiction

Some fiction titles
Curtain Call
The Ladies of Hanover Square
The Mating Dance
Dragonmede
The Watchman's Stone
Glenrannoch
The Frozen Ceiling
The Arrogant Duke

The Potteries series
The Drayton Legacy
The Potter's Niece
The Rival Potters
The Tower Room

The Tower Room

Rona Randall

ORION

An Orion paperback

First published in Great Britain in 2001
by Orion
This paperback edition published in 2001
by Orion Books Ltd,
Orion House, 5 Upper St Martin's Lane,
London WC2H 9EA

A CIP catalogue record for this book is available
from the British Library.

ISBN 0 75284 420 2

Typeset by Deltatype Ltd, Birkenhead, Merseyside

Printed and bound in Great Britain by
Clays Ltd, St Ives plc

One

Complacency sat on Cynthia Frenshaw's elegant shoulders. If she'd been a cat, she would have purred. Young, lovely to look at, wife of a leading pottery tycoon and mistress of his inherited estate of Dunmore Park and the ancient pile which was still known as Dunmore Abbey – she had done well for herself and would continue to.

Occasionally she was honest enough to acknowledge that she owed much of it to her father, though she took the greatest credit for herself; her looks, her alluring (and useful) body, her intelligence, her early desire to escape from the background into which she had been born – all had been responsible for her marrying Daniel Frenshaw and stepping into the moneyed ranks of Staffordshire's industrial society. The fact that her father's ambitons had coincided with her own had also been useful, especially when she had needed help out of a tricky situation.

When it was over all he had said was, 'Put it behind you, girl. You'll marry well, I'll see to that, and then you'll forget the whole thing.'

'But will you, Dad?'

'I already have.'

'I doubt if Ma ever will.'

His bulky shoulders had shrugged, dismissing anyone so unimportant as her mother, whom Cynthia had since learned to call Mamma. The costly Droitwich finishing school, to which Alfred Collard then chose to send his daughter, had rid her vocabulary of working-class usage although, despite his own climb in the Nottingham lace industry and his ultimate ownership of a house in Wollaton Park (now eclipsed by a stately home in Rutland, the Wollaton residence being donated to the wife who had failed to keep up with him socially) his own speech was still peppered with flat Midland vowels. Not that he cared about that. The Great War and his astute brain had enabled him to make enough money to buy out his late boss's sons who had entrusted their family lace factory to his care when they were called up. At the end of it he was sitting pretty and they were not.

Neither had he worried about his daughter's unfortunate teenage experience. After all, things like that happened all the time and the best way of dealing with them was to sweep them under the carpet. In her case that had been particularly necessary, the end result being rather worse than expected, so he had dealt with that too.

'And now don't think about it, lass. Don't look back. Look forward.'

This she did and continued to, except on rare duty visits to her mother when the woman's resigned eyes were an uncomfortable reminder. For this reason Cynthia combined the visits with couturière appointments in Nottingham; an excellent excuse to leave early, and an excellent opportunity to order gowns as stylish as any from London or Paris. Ever since the importation of French lace machines from Calais and male operators to use them, men who either married or mated with the local women, a French touch had grown and flourished in that provincial town. Naturally, Cynthia let Staffordshire friends believe that she dealt exclusively with London and Parisian fashion houses.

It was annoying that memories of her early life should enter her head just when she was gazing out on Dunmore's sweeping acres and relishing her present situation. On days when she wasn't involved with social affairs or matters to do with the estate, on which she kept an eye with all her father's astuteness, she would sit by her bedroom window around the time when Bruce, her brother-in-law, would be likely to drive across the park on his way home from the Frenshaw potbank. She knew which route he would take – the western drive running close to the main part of the abbey occupied by herself and Daniel – choosing it deliberately so that he could catch a glimpse of her.

It was a well-established pattern to which she looked forward. She knew he would glance up expectantly, smiling that half-smile which implied so much and promised more. In return, she would give the merest nod, but he knew what lay behind it – the promise, the desire, the impatience – then on he would go to his own roomy apartment on the ground floor of the east tower where he lived his own life in his own way. The rest of that tower was unused; even the empty room at the top which, besides having a door opening on to the tower stairs, had another giving direct access to the abbey. This Bruce kept locked. It was wiser to use

3

the main tower door at ground level, tucked away at the side and less detectable.

Cynthia had no doubt he would be on time. Daniel, of course, would be late, even though he was now chauffeured to and from the potbank, due to the tiresome relic of a war-battered leg which he dismissed as a bloody nuisance and was determined to master. And, no doubt, he would, being the stubborn man he was. No one had expected him to be able to drive again, but within weeks of his discharge from hospital he had bought a two-seater Austin to which he attached a self-designed, self-help gear device which enabled him to. With this he practised within the confines of Dunmore's vast park. Cynthia only hoped that the scars would disappear as rapidly as his determination grew – wounds were such distasteful things for sensitive people like herself to look upon. A room off their bedroom made a convenient boudoir in which to prepare for bed and so avoid seeing him undress. Once in bed the scars were unseen and his manhood in no way marred.

But the real reason for Daniel returning home later than his brother was his obsession with the Frenshaw potbank. He loved the whole process of pottery-making. 'God knows why,' Bruce often said. 'I can think of more attractive occupations. Still – mustn't grumble. Being in charge of Export and Dispatch keeps me away from all the muck and mess.' And he would laugh his attractive laugh and smile his devastating smile and she would wish she had met the younger brother first, even though she knew her father considered Daniel to be the far better catch.

'*He'll* not waste his time at Aintree or Epsom or Ascot and every other minor racecourse in between.'

Dunmore's stables contained three of Bruce's prized horses and a gentle animal for herself. Cynthia's early years in the less salubrious area of Nottingham, ironically called The Meadows, had not offered a child the luxury of early training in the saddle, but at least she now knew how to look well on a horse and impress the estate workers on her daily rounds. And it was a convenient way of meeting Bruce well away from the abbey.

The brothers differed in every possible way. Daniel had rarely gone out with the hunt even before he was injured, preferring solitary cross-country gallops, whereas Bruce never missed a meet. Daniel also loved motors – in fact, anything mechanical, which was why he was forever trying out new forms of mechanisation at the potbank. 'And a damned waste of money most of them are,' Bruce said frequently. 'He spoils those workers. Frenshaws could get by well enough with a lot of the old methods. Other potteries do.'

'Perhaps that's why he's outstripping them. Anyway, what would you know about it, being only on the executive side?' She was careful to put a teasing note in her voice. 'You wouldn't know what to do with a lump of clay if Daniel offered you a bonus just to try.'

'Well, one thing I would *not* do if I were boss is neglect my wife. I'd down tools on the dot and drive at the double to get home to you. And I'd fuck you so often you'd have no need for other men.'

Despite being well born and public school and university educated, Bruce could be defiantly coarse when he chose to be. It amused him to ape the rough workers' speech. He liked shocking people, and although it amused her she said coldly, 'I thought gentlemen didn't use disgusting words like that.'

'Come off it, sis-in-law. Don't pretend with me.'

He could be disconcerting at times, damn him, but the moments would pass and their sexual awareness would quickly stir again. He was so devilishly handsome; light brown hair flowing back in waves from his forehead and long in his neck, defying the twenties respectable short back and sides; mouth curving sensually, eyes deep blue beneath a well-shaped forehead – unlike Daniel, who paid far less heed to his looks, although when she first met him she was struck by the excellence of his tailoring and found his looks very acceptable. He had the craggy, ill-matched sort of features which should have added up to ugliness, but were fascinating instead.

But now she found them less so. She had become accustomed to so much about Daniel that she took everything about him for granted. And she didn't really mind Bruce's criticism of him because much of what he said she agreed with. Daniel *did* devote too much time to the family industry, although, of course, she had every reason to be glad of that. It was devotion like his and his forefathers' that had brought wealth and renown to the family, and was continuing to do so.

What really did bore her was Daniel's obsession with the history of the place. One of the ancient bottle ovens in the great forecourt bore names of valiant workers from the past; men who had been maimed by fire and accident. And one in particular, George Willcox, whose terrible death he had never forgotten. He still cared about the welfare of old Kate Willcox, George's mother, a woman prematurely aged and too arthritic now to handle clay. She had struggled on in a menial position until Daniel inherited control and immediately provided her with a pension and accommodation in one of the new almshouses which, considered Cynthia, must seem like heaven to her after the shack she had been accustomed to.

Then there was his interest in George's daughter Sarah, now almost fifteen. He often declared she was the image of old Kate when young. Cynthia found that hard to believe for although Sarah Willcox was gauche, all gangling arms and legs and great dark eyes too big for her face, there was a promise of beauty there and the old woman could never have been much to look at. Once Cynthia had even said as much, whereupon Daniel had retorted, 'Don't you believe it. Kate Willcox was beautiful when young. Legend has it that an artist who visited Staffordshire to make studies of the Potteries and the countryside was so struck by her that he painted her portrait.'

'Not in the nude, I hope,' Cynthia had quipped, and changed the subject because she wasn't interested in an old hag like Kate, or in the granddaughter whose widowed mother had wasted no time in marrying again. Many said Mabel Willcox had done well for herself in getting Frenshaws' chief thrower as a husband, but Cynthia wasn't interested enough to speculate on that. All she knew was that Joe Boswell was a handsome hunk of a man, but the kind she had learned to beware of in her early Nottingham days. There had been plenty of such men working the lace looms. Thanks to her father, she had learned to recognise and avoid them. Or so he had thought until her early disaster jerked him into action and set her on to the course he determined for her.

Dear Dad. Dear Papa, she corrected herself hastily. She had fulfilled his every ambition. He had every reason to be as proud of her as she was of herself. And he was always so confident, so reassuring, though he'd been less so when dismissing talk about the Kaiser and war with Germany. 'Scaremongering, that's all it is,' he had insisted. 'Only fools heed the newspapers.'

But he had done well out of the war himself, her clever father. And in the aftermath he had prospered even more until now he was kingpin in Nottingham's lace industry.

Since there was still no sign of Bruce she turned from the window petulantly. Serve him right if he looks for me now and is disappointed, she thought as she crossed to a cheval mirror on the opposite side of the room. The swing of her mid-length grosgrain skirt pleased her, as did the silk-stockinged ankles and high-heeled court shoes below it. The matching grosgrain jacket lay tossed over a chair, the better to display a French-designed blouse of ecru lace in which Bruce always admired her. But he admired whatever she wore. 'With a body like yours, you'd look ravishing even in a sack.'

The thought appeased her. Serenely, she viewed herself. Her features were lovely, her face a delicate oval, her nose delicious, her mouth full and soft. Her naturally blonde hair shone, her skin was flawless. She had learned how to present herself so that whatever she did, wherever she went, whether socialising or officiating at some local event, she was eye-catching.

Satisfied, she returned to her seat beside the window. There was still time to catch a glimpse of Bruce before her husband returned. Daniel never left for home if there was some problem at the potbank. She had even known him to be late through concern for some tiresome worker — folk like the Willcoxes, though heaven knew why he should feel a particular responsibility for *them*. Other workers had problems too. She could see no reason why her husband should take such an interest in people like that old Kate Willcox and her gauche granddaughter. Hadn't he done enough for them already?

Two

Early on the morning of her fifteenth birthday Sarah
Willcox crept downstairs, carrying her heavy lace-up
boots and avoiding the third tread in case its customary
creak rang out like a pistol shot. Even in stockinged feet
the bare treads were cold, but this she endured until
reaching the stone-flagged kitchen. There she lifted the
wooden door latch as quietly as possible, thankful it
wasn't an iron one or that sleeping hulk upstairs, who
seemed to have ears for every sound she made, might
jerk awake and then there would be no escaping him.

After hurriedly lacing her boots, she took bread from
the larder and cut a thick slice, buttering it sparsely even
though butter had not been scarce since Joe Boswell
persuaded her mother to buy the cow called Flossie.
But Sarah's thoughts shied away from any reminder of
poor Flossie. Doing that had become a habit since the
day her stepfather had taken her to see the hired bull
being put to the heifer for the first time.

That day had also been her birthday – her ninth. 'I've
summat to show ye, lass – come 'n' see,' he had said,
smiling and holding out one of his huge hands, and she
had gone with him willingly, anticipating a birthday
treat. Then he had stood with his great hand gripping
the back of her neck, forcing her to watch.

'See that, young Sarah? Know what the bull's doing? Fucking 'er, the way I do your mam and the way I'll mebbe do to you, one o' these days.'

Despite the strength of his hands – he was the strongest thrower at the Frenshaw potbank – she had wrenched free and fled across the yard, hands over her ears to dull the sound of the bull's bellowing and in her memory the indelible picture of a terrified Flossie being forced to submit. Joe Boswell had roared with laughter and shouted something after her which, mercifully, she scarcely heard. And because, at that time, she knew little about the mating habits of man or beast, only that a man and a woman 'loved' each other in bed and babies came as a result, she had never paused until reaching the sanctuary of her box room beneath the eaves. There she had flung herself face down, trying to blot out the memory.

Never would her gentle father have treated her mother so violently! He had been kind and protective toward his womenfolk – Gran, Mam, and herself. Too protective of his little girl, perhaps? More knowledge might have spared her such a shock and she would certainly have understood the sniggering jokes of fellow pupils at the Board School. Many came from outlying farms and were accustomed to animals, others from overcrowded potters' homes in Longton and Stoke, where little had been hidden. But she had been reared as a sheltered only child in a terraced cottage in the centre of Burslem, from where Dad had journeyed to the Frenshaw potbank daily. In that happy home her mother and father had slept in the built-in wall bed in the living room and she in the small loft above. It had been entered through a trapdoor at the top of a ladder, and always carefully closed after she was tucked up for the night, leaving her safe and protected.

In contrast, her room beneath the eaves of this cottage off the main country road to Longton was little bigger than the boot cupboard under the stairs, but at least it was her own private world. Not even Joe Boswell would dare molest her there, with Mabel always within earshot, but Sarah often recalled that tiny loft where Dad used to tuck her up and drop a kiss on her brow and say, 'Sleep well, luv. Sleep well . . .' And then he would lower the trapdoor gently, sometimes thrusting his head back to say, 'I like those drawings you did today, Sarah. You've got talent. It'll see thee well at Frenshaws.' Or if she had been using his annual birthday present of cheap watercolours he would say admiringly, 'The lady paintresses there have class, and you'll be like 'em one day, mark my words.'

Dad had dreamed of his daughter being educated and rising above their station, but it didn't do to think about her father and his dreams. It brought back memories of his terrible death and the instant change in their lives.

Looking round the kitchen now, as she drank a mug of hastily brewed tea and packed a hunk of bread and cheese into her tin box for midday dinner, Sarah saw the signs of neglect which had never been part of the Burslem cottage. Since wedded to Joe Boswell her mother had lost her household pride, but developed an overweening one in herself. Her light brown hair was now a bright and unbecoming red and when Joe took her into Stoke for an evening at the Brewer's Arms she wore powder and rouge and cheap jewellery and gaudy clothes.

Dad would have hated to see her like that. So did Sarah. She vowed to get out of this place, soon as she could.

But that was a pipe dream. She had two more years of her apprenticeship to serve and, until then, her traditional token wage of five shillings a week, less the customary deduction of sixpence for her training, was, as in all potters' homes, handed over for her food and keep. The deduction at source was still customary in the Potteries. Gran had once told her that when Daniel Frenshaw first became master of his family's long established potbank he had tried to overrule this unwritten law, but his action had created such antagonism from other pottery owners that in the end he had to toe the line. Wise potters did not make enemies of their fellow manufacturers in this prospering but cut-throat Staffordshire industry.

The fingers of the kitchen clock pointed to seven. She had to sign on at eight and there were four miles to walk if she failed to catch the workers' bus. On fine, dry mornings she could do it easily, but on wet and windy days, such as this one threatened to be from the look of the sky, she would be hard pressed. What's more, she'd better hurry before Joe Boswell lumbered downstairs, heavy-eyed and demanding his breakfast. If she didn't get away before that she would have to travel with him on his unsaddled horse, his muscular body pressed against her. He always made sure that she never sat behind him, but in front between his legs.

'Safer this way,' he would say if she asked why she couldn't ride behind, and of course her mother would agree with him.

Mabel could see no wrong in the man, so considered Sarah's latest protest to be nothing but ingratitude.

'But I'm not a child now. Look at me, Mam!'

But all Mabel could see was a thin girl, long-legged, black-haired, big-eyed, high-cheekboned, with immature young breasts and a body which could do with a bit of rounding out – but that would come when she matured a bit. Sarah wasn't going to be one of those buxom wenches men had an eye for. Joe had said that many a time.

'You needn't worry about any of them lusty potters at Frenshaws taking a fancy to her. She ain't the kind that catches a man's eye. Not like her mam,' he would finish, slapping his wife's big bottom and letting his hand linger there. 'My, but you're a fine figure of a woman! A pity that girl o' yours don't take after ye, but that she never will. She won't be rolled in the hay afore she's wed, take my word on it. Not even the boss's randy young brother would take a second look at her, and everyone knows Bruce Frenshaw ain't all that fussy.'

Sarah had overheard him say that many times and knew it was only to pull the wool over Mabel's besotted eyes, just as she knew it would be useless to describe to her mother how Boswell pressed himself against her as the horse jolted along to work. Not only would Mabel refuse to believe it, she would call her a liar and dirty-minded into the bargain. 'Joe rides saddleless because he's a fine horseman an' needs no saddle. Look how he wins the bareback riding races at the county fair!'

Once Sarah had dared to say that that was his reason for riding that way to the potbank. 'To show off! That's why he doesn't use the council's bus for workers though it stops little more than a mile away.'

'You been visiting your gran again?' Mabel had demanded instantly. 'That old woman's got an evil tongue. Sees the worst in everybody. I've told ye afore and I'm telling ye again – keep away from Kate Willcox. All she aims to do is poison your mind against me 'n' Joe.'

But nothing would ever stop Sarah from visiting Gran, and after work this evening she would do so again. The old lady would be expecting her. She always looked forward to a visit on her granddaughter's birthday and a cosy little party together.

A final gulp of tea and Sarah was off. No time to inspect herself in the cracked kitchen mirror; no time to check that her mane of black hair was as tidy as it should be; time only to get to the one place where she felt safe these days (apart from Gran's almshouse). Sarah looked forward to her days at the potbank. She felt at home there, like her father before her.

Picking up her tin box, she snatched her cloak from its peg behind the back door, and let herself out silently. Cloaks were provided by the Master Potter for workers who had a distance to walk to the bus stop, from where apprentices travelled free. The thought that Boswell would be livid when he discovered she had dodged him again lent spurs to her feet.

'You've gotta travel to work with me, m' leddy, and none o' this jaunting off on your own. Walking by yourself ain't safe for a girl of your age, any time o' the day. Too many tramps around. Too many down 'n' outs sleeping in ditches. See how I look after your lass, Mabel? Couldn't have a better dad, could she?'

And Mabel would agree and tell Sarah she should be grateful to her stepfather, any lingering maternal love in her eyes eclipsed by a stupid trust in the man she had wed.

Sarah didn't slacken her step until well on to the Longton road. Into her roaming thoughts came the realisation that not only was today her birthday, but the first anniversary of the day she had started her apprenticeship. She wondered if her mother would remember, and if there would be a birthday present waiting for her when she reached home tonight. Last year Mabel had seemed genuinely upset when she realised that she had forgotten. She had promptly given her a whole shilling out of her token wages, and Joe Boswell had told his wife not to be so bloody extravagant.

Sarah made good headway for the first fifteen minutes, but increasing wind and rain made the going difficult as she neared the massive wrought-iron gates of Downley Court, home of the wealthy Petersons who owned extensive lands in these parts, as well as coal mines at Spen Green and valuable clay grounds surrounding them. Centuries of digging had robbed Staffordshire of many clay sources, so the Petersons were 'sitting on hatching eggs', as Gran would say.

Although the old lady was unaware of it, she had a lot of sayings which dated way back. Dad had been surprisingly knowledgeable about such things. 'I were never educated,' he would say when Sarah asked how he came to know so much, 'so I had to teach myself and that meant reading books, any I could lay my hands on. As a boy, Preacher Latimer took an interest in me, even wanted to coach me for a scholarship to Worksop, but 'twere time for me to follow the family footsteps into the potteries. So he gave me free use of his library. "Come any time you can get away from that goddam place," he used to say. Not very reverent was the Reverend.'

At that point her father would smile, a trifle wistfully, Sarah sometimes thought.

The knowledge her father had harvested from books had occasionally made him pounce when Gran used some of her well-known sayings. 'Cheer thysel'!' she would pipe when anyone was feeling down.

Then Dad would announce, 'Fifteenth century, tho' you wouldn't think so. Not much different from "cheer up", as we say now.'

Oh, to have been born with Dad's brains! His hunger for knowledge had been passed on to Sarah, but access to books was something denied her. 'Books!' Mabel would exclaim. 'The pittance Frenshaws gave me when your dad were killed won't stretch to things like that!'

And local Board Schools never gave books as prizes, only certificates with fancy writing on them, which was why her father had left only a battered old atlas, a Bible and a much-thumbed copy of *The Legends of King Arthur*. Sarah had read that over and over again, also certain passages from the Bible which seemed to have some meaning or sounded nice when read aloud – like the thirteenth chapter of First Corinthians.

Now, head down against driving rain, she kept her mind occupied by reciting those sacred verses in her mind. 'And now abideth faith, hope, and charity, but the greatest of these is charity . . .' And charity, Dad had said, was another word for love, so she supposed the Master Potter's handsome wife, who was known to be a very charitable lady, must have a very loving heart indeed.

Letting her thoughts ramble this way prevented Sarah from worrying about the possibility that at this rate of progress Joe Boswell would catch up with her before she reached the bus stop and that if a ditch was handy she would have to leap into it to hide. Anything rather than see her stepfather's face when he spotted her by the roadside. Physical resistance would be no match for his strength when he seized her and dragged her up before him, and from then on she would have to endure unpleasant contact with his body.

The first sound of oncoming hooves made her spring from the road on to the verge. Unluckily, there was no handy ditch so she headed for a tree standing back from the road, a massive oak with a trunk which, please God, would prove wide enough to crouch behind. Wild, untended grass hampered her steps and she reached her goal with barely moments to spare, breathless, heart thumping, clutching at any thought to still her fear . . . a pity the wealthy Petersons weren't responsible for the highway beyond their boundaries . . . folk so rich could surely afford it . . . and, dear God, don't let this wind whip my cloak into view . . . and why couldn't the Petersons provide deep ditches outside their boundaries big enough to hide in?

Sarah didn't dislike the Petersons (how could she, since she had never met them and was never likely to?) but she resented them because all the working poor in these parts resented anyone rich, but greater than resentment was her envy of Annabel, the indulged daughter about whom everyone was talking these days because she had broken with tradition, defying the unwritten law of her world which said that well-bred young ladies didn't go out to work. They went to fine finishing schools for young ladies in Buxton or Droitwich or faraway London, or even to costlier finishing schools in Paris or Switzerland and, when finally polished, came home to lead elegant social lives until they married well and maintained the tradition by bringing up their children to the same pattern.

But now rumour had it that Annabel Peterson had thumbed her nose at all that and declared her intention to study at the Potteries School of Design. It was also rumoured that her parents were opposed to the idea.

'An' no wonder,' Gran had chortled. 'That there place were started way back by the Potteries Mechanics Institution to spread knowledge 'mongst the working classes. They'll make short shrift of a posh young leddy like the Peterson wench. Not that she don't seem very nice, always smiles as she goes by and sometimes stops to pass the time o' day, but the toffs' class an' ours don't mix, nor ever will, so Miss Annabel 'ad best stay in her own.'

With her body pressed against the massive tree trunk and her mind spinning, Sarah waited. It wouldn't be long now. Any second her brutal stepfather would catch up with her. The hoofbeats were nearly level with her hiding place, loud and unmistakable. She had perched on that animal often enough to be familiar with the sound of its tread. A horse's step, like a human being's, was individual and therefore recognisable to those familiar with it. Clutching her cloak about her, Sarah tried to still her fear while waiting for the beast to be reined in – or, please God, pass by. Rigid as a frightened mouse, she waited, trying to calm herself in thought again by focusing on the girl who had startled everyone by announcing that to become a professional painter on porcelain was what she wanted to do more than anything else. Gran was right in saying that everyone knew what that would mean if she got her way. 'She'll be taking a job some needy young woman like my granddaughter could do a damn sight better, that's wot!'

Gran was as proud of Sarah's skill with pencil or brush as her son had been. He had never called her pictures daubs, the way that bastard Boswell did, persuading the besotted Mabel that it wasn't worth trying to get the girl into that so-called 'school of design' to learn porcelain painting. If George had lived, declared Gran, he would have scraped the weekly payments together somehow, had Sarah failed to qualify for a Benefit. And, Kate had continued ferociously, if any potbank owner in Staffordshire dared to employ that Peterson girl as a paintress, she'd shoot the lot of 'em herself, damned if she wouldn't.

Gran could be a real old tigress at times.

But now there was no room in Sarah's mind for anything but this moment because the hoofbeats were loud and strong. The thought of Joe Boswell finding her like this numbed her heart. 'Dear God . . . dear God . . . make him ride past . . . make him ride past . . .' The prayer filled her brain and stilled every nerve in her body.

But now horse and rider were level, the clang of horseshoes indicating a lumbering and difficult gallop in weather like this. Louder still was her stepfather's voice, urging the beast to go faster and hurling obscenities and threats which the long-suffering animal struggled to heed, breath straining. The lash of a whip caused it to stumble and Sarah's heart to quail. Then the hooves steadied and renewed a gallop which grew fainter and fainter as the horse struggled on its way and was finally heard no more.

Relief made Sarah slump to the ground. Joe Boswell was plainly after her, enraged because she had left before him. He would make her suffer for it, first chance he got. I'll face that when it comes, she resolved. Meanwhile I'm staying here until he's well out of sight, even if it means missing the bus and walking all the way. If I'm not in the bus queue he'll go straight to work and corner me when he can. And I'll spend the day dodging him. She relished the thought.

However, it was folly to remain on this damp ground. She rose and removed her cloak, giving it a thorough shake before donning it again, too concerned with restoring her appearance to heed the sound of an engine zooming along the road until it roared by, slowed, stopped and reversed.

'What the devil are you doing, walking to work in weather like this?'

With a mixture of consternation and relief Sarah recognised the voice, also the driver at the wheel of the latest Lanchester. It was Bruce Frenshaw, the Master Potter's younger brother who had taken his hereditary place in the family business some time after Sarah had started her apprenticeship. She had also learned from her grandmother that the elder brother had taken the helm on the sudden death of their father shortly before the war ended in 1918, and that six months before that Daniel Frenshaw had been invalided out of the army. After the horror of the trenches in his youth Daniel had found himself the youngest potbank boss in the industry.

In contrast with Bruce's exuberant personality, the horror of war, followed by early responsibility had turned Daniel into a quiet, reserved man whom everyone respected, but they warmed to young Bruce. Somehow the rumour that he had been sent down from Cambridge because of some serious scrape only made him more human in people's eyes. And his way of greeting folk with a nod and a smile, even pausing for an occasional chat, endeared him even more.

The Master Potter's manner was more distant, as was his fashionable wife's despite all her charitable works. 'The dif'rence there,' said Gran, 'is that the war's made Master Dan kinda withdrawn, while she's bloody high an' mighty. Her forebears were loom operators in Nottingham lace factories until 'er dad got to the top an' managed to buy out the bosses.'

Now the younger Frenshaw's voice echoed in the morning air, amused and compassionate.

'You won't get much shelter there! Come here – or do I have to drag you out?'

Hesitantly, she obeyed. That he should stop to give her a lift was an unexpected gesture. When he held out a hand to help her aboard she hung back, conscious of her wet cloak and streaming hair, for the wind had long since blown back the cowl hood. 'Oh, sir, I couldn't—' she began, but he brushed that aside.

'Of course you can! I know you work at Frenshaws, so in you get.'

In a moment she was in the front passenger seat and he at the wheel. She was awed by the luxury and overcome by shyness. He gave her a sidelong glance and, guessing she had never been in a motor car before, said kindly, 'Don't worry, I won't land us in a ditch. Just relax and enjoy the ride. This is Lanchester's 22 – its newest. It goes like a dream, even at fifty.'

'Fifty what?' she asked, feeling she ought to know and wishing she wasn't revealing such ignorance.

He laughed. 'M.p.h. In other words, miles per hour.'

The thought of anything going so fast astonished her. 'I should think only the birds can fly so fast!'

He smiled. He didn't know who she was, only that she was one of the apprentices he'd seen around the potbank and, now seen at closer quarters, damned attractive – might even be beautiful one day, what with those eyes, and features well worth a closer study. Same with her body. A bit too thin at the moment, but time would tell . . .

She was studying the car appreciatively, her expression awed. She caught his glance and flushed a little. 'You can tell I've never ridden in a motor car,' she said.

'Then you're having your first experience in one of the best. That chap Morris in Oxford will have a job to compete with this.'

She didn't know who 'that chap Morris' was, but decided not to admit it. All she wanted was to listen to the Master Potter's brother and searched her mind for questions so she could hear his cultured voice. He spoke in the way she longed to speak. Neither had she ever seen him at such close quarters before. His features were handsome, more so than the Master Potter's. She could also see the brilliance of his eyes. They sparked with life and enjoyment. She wondered why her legs suddenly seemed weak. What a start to her birthday! When the clear road ahead revealed no sign of Joe

Boswell and no waiting passengers at the bus stop, Sarah's relief was almost physical. Undoubtedly he would have been in time to see the queue board the bus; he would also have been enraged because she was not in it. That would have sent him galloping on to the next stop, convinced she had caught the earlier bus and determined to drag her off it and vent his anger whether people looked on or not. He never cared if fellow potters heard him round on her at work, and to avoid that she resolved to steer clear of him today. With that resolve, relief claimed her, and from sitting bolt upright and self-consciously she sank back into the luxurious passenger seat.

'That's better,' said Bruce Frenshaw, smiling. 'Relax and enjoy yourself.'

She smiled back, and obeyed, lulled by the purr of the car's engine and the comfort of fine upholstery, but gradually the audacity of what she had done overcame her – she had accepted a lift from the boss's brother, and everyone at the potbank would see her drive into the yard with him. There would be whispers and titters in the workshops, and pointed comments when she ate her midday meal alongside fellow apprentices. Even worse, the news would spread through the place, the way all gossip did, inevitably reaching Joe's ears. God help her when he learned how she had actually arrived.

The chief thrower ruled the roost in the throwing shed, for a man in such a position was highly valued in the clay world. Throwing on the wheel demanded skill, and the Frenshaws were envied for having a man as expert as Boswell. He could take a mammoth hunk of clay, kick the treadle which set the throwing wheel spinning, and drop the massive lump dead centre. Then his strong hands would control it as it spun, forcing obedience like a man handling a reluctant beast, then a brief dip into a bowl of water and back to the whirling mass, his great thumb plunging into the middle to start an ever-widening hole. Then up would rise the walls until a perfect pot emerged, sometimes so big that only a man of his size could lean over and place a forearm within its depths.

But those hands could be brutal, too. Workers beneath him were afraid of them. So was Sarah, but not Mabel. 'My magnificent animal!' Sarah had once heard her mother whisper to him, her breathing heavy, her eyes filled with longing.

Animal, yes. Magnificent, no, thought Sarah now as another thought disturbed her. Being conveyed in Bruce Frenshaw's handsome Lanchester would get her ahead of the workers' transport, but those on board would see him go driving by with a girl apprentice beside him. At least one of them would blather about it in the turning shed or the slip house or the wedging workshop or anywhere else within the pottery walls, and not a word would miss Joe Boswell's ears.

Nor would he wait until they were home that night to give her a piece of his mind. He would corner her somewhere in the potbank and do it then, unsparingly – but not within sight or sound of the Master Potter or any supervisor.

Calming herself, she said, 'If you'll kindly put me down, sir, I can catch the next bus. They stop at that junction ahead.'

Despite her attempt to hide anxiety, Bruce Frenshaw sensed and understood it. To a lesser degree, he even shared it for, although it was acceptable for the pottery hierarchy to know every employee individually and to talk with them in the course of the day's work, in his opinion travelling with them or mixing with them socially was another matter.

Giving this girl a lift had been a natural impulse and one he didn't regret but, now he came to think of it, perhaps he had been a little hasty. But what was wrong with that? Impulsive actions were often enjoyable and, after all, how could he let the poor young creature trudge on in the rain?

'Please, sir . . .'

Without answering, he took a left turn that would eventually link up with the Longton Road again, a meandering route but one which finally emerged opposite the Frenshaw potbank. The going was uneven and muddy. Once or twice a jolt flung her against him and when he laughed and steadied her she flushed with embarrassment. When that happened he smiled at her indulgently and she would turn her head away to hide her reaction. Sarah was unaccustomed to men. As an only child she had experienced nothing but paternal gentleness from her father, then only brutality from the man who replaced him. Near contact with a young man of culture was a new experience, and the proximity of Bruce Frenshaw's strong young body made her suddenly self-conscious.

Turning her head away to avoid self-betrayal, she had another passing glimpse of his features, the chin with a slight cleft in it, the mouth inviting, and beneath a pair of well-defined eyebrows, deep-set eyes of a startling blue. She felt hot colour rush to her face. She did not see his amused, indulgent, and faintly satisfied glance.

'Here we are at last . . .'

His words surprised her, for they were some yards from where the rambling cross-country track linked again with the main road. Through a screen of trees ahead she could glimpse the tall necks of Frenshaws' bottle ovens. They all looked alike to the untrained eye, but long ago Sarah had learned the subtle differences in their construction. Much depended on the firings they were individually designed for – earthenware, china, or porcelain and stoneware. The last two demanded the highest temperatures of all and these Sarah always avoided looking at, for one enclosed the high-firing kiln which killed her father.

She had schooled herself into seeing these giant shapes only as a group of smoke-blackened buildings from which delicate cups and saucers and dinner services and jewel-bright vases and bowls miraculously emerged. That was the beautiful side of their function which her father had taught her to appreciate. She yearned to create such things herself and, even more, to be rich enough to own them.

But now the Master Potter's brother was pointing out that she had only a few yards to walk. 'I'm afraid I must head for the garages.' He sounded apologetic, a little embarrassed. 'If you run, you shouldn't get too wet . . .'

Bleakly, she realised that he was dropping her here. He had alighted and was holding the passenger door open for her.

It was silly to feel rejected, even sillier to wonder if he didn't want to be seen with a common little apprentice from the works.

After that first sensitive stab, she pulled herself

together. He was being kind again, wanting to spare her the comments of fellow workers. Such thoughtfulness was typical of so amiable a young man.

Stifling disappointment, she watched him drive away. She still had the friendliness of his farewell smile to remember, and hadn't there been something else in it, a hint, a promise, a wish of some kind? Tremulously happy, she walked on.

Across the main road the massive gates of the potbank stood ajar. Workers were streaming through into the cobbled yard. Head down against the rain, she hurried to join them and came full tilt against Joe Boswell, blocking her path. Her startled eyes looked up into his florid face and saw rage there, and triumph, and the familiar fear shot through her.

Three

He grabbed her shoulder.

'So ye be here at last, miss! And in style, from the look o' things. I saw ye following the Master Potter's brother out o' that side lane. Picked ye up along the way, did he? So that's why ye scarpered so early – to waylay the young gentleman.'

When she tried to break free, the grip tightened.

'Now you listen t' me, miss. Running after lads of your own class be one thing, but ye'll fall flat on your face if y' think ye can do it with your betters – though mebbe ye wanted 'im to take ye face down? Or how about on your back? Did ye have any luck? Some wenches fancy it either way in the morning.'

She blazed, 'Let me go!' But his grip tightened and, uncaring about the passing stream of workers, he lifted his other hand to strike her.

'Stop that, Boswell!'

Neither had seen the Master Potter stepping down from the chauffeur-driven Daimler which was traditionally used by the head of the company. Daniel's father had driven in it daily, and although in appearance it was no longer the grandest motor car in existence it was still impressive, still immaculately cared for, and still ahead of many potential rivals in the current competitive automobile market. Compared with the modest Austin Daniel had purchased to encourage his wounded leg into normal service again, the company Daimler was equal to anything from Buckingham Palace in the eyes of Frenshaw workers, and anything less only on a par with that Crystal Palace place outside London and therefore unworthy of this century-old firm. They respected the Master Potter for still using the Daimler and respected him even more for working the same hours as his employees, arriving dead on time each morning – which, said the expression on his face at this moment, the chief thrower had been unwise to forget.

Daniel Frenshaw's glance then went to Sarah. He saw her hasty curtsy and the proud way in which she tried to pretend that her stepfather's grip had not hurt.

Frenshaw said quietly, 'Get inside, child. You are drenched.'

With a bob, she hurried away. He saw the swinging grace of her step, and watched for a moment. It recalled the beautiful walk of Kate Willcox when young. As for the girl's dark looks and amazing eyes, they, too, were clearly inherited from her grandmother.

Nostalgia gripped him, a longing for the days before Kate's son had been so tragically killed and the rift had sprung up between them. He yearned for the days when he had run to her as a small boy, begging her to show him round the potbank because his father was too busy, and she would wipe her clay-covered hands and take hold of one of his and risk a telling-off from her foreman for neglecting her work. 'I'll make it up and he knows I will,' she would say happily, and off they would go, like mother and child, each enjoying the wonders of the clay world.

But the past was over and it was unwise to let the sight of a young girl recall it. Abruptly, Daniel turned back to his chief thrower, only to find the man had beaten a retreat.

Walking across the cobblestoned yard to his office, Daniel caught a last glimpse of Sarah Willcox as she vanished into the main workshop. Although she reminded him of the young Kate, there was a subtle difference, one he could not put a finger on. Sarah might bear a physical resemblance to her grandmother, but there was an added quality. He had first become aware of it when her mother brought her to be interviewed for an apprenticeship, though she had sat there like a scared kitten, scarcely speaking even when spoken to, big eyes downcast, darting occasional sidelong glances at the display of Frenshaws' finest majolica in his office.

Every month Daniel changed the display to feature the best of their current products. He had been on the point of telling the girl to take a closer look, even to handle them if she wished – that was always a good test of a potential potter, an indication of how much interest they had in the product and whether they had an instinctive feeling for beauty or quality – but somehow he had sensed that the inhibiting presence of her mother would make her shrink further into her shell.

It was customary for the first discussion of an apprenticeship to be conducted only with the parents. So the fathers would spruce themselves up to go before the master potters on behalf of their sons, and mothers would appear in their Sunday best to speak on behalf of their daughters. At these preliminary interviews a date and time would be arranged for their offspring to be seen by the supervisor of the department they were to start in. But Mabel Willcox (Mabel Boswell, as she was by then) took a short cut by bringing her daughter to Daniel Frenshaw's office without any preliminary appointment.

It was as if she said, 'Well, here she is – she's reached school-leaving age and I don't expect to go through any hoops about her apprenticeship. I expect a job for my girl and there'll be no shilly-shallying, because it's owed me – remember?'

Despite Sarah's silence, Daniel had been strongly aware of the girl. Later, he had attributed this to her physical resemblance to her grandmother, the same immense dark eyes, the same glossy black hair, the same bone structure that had been the basis of Kate's beauty.

But there was no beauty in the girl's mother. Daniel had been shocked by the change in the woman. She no longer resembled George Willcox's wife. She had coarsened. She had become Joe Boswell's woman all right. And he could well believe that when the news spread about the provision Frenshaws had made for her, the uncouth Joe had declared it should be a damn sight more.

Studying Mabel Boswell that day, Daniel had reflected that perhaps there had been one merciful thing about George Willcox's death – the man had never seen his wife look like this. Her over-painted face was bold and confident and crowned with a pile of brassy hair. Would such a change in her have come about had Willcox lived? Had the potential always been there, hidden beneath a false veneer – and, if so, for how long would it have remained hidden?

Daniel had accepted shy Sarah Willcox as an apprentice without any further discussion, not merely because he already intended to, but to get rid of her mother.

At ten o'clock the chief thrower was summoned to the Master Potter's office. By that time Joe's confidence had returned because he knew that in the pressure of work any trivial outside incident would have been forgotten.

Squalls between workers could happen in any potbank, often between relatives. It was one of the risks attached to the employment of families; domestic squabbles could be carried to the workplace and wise managements only interfered when necessary. Parents were as entitled to reprimand their children as foremen were entitled to reprimand their workers, so Joe was confident that this morning's incident at the gates was nothing to worry about.

Wiping his thick hands on a fistful of sisal fibre, he decided there must be some other reason for this summons, a new order for a particular type of thrown ware, or a request for his opinion on that new consignment of Cornish china clay – did it throw well, was it as pliable as that load from Devon, did he think it contained too much or too little kaolin? Or perhaps the Master Potter wanted a report on the work of his subordinates, how they were shaping up and did any show the outstanding promise he himself had shown from the start?

Joe Boswell knew how to behave at such moments,

praising subordinates who represented no threat to himself, but less so if he sensed a potential rival – such as that handsome young devil Jacques Le Fevre, whose ancestors had come over from France at the time of the Peninsular War with others who had worked at the Sèvres Manufactury, seeking work in the only English region that could utilize their skills.

The Le Fevres were now as English as anyone, French only in name, speaking with Midland accents and as skilled as their forebears had been. Too skilled for Joe's liking. In Jack Le Fevre he sensed a future contender for his job, but he would take bloody good care the young devil shouldn't get it.

And there was another thing. The arrogant young devil had an eye for that posh young lady from Downley Court, Annabel Peterson, and Boswell wasn't so sure the girl didn't reciprocate. Ever since the Master Potter had invited the Petersons to a tour of the potbank and the girl had watched enthralled as the Frenchie had thrown a delicately spiralling vase which he had the nerve to promise he would put aside as a memento of her visit (and how her hazel eyes had lit up!) she had made many an excuse to drop in to enquire how it was coming along.

'Is it fired yet? What colour will it be?'

'Whatever colour you wish for, Miss Annabel.'

She had asked for blue and the cheeky young sod had produced a dazzling turquoise which the Master Potter then decided to include as one of Frenshaws' regular glazes. That was a feather in the blighter's cap.

Well, if the Master Potter was now wanting a report on the progress of the throwers under him, now was his chance to take the Frenchie down a peg or two. It was easy to damn someone with faint praise, to imply doubt with a slight shrug and a purse of the lips. He had nothing to fear from young Le Fevre.

Confidently, he knocked on the office door.

It was a typical pottery manager's office, the floor covered with glazed tiles made on the premises because glazed wore better than unglazed, leather-covered mahogany desk and leather-seated revolving chair to match, wall racks displaying samples of the latest and best Frenshaw ware, shelves holding ledgers, others with hand-written books of recipes for pottery bodies and colours, wooden cabinets for records of clients, and others housing pattern books of old and new designs.

In one corner was the book-keeper's desk and in another an iron press — a new acquisition for printing copies of the latest products for mailing to existing clients and prospective ones. In this respect, as in most things, Daniel Frenshaw kept well abreast of his rivals.

Joe was surprised when Treadgold, the book-keeper, left the room on his entry, almost as if he had already been prepared to. That surely meant that the Master Potter wanted to discuss something privately, something important. Joe's confidence soared.

A seat was not offered him, but he remained unworried. He could talk just as well standing.

Daniel Frenshaw came straight to the point. 'I want to know why you were threatening George Willcox's daughter this morning.'

Joe's pugilistic jaw dropped. Before he could recover, the Master Potter continued, 'Your fist was raised. Do you make a habit of abusing her?'

'I – I dunno wot y' mean – sir.'

'You should. It's plain enough. Is it your custom to threaten George Willcox's daughter physically?'

Joe didn't like that. Insulting, it was. He answered sullenly, 'She be my stepdaughter. That gives me the right to control her, teach her wot's right and wot's wrong.'

'I am sure her father did that. He was a good man. But you haven't answered my question. Why were you going to strike her?'

'I were doing no such thing, sir. I were joking, play-acting, the way parents do with their childer – teasing – ye know the way it be, sir.'

Daniel Frenshaw didn't. Parenthood was the one thing life had so far denied him, and the one thing he longed for. He still believed a child could bring himself and Cynthia closer.

'It didn't look like play-acting to me. It was too ugly. Differences of opinion between employees I can tolerate. Threat or physical abuse I will not, especially of the young.'

'Sarah be all of fifteen now, so oughta know better.'

'What should she know better?'

'Than to pester they who *be* her betters, sir.'

'And who exactly do you mean by that?'

With feigned embarrassment the man said, 'Master Bruce, sir. The wench had no right to waylay the young gentleman, and so I were telling her. 'Ye'd best be knowing your place, young woman,' I sez, and I meant it too, but she give me a piece of her lip and that made me see red—'

He broke off, disconcerted by the Master Potter's expression of bland surprise, even of amusement.

'You mean your stepdaughter accosted my brother?

I'm sure it was the other way round. No doubt he was passing the time of day and she was polite enough to acknowledge it.' The hint of amusement vanished. 'Simple courtesy deserves neither abuse nor the threat of it.'

'She did more 'n speak to him, sir. She stopped him on the way t' work an' asked for a lift and he, being the gent he is, brought her all the way. Some o' the workers saw them turn off the Longton road afore reaching the next pick-up stop. My guess is she persuaded 'im to. I were right shocked an' wanted to know why she hadn't taken the workers' bus same as everybody else, but all she did was laugh an' say she preferred to be seated alongside Master Bruce an' she were sure he liked it too. Such impudence! She be badly in need of a setdown.'

Daniel Frenshaw was looking amused again.

'Sir – surely ye can't be thinking I should take such lip from a chit of a girl who thinks 'erself as good as 'er betters?'

'I was thinking that, no doubt, my brother did like it and that he was the one to do any "accosting".'

'Ye can take it from me, sir—'

'But even if she did, it deserved no threatened blow. If I had not arrived at that moment it would have been more than a threat. You would have injured her.'

The amusement was gone. The censure was back. Joe Boswell's anger rose. He would get even with that stepdaughter of his for putting him in a bad light with the boss, and he'd do more than that if he ever managed to get her alone. Trouble was, Mabel was always around and when he'd taken the strap to her daughter one day she'd made a hell of a to-do, screaming that

George Willcox had never touched a hair of the girl's head, and he had yelled back that the man had been a weak sort of bastard, and that had made everything worse.

'I never thought ye could be like this, Joe Boswell!' Mabel had sobbed, but, of course, he knew how to shut her up. Off upstairs and on to the bed. Worked like a charm, it had, and there'd been no more reproaches after that.

Even so, he'd been wary since then and knew he must continue to be so long as the smallholding was in her name. The place was Frenshaws' pension to the widow so it was best to go carefully for the time being. Meanwhile, he could at least seize this opportunity to queer her daughter's pitch. He was sick of the way the girl was always dodging him.

Clearing his throat to indicate reluctance, he said, 'I be afraid there's summat worse, sir. Summat I've bin keeping quiet about, but her impudence this morn made me temper rise and I b'aint sorry. She's gotta learn the dif'rence twixt right and wrong. And stealing be mighty wrong.'

'Stealing?'

'Aye, sir. She's bin at it for a long time an' I be fair at me wit's end to know wot t' do about it. I daresn't tell her mam, for fear o' breaking her heart, but when the wench spoke to me so brazenlike this morn I couldn't hold back no more. An' she dared deny it! That angered me. Right shocked, I were.'

The concern sounded genuine, but the master's penetrating glance was disconcerting.

'And what has she been stealing?'

Joe Boswell looked pained. 'I fair hates t' tell ye, sir—'

'You were telling me things willingly enough just now, so why hesitate? Accusations of theft need substantiating.'

Boswell didn't know the word, but got its meaning. He glowered.

'If ye think I be making this up, sir, ye be wrong. I'm giving ye the truth. That stepdaughter o' mine's been stealing crocks and stashing 'em away. I've bin watching for some time, saying nowt for fear it might be the end of her apprenticeship an' wot her poor mam would do then, the dear Lord knows. Wot other female employment be there in the Potteries 'cept domestic or the streets? An' domestic the girl b'aint no good at. She's allus lolling about painting silly daubs. And for her mam's sake the other thing don't bear thinking of. I've bin hard pressed, wondering wot t' do for the best, but when I tackled the wench this morn she lied. Bold as brass! Maybe I shouldn't've lost me temper, Master Potter, but lying an' thieving be two things I won't put up with. I'm an honest man, as well ye know, sir.'

Do I? thought Daniel. I know you're the most skilled thrower in the Potteries and too valuable to be got rid of, and in all the years you've been here you've never put a foot wrong, but as a man I know nothing about you – except that I dislike and mistrust you.

He said briskly, 'You say your stepdaughter has been helping herself to pots. What kind? And what does she do with them? Take them home?'

'She daresn't do that, sir, knowing her mam an' me would make her bring 'em straight back. No, sir – she hides 'em.'

'*Hides* them? Whatever for? And where?'

'Right 'ere in the potbank, sir. For painting on. I ain't joking, sir, though t' see the daubs she does at home is enough t' make anyone laugh. An' that be another thing, sir. She steals the paints. Must do, since we ain't got spare money to buy 'em. I'll warrant she's taken a good look around to see where the paints be stored when taking a billy-can o' tea to the lady paintresses. Wot's more, she brews that tea beside whatever firemouth is alight.'

'That isn't against the rules. It's an old Potteries custom. Let's get back to the thefts you're accusing her of. You say she hides them, but where?'

'The place where she eats her midday dinner, sir.'

'With other apprentices, in a corner of the turning shed? There can be no hiding place there. There's nothing but a few feet of empty storage space, with stools for them to sit on. So what cock-and-bull story is this?'

Boswell answered sullenly, 'T' ain't no story, 'tis the truth. Why don't ye take a look for yourself, sir? Ye'll be surprised, that ye will. As to why she does it, I can answer that well enough. To sell. Behind your back. An' *that* be summat no pottery worker be allowed t' do. But I've kept quiet 'cos she be my wife's daughter and it'd fair break 'er mother's heart to hear of it. So if ye please, sir, go easy on the lass. I take me responsibilities to the wench very seriously. Would I be telling ye all this if I didn't?'

The Master Potter didn't seem to hear that. His next remark was another surprise, but at least it changed the subject.

'By the way, Boswell, Jacques Le Fevre seems to be

becoming as expert a thrower as his forebears. I've noticed the strides he has made this past year. You must be pleased with him.'

'Aye,' agreed the chief thrower, but with evident doubt. 'I dessay he'll do well enough when he can throw a good pot every time, which he ain't doin' yet by a long chalk.'

'I never overlook the progress of a single potter, and it seems to me that Le Fevre's potential is being rapidly fulfilled.'

Having only the vaguest idea of what 'potential' meant and not liking the sound of it, Boswell said arrogantly, 'Well, he's still got a helluva lot t'learn, but I'll learn 'im, sir. Ye can rely on me for that.'

'I'm sure I can,' said Daniel Frenshaw smoothly, and there was really no reason why his tone should increase the uneasiness in Boswell's mind.

Try as he might to reject thoughts of the past, the sight of Sarah Willcox had brought it so alive that it haunted Daniel increasingly as the day went by. Despite all his wife might say about fatal accidents being a risk in many an industry, he had never forgotten the horror of George Willcox's death.

A kiln fire that got out of hand was every potter's nightmare because it could spread to the hovel, the space within the bottle oven which formed a passage between the walls and the brick kiln in the centre. It also directed the belching smoke through the bottle-neck chimney towering high above. Within this narrow, unventilated area there was scarcely room for the fire stokers to pass each other in their task of feeding the oven mouths built at intervals in the kiln walls. The

41

whole place was a black hell-hole of heat and dust and smoke, with coal ground underfoot from constantly replenished supplies.

In these circumstances, one uncontrolled draught could make sparks fly and herald disaster. Under Daniel Frenshaw's command strict supervision had become a round-the-clock law. The smallest repair job was promptly attended to and, when a firing was under way, temperatures had to be strictly controlled day and night, especially the highest ones like stoneware and porcelain.

A lower temperature on the night of George Willcox's death would have been unlikely to flare up so violently when a freak gale swept through the yard and through the entrance of the bottle oven, fanning the flames beyond the open firemouths and showering sparks on to the coal-covered floor and up the coal-dust covered walls until the men fled and the place became an inferno.

Coupled with the hideous memory in Daniel's mind was the perpetual wish that he could have done more for George Willcox's family.

'Nonsense, Daniel! You did more than enough, moving his widow out of that wretched little place in Burslem into a cottage with its own smallholding, *and* the means to run it.' Cynthia's voice echoed in his memory. 'Employers are under no obligation to pay compensation for accidents and the man's attempt to extinguish the fire in that insane way was his own mad choice. No one ordered him to. And the official inquiry cleared Frenshaws of negligence, which was indisputably the fire chief's. I recall you telling me that the weakening brickwork had been reported to him after the previous firing, and he had not even bothered to examine it.'

True though that was, and that restacking the kiln with a full load before it had properly cooled had been further irresponsibility on the chief stoker's part and well deserving of dismissal even in the eyes of the current Workers' Union, the disaster still scarred Daniel's memory.

He could not share his wife's philosophical dismissal of it. He would forever remember George Willcox's courage in placing the tallest loading ladder against the outer walls of the bottle oven in an attempt to direct a hosepipe through a widening gap in the bricks, while waiting for the fire brigade to come all the way from Stoke. No one could have predicted that the weakening area would suddenly cave in, pitching the man into the inferno. His body was found impaled on the crown of the red-hot kiln within, and the horror of it would live with Daniel for ever.

Nor could he forget his meeting with Kate Willcox later. He had visited both the widow and the mother, but the visit to Kate was the most painful. He loved the warm-hearted, garrulous old woman she had become.

But her son's death had left her numb. Even so, he had known what she thought and felt and what she would say, later, when people remarked that the Master Potter had been generous as well as compassionate.

'So he oughta be, the young bugger!' No doubt she had said worse than that, in the storm of her grief. 'Shouldn't have left it to that dolt Sam Gurney to check everything – everybody knows wot a bloody useless foreman that man be. So were 'is dad afore 'im. *I* oughta know. He were my boss in the sliphouse afore Master Danny were scarce breeched.'

Every word was justified, and he knew it – and so he told her when he called at her shack. He had wanted to rehouse her in something a great deal better, but to his surprise all she wanted was one of the new almshouses. Daniel was on the local committee responsible for their construction. 'Get me one of 'em, Master Danny, and I'll lack for nowt. Then ye can consider your duty done and bother with me no more.'

It was dismissal; he understood it and accepted it, but it hurt because it was more than a sense of duty that prompted his concern for the old lady.

Cynthia frequently lost patience with him, though kindly. 'You're far too charitable, darling. Remember that *I* do enough charitable work for both of us. There's scarcely a deserving cause my name isn't linked with, and that should be enough. As for the Willcox family, you've looked after the old woman well, and the widow has flourished. Nor did she remain a widow for long. Have you *seen* the creature these days?'

Not since that memorable visit to his office with her daughter. By tradition, the families of pottery workers followed their forebears into the industry, generation after generation working for one establishment. For the hundred years of its existence the Frenshaw potbank had maintained a steady line of employees in this way. George Willcox's father had been a fire stoker before him, his mother advancing from the slip house to mould-casting, and very good at her job had Kate Willcox been.

Daniel still remembered his first encounter with her. He had been a youngster then, on his first visit to the place. He had dodged authority and wandered into the sliphouse where she was shovelling lumps of solid clay into a huge sort of drum, periodically adding water while the thing chugged and vibrated. She wore a loose potter's 'slop' over her long clothes. It had wide, elbow-length sleeves beneath which her own were well rolled up. Her hands and forearms were covered in wet clay. She also wore a big mob cap on her head, as all the women workers did, but errant strands of her shining black hair refused to be restricted. They brushed her beautiful face, no matter how persistently she pushed them aside.

When she saw him she didn't tell him to run away and play, as grown-ups usually did. Instead, she gave him a smile so lovely that he ran to her, pelting her with questions . . . what was she doing . . . and what was all the water for . . . and what was that strange chugging thing . . . was it making something, and would it come out of that hole at the bottom, and when? And not once did she say, 'You're too young to understand,' or 'Wait until you're grown up – run along now.' She laughed instead and said, 'One at a time, Master Danny, one at a time! Oh, yes, I know who you are – you're the boss's son.' Then, wiping her clay-covered arms with sisal, she picked him up to take a closer look.

'It's called a blunger, me luv, because the clay must be blunged with water till it's all creamy and smooth with not the tiniest lump or one speck of grit left.'

'Then what happens?'

'Well, by then the clay's become "slip" and it's poured into this funny-looking tub – only it ain't a tub, it's an ark.'

'Like Noah's?'

'Nay,' she'd said in her broad Midland accent. 'Poor old Noah'd 'ave a bad time trying to sail the flood in that there thing!' Her laugh was as lovely as her smile. The next moment he was astride a high stool, looking down into the ark and watching paddles stirring the thick, smooth liquid.

'That's to stop it settling,' she said, 'an' after that it be sieved and sieved and *then* wot's the next step, d' ye think?' (How did she know he was wondering exactly that?) 'Well, Master Danny, I'll tell ye. It's poured over that great big magnet over there to get rid of any bits of iron — it's iron wot makes the clay that red colour, d' ye see? But if any grit were left in, the clay would blow up in the kiln an' the whole load could be damaged by flying pieces. Then it could be the sack for the likes o' me. *And* I'd deserve it for not mixing the slip proper.'

That had been his first lesson in potting and he had never forgotten it. Whenever he had earned the treat of a visit to the family potbank as a child he had sought her out, racing to greet her, shouting her name, and he would fling himself upon her, wild with joy. And she always called him Danny, never Daniel, albeit with that silly word 'master' before it.

'I'm not your master, Katie,' he would insist, but she would laugh and say what a pity she wouldn't be here when he was, because she'd like nothing better than working for him. 'Though I'd not answer to Katie then, young man. The name's Kate, so see you remember that.' As always, the words had been softened by her smile.

Now he often stopped at her door to see how she

46

was and if she needed anything. She never did. 'I've everything I need, Master Danny, thankin' ye kindly.' But her tone would be stilted because he was now Master Potter, not a lad she was pally with.

Cynthia never knew about these visits to a woman whom she sometimes called 'that old hag'. But Kate had been lovely once, and that was the Kate he remembered – tall, straight-backed, raven-haired, magnificent dark eyes fringed with black, curling lashes, her beautiful complexion flushed with the heat of the works, her classic features glistening with sweat but forever beautiful.

He wasn't surprised that an artist had once painted her, though the locals didn't believe it. Who would want to paint a working potter's wife, herself a slavey in the sheds? said the sceptics. Besides, Kate Willcox had been nothing but the daughter of a mining family from Burslem, thinking like them, talking like them, her rough upbringing stamped on her. No one of culture would have looked at a young woman who swore like a trooper and whose laugh was so loud it could be heard the length of the potter's yard.

But no longer. Age had not extinguished the light in her – grief had done that, a grief he shared, but hid. A few days after the disaster the company's book-keeper had reported that the financial loss of such a valuable porcelain load was beyond estimation, whereupon Daniel had scalded the man with his tongue.

'You talk to me about the loss of a load of pots when a man has been *killed*?'

He had resolved at that moment that no one should hurt George Willcox's mother or child ever again and now, driving home from the pottery, the recollection of Joe Boswell's upraised fist renewed that resolution.

Four

The Frenshaw potbank had the advantage of being situated right on the canal network built in the late 1700s by the unschooled genius, James Brindley, to enable supplies of Cornish china clay to travel direct to the Potteries instead of by the long sea route to Liverpool and thence by road from Merseyside. When the weather was fine, many potters would eat their midday meal by the canal, making the most of the half-hour break in a ten-hour working day, at the end of which relaxation was badly needed. When tired apprentices were cleaning workshop floors, most of the potters were drinking in the nearest pub.

Drunkenness had long been a problem in the Potteries. It was accepted philosophically by women-folk because after a hard day's labour what else was there to do since dog-fighting and cock-fighting had long since been banned and places in which to enjoy them illicitly were hard to find? Innkeepers accepted biscuit-fired pots for payment and asked no questions about the rights of workers to help themselves to their employers' stock because such items could be resold for a greater price than a slug of gin.

So public houses offered welcome relief after hours of labour at the benches. Life was harsh and solace was to be seized in any available way. Drink and women were the cheapest, and Joe Boswell made the most of them.

This evening he planned to do precisely that. He would drink his fill at the Boar's Head before picking up that stepdaughter of his and taking her home in his own time and by a carefully chosen route. Why not that cross-crountry track she had emerged from in Bruce Frenshaw's wake this morning? There were plenty of isolated spots along the way, and by then she would be tired after the extra cleaning. Even so, he wouldn't put it past her to fight like a she-devil. That would add spice to it. He would also enjoy paying her back for that summons to the Master Potter's office.

For Sarah herself the day held nothing but promise. Not only did it mark the completion of her first year but the end of nightly cleaning-up duties, so she would be off to Gran's place earlier than usual.

It also meant promotion to the turning shed for her first lesson in putting an upstanding foot on the base of a pot.

The worst of her early training was over; the hand-riddling beneath running water to extract grit from clay until her skin was raw and her fingers numb, then hand-wedging to remove air bubbles, a job which strengthened the muscles of her forearms but left the shoulders aching. Although mechanisation now handled these operations, the Frenshaw potbank made skilled potters out of its workers by teaching them to master the basic skills. Only by handling clay in the raw would they become familiar with its qualities.

Expert throwers appreciated nothing so much as

hand-wedged clay. It beat anything out of a pug-mill, and the day when Jacques Le Fevre complimented Sarah on a batch she delivered to his bench had been a red-letter day in her life. She had lingered to watch him throw a tall, delicately shaped vase, marvelling at its beauty. She had still been marvelling when Joe Boswell yelled at her to get back to her own work.

It was rumoured in the workshops that Jacques would be as good a thrower as Boswell one of these days. Some said he was already, for although lacking the older man's powerful physique, he had strong wrists, a deftness of touch and an eye for elegant lines. He had also devised a new way of producing immense orna-mental garden urns, big enough to adorn the terraces of huge country houses. His method was to throw them in separate sections then bond them.

Jacques made no secret of the fact that he had been staying behind to develop his idea after the potbank closed. If a worker wanted to do that, he was free to, and his foreman could not forbid it. Alone on the premises, except for the fire stokers who worked in shifts day and night, Jacques had been working to perfect the system. And when he proved that it was not only workable but speedier and therefore more eco-nomical, his workmates were behind him to a man for it meant that three of them could simultaneously produce the separate sections, with a fourth doing the bonding.

Throwing the individual parts demanded skill because each had to be produced to exact measure-ments to dovetail with the others, but by this method six items could be produced in the time it took Joe

Boswell to complete one. There wasn't a man in the throwing shed who didn't relish the thought.

But Jacques had a greater goal. He wanted to produce the immense urns of ancient Greece, with all their grace and power, and on the very day that Sarah started her training in the turning shed, he displayed his first completed one, the clay leather-hard and standing firm.

'And who the hell's going to buy pots that size?' sneered Boswell. 'And how many could be packed into the kilns – thought of that, Jack Lefever? Thought of the cost of firing only a few at a time? They'd be too big to stand in saggers on the shelves; they'd have to stand free on the kiln's base, and all space above go to waste. Thought of the heat loss? Thought of how much clay each one would use?' Laughter bellowed from his mighty frame. 'Ye'd never get the idea past the Master Potter and ye damn well can't get it past me. There'll be no freak stuff like this made at Frenshaws so long as *I'm* boss of this shed.' And with one mighty swipe he shattered the unfired clay and laughed at the angry faces around him.

In the quiet atmosphere of the turning shed, Sarah was far removed from all this. To be adding a foot to a pot gave her the feeling of actually creating something. In the deft hands of the experienced turners it looked easy, long ribbons of clay curling away from beneath their small, hand-held tools. She found it difficult, but challenging and absorbing. Lost in it, she forgot this morning's ugly encounter at the gates.

Her enjoyment was increased by the patience of Hobson, the chief turner, who looked with a kindly eye on her first fumbling attempts and told her not to fret when she peeled away too much of the leather-hard clay, or pierced the base with the pointed arrowhead of her turning tool.

'Patience, lass. That's what's needed in potting, whatever stage we're at. Rome weren't built in a day and nor were a good foot on a pot.'

By the time the dinner-break came, she had ruined more than she cared to count, but the man remained benign. 'It isn't easy to judge the thickness of a base – that's summat you learn with time. If you jab your tool in too sharply, you'll pierce it right through or split the clay before you get there, so gently does it.'

So again and again she centred an upturned pot on a banding wheel and again and again she poised her turning tool above it, lowering it to trace the outer and inner lines of the foot as the wheel revolved, then peeling away the leather-hard clay from either side of the ring. In the main workshops, where mass production had been introduced, the new jigger and jolley tools did the work mechanically, but here at Frenshaws self-made ware was a speciality sideline and no apprentice would finally qualify unless schooled in the old skills.

'The Master Potter says that if we allow the ancient rudiments of the craft to be forgotten, the whole art will die, and he's right,' said Hobson. 'Knows what he's talking about, does Daniel Frenshaw. Dedicated, he is. Like your dad. I remember him well, lass.'

The warmth in his voice lifted her heart. Meeting someone who had known and liked her father never failed to do this. At the dinner-break she went to meet other apprentices at the far end of the shed feeling much happier than when she had signed on this morning.

Marie Le Fevre was the first to join her. Despite the length of time since her forebears had settled here, traditional French names continued in her family – Pierre and Jacques and Marcel for boys and Germaine and Solange and Marie for girls, all commonly mispronounced, as was their surname. Here in the Potteries, Le Fevre had become Lefever long ago. Thus Jacques was called Jack and Marie Mary – except by Sarah, who liked pronouncing it the French way. A smattering of their native language survived in the family, though the young ones felt self-conscious about speaking it outside the home.

'But *why*, Marie? I wish I could speak French. I'd feel proud then. Educated. A cut above everyone.'

'Why d'you want to be, Sarah?'

'I just do. I want to get somewhere. *Be* someone.'

'I can't see anything wrong with the way you are. I think you're clever. Look at the way you paint on china! Good as any of the paintresses upstairs.'

'I wish I were! Little chance I've got, though. You need teaching to be as good as they. All them – I mean those – ladies in the painting room have been taught at the Potteries School of Design. I can only brush paint on somehow because I don't really know how to use it. And the stuff I use is wrong – it has to be glaze-mixed. You won't go telling on me, will you, Marie? I might be in trouble if found out. I've a feeling my stepfather suspects, anyway.'

'I wouldn't be surprised. He's lynx-eyed, my brother says; gives his workers hell sometimes. Jacques doesn't grumble, but I suspect Boswell picks on him in particular. I'm sorry, Sarah, but I don't like your father.'

'He's not my father. Not my real one. And you can say what you like about him 'cos I don't like him either.' Suddenly aware that they were alone in their corner because all the qualified turners had departed with their meal boxes, Sarah finished, 'The other girls are late—'

'Here they come across the yard. What a nuisance! I wanted to see your things again. No hope of that now, I s'pose?' Marie glanced toward the box partially hidden beneath Sarah's stool and covered by her potter's slop. 'Funny none of them have never noticed that.'

'Too busy eating and talking. And they wouldn't be interested anyway. Teach me a few words of French, Marie.'

'Not right now. They'd all jeer and say I was swanking.'

'Let them! It seems to me that if you want something badly you've got to put up with people's mocking. My gran says you've got to fight for what you want in this world and to hell with what folks say or think.'

'I've never heard you talk like that before. You're always so quiet and gentle.'

Before Sarah had a chance to answer, the other girls trooped in, chattering like magpies, and soon they were all eating and laughing and grumbling in unison, moaning about the supervisors, particularly any bossy female ones, and exchanging bits of overheard gossip.

The difference between them and me, mused Sarah, is that they're not really interested *in* pottery, only in getting through their apprenticing and on to piece-work to earn money. If I showed them the things in my box I doubt they'd think much of them. No one would, except Gran. I'll take one or two to show her tonight.

Sarah had become expert in letting other people's conversation flow over her head while pursuing her own thoughts. She wanted nothing so much as to create beautiful things out of clay, to see the drab substance emerge from the kilns sparkling with colour, transformed, glorified.

She hoped that now the war with Germany was over Frenshaws would produce more ornamental products but, in common with the rest of the potteries, survival had depended on good, utilitarian ware which would last until better days came. Only now were there signs that people were beginning to afford quality ceramics again, and only now were export orders beginning to increase. Thinking of that reminded Sarah of Bruce Frenshaw, in charge of that department, and back came the memory of this morning's enchanted meeting.

'What are you thinking about, Sarah?' Marie's elbow was nudging her. 'Wake up – you're miles away.'

'She's allus dreamin', that one!' It was poor Daisy Wilkins, whose mam was no better than she should be. It was well known that the woman was a fair lay for any man. Poor Daisy – what chance had she, with a mother like that? She didn't even know who her father was and her apprenticeship at Frenshaws was due to the Parish Charity Visitor who had put her case before the Master Potter. Daniel Frenshaw had taken Daisy on at once.

'So wot be ye adreamin' about this time, eh, Sarah?' Daisy persisted. She enjoyed teasing folk, but today Sarah found it difficult to shrug off her next words.

'Could it be Master Bruce – eh, Sarah? It be all over

t' works that ye've bin in trouble with yer dad for chasin' after 'im . . .'

'I did no such thing. And Joe Boswell's *not* my dad,' Sarah said sharply.

'Orlright, luv. Keep yer 'air on. I be only jokin'. Anyways, there ain't one of us as wouldn't like the chance to catch Master Bruce's eye!'

Marie seized on the first thing she could think of to change the subject.

'Show us your things, Sarah. Do.'

'Wot things?' piped Daisy.

'Things she paints when no one's looking.'

'Not *pots*?' said another. 'Lord luv us, Sarah, you'll fair cop it if ye're ever found out!'

'I ain't – I mean I'm not – going to be found out.'

''Ark at 'er, trying t' speak proper! Quite the little lady is our Sarah, ain't ya, luv?'

The words were well meant, but they jarred as much as the jibe did. They'd accept me willingly enough if I spoke the way they do and talked about the things they talk about, Sarah reflected, but I don't want to. It takes me all my time *not* to speak their way. Dad's voice was quiet and he taught me to speak the same. A dialect docsn't matter if you speak clearly and quietly and grammatically, he used to say. A dialect tells people where you come from, and that's no disgrace, but you still don't have to drop your aitches and speak roughly.

Suddenly she recalled Bruce Frenshaw's voice, close to her ear this morning; cultured and pleasant. That's how *I* am going to speak one day, she resolved, and if these girls don't like it they can make fun of me as much as they like.

'C'mon, Sarah – show us yer things,' Daisy pleaded

and, suddenly curious, the others took it up. Reluctantly, Sarah picked up her box and removed the lid, and at that precise moment a shadow fell through the open door. Startled, they all looked up and saw the Master Potter standing there.

Later, Daniel reflected that if anyone had been embarrassed it was himself. Although the owner of a potbank had every right to tour the works at any time, only a tactless one would intrude on any worker's brief spell of privacy.

Inspecting the sheds when workers were absent enabled him to assess improvement in the work of individual potters without standing over them and making them feel self-conscious or apprehensive, the diffident ones in particular, but now he was faced with a group of young women amongst whom only Sarah Willcox looked nervous. Hastily, she thrust a lid on to a box she was holding, but Daisy piped cheerily, 'Ee, Master, y' orta see wot our Sarah does! Paints summat *luvly*!'

He said, 'I would very much like to,' and went over to join them, controlling a reluctant fear that he was about to see proof of Joe Boswell's accusations.

When the lid was removed he didn't touch the contents. He gave one glance and smiled. 'You should practise on something better than broken pieces,' he said. 'I take it these came from the pile of throwaways waiting to be ground into grog?'

'Yes, sir. It ain't – I mean, it isn't – against the rules, is it, sir?'

'Certainly not, but you should practise on whole pieces and with proper paints. Watercolours will do for practising on biscuit ware, though the colours will be absorbed and then fade. They can even wash out if soaked. For glaze you need the right paints, underglaze or overglaze, specially prepared for firing.'

'I know, sir. I've found that out. But watercolours be all I've got. My dad used to give me some every birthday but I've hardly any left now . . .'

Her voice trailed away. She was afraid she had said too much and spoken for too long. The most one did in the Master Potter's presence was to curtsy and murmur, 'Yessir', and she did it automatically when he said, 'Bring these along to my office when you've had your meal. I want to talk to you.'

Then he was gone and the girls were whooping and laughing and chattering, and Marie was hugging her and Daisy dancing a jig, kicking up her bare legs from beneath threadbare petticoats and screeching as loud as her mam. Her legs were blue with cold and despite her own relief and excitement Sarah found herself thinking, If only summat could be done for Daisy, summat to give her a real chance in life . . .

Now freed from cleaning-up duty at the end of the day, Sarah was able to hurry along to Gran's as soon as the potbank closed, but she was wise enough to wait until she saw Joe Boswell striding off to the Boar's Head. He had either forgotten or was unaware that today marked the end of her first year's apprenticeship and her elevation to second-year privileges. He would return to the potbank to pick her up at the time she normally left, and she relished the thought that he would find her gone. He would then remember that this was her evening for visiting Gran, and go home without her.

Kate's almshouse was in Colney, a village three miles away. It was one of a row of single-roomed dwellings provided for the needy. It was dry, warmed by thatch and an open hearth with a bread oven built into the wall beside it, but the only sanitation was a line of communal earth closets at the back, shared with neighbours. There was also a communal washing line strung across a patch of green earth; 'the gossip club', Kate called it and tried to get her laundry hung out first to dodge the ribald catcalls of that Nosy Parker Ted Carter, who lived at the end of the row and delighted in spying on his neighbours.

But within her diminutive cottage she was happy and content. Sleeping accommodation was the traditional wall shelf, but instead of the usual straw-filled palliasse Kate had a good flock mattress, proper bedlinen and an eiderdown. They'd been there when she'd moved in, with no indication as to why she was so favoured. Almshouse bedclothes were usually utilitarian and harsh, of the kind donated to the poor by one of Cynthia Frenshaw's charities, but Kate was under no illusion regarding the source of her own furnishings, all a cut above her neighbours'. There were lined curtains at the two small windows, an oil lamp with a pretty glass globe to shed a warm light on dark winter evenings, and a gate-leg table with a couple of good ladderback chairs. There was also a rocker beside the hearth, with a knee-rug knitted by Sarah, a log basket easily replenished from the woodlands hereabouts (a task Sarah attended to every Sabbath) and a footstool for her tired feet. There was also an ample supply of Frenshaw domestic crocks in a built-in cupboard.

Best of all was a carpet completely covering the stone

floor. She had lied to everyone about that, saying it had come from parish charities when actually it had come anonymously, along with the pottery supplies and the rest of the furnishings. It didn't take much guessing to identify the donor. She had guessed it was Daniel Frenshaw because when she ventured to thank him he had turned an uncomprehending glance on her, indicating total ignorance. That hadn't deceived her in the least.

To this tiny cottage Sarah now raced with wings on her feet, seeing nothing of the beautiful countryside which started dramatically at the point where the blackened potteries ceased. Staffordshire had been a sylvan county until its coal and its clay had been discovered and its six towns – Tunstall, Burslem, Hanley, Fenton, Longton and Stoke-upon-Trent, all little more than villages then – gained prosperity and lost their beauty.

Since then the social levels had been marked by the sharp division between wealth and poverty, with the mine owners and potbank lords living on the grand scale in homes like the Petersons' Downley Court or the Frenshaws' Dunmore Abbey, once a monastery dissolved by Henry VIII and presented to an early baron who had supported him in his battle with the Church. The Frenshaws' acquisition had come later, when their hereditary wealth had been increased by the boom in the pottery industry. For succeeding Frenshaws to live anywhere but in the stately family home was now unthinkable and so the tradition remained.

Despite her haste to reach Gran this evening, Sarah paused at one point to gaze across the fields at the four round towers of Dunmore Abbey. One tower in

61

particular caught her eye because it differed from the rest. Instead of closed stone walls immediately beneath its crenellated roof, large windows encircled it. Someone, at some time, had turned it into a tower room commanding peak views north, south, east and west. The windows now sparkled like jewels in the late evening sun, so beautiful that Sarah caught her breath. Surely they encircled a magical room, a room she longed to enter but, of course, never would. She had never been near the abbey and was never likely to. Even so, today the unbelievable had happened – she had met the younger son of Dunmore's reigning family and, even more unbelievably, she had been befriended by its present lord.

Gazing across the fields to the abbey's faraway beauty, she was held in a breathless excitement. Fancy anyone who lived in so grand a place taking an interest in *her*! She had expected to be put down, but instead the Master Potter had said – what *exactly* were his words? She had to remember so she could tell Gran.

'A talent like yours, Sarah, must not be wasted.'

A talent! A word like that applied to *herself*? She had been so astonished that she had almost missed what he said next, but now it danced back into her memory and wings attached themselves to her feet again and on she raced, pausing no more until she reached Kate's cottage and tumbled through the unlatched door, crying, 'Gran! *Gran!* Guess what's happened – no, don't try because ye'll *never!*'

Seizing the old lady, Sarah skipped her about the room until the frail figure cried, 'Stop, for land's sakes! D'ye think I be spry like y'rsel'? Mind me aching old bones, luv – I need 'em yet a'wile!'

'Your bones aren't old and you're as spry as I am!'

Even so, the body seemed fragile in her arms, an impression that belied the truth. Her grandmother was a tough old lady who had weathered all the knocks life had dealt her. And she still had a zest for living.

'Well, me luv, come on, come *on*! Since ye say I'll never guess, ye'd best be tellin' me – though I admit I do enjoy a bit o' guessing now an' then. Cain't be that your mam's come to 'er senses and kicked that bugger out? No – I were afeared not. Summat else, then. 'E's fallen an' broke 'is bloody neck? Ye couldn't bring better news than that, could ye, m' dear?' Her full-throated laughter echoed loudly in the small room and Sarah joined in.

'Oh, Gran, you *are* a one! But 'tis better news even than that.'

'Cain't be!'

'Listen an' *then* tell me what couldn't be better.' Sarah took a deep breath and announced triumphantly, *'I'm to be sent to the Potteries School of Design for two full days a week!'*

Kate sat down abruptly, mouth agape. 'Y'ain't kiddin' me, our Sarah?'

'Would I kid about summat like that, summat we could never raise the money for? 'Tis the Master Potter's doing, Gran, and I still cain't take it in . . .'

Tears were running down Kate's lined face. She was laughing and crying and declaring, 'Well, *I* can take it in orlright, luv, 'cos I knows Master Danny. 'E ain't the kinda man t' do summat for somebody unless 'e not only wanted to, but knew 'twere the right thing t' do. 'E must've bin watching thee at work, luv, an' summed ye up right well.'

"Tweren't like that, Gran. It were these.' Sarah fished out of her pocket a handful of broken china pieces. 'Remember how Dad useter say I'd make a paintress one day?'

'Am I likely t' forget?' Gran was turning over the pieces, eyes alive with interest, voice alive with pride. 'I've said it meself many a time – and to that Mabel. 'Y'oughta send our Sarah t' be taught proper,' I've said, but would she part with a penny of that pension? She would not. Leastways, not since she took up with Joe Boswell.'

'Never mind that, Gran. Frenshaws are paying. They do it "for exceptional talent", the Master Potter said. I couldn't believe my ears!'

' 'S wonderful, lass. 'S wonderful. An' well do ye deserve it. My, but I wish my George could see these. Mighty proud would 'e be.'

'They're not all *that* good, Gran. The paints are wrong. And the brushwork. "You've got to be properly taught, Sarah. A talent like yours should not be wasted." That's what he said – his very words, Gran.'

'And when do ye start?' Kate asked eagerly.

'Well, Mr Treadgold – that's the gentleman who does the book-keeping—'

'I know, I know – useter work there meself, remember. Treadgold joined the company a coupla years afore this damned arthritis made me stop, or I'd be there still. So Treadgold's going to fix it up?'

'Only the first step. He's going to see the Principal tomorrow and take the rest of these broken pieces – the Master Potter's kept the best – and he'll fix a date for me to take whatever tests be set me. Drawing, for one. I'll like that. I enjoy sketching. Specially people.'

'People! Don't go wasting time on people, lass. Flowers an' leaves an' birds an' things. That's wot them lady paintresses do on dinner services an' that's wot ye'll be taught. Designs that'll never go out of fashion – that's wot sells in the pottery line.'

'The Master Potter's lent me this book. Take a look, Gran. He said I were to study it an' see how I felt about the ideas in it. I've never seen anything like it, an' I dessay you haven't neether.'

Kate was already turning over the pages, looking at designs which were strange and, to her mind, unlikeable. Surely Master Danny couldn't be thinking of using this sort of thing on Frenshaws' best china and porcelain? All the pictures were of vaguely mingled colours, patterns which weren't really patterns – all fantasy-like. But somehow they made you keep on looking, turning the next page and the next.

Eventually she went back to the beginning and looked at what her son had called the title page of a book (my, how George had loved to read, forever browsing in secondhand bookshops, sometimes for hours at a stretch until the owners began to look at him askance!) and there she saw the publisher's name. She couldn't read, but she could tell it wasn't English.

'Foreign!' she said in a tone implying that *that* was why it was all so weird. She laid the book aside with a sniff, and Sarah laughed and hugged her.

It was an evening of happiness. Heaven had opened and showered sudden blessings on them and Kate poured two glasses of her wild raspberry wine in celebration. She was forever gathering things from hedgerows and fields and making good use of them. Now she toasted her granddaughter's fifteenth birthday, and then her future.

'You're goin' to do great things, lass. Great things.' And while Sarah set the table the old lady brought food from the oven and then a small fruit cake from a cupboard. It had '15' outlined in cob nuts on the top. Then came the surprise. Something small, wrapped in a crumpled paper bag, was laid on Sarah's plate.

''T ain't much, luv, but that tinker at the Saturday market let me 'ave it special.'

It was a cheap chain bracelet with the initials 'S' and 'W' dangling from it.

'Oh, Gran – 'tis *beautiful*!'

Ecstatically, Sarah slipped it on to her wrist. It was slightly big and threatened to slip off but she took care not to let her grandmother see that.

'I wish it coulda bin reel silver, lass.'

'Well, *I* don't – 'tis lovely as it is. Anyways, it *looks* reel silver an' the girls at the potbank ain't half going to be jealous.' She kissed her grandmother's cheek tenderly. 'Ye shouldn't have spent your money on me when ye be needing things yourself.'

'I need for nowt, lass. Look at this place – did ever a woman want for more?'

She was now wrapping up the rest of the cake for Sarah to take home, but Sarah stopped her.

'No, Gran – keep it here. 'Tis you I like sharing things with.' A sudden sadness claimed her. She hated the thought of leaving. 'Oh, Gran, I do wish I hadn't to go! I want to stay here with you.'

'Aye, an' that's wot I'd like too, but I be bound by wot they call the law of single habitation – meaning these places were built for one person only an' no

66

sharin', and it'd soon git around if ye joined me. Folk enjoy splittin' on others. 'Sides, I don't want eether o' *them* comin' after ye – which, mark me words, they would, seeing as 'ow they've got the law on their side. Leastways, your mam has. An' I do believe she still loves ye. Trouble is, she loves that bugger more – at the moment. One day she'll come to 'er senses, an' by that time ye'll be well on your feet. Best be on your way now, me darling. 'Tis well past dusk and you've a long walk ahead.'

The wings were back on her feet as she set out, heart singing, mind alight. What a birthday it had been, first the drive with Bruce Frenshaw, his friendliness, his exciting nearness, and her feeling of triumph because she had outwitted Joe Boswell – and then the incredible interview with the Master Potter, a man to whom she had only bobbed a curtsy before, a man who, like his handsome young brother, lived in another world, and one she was never likely to enter. But now unexpected doors were to open and the promise they held made her giddy to contemplate. For two whole days a week she would be able to call herself an art student.

Confidently, she stepped out. Country folk were accustomed to walking alone along country roads after dark, and she welcomed the solitude because it gave her the opportunity to dwell on the day's events, reliving them and marvelling over them.

She had left Kate's cottage, and the village, well behind and was traversing an isolated stretch of country road when a figure loomed up, reeking of gin and staggering. She was repelled but not afraid – you couldn't grow up in the Potteries without becoming inured to the rougher side of life. She was crossing to

67

the other side to avoid the man when she was suddenly grabbed and flung on to the verge. His strength was as enormous as the weight of his body on top of her.

Terror seized her. She heard curses and abuse pouring from the man's mouth before it settled on her own . . . slobbering, sickening, reeking. With every ounce of her strength she writhed and fought, but the more she did so the more heavily she was pinned until her flailing arms were rammed against the earth and her legs thrust wide and she lay spreadeagled beneath him. Trapped. Ready for the raping.

It came swiftly and violently . . . clothes ripped from her . . . thighs wrenched . . . pain screaming through her body, fiercer and fiercer as her flesh was torn by thrusting male hardness . . . violent, merciless, seering, savage, splitting her flesh until blood spilled between her thighs . . . more blood choking her as the man's teeth savaged her mouth . . . and the roar of a bull bellowing in her ears and the long-forgotten cries of a helpless victim, but this time it was the roar of a beast raping the animal he most wanted and hated . . . and beneath its weight she lay crushed and battered while in some black corner of her mind she was praying for an oblivion which never came.

On he went, and on, insatiable, unquenchable, babbling, *'Bitch . . . bitch . . . fucking bitch . . . damn fucking BITCH!'*

And the voice penetrated her reeling brain and she knew who it belonged to and her hatred was as violent as his attack, a hatred that would be with her for ever, screaming for vengeance.

Then came the blows. On her head, her face, her breasts, her half-naked body. Fists rained until she was half-senseless, unaware that the distant screams echoing in her brain were her own.

Silence. Stillness. A dreadful collapse of dead weight upon her. She was rigid, unable to move, her body numbed yet pain-racked. Breathing was a knife-thrust in her lungs. There was a searing soreness between her legs and worse piercing upward inside her. Pain was scorching through her body and there was wetness between her thighs and in the stunned recesses of her mind she remembered it spurting into her like a hideous fountain, mingling with her blood.

Above her the collapsed body was immovable, and the dark night covered them.

Five

Time was blurred. It was consciousness receding, returning and receding again. It was darkness and silence through which a remote instinct urged her anguished body to escape. Her spirit struggled to obey, but the weight pinioning her to the ground was unyielding.

Terror spurred her on. The hulk would not remain supine indefinitely. It would waken from its drunken stupor, senses clearing and brutality returning. Her trapped limbs fought for release, tautening when the man's grunts suggested he was waking. Panic strengthened her and with a desperate lurch she heaved his body sideways. There was a sickening sound as he rolled away – a heavy, metallic thud – but she was aware only that the brutal weight was gone.

On hands and knees she crawled through the grass, hampered by shreds of clothing but driven by desperation. She gulped great spasms of air through agonised lungs and a throat made raw by screaming. Her instinct was to sink to the ground and remain there, but a stronger instinct clamoured for escape.

After a while she ceased crawling and dragged herself into a sitting position, pulling her tattered garments around her. Then, forcing herself to stand, she began the long, slow, agonising drag back to Gran's cottage.

One of Kate Willcox's frequent observations was that when people grew old they either slept longer or shorter. She was among the latter. Her nights were patchy, as were her days. She could nod off in her rocking chair at almost any time, but nights often found her listening for the boom of the church clock heralding the early hours.

Tonight it was striking two when the sound came at her door, a scrabbling noise as if an animal were scratching at it. A night fox again? That blasted Ted Carter at the end of the row must have been putting out scraps, though he really had no love of the creatures. He did it to get them prowling round his neighbours. He enjoyed doing that. Someday she would think up some way to retaliate, and then the enjoyment would be hers.

The noise came again, this time with a feeble cry. That was no fox! That was a human being. She tensed. Whoever was there, they could go away. She wasn't drawing the bolt at the dead of night to a mortal soul.

The sound persisted; a hand was struggling with the heavy iron knocker, accompanied by desperate thumpings on the wood as the cry rose to a heart-rending wail. Kate jerked awake, alert, tumbling out of bed when the feeble cry became stronger.

'*Gran! GRAN!*'

The old woman stumbled across the room, snatched at the bolt and caught Sarah as she fell across the threshold. One glance was enough. The torn and earth-stained clothes, the half-stripped body, the signs of brutality – all told their damnable story.

Daniel arrived late at the potbank. After his wife's supper party last night, guests had lingered until well after midnight for she was a superb hostess. The menus Cynthia planned were second to none and this one had been no exception. A fine Hessian soup had preceded hot crab flavoured with nutmeg and browned in a salamander – both excellent forerunners to a tender roast tongue served with currant jelly and vegetables cooked to perfection. Sorbets then refreshed the palates before a delicious Souster was brought to the table to vie with an equally tempting Flummery, supplemented with *Puits d'Amour* and Imperial and Codlin creams placed judiciously about the table in a chain of silver dishes.

And, as always, Cynthia had been elegantly gowned, her pale blonde hair immaculately dressed by the best hairdresser in Stoke, who naturally journeyed out to the abbey to serve her. Her lovely complexion had been enhanced by the lightest and most subtle make-up and, as always, her beauty stirred him. From their first moment of meeting Daniel had been captivated by Cynthia's perfect features – the straight nose set beneath a low brow from which her lovely hair swept back from a widow's peak, a small but firmly chiselled chin, almond-shaped eyes of amber brown and a full, sensuous mouth. She had the kind of beauty which enchanted a man.

Ruth Peterson always said that not only was Cynthia beautiful, but the best-dressed woman in Staffordshire – not that Daniel had ever heard this prematurely silver-haired woman criticise anyone adversely. If Ruth could not praise, she kept silent, and last night her admiration of Cynthia's fashionable tunic gown with its lace godet insertions had been spontaneous and sincere.

It had been Annabel, her daughter, who added, 'That blue watered silk is beautiful – *and* the lace. Honiton, is it, or Nottingham?'

And Cynthia had said, 'Nottingham, of course. Dear Papa would never forgive me if I ordered anything else!' But her light response somehow conveyed that no one could influence her once she had made a choice in any way.

Ruth had also admired the expertise of Cynthia's dressmaker.

'Couturière.' The quiet correction had jarred on Daniel. He hoped it was heard by no one but himself. 'If she were not so expert,' Cynthia had continued blandly, 'I wouldn't journey to Nottingham to employ her. And I certainly wouldn't pay her outlandish charges. She costs me a fortune, but one has to pay to get the best, don't you agree?'

Cynthia's references to the prices she paid for everything frequently embarrassed her husband, who had been brought up in a household where ostentatious talk was unnatural, but Cynthia came from a hard-headed lace-making background, influenced by a father whose conversation was always dominated by pounds, shillings and pence. It was ingrained in Cynthia's upbringing and her husband had learned to tolerate it.

If there was one thing his wife expected, and made sure she obtained, it was value for money. Household accounts were meticulously examined and no item of expenditure missed her sharp eye. And not a thing went on in and around the estate that she failed to notice. If a barn was being reroofed or an estate worker's cottage repaired she would demand to know what was being done, and why, and how much it was costing, and why she had not been consulted, but always with the charm and poise which an expensive finishing school had provided.

The entire running of Dunmore could have been left in Cynthia's capable hands, had Daniel felt so inclined. Sometimes he wondered why he didn't, and why her efficiency occasionally jarred, and why he sometimes felt disloyal for feeling that her vigilance had a mercenary touch.

In contrast, she never criticised Bruce's extravagances. She had even been indulgent about him being sent down from Cambridge. 'A few gambling debts! What do *they* matter? Every young man is entitled to sew a few wild oats.'

But they had been more than a few, and others had been linked with them, and when he took Bruce to task about the whole affair Cynthia had told the boy to take no notice. 'My dear husband can be stuffy at times,' she had said, smiling at her young brother-in-law, and the fleeting glance Daniel detected between them – amused, almost conspiratorial – had shut him out.

Bruce had not been at last night's supper party. For the most part, the only contact the brothers had was at work. Although Cynthia sometimes included Bruce among her guests, last night's affair had been mainly for people who were becoming accepted in Staffordshire society, or were visiting their country houses as a break from their London ones, or whose businesses were growing and consequently their social standing. To Daniel, these were the wrong reasons for inviting people to their home, but he let her have her way.

Mercifully the Petersons, their nearest neighbours and long-standing friends, had been there. 'They give tone to any event, and that impresses newcomers,' Cynthia said. Once upon a time the comment would have amused him.

Daniel liked Charles and Ruth Peterson and their daughter Annabel, and if it were true that the girl was determined on a career in the clay world he would happily give her a trial when the time came.

'She'll outgrow the idea, and the sooner the better,' Cynthia had said when the rumour first went round. 'Imagine a girl of her breeding working with those rough women! *So* demeaning. Her parents will never permit it, and a good thing too.'

After everyone had gone last night, she had reproached him for encouraging the girl. 'I heard your conversation when the two of you were sitting apart on that window seat.'

'I was interested in her ideas and concerned about the opposition she is facing. It's so unlike Charles and Ruth because there's no snobbishness in them. The truth is that they think she should try for the Royal College of Art in London because they fear her social standing locally might be resented and therefore give her a thin time.' He was annoyed with himself for feeling he had to explain.

'But I heard you offering to employ her when she graduates. Why, for heaven's sake? You wouldn't expect a girl of her background and education to work in a filthy potbank?'

75

'If she wanted to and was equipped to, I see no reason why not. And Frenshaws' is not filthy. Cleanliness standards are high, though no clay workshop can totally eliminate dust.'

But that was the only discordant note in the evening and when, later, Cynthia complimented him on the wines he had chosen she meant every word. 'I'm so lucky to have you to handle that side, darling. Your choice is always excellent.'

Mellowed by the party's success and the flattery of her newest guests, she had rewarded him in bed with an unexpected demonstration of passion, but in the morning she was indifferent, offering no more than a cool cheek to be kissed. He had descended the sweeping stone staircase to the ancient refectory hall feeling like an accommodating servant who had been graciously (or merely usefully?) admitted to the mistress's bed.

All thought of his marital problems fell away the minute he entered the potbank. This place was his life. The enthralment he had felt on his first childhood visit had never left him. He felt it now as he walked to his office, past the sheds and the workshops and the bottle ovens towering above the potters' yard and, last of all, the big throwing shed. The doors stood open and his eye fell on a pile of broken clay awaiting transportation to the sheds where discarded clay was reconstituted.

There was nothing unusual about that. What *was* unusual was the size of a shattered base and the curved shapes of other broken pieces, all of which appeared to have been very skilfully thrown and none of which seemed to justify rejection. Promptly he was inside the shed and examining them, his experienced eye noting not only their exceptional size but the excellence of their design and the clever way in which they had been thrown, each to its own shape and depth so that they would dovetail exactly. There were even signs that they had been bonded before being discarded. That puzzled him further.

'Whose work was this?' he asked. 'And what caused the accident?'

After a brief silence, one of the men spoke up.

''Tweren't no accident, sir. The boss destroyed it.'

'*Destroyed* – skilled throwing like this?'

The pieces must have matched without a fault – a new way of producing large-scale work, it seemed, and one worth pursuing. Glancing round the shed, he asked where Boswell was. It was unusual for the man not to be at his wheel at this hour.

Feet shuffled. Glances turned away. Someone mumbled that he had not turned up yet, then the wheels began to spin again. He ordered them to stop.

'If none of you knows where he is, at least you must know who made this. No inexperienced hands could have done it.'

That was different. Answering questions which could lead only to trouble was one thing; talking about work and allotting praise where it was due was quite another.

''Twere Jack, sir. Jack Lefever. But the boss didn't like it. 'Tweren't practical, he said. Waste of time and materials an' no one were likely to want anything that size, so into the slip bins it goes.'

Daniel had heard enough, and guessed more. Boswell was getting above himself. The man had always been over-confident and too full of his own importance. Anger stirred, but for the moment Daniel was more interested in Jacques Le Fevre. While all this conversation was going on, the young man had scarcely glanced up from his wheel.

Daniel called him over.

'What gave you this idea, Jacques?'

'It wasn't mine, sir. It belonged to the ancient Greeks. There are books in Stoke's public library, showing their art and their working methods. Their enormous garden urns are shown in detail, including the measurements they worked to and their method of assembling separate sections. I wanted to try it, just to prove to myself that it could be done. I wasn't aiming to push myself forward, sir.'

Daniel thought wryly that pushing himself forward was the last thing this good-looking and unassuming young man could be accused of.

'You've done splendidly,' he said. 'We'll go into production without delay. Ask Boswell to come to my office as soon as he arrives.'

There was an uncomfortable silence. When he asked what was wrong, the silence continued.

'Come *on*, men. Answer me.'

The earlier speaker said uncomfortably, 'He won't be turning up today, sir. Truth is. Constable Bailey be waiting for ye.'

Young Charlie Bailey looked out of place in the Master Potter's office, and felt it. His own small police depot, if such it could be called, housed nothing as well furnished as this. Stoke boasted a Chief Inspector and a full staff occupying impressive quarters, but Charlie was a village policeman in sole charge of a one-man station and therefore had to live on the premises.

The front room which, his wife declared, ought to be their parlour, was the official office, and the scullery at the back had been converted into a well-barred cell in which miscreants were locked before being carted off to higher authority in Stoke. The cell was mainly occupied by village drunks on Saturday nights, but his wife hated such proximity with local rabble.

But last night Millie had had no cause to complain about rowdyism, for Joe Boswell had been unconscious.

Charlie Bailey waited in an empty office, for Treadgold had been told to make his visit to the Potteries School of Design his first task of the day. Daniel greeted the constable and asked what brought him here, though guessing that it had something to do with Boswell's absence. The man had probably been arrested for being drunk and disorderly and Bailey had come to report that he had been locked up until sober. No doubt he was now sleeping it off.

'Well, sir . . . it's like this, sir . . .'

'It's Boswell, I take it. He's locked up in your cell, hence his absence.'

'Not exactly, sir. He were only there until the ambulance came to take him to hospital in Longton. He were found by the roadside, on a lonely patch on the way to Colney village. Must've been lying there unconscious for quite a time. Head badly gashed. A farm hand found him at dawn and yanked me out of bed . . .' Charlie dodged that because it recalled Millie's fury at being wakened so early. 'His head had apparently struck the prongs of a broken old pitchfork nearby. You know the way folk chuck things away in the country, sir, not giving a damn if others trip over 'em.'

'You say the pitchfork was lying "nearby". That could mean close, but not underfoot. It seems to me that if he had fallen where he stood, his head would have struck the ground. Instead, he fell "nearby", which suggests that he staggered there, or rolled there . . .' Daniel added thoughtfully, 'How bad is his injury?'

'I can't say, sir. All I know is, he needed stitching up and they're keeping him a while.' Bailey added confidentially, 'What's puzzling, sir, is what he were doing on the way to Colney, seeing as how he lives in the opposite direction. And there's another thing – everyone knows he rides to work daily on that nag of his, scorning the workers' transport. Some say he likes showing off his skill as a bareback rider—' Sensing that Daniel Frenshaw was not a man to respond to gossip, he amended hastily, 'What I mean, sir, is that his horse weren't nowhere around and when I checked I found he'd left it in the potbank's stable block. Unusual, isn't it, sir – keeping the old stables in use? Shouldn't think there's a potbank left that doesn't use 'em for other purposes now.'

'In this country area a few people still ride to work.'

Daniel rose, indicating that the meeting was over. He liked the police constable, but was in no mood to encourage further conversation. He was more disgusted than surprised by the news. It wasn't the first time Boswell had been taken into custody, the only difference being that this time there was apparently no charge of disturbing the peace.

'Any idea what time it happened?' he asked, sensing that the constable was expecting questions, but Bailey merely shook his head and said no doubt the hospital could answer that one. He had gone in the ambulance with his charge, but hadn't waited because there was nothing further he could do once the admission formalities were over. ('For God's sake don't hang around there, Charlie! And come in quietly when you do get back. I don't want to be wakened twice in one night!' Real irritable, Millie had been.)

To Daniel, the matter was closed. Boswell had no doubt been drinking at some hostelry other than his local one and, on returning to pick up his horse, his unsteady legs had deserted him when reaching the abandoned pitchfork. That was a logical explanation for him striking his head on it. Tomorrow the man would turn up for work slightly the worse for wear, sporting a dressing on his head but as cocksure as ever.

'Thank you for reporting the matter to me, Constable.'

That closed the interview, but Bailey lingered. Shuffling uncomfortably, he said, 'There's reason to believe he'd not been alone, sir.'

'You mean his drinking companions had left him to sleep it off? One can hardly blame them.'

'No, sir.' The constable's fingers were unfastening the breast pocket of his tunic, then producing something. 'This were found, sir. Caught in his clothes.'

He placed a trinket on the Master Potter's desk. It lay there, winking in the sun. A cheap little chain bracelet with tiny charms dangling from it.

'Tells its own story, don't it, sir? So did the earth, the grass all mangled as if two people 'ad been – well, you know what I mean, sir. I thought mebbe the woman might work here and want the bracelet back. That's why I brought it.'

'Do you really think any woman would come forward? The best thing you can do is lock it up with lost property until an enquiry comes along. If it does. I imagine few women would draw attention to the fact that they had been with the man in such circumstances. With lost property, isn't it the rule to pass it on to the finder if it remains unclaimed? Or, in this case, perhaps Mrs Bailey might like it?'

The constable refrained from quoting his wife's opinion of it.

'I can't lock it up, sir. One-man stations like mine aren't fitted with safes.'

'But surely—'

'And there's no one in charge when I'm out on my beat, sir. I can't expect my wife to deal with things, what with the kids and the housework an' all.' ('I'm not having any truck with local tarts!' Millie had declared, tossing the thing aside after first examining it to see if it was likely to fetch anything.)

So that's the way it is, thought Daniel intuitively. Poor devil. The rumours of Millie Bailey's sharp tongue were apparently true. The constable's brother was a forestry hand at Dunmore and lived on the estate; in such close communities items of gossip filtered through to all levels.

The door finally closed behind the constable, leaving the cheap little bracelet on the Master Potter's desk. And what the hell do I do with it? Daniel thought as he swept it unseeingly into a drawer.

Early in the afternoon, Kate Willcox limped through the gates.

'Good day t' ye, Todd,' she said to the gatekeeper and, giving him no chance to answer, continued on her way. Even with the support of sticks she maintained a proud, almost militant air. When young she had walked tall, head high, carriage graceful, and somehow the bent body still conveyed the same air, though she must be into her seventies now. She'd had a brace of kids before her last one, George, was born.

Simon Todd let her pass with an almost deferential touch of his cap. He knew she could find her way round this place blindfold and no one would say her nay. Other workers from the past could be forgotten, but never Kate Willcox. She had been the queen bee here long ago but the smile she gave him now was that of a tired old woman.

Sadly, he watched her go, wondering if those long-ago rumours about her had been based on truth. People always thought the worst of beautiful women . . . that they were no better than they should be, that there were always plenty of men in their lives, even, in Kate Willcox's case, that there had been one in particular and famous at that, though how painting pictures could bring a man fame was something local working folk couldn't understand. Anyway, the rumour had died and there had never been any proof that she had ever been anything but a good wife, and a good mother to the six Willcox children she had borne – all long since scattered, or dead.

He thought now, as he had always thought, how sad it was that a woman such as she had been born into a background of stark poverty, rough to a degree.

Coming from a family of miners and marrying into a family of labouring potters, she had never risen above her environment, though looks like hers could surely have lifted her way beyond them.

Todd watched her bent figure cross the cobbled yard and disappear in the direction of the Master Potter's office. Not that she could be heading there – there were other buildings in the same direction and many a workshed she could drop into for a chat. Such intrusion might not be tolerated at other potteries, but that a former and much respected worker should be welcomed was typical of Frenshaws.

The door of Daniel's office was ajar. After rapping on it with her bony knuckles, Kate called across the threshold, 'Mornin', Master Daniel. I wonder if ye can spare a moment of your time?'

He looked up from his desk with a smile and said, 'For you, Kate, always.'

Then he was helping her over the step and across the room to a chair.

'Lawks, sir, I don't need helping! Me pins still git me around.' But she sank into the chair gratefully and somehow he knew she wanted nothing so much as to rub her knees to relieve the ache in them, but wouldn't give in.

He noticed, too, that she looked haggard this morning.

There was a brass-ornamented, upright telephone on his desk. Unhooking the earpiece, he then pressed a button and ordered tea. Kate smiled faintly. 'My, Master Danny, you must be the first manager of

Frenshaws to have a smart thing like that on his desk, just for ordering tea.'

He laughed. 'It has more important uses than that, Kate, and greater forms of communication have yet to come.'

'And *you*'ll be the first to have 'em, sir. You allus were a one for progress. Look at that steam engine driving the sliphouse machinery now – bigger an' more powerful than the one afore, from the looks of it.'

'So you remember that one, do you? Then you'll also remember how everyone predicted it would be a waste of money, and you won't be surprised that the same was said of this one. Instead, it's worth its weight in gold. And soon it will be replaced by the latest and most modern. I have other improvements in mind, other advances – in particular, expansion that will surprise everyone. But why are we avoiding things? There's something on your mind.'

Couldn't hide anything from Master Danny, you couldn't, thought Kate with relief. Even so, she found it hard to begin.

'It's not like you to hesitate,' he said gently, 'but take your time. We won't be interrupted. Treadgold has gone to Stoke this morning. And now here comes our tea.'

It was hot and sweet and merciful. It eased Kate's weariness. She was so grateful that she was unable to speak, but Daniel Frenshaw appeared not to notice. He was a patient man. He would wait, even though he knew that only something vitally important could have brought her here. She wouldn't have trudged so far from her village without very good reason. Inevitably, his mind turned to Joe Boswell, then dismissed him.

Kate Willcox had no time for her daughter-in-law's husband and certainly wouldn't take such a walk to plead that his latest scrape should not cost him his job. She'd be more likely to wish that it would. ('. . . *and good riddance to 'im! Should've bin kicked out long ago, that 'e should.*') If she hadn't heard the news already, she would hear it soon enough, and he could imagine her saying those very words.

'Are you still comfortable in your cottage?' he asked to ease the moment.

She nodded, but said nothing. She just sat there, staring down at her gnarled hands. For Kate to be lost for words was unusual. Wasn't she well? If not, how had she managed to walk all the way from Colney with the prospect of the same walk back?

He said abruptly, 'What is it, Kate? Tell me.'

A moment's hesitation, then it came in a rush.

'It's my Sarah — and 'er bastard stepfather.'

He saw then that her hands were shaking. He had never seen the laughing Kate close to tears, but the faded eyes were suddenly brimming and sobs were racking her shrunken frame. He was immediately on his feet and round the other side of his desk, his hands on the bent shoulders, his touch compassionate.

'Tell me, Kate. Whatever the trouble is, *tell* me.' Even as he spoke he was remembering Boswell's raised fist yesterday morning and the girl's instinctive shrinking. 'Has the man been ill-treating her?'

'Worse.' Kate choked, tried again, and at last the words poured out. 'The swine raped 'er. Last night. *She* . . . a virgin . . . innocent as they come . . . an' the bastard *raped* 'er! God knows how she dragged 'erself back to me. I've seen other rape victims in me time, *and* tended 'em, but never the likes o' me poor dear lass after Joe Boswell 'ad finished with 'er.'

Had her eyes not been tear-dimmed she would have seen the raw shock in Daniel Frenshaw's, the outrage and disgust and the surge of blazing anger, but he was a man who had learned self-control and knew he had to practise it now although, coupled with deep compassion for this distraught old woman, he was filled with horror at the thought of her granddaughter's vile experience. He visualised the agony and the terror of it and mentally recoiled from the thought of Sarah's young body being defiled and her innocence destroyed by brutality. Simultaneously the memory of her facing up to Boswell's threatening fist leapt into his mind, followed by a picture of her walking away across the potters' yard, her slim young back erect, her carriage graceful. Like a flash the memory came, revealing how strongly it was embedded in his mind – as she was.

With an effort he stifled his storming reactions and listened to Kate's voice saying, 'She allus comes to me on 'er birthday an' we 'ave a party like, just the two of us. She wouldn't miss it for the world, an' yesterday were special 'cos it were 'er fifteenth, which meant the end of 'er first year's apprenticing an' the end of extra work after the potbank closed, so she could get to me even earlier and dodge going home with that bastard. Fifteen may be grown up with some wenches, but not with our Sarah. She were an innocent lamb and me heart's treasure, an' so she will for ever be, but this 'as done summat to 'er wot even *I* can't cure. She couldn't utter a word, an' no wonder. When I saw what'd bin done to 'er I took a fair guess at who'd done it, an' the look on her face told me I were right. Brutalised, she were. So badly she'll bear the memory for ever.'

Swiftly Daniel asked if she had called a doctor, but Kate shook her head, saying that the doctor's Ford at her door would set tongues wagging 'mongst the neighbours, who never missed a thing.

'Got eyes wot can see through walls, those gossiping neighbours o' mine, an' seeing me up and around as usual would prove 'tweren't *I* as needed doct'ring, an' then they'd soon be telling everyone that old Kate Willcox were breaking that there single occupation law an' the cat'd be in the fire. 'Sides, I've me own cures for everything, *and* they work. Nobody knows better 'n I wot t' do at such times, an' I didn't leave the lass alone 'till I'd done everything that had to be done. I doctored 'er thorough, then gave 'er one o' me herb draughts for sleeping, and out she went like a light. She be safely locked up an' away from prying eyes, but I must get back afore she wakes, an' when she does she'll be ahungered, please God.'

The aging voice rallied. 'For miles around I be known for me nature cures, an' many's the woman I've tended when needed. That's why they call me the Witch Doctor, an' think I don't know. Any old woman growing herbs an' making special mixes gets called that, but folk come t' me just the same, specially for troubles I keep quiet about an' dealing wi' things they never want known, like the gypsies do. *They* never need no doctors, for childbirth or nowt. I keep me mouth shut an' never say nay. I were able t' do all that were needed to make me poor lass safe from what could've followed on, but there's nowt I can do for the state of my Sarah's mind or the memory of that brute's violence . . .'

Daniel remained silent, the muscles of his face taut and his eyes hard. Kate had never seen him look like that – steely, relentless.

'So that's why I've come to ye, Master Potter. I can't let me poor lass come face to face with that man agin, which means she won't be coming back to Frenshaws so long as Boswell works there. I'll not be letting 'er go back to Mabel Boswell's place neether, even if the woman fights to get 'er back. Sarah's staying right where she be, in that cottage o'mine, an' if I be turned out for breaking the rule it'll 'ave t' be done bodily. Either which way my Sarah stays with me. *There*, now – I've said me piece an' all I ask is that ye tell nobuddy why the girl's left this potbank. As for 'er apprentice indenchers, I ask ye now to tear 'em up as a favour t' me an' my Sarah. 'Tis the first favour I've ever asked o' ye, Master Danny, an' I promise it'll be the last.'

Controlling his thoughts, Daniel promised that whatever he could do to help would be done, but indentures were binding. 'I'll file them away until Sarah is ready to talk to you and, I hope, to me. If it's her wish, I will destroy them and of course tell no one because she would not be admitted to the Design School were it known that her apprenticeship had been terminated. Except for fee-paying students, of which only a limited number are accepted, admission hinges on candidates being sponsored by their employers, which means that Sarah's apprenticeship must still stand. I'm thinking of her future, as you are, but we must create no problems.'

'And wot about that swine? 'E keeps 'is job, I s'pose?'

How could he tell this distraught old lady that to do the one thing he most wanted to do would bring him up against an unyielding obstacle? His instinct and his desire was to sack Boswell immediately, but the latest move in trade unionism was being more successful than its forerunners. The voice of The National Amalgamated Union of Male and Female Pottery Workers was proving more effective than the stormy rantings of its predecessors, and one of the things this new group had successfully campaigned against was the instant dismissal of workers without the justification of consistently bad workmanship.

To this and other demands, the Frenshaw potbank had felt compelled to agree. Competitors commented wryly that the place had indulged its workers ever since Daniel had become Master Potter, but at the time it had seemed to him a matter of fairness. Even before the new union was formed, he had introduced a system of demotion rather than dismissal, delegating them to lesser positions and lower wages until they proved themselves deserving of reinstatement. In nine cases out of ten the policy had worked, but when it came to offences against workmates, unless these were committed on the premises no employer could sit in judgment. Whatever a man did in his private life was his own affair.

As for women, the day had yet to come when they could accuse a man of sexual offences and get away with it. Separate moral laws for men and women had always existed. As for rape, it was as old as time and the woman was invariably blamed for inviting it. Few would believe her if she swore she had not. Besides, declared the majority of potbank owners throughout Staffordshire, all that had nothing to do with the bosses.

It was the one area in which no one could interfere,

so in every respect but one Daniel's hands were now tied. Unless he wanted to make matters worse for Sarah Willcox and expose her to gossip and even condemnation, he had to conceal his abhorrence of Boswell. He had to make sure that the ugly truth remained known only to the girl, her grandmother and himself. Even now, in the twenties and after a hideous war, rape was something to be hushed up, particularly in country areas where traditional attitudes died hard.

So how to deal with Boswell? Sacking a man who was an expert worker would have this new Union and all its members campaigning for justice, no matter how greatly disliked the man was.

It could even build up sympathy and support for him. Just because he had been found drunk by the roadside (and with a head injury, poor devil) that was no justification for kicking him out of his job. Even if he came before the magistrates, he had committed no crime for which he could be indicted.

And how could rape be proved? More often than not it would be dismissed as malicious gossip, or the woman be accused of courting it. The best thing she could do was to keep quiet.

And here in the Potteries arrests for drunkenness and disorderly behaviour were quickly forgotten. High spirits on pay night merited a night's lock-up and a fine for any damage caused, but no more, and absence from work because of it was considered punishment enough since the majority of pottery workers were paid piece-work rates, so the culprit inevitably lost financially. It was therefore up to him to stay sober.

Much of this was already known to Kate, but the rest had to be explained. 'Believe me,' said Daniel when he had finished, 'I share your feelings, and by all means we must keep Sarah from any contact with the man. Only time will help her to to get over such an experience—'

'If she ever do, Master Danny. My lass ain't like others. She be mighty sensitive; don't show 'er feelings much, but they go deep. An' she remembers things. Many's the time I've bin astonished by wot she remembers. An' I knows well enough that folks would look at 'er askance if a whisper o' this vileness got out. *I* know wot they'd say, and the way they'd brand 'er. But one o'these days I'll get that bastard. One o' these days he'll get his deserts.'

Daniel reached out, took her hands, and said urgently, 'Dear Kate, believe me when I say that if it were in my power to get rid of the man at once, I *would*, but for now there is only one thing I can do, only one step I can take. I can downgrade him and promote another man to chief thrower above him. And that I will do and waste no time about it.'

He found himself relishing the thought. All he needed was one good reason, one perfect excuse, and he already had it. Boswell had destroyed a potentially valuable piece of work which was legally the property of Frenshaws. He had gone even further than that in rejecting what could have been a splendid selling line, without consultation with the management. He had taken it upon himself to dictate what could and could not be produced by the Frenshaw potbank and dearly would he pay for it, though not as dearly as he deserved for his abuse of Sarah Willcox.

'At least I'll get *some* satisfaction, though not enough,' Daniel admitted to Kate, 'and I'll give him the news the moment he returns. Right now he's in hospital with a head injury—' At Kate's surprise he related how the man had been found, and the presumed cause.

'Presumed?' pounced Kate. 'That means guessed at, don't it?'

'Yes, but it seemed obvious at the time.'

'At the time! D' ye mean ye think else now?'

'No, Kate, I do not. Plainly the man fell, or rolled over and struck his head on a broken pitchfork.'

'Who told ye all this? Who found 'im?'

Daniel told her of Charlie Bailey's visit.

'So folk *do* know,' she quavered.

'Only that Boswell was picked up by the wayside. He was alone and injured and taken to hospital and that's the whole of it.' He hesitated, then reached for a drawer in his desk and withdrew something. She saw it glitter in his hand and her face whitened.

'It was caught in his clothes,' Daniel told her gently. He saw now that the tiny charms were the initials 'S' and 'W', and the picture of Sarah Willcox's face came vividly to him once again.

With an effort he said, 'Constable Bailey brought it. He thought it might belong to some female worker who might lay claim to it.'

Kate reached out a shaking hand, and took it. ''Twere me birthday gift,' she whispered. 'Must've caught in the bastard's clothes.' She thrust it into a pocket. 'Thanks for giving it t' me, Master Danny. I'll keep it hid until she misses it, then I'll say it fell off 'er wrist as she stumbled over me doorstep.' She struggled to her feet. 'I've taken up enough of your time, sir. I've said what I came t' say, an' I mean it. Keep her indenchers if ye must, but no way will I agree to our Sarah coming back so long as that bastard's here.' She added urgently, 'My lass don't know I've told ye, Master Danny . . .'

'Nor ever will. Trust me, Kate.'

She tried to thank him, but could find no words. She could only look at him and stammer, 'Well – I'd best be on me way.'

'Not yet. There's a way of keeping Sarah away from Boswell, and I will arrange it. She can be enrolled at the Design School full time instead of part time. Treadgold has gone there today to make preliminary arrangements, but full time can be applied for instead. The snag is that admission can only start with the opening of a fresh term, for which we'll have to wait. Even I can't overrule that, though I happen to be one of six leading potbank owners elected to the Board of Trustees this year. The full course lasts three years and can be extended to other branches of ceramics if a pupil shows a particular bent. My own assessment of those broken samples of Sarah's is that she has talents yet to be explored, and that takes time, so once she's there she'll be far away from the potbank until she finally qualifies. When that happens and she returns to Frenshaws I'll see that she works nowhere near the throwing area and that space beyond that will be strictly out of bounds to Boswell. Meanwhile there's the present to think of. Plainly, she must not go back home but on no account must the Housing Board find out that she is living with you.'

'I've already thought o' that. It'll be a few days yet afore she'll want to step outdoors with 'er poor young face all swollen an' bruised, an' I don't want folks staring an' asking how she got that way. Mercifully my treatments work faster than most an' scars disappear quicker in the young than in the old. Meantime, we can take a breath of air together after dark, when folks' curtains be drawn.'

Such a picture disturbed Daniel, but the only practical help he could give as yet was to arrange for the apprentice money to continue.

'Once she's at at the Design School it will be replaced with a larger retaining fee and guaranteed employment on graduation,' he said. 'Meanwhile, do nothing to risk losing your home, and keep me informed about Sarah. And don't forget you can always turn to me.' He smiled. 'Our friendship goes back a long time, doesn't it, Kate?'

When Daniel smiled his whole face changed, obliterating the serious and sometimes tense lines. With the intuition of the old, Kate had sensed for some time that all was not right with his marriage and that his reserved air hid much, but his smile now was almost reminiscent of the boy who used to come striding through the workshops.

'Aye, it does indeed, Master Danny.' She added slowly, 'Why are ye always so ready to help?'

'Because I want to. Because I wanted to a long time ago and your stiff-necked pride wouldn't let me. Because I thought highly of your son, as I do of you. And because the promise his daughter shows should be given every chance to develop. Aren't those reasons enough?'

Six

Joe Boswell returned to the Frenshaw Pottery with his head bandaged and a scowl on his face. It deepened when he saw Jacques Le Fevre working at the chief thrower's wheel, and even more when he saw what he was making.

'What the bloody hell are you playing at, Lefever?'

'Master's orders,' Jacques said absently, lost in his work.

Smothered laughter made Boswell spin round. To his further outrage he saw the rest of his men working on graduated sections, all plainly designed to become part of the kind of monstrosity he had thrown out the other day. In one stride he reached Jacques Le Fevre, who glanced up and said, 'We're working on a new Grecian line Frenshaws are launching,' and then got on with his work.

One of the men, a cheeky devil named Luke Walker who had long been a thorn in Boswell's flesh and whose chirpiness seemed to make him impervious to reprimand or snub, piped, 'I reckon the Master Potter'll be pleased to tell ye all about it, so why don't ye pay 'im a visit? I'll bet he'll gladly welcome back a battle-scarred hero!'

Loud laughter was Boswell's first warning that things

were different, that something had happened behind his back and, whatever it was, he was not going to like it. Beneath his anger, uneasiness stirred. This damn Frenchie was responsible, of course, selling his own ideas, pushing himself forward, trying to grab his job.

Jacques' wheel slowed to a stop. The broad clay base, with gradually widening walls rising nearly three feet above it, was perfectly thrown and of consistent thickness. It was not only equal in quality to anything Joe had thrown in all his years at the pottery, but an honest man would have admitted that it was even better. But not Boswell. No one had ever excelled him and nothing would ever induce him to admit that this man now had.

Carefully, Jacques sliced off his work, set it aside, seized another lump of prepared clay of equal weight so that uniformity would be maintained, slammed it on to the revolving wheel, centred it expertly, touched the foot treadle to increase the speed, and ignored Boswell.

The man's temper rose. He'd had enough of opposition, what with those tykes at the hospital giving him a piece of straight talk about drunks like him taking up time that could be better spent on sick people who were there through no fault of their own. And then, on the way home in the bus that took them to the nearest point to the smallholding, there'd been Mabel's narking about the shame he'd brought on her. For an alarming moment he'd thought she meant the shame of what he'd done to her girl, though what shame there was about that he failed to see, but all she was moaning about was the drinking binge he'd been on and the talk she'd had to put up with from neighbouring folk.

'Made me feel right shamed, they did, right

shamed . . .' To which he'd said to hell with them and that he drank no more than anybody else and to shut up, for God's sake.

But she didn't. He had counted on sympathy from Mabel, but all she went on about was the disgrace he'd brought on her, until he'd wished she hadn't bothered to come to the hospital to bring him home.

The word 'disgrace' had startled him. Since none was attached to getting drunk and passing out, what was she complaining about? Not the other thing! Surely she couldn't know about that? Young Sarah would be too scared to talk, and even if she did she wouldn't be believed. Everyone knew she was a strange sort of creature, quiet, sort of buttoned up. Shy, some called it, which he considered rubbish. Anyway, she'd be too frightened to open her mouth because if she did, she'd get no sympathy. Women got what they asked for, didn't they?

After a while he had let his wife's plaintive reproaches run over his head in an unheeded stream, until a string of words jerked him to attention.

'What d' ye mean – she's gone?' he demanded. 'Where to? And how could she?'

'Like anyone does – walk out and not come back. Went off to work that morning an' didn't come home that night. Real feared, I were. Thought she must be on her way home with you, so I didn't worry till *you* didn't turn up neether. An' then I remembered 'twere her birthday and she always goes to her gran's that day, so as the night wore on I knew she must've stayed there, though I were ready to give her a good ticking off for worriting me like that. You too, Joe, till I heard ye'd bin lying injured by the roadside. The shock of that drove all else from my mind. I've bin through a bad time, wot wi' the news about you and hearing nowt from Sarah until the old woman arrived, cool as a cucumber, and told me the lass were staying with her an' if I tried to interfere I'd be sorry. The bare-faced cheek of it! I've never liked that old woman an' she's never liked me, but I'll be crossing no swords with such a one. She's got the evil eye.'

Joe's guffaw had jolted his bandaged head, hurting so much that his laughter was cut off and he avenged the pain on his wife, calling her a witless fool. 'All the silly cow can do is make threats. Try threatening her back.'

'What for?'

'Enticing your girl away. As for Sarah, let her go. Who cares?'

'*I* do. I'm her mam.'

'Well, I bain't her dad an' *I* say, let the wench go and good riddance. She's nothing but a cheap little whore.'

'How *dare* you, Joe Boswell?' Despite her mind-blown obsession with him, latent motherhood still stirred occasionally in Mabel and she really flew off the handle then, pouring rage on his head until he told her to shut up, for God's sake, and if she didn't, he'd get off this bus and walk all the way to the potbank, and by the time he got home tonight she'd better have a still tongue in her head . . . 'Because I'll be tired after pot-throwing non-stop an' I'll need some home comfort.'

'Oh, Joe,' she pleaded, 'you don't need to go straight back to work!'

'Course I do. I'm paid piece-work, so I've gotta catch up. This accident's cost me money, but I bain't one to shirk me duty. They'll be needing me at Frenshaws. Must be in a right mess without me.'

'We-ell, if ye really feel up to it, Joe – though I do think ye should rest awhile.'

'*Rest?*' he had scoffed, as if he couldn't spare time for such luxury. 'I've gotta get back to my wheel or the devil only knows what delays there'll be. I'll bet those lazy sods under me are sitting on their backsides, doing nowt. Frenshaws cain't git along without me.'

'Then look out for Sarah, will ye? Tell her I don't mind her staying with her gran but I do wish she'd come home.' Mabel finished fretfully, 'I really cain't think why she took it into her head to do this at a time when you be injured and *I* left all alone.'

'Don't you worry, Mabel. She'll come back. Where else can she live? Not with the old woman. There be rules about almshouses.'

The bus from Stoke terminated a mile from the potbank in the opposite direction from the smallholding. Here they parted company, Mabel still protesting that he wasn't well enough to walk that distance and he only too glad to prove that he was. He was helped on his way by thinking of the power he would now enjoy with the girl available to his will. He'd have to go carefully, of course – Mabel's eyes could dart suspiciously sometimes. He'd have to find a place for regular use of the girl, but there was really no problem there with so many broken-down barns and outbuildings scattered around.

But she had to be stopped from seeing too much of old Kate. The closeness between those two was the only thing that vaguely disturbed him. Mabel had said she was now staying with the old woman. If so, just when had she gone back there? He knew Sarah had been to see her grandmother before he finally tracked her down, because he had left the Boar's Head to pick her up as usual after the apprentices had finished their cleaning, and had met that pert little piece, Daisy. She had asked why he was waiting.

'Not for Sarah, is it? She don't 'ave to stay on like the rest of us now, so she's gone to her gran's. She allus do on 'er birthday, don't she?' So he had headed for the village of Colney, stopping a few times to wet his whistle at taverns along the way and anticipating the moments to come. He couldn't fail to catch her on her way home.

And it had all gone according to plan until he fell on that rusty old pitchfork, and when the police constable had roused him, the girl had vanished. After that, he hadn't wasted another thought on her – until now.

'Didn't come home all night,' Mabel had said, but surely, after he'd had his way with her, she wouldn't have gone back to old Kate's place? From that point it was the longer walk, so she *must* have gone home and avoided Mabel somehow. He could picture her creeping up to that poky room of hers, drawing no attention to herself and saying nothing, and he hoped to God she'd said nothing to Kate Willcox later, or to anyone else – though who would heed the tittle-tattling of a young lass or the rantings of a crone in her seventies?

These thoughts had been on his mind when he entered the throwing shed, but were driven out by the sight of Jacques Le Fevre working on *his* wheel and by the jibes and laughter of his men. But worst of all was the realisation of what was going on. At Luke Walker's taunt, he turned his back on the lot of them and strode off to the Master Potter's office.

That old pen-pusher, Treadgold, was there, seated at

his ledgers like a thin black crow, grey and black pin-striped trousers hidden beneath his desk and his black jacket relieved only by a stiff white celluloid collar rising to his chin. Its two small wings stuck out above a black bow which was anchored by an elastic band round the collar. His hair was grey and his complexion almost matched. Rimless spectacles were a permanent fixture on his hooked nose. He looked as if he'd been sitting at that desk and writing in those ledgers all his life, and there was an air of contentment about him suggesting that he never wanted to do anything else.

Not that Boswell noticed any of this when his knock on the door brought a command to enter. The only time he ever heeded the book-keeper was when lining up for the pay envelope which bore his piece-work earnings listed on the front, plus the extra emolument as chief thrower, all penned in the man's laborious copperplate writing, and he ignored him now as he approached the Master Potter's desk, his heavy boots scuffing the floor.

To his chagrin Daniel Frenshaw didn't look up. He was absorbed in a batch of papers which Boswell recognised as labour sheets, weekly analyses of work throughout the pottery, broken down into day sheets which supervisors returned to the Master Potter's office at the close of work.

Somewhere among those labour sheets was one from the throwing shed, *his* department. At the end of each day he signed it, indicating the number of items each man had thrown, and of course he never over-assessed his own output or under-calculated another's. He would never be so dishonest! Yet what he had seen in the shed just now showed how dishonestly *he*'d been treated during an absence that was no fault of his own.

Daniel Frenshaw let him wait. He had recognised the man's footstep, even his heavy knock on the door. When he finished studying the last report he said absently, 'So you're back, Boswell,' and didn't even bother to look up. Boswell grunted in acknowledgement, trying to sound like a man still suffering, but Frenshaw was collecting the papers into a batch and didn't seem to notice. Unfeeling devil.

'These all seem to be in order, Treadgold, but here they are for double-checking. Hobson's shed seems to be getting record results. He's turned out more expert turners than any man before him.'

The bulky concertina file was passed to Treadgold's desk, and still Boswell was left waiting. The bugger's doing it on purpose, he swore inwardly, his eyes fixed on the Master Potter's fine Norfolk suiting and estimating that it must have cost a fine penny. Unlike other pottery lords, Daniel Frenshaw never wore the traditional formal wear. He was a countryman and favoured well-tailored tweeds. When doing the rounds of the sheds he discarded his jacket and donned a potter's slop like any of his workers, and examined clay and slips and oxides expertly and talked to the potters man to man, and they respected him for his knowledge and his understanding of their problems.

But right at this moment he seemed indifferent to Boswell's. From the way he ignored him anyone would think he didn't even know about them, but that couldn't be so. He was the boss, wasn't he? He knew everything that went on in every shed. Then what about *my* shed? fumed Boswell, shuffling impatiently and adding a faint moan of pain to attract attention. It seemed to work this time for Frenshaw looked at him at last, but all he said was, 'So you're back,' as if he hadn't said it already, then continued, 'There was no need to report to me. You clocked in in the usual way, I take it. However, since you are here, I can tell you that you have been replaced as chief thrower. Had you gone straight to your shed, you would have realised that.'

His voice and his eyes were cold, unusual in a man who was normally courteous to his workers, though firm when necessary and just in punishment. But not this time! And what in God's name am I being punished *for*? Boswell growled to himself. Not because of a drop too much outside working hours – the job can't be taken away just for that. The Union won't allow it. They'll see me reinstated, and quickly.

The thought revived his confidence. 'Ye cain't do this, Master Potter. Ye cain't take a man's job away from him just because he's injured in an accident.'

Boswell touched his bandaged head and winced expressively, but the Master Potter merely said, 'That isn't the reason. And the Union cannot protest because I am within my rights in downgrading you. Without permission you destroyed a fine piece of work which was the property of this company, and dictated that Frenshaws should produce nothing of its kind again. The management decides what shall and shall not be manufactured here, and it is *I* who gives such orders.'

Beneath the anger was something stronger, a hint that the Master Potter held something worse against him. A less obtuse man than Boswell would have recognised it as contempt combined with disgust, but all he was aware of was the anger. He took a step backward, hesitated, then blurted out defiantly, 'It were bad work, badly thrown, only fit for chucking out! I be the best thrower in the Potteries an' I know bad work when I sees it. And Jack Lefever had no right to make summat like that off his own bat.'

'He had as much right as you or any potter in this place who chooses to develop an idea after working hours. Enterprise like that, keenness like that, is what makes a successful potter. And the work was *not* bad. I examined every broken piece myself. You smashed it for a reason of your own. Jealousy, because it wasn't your own work.' The Master Potter made a dismissive gesture. 'You have the choice of going back to work with the other throwers, under Le Fevre, or working elsewhere in this potbank. How about the dispatch department? I'm sure they could do with extra hands, and you've been in the business long enough to know how china has to be straw-packed in plaited willow crates. Of course wages would be lower so if you dislike the idea, Boswell, you are free to seek work elsewhere. I am acting in accordance with Union rules.'

For a moment the only sound was the uninterrupted scratching from Treadgold's desk. That all this should take place in front of that pen-pusher was the final insult and tipped Boswell's rage over the edge. He opened his mouth to shout abuse, but was forestalled again by the Master Potter.

'Alternatively, you may prefer to help your wife run her neglected smallholding. Whatever your choice, remember my warning about threatening your step-daughter. She is a young lady of talent and is to be a protégée of this establishment for the next three years. I see from your face that all this is news to you. Don't forget to close the door on your way out.'

Boswell slammed it behind him. Outside, he walked unseeingly between the maze of worksheds until he reached the canal and stopped dead, staring at the water. Rage was subsiding beneath fear. There had been something in the Master Potter's tone that he had never sensed before. Threat. Knowledge. Even disgust. But what kind of threat? And what kind of knowledge? And above all, why disgust?

Alarm clamped tightly on Boswell's mind. He slumped to the ground and stayed there, unaware of time and equally unaware of the stares of bargees unloading supplies and the derisive jeers of Frenshaw workmen carting them away. 'Ain't yer got nowt t' do, Joe Boswell?' Even the catcalls about his bandaged head fell on deaf ears. 'Bin knocking ye about, 'as she, Joe?' He was aware of nothing but a seething fury, a desire for revenge. He had to hit back at that lot in the throwing shed and, by God, at the Master Potter too, but equally strong was an instinct to walk out of this place, shouting, 'To hell with the lot o' ye! There ain't a potbank in Staffs that won't jump at a chance to get Joe Boswell!'

But would they if the Union didn't oppose Daniel Frenshaw?

It was a sobering thought and made him think again. The world was a harsh and unfair place and he felt profoundly sorry for himself, but that brought him no nearer to a solution. To walk out was tempting, but through his sore head common sense began to penetrate. What would he be walking out *to*? A wife bossing him around, reminding him constantly that the place was hers and not his. Like hell I will, he vowed, and faced the alternative – to stay where he was, take whatever this potbank had to offer, and bide his time. He was good at that. He'd hankered after Sarah Willcox since she was ten, and at last he'd had her. And enjoyed it. And would again.

Wearily, Joe dragged himself to his feet. His head was aching and the day had gone sour on him, dampening his rebellion. His dominant need now was to decide what to do, and logic forced it on him. He had to accept or reject the Master Potter's alternatives, so it made sense to choose the best one. And when it came to it, there was really no choice – he was a pot-thrower, not a turner or a finisher or a wedger or a sagger-maker or a packer or any other lesser degree of pottery worker. He could do only one thing, and there was only one place where he could do it – back in the throwing shed, with that Frenchie lording it over him (*and* earning the chief thrower's emolument). And there'd be no more kow-towing from the rest of the men. The thought stung, but it also fired his determination and his arrogance. I'll damn well show 'em that no one has ever bested Joe Boswell!

And *that* would put the handsome Jack Lefever back in his place.

Brushing mud from the seat of his trousers, he made his way back, strode into the shed, glanced round at every wheel and shouted, 'A bloody lot of sluggards you lot are! You're no further on than when I left ye.' He then carried a hunk of clay to Jacques Le Fevre's former wheel, slammed it down, spun it into position and called over his shoulder, 'Well, Master Thrower, let's see who does the better job, shall we?' But there was no geniality in his voice.

Jacques, smiling inwardly, accepted the challenge.

'Right, Boswell. You're on.'

Seven

A wedge of light from between drawn curtains pierced Sarah's eyelids, urging her to wake, but an inner resistance held her back. She didn't want to return, to remember, to *feel*. Unaware that for nearly twenty-four hours she had lain traumatised, nightmare recollections intermittently possessing her until Kate's merciful administrations had finally brought prolonged sleep, her brain now told her that there was a powerful reason for her inner resistance and when physical pain stirred her, memory plunged her back into reality.

She lay quietly until movement made her aware of dressings between her legs; then came recollections of Gran's gnarled but able hands cleansing her. They had been as gentle as a mother's with her babe.

Obediently, Sarah had drunk the bitter potion her grandmother finally mixed. '*That*'ll take care of ye, me luv. No risk of the worst now . . .' And Sarah knew what she meant.

But now, between the ebbing and flowing of induced sleep, came the agony of torn flesh and the recollection of Joe Boswell's besieging body, and at once the hideousness came alive, and the hatred, and the degradation.

She closed her eyes again, seeking oblivion but

finding none, so against her will she opened them and scanned the empty room. Had Gran deserted her, leaving her alone like this? The thought shamed her as she recalled the wrinkled face forcing a smile through tears, and the arms cradling her and the rough voice saying, '*I*'ll take care o' ye, little luv. *I*'ll see thee well. There be nowt t' beat old wives' cures. Penniless women've allus had to fend for themselves an' none knows better 'n me how t' do it. Ye've nowt to worry about, me blessed one. In a few days ye'll be yourself agin.'

But she would never be herself. Not as she had once been, only as she had become – a young woman befouled by a man on the wayside. A creature of shame. Vaguely she recalled murmuring this as Gran covered her, and the old woman telling her, sharply, not to go thinking that way.

'*You*'ve done nowt wrong, our Sarah. T'was that stepfather o' yours, an' I swear to God nobuddy in this world'll ever be allowed to point a finger at ye so long as *I* be alive. An' now that drink'll make ye sleep the clock round and then ye'll face another day, and another, and another, safe with me. Ye'll not be going back to your mam's place and nobuddy's going to cross this doorstep to take ye away from me.'

On she had gone, and on, her love calming fear as expertly as her ministrations healed wounds.

'I've done this for many a woman, lass, an' all were fine afterwards, same as you're going t' be. Those comfrey poultices will cure the bruising an' my dressings will heal the wounds an' the bleeding, and inside ye I've taken care of all else. As for the shock an' what ye be thinking of as shame, ye've gotta be patient.

In time all that will go too, even though ye'll nivver forget. And one day ye'll learn that not all men are swine.'

Now Sarah realised that her neck and shoulders and jaw also bore dressings from which came a faint but familiar country smell – comfrey, one of the healers Kate swore by. 'Used proper, mind ye. Used as it oughta be.'

When Sarah tried to move her jaw, pain intensified. Her stepfather's blows had been as brutal as his sexual assault. She recalled Gran's examination of her jaw and the relief in her voice when she prounounced it unbroken. 'Praise the Lord for strong young bones,' she had muttered to herself. ''Tis the wounding of the spirit that lasts longest, alas.'

Gingerly, Sarah stepped out of bed, swayed, waited for the dizziness to pass, then dragged herself across to the only mirror in the place, a cracked thing hanging near the window, and into her weary senses came the memory of Gran saying, 'I keep it there for the benefit o' ladies who like to take a decko at themselves after I've treated 'em.'

'Treated them for what, Gran?'

Kate had smiled and patted her head. 'All sorts o' things ye be too young to know about, little lass.'

But now she did. One of the things. One of the worst.

Stepping painfully across the room, Sarah's foot caught in the hem of one of Kate's nightgowns. It was the old lady's proud boast that she kept one 'for best' in case she were ever run over in the street and landed in hospital. She had shown it to Sarah once. 'So ye'll know which one to bring if them tykes keep me there.

*I'*ll not be seen in one o'them coarse charity things they put folk in.'

And this was it, with frilled cuffs and flounced hem, but now it was blood stained. Sarah felt she had defiled this precious garment. *I must wash it before Gran comes back.* She stumbled to a chair and, sinking into it, felt pain corkscrew upward inside her, piercing her like a renewal of Joe Boswell's brutal thrusting. Lifting her hands to cover her face brought further realisation – her wrists were bare; her precious bracelet was missing. Pray God Gran had found it and put it somewhere safe.

Brushing tears aside she touched dressings on her cheekbones. She dragged herself back to the mirror and lifted a corner of one dressing and glimpsed a shocking discolouration of purple, but not so dark as it would have been without Gran's nursing. Sarah's heart swelled with gratitude, but more to Gran than to a God who allowed beasts like her stepfather to batter a woman to satisfy his lusts.

She wondered how her mother escaped his brutality. If the man had ever treated Mabel in such a way the evidence would have been there to see. So why me? *Why me?*

The answer leapt at her – because the man hated her, because she was not pliant and submissive, like her mother, and therefore enraged him. And angering a man like Joe Boswell roused a vengeful hatred which he would never miss a chance to satisfy. Last night had been only a beginning. From now on he would corner her whenever possible.

The realisation took Sarah in one giant mental step into adulthood. She was no longer a virgin, innocent, trusting. Without reason, the recollection of Bruce

Frenshaw's handsome face came to mind. She had never trusted her stepfather but she did trust the Master Potter's brother and she clung to that. Hard as it was to believe that any man could now waken anything but hatred in her, she recalled Bruce Frenshaw's friendly voice, his smile, the liking in his eyes, and the protective way he had helped her in and out of his costly Lanchester. Surely Dad would have liked him, because Dad had been a kind man too. She was glad her father was not alive to know what Joe Boswell had done to her, and hard on the thought came the realisation that if Bruce Frenshaw ever heard of it she would be too ashamed to meet his eye.

That thought thrust another unwelcome one into her clouded senses. Had he turned off the main road because he didn't want any Frenshaw workers waiting at the next bus stop to see him in the company of a mere apprentice, and had he dropped her for the same reason before reaching the potbank? She felt hot tears pricking her eyelids and in a desperate attempt to dispel them she focused attention on her unkempt hair. Gran mustn't find her like this, untidy and unwashed. Gran was a fighter and would expect her to be the same.

Where the old lady had gone, Sarah had no idea, but the bolts had been drawn and the great iron key was missing. That meant Gran had taken it with her and locked the door from the outside to keep her grand-daughter safe while she went on some errand – to get food, most likely, though there was still some left over from last night's birthday party; that memorable party, that memorable day! Even the hideousness that fol-lowed could not tarnish it nor destroy the reason for the celebration and the excitement of a new chapter opening in her life.

But would it, now? The disturbing question presented itself unbidden. She was unlikely to be accepted by the Potteries School of Design if she failed to turn up for the interview Mr Treadgold was arranging, but how could she go in this state, looking like some brawling creature from the backstreets of Burslem or Stoke?

And something else had to be faced. The death of her father had taught Sarah to accept the inevitable, but the prospect of seeing Boswell at the work sheds every day repelled her. She could imagine the knowing smirk on his face and the triumph in his bloodshot eyes when he looked at her, hinting at repetition. She sank into the chair again, her hands clutching its arms, but the sweat on her palms prevented any grip.

Panic threatened. She jerked to her feet. Driven by the need to be moving, *doing*, she stumbled across the room and seized the big black kettle that stood in the hearth, always filled. Placed on the hob, it would be ready to brew a pot of char the minute Gran returned.

She had no idea of the time because Kate's old clock had ceased to work. That never bothered the old lady because she could tell the time of day by glancing at the sky. She had taught Sarah how to do it, but now was not the moment. It would mean drawing back the curtains, and doing that would tell the neighbours that someone was in Kate Willcox's almshouse, and if they had seen the old lady go out they would know it was someone else, and wonder who. So keep the curtains drawn, Sarah warned herself. Don't attract attention. Gran wouldn't have locked the door and taken the key without good reason.

Slowly, her head began to clear. By God, that drink Gran had mixed for her must have been a powerful one, for not only was thought erratic, but her movements were clumsy and slow. Frustration angered her, but also made her resolute. She would *not* give in to a body that hurt, much less to one that wouldn't obey her. She would *not* surrender to what her dad had called apathy or inertia.

(What words you knew, Dad! What knowledge you were forever seeking! You were always hungry for it and full of dreams for me . . .

'And you'll make them come true, little lass. You'll get to the top one day. I feel it. Know it. It'll take time, of course. Nothing in this life comes quickly or easily, and when it doesn't — why, you just have to pick yourself up and start again.')

Waiting for Kate's return, Sarah clung to thoughts of the past. They kept reality at bay and acted as a lifeline pulling her back to self-control. Another day had come and she had to live it. She couldn't hide or flee from it or rely on Gran to get her through it. She had to do what she did every day . . . get washed . . . get dressed . . . go forward with the hours.

Shedding Gran's nightgown was an effort. After the abuse she had taken her body protested against movement. Even washing herself from a pitcher of cold water kept on a table near the back door — for every drop had to be drawn from the communal pump outside and carefully hoarded — seemed to drain her energy. Her movements felt heavy and hampering as she searched for her clothes. In the end she wondered if they had been so badly torn that Kate had thrown them out, though it would be more characteristic of her to put them aside to wash and mend. She finally made do with some of Kate's ill-fitting underwear and an overall as a substitute for a frock. Conveniently, it had sleeves which covered her bandaged arms.

With difficulty she tidied her hair. Next, she washed Gran's nightgown, put it slowly and painfully through the mangle standing just inside the back door, then glanced between the drawn window curtains to check that no neighbour was anywhere near the communal clothes line. Mercifully, no one was in sight, but the wind was high and that was her undoing for when pegged on the line the garment billowed in the air, attracting the attention of a man lolling against the lintel of a back door at the far end of the row. For one still moment she met his stare then turned with assumed composure and went indoors, shooting the bolt behind her. Even at that distance she had sensed surprise and speculation beneath the man's interest and a calculating sort of relish that had nothing sexual about it but alarmed her even so.

She sank into Gran's rocking chair and to rid her mind of the incident, and even more to repel recollections of her stepfather's violence, she forced her mind into other channels – to the girls at the potbank, the whole chattering-magpie lot of them, with Daisy screeching in admiration of the contents of her secret box and blurting out to the Master Potter, 'Y'orta see wot our Sarah does! Paints summat *luvly*!' – then on to the turning shed with chief turner Hobson watching with a kindly eye as she struggled with an unfamiliar tool, over and over again until at last she actually produced a foot on a pot . . . and the thrill she had felt, and the smooth texture of the clay as she gathered up the curled, discarded shreds and moulded them into a ball for re-wedging and re-use, and the irresistible longing to create something out of it – an animal, a bird, *any*thing so long as it was made by *her* hands, *her* fingers, from *her* mind. At that moment it had even eclipsed her desire to paint on porcelain.

Suddenly she wanted to be back at Frenshaws, where she felt at home as much as her father had done, but the thought of Boswell's menacing presence there jerked her back to the present situation. She thought wretchedly, I am hiding here like a fugitive, someone nobody should set eyes on. Then, Stop being so damned self-pitying! Rouse yourself and *DO* something! Do what Dad urged you to do when he took you for walks in the countryside. *Draw* something. Birds. Trees. *Any*thing!'

Rummaging in Gran's sideboard produced a paper bag and a blunt pencil. Both were better than nothing. She slit two sides of the paper bag so she had an oblong piece to draw on, and began sketching despite her injured hands – a branch from which leaves were beginning to sprout and an offshoot on which a bird perched, its head lifted to the sky, its bill wide open, its throat extended as he sang. A thrush, or a blackbird? She recalled both; they weren't all that dissimilar in size and shape, and they were both songsters. She could speckle a thrush's curved breast for instant recognition; she could darken a blackbird's head, create light on its glossy black wings, and leave the outlined beak white since she had no yellow crayon. Eagerly she worked, troublesome hands forgotten, and both birds came alive.

Excitement gripped her. Oh, to create them in solid

form, to pick them up and handle them and feel a smoothness and gloss on their bodies – something more tangible and real than sketches on a torn paper bag.

For well over an hour she became absorbed and by the time Kate turned the front door key and walked into the room carrying the milk can she took to Maynard's Farm for her daily pint, Sarah had herself in hand. The kettle was singing and on the gate-leg table were set cups and saucers and sugar and milk, bread and butter and Kate's home-made jam, and the remainder of her cob-nut birthday cake.

The old lady took one look and nodded approval. 'Glad to see you've gotta brew going, our Sarah. I can do with a cuppa.' She betrayed nothing of her relief, nor revealed that she had left the pewter can at Maynard's to pick up on her way back so her granddaughter would think she had merely been on an errand. No need to tell her where she had really been, or that Daniel Frenshaw had personally driven her home, dropping her a few yards from her door because she asked him to.

Kate hung up her shawl and said, 'My! I see ye've been busy, luv,' but she wasn't referring to the meal but to Sarah's bird sketches, left on the sideboard while she set the table. Kate picked them up and beamed. 'Dear George were right about thee, lass, and so were the Master Potter – I'll make sure 'e sees these so ye get another chance to try for the Design School. That is,' she added hastily, 'if ye b'aint well enough to try this time.'

'I must be, Gran. I'm *going* t' be.'

'That's the spirit. An' now let's sit down an' enjoy this feast.'

'Before we do, there's something you must know. I – I've lost my precious bracelet!'

'No, you ain't, luv. It dropped off your wrist when ye fell across the doorstep.' Kate produced it triumphantly and held it up, shining like the most precious piece of jewellery in the world, and saw her grand-daugher's wounded face smile again.

She said practically, 'Glad you be making use of that overall o' mine, lass.'

'I couldn't find my clothes.'

'I didn't mean you to. I've rescued what little can be washed and mended, an' wrapped the rest in old newspapers an' thrown them in the midden. By now they'll be well nigh covered with neighbouring folks' rubbish an' tomorrow the midden'll be emptied an' that'll be that. It's about time the Council provided dustbins like they do for the better-offs. I 'ates that smelly midden. Ted Carter's empty gin bottles stink it to high hell.' Kate talked on, relieved to find Sarah up and about and with colour in her cheeks. 'Come Saturday we'll see wot the market's got in the way of clothes to carry ye over. I bain't going to Mabel Boswell to pick up wot little else ye've got, an' nor be you. Liz Jones's stall's good for jumpers, an' there be plenty as sell stuff for blouses an' skirts. I've still got me old Singer to run things up on an' ye'll be needing summat neat-like for the Design School.'

'If I get there.'

'No "ifs" about it, lass. Now tell me how else ye've occupied y'rsel' while I bin away.'

'Idly, I'm afraid.' Sarah sounded ashamed but Kate was pleased, and said so. Rest was what the girl needed.

'But I've not been entirely lazy,' Sarah added. 'I was

shocked when I saw I was wearing your best night-gown, and the state of it, but it washed beautifully—'

Kate set her teacup down sharply.

'Y' shouldn't've done that, luv. Where've ye put it? Left it by the mangle, I 'ope, since I see you ain't used the airing rack.' She nodded toward the ceiling.

'No need, Gran. I pegged it out. No one was using the line so I seized the chance.'

'Eh, Sarah, ye shouldn't've run a risk like that. Summun might've seen ye an' made mischief by telling the Board I ain't living alone, an' ye know what that could mean.' One glance at Sarah's face made the old lady add in concern, 'Oh, m' dear – *did* summun see ye?'

'Only from a distance – a man from the far end of the row.'

'Not that ferret-faced Carter! There couldn't be nobuddy worse – but there, m' dear, don't fret. We've just gotta be careful, that's all. I know it sounds hard, but I've gotta protect ye from prying eyes until we can plan the next step.'

'But surely you can't be punished just for having a visitor? And I'll go soon, I promise.'

'That ye won't! Where would ye go to, anyways? Not back to those two, by God. Ye stay right where y'are until ye're fit agin an' *then* we'll think o' wot to do next.'

Sarah said firmly, 'I must get back to work. I'm still an apprentice, and tied. And though it sickens me to think of bumping into Joe Boswell again I'm not fool enough to think I can avoid him.'

'Ye won't meet up with the bastard once ye start at that Design School.'

'Which isn't likely to be soon, however much we hope. How can I go for an interview looking the way I look now? I've missed the chance for next term.'

'We'll see,' Kate answered complacently. 'We'll see. Put some faith in me, Sarah. Anyone meeting with an accident shows signs an' all we need say if folk ask questions is that ye fell down them wooden stairs at your mam's place. Meantime, I've plenty of possets to speed on the healing an' *you*'ve got youth on your side, and a brave heart like your father's, so ye'll stay right here with me an' stop worriting.' A wicked grin spread over her lined face. 'Think o' the fun it'll be, hoodwinking that Board!'

But a few days later the knock Kate feared sounded on her door.

'Good morning,' said the caller, smiling a toothy smile. 'I am—'

'Miss Jennings,' said Kate tonelessly, pulling the door half-closed behind her. She recognised the neat lady who inspected the almshouses every three months. Not an unkindly soul in her way, just one who thought the word 'duty' meant 'law' and expected everyone to think the same. Her severe hat, anchored with a hatpin through the heavy bun at the back of her head, coupled with steel-rimmed pince-nez on the sharp bridge of her nose, gave her the air of a Victorian schoolmarm.

'I didn't realise it was inspection day,' said Kate.

'Oh, it isn't, Mrs Willcox.' The caller's protruding teeth projected even more when she attempted a smile. 'I am no longer in that Division. I am in Administration and part of my duties, alas, is to investigate complaints and reports.'

'Wot sorta complaints 'n' reports?'

'Not always pleasant, alas. In fact, this part of my new appointment is one I do not enjoy—'

'Then I'm sorry for ye, ma'am. Must be nasty, doin' things ye don't enjoy. There I be luckier than thee, 'cos I enjoy me own life very much an' mean to go on doing so.'

Miss Jennings bridled faintly. 'Then I am sorry to be the bearer of bad news. It has been brought to our notice that you are infringing the single-occupancy clause in your tenancy.'

'Infringing?' stalled Kate, pretending ignorance.

'Breaking the rule, if that is simpler.' The woman glanced right and left, aware of inquisitive faces at neighbours' windows. 'It would be simpler, too, if we discussed things indoors.'

'I'm afraid the floor's just been swilled down, ma'am. I wouldn't like ye t' get your shoes damp any more than I'd like footmarks messing up me quarry tiles.'

So she was going to be difficult, was she? Miss Jennings had never experienced it when inspecting the woman's spotless premises, but had heard that she could be difficult indeed if and when it suited her.

'No matter – we can talk just as well here. It is reported that you are sharing this almshouse with another occupant. That is what infringing the single-occupancy clause means.'

'A visitor ain't an occupant, ma'am.'

'Then you admit there *is* someone else here. A single weekend annually is the concessionary time permitted for visits from relatives, but reports confirm that you have had a lodger for longer than that.'

'Not a lodger, ma'am. Lodgers pay rent and I'd

nivver charge any relation o' mine for board 'n' lodging. But since neighbours seem to've been spying – an' I can guess who – ye may as well know that me granddaughter's here, temp'ry. I'm looking after 'er following an accident. Nothing in the lease forbids me caring for those as belongs t' me.'

'But your granddaughter has parents to do that. She is the daughter of Mr and Mrs Boswell who live out on the Longton road, is she not?

'Boswell's daughter she *ain't*.'

'Stepdaughter, then, which means he has responsibilities toward her, as does her mother. Her home is with them so she must return to them.' Miss Jennings spoke firmly but curiosity made her add, 'If she was involved in an accident, where did it happen and why was she brought to your home instead of her own?'

Kate had had enough of this cross-questioning.

'Miss Jennings, ma'am, you've said your say, but I've not. The lass stays with me 'cos I say so. She be paying no rent, so she ain't no tenant. *I* am.'

'And therefore liable for eviction. But the Housing Board handles these situations humanely. You have twenty-four hours to pack your possessions, which will then be stored on your behalf while you yourself will be moved to St Bartholomew's Home for the Destitute—'

Kate interrupted, 'It bain't called that now, ma'am, an' a good thing too. Just St Bartholomew's. The name's up on the gates, thanks to Daniel Frenshaw who's a member of the Board and fought for the change.'

'*Mr* Frenshaw,' the woman corrected. 'The fact remains that you will be accommodated there until another place can be found for you. And make sure you leave these premises in as good a condition as they were when you moved in.' She held out a printed sheet. 'These are the evacuation rules for you to read. Meanwhile I will report the matter to the Board. They meet tomorrow morning, so no time will be wasted in notifying them that I have carried out my duty—'

Her words stopped in midstream when a girl pulled open the half-closed door.

'*And* bossed a fine old lady!' Sarah cried. 'I'm sorry, Gran, but I can't keep out of this even though you told me to. As for you, madam, you may be interested to learn that I'll be back at Frenshaws tomorrow, and now please go away and leave my grandmother alone.'

The surprise of seeing a girl bearing evidence of injury silenced the woman, but only briefly.

'I have done nothing but my duty, young lady, and the requisite penalty will be carried out according to the law. Don't forget that, Mrs Willcox, and good day to you.'

The minute the door was shut, Kate declared, 'Back to work tomorrow! That ye will not, lass. I'll not 'ave ye coming face t' face with that swine—'

'I'm sure to some day, Gran, and the longer I leave it the more afeared I'll be.'

The dread of meeting her stepfather again was a nightmare Sarah had concealed successfully these past days, but it dominated her dreams at night and haunted her intermittently by day. It was worse when Kate's vigilance forced her to be alone, for never by daylight had the old lady allowed her to step outdoors. It was Kate who went to the Saturday market and brought back food and essentials and decent second-hand clothes she could wear. But now reality had to be faced.

'We can't go on like this – don't you see, Gran? You told me yourself that I'd have to live each day as it came, and that's even more true now you're threatened with eviction. If I go you won't be turned out of your home.'

'An' just *where* will ye go? Not back to that smallholding.'

'I'll think of something. Find somewhere.'

Sarah hid the fact that she had no idea how to. Without money she could pay no one to take her in, and the most kindly person in the world would fight shy of befriending the stepdaughter of a man like Boswell. Fear haunted her, but she had become skilled in hiding black moments when recollections of his assault set her body shaking and her mind ablaze with disgust. Such moments were less frequent when Kate was near and, when alone, Sarah fought them by busying herself with tasks in the almshouse, thankful for its refuge. But now its protection was over. There was no salvation except in work at the potbank with kindly Mr Hobson and friends like Marie and Daisy, but that would only be by day. When work ended, where could she go?

Twenty-four hours, the toothy lady had stipulated. Twenty-four hours for Gran to vacate. Despite all Kate's bravado, her declaration about having to be turned out bodily would come to naught. She would be conveyed to the shelter of St Bartholomew's until accommodation of some sort was found for her, nothing like so good as an almshouse.

But at least Sarah could return to be with Kate until

the final separation. It would be painful, but they would face it together when it came. *One step at a time . . . face each day as it comes . . .* The words chanted in her mind throughout a sleepless night and were with her next morning when she rose before Kate wakened. Quiet as a mouse, she washed and dressed, donned the second-hand skirt and jumper Kate had purchased in the Saturday market, helped herself to gruel from the pot kept warm overnight in the bread oven, then cut a thick slice of home-baked bread to eat at midday. This she wrapped in a cloth because she had no dinner tin now.

Because the sleeves of the jumper were short, she added Kate's long-sleeved overall to hide betraying marks on her arms. Those on her body could be seen by no one, thank God, but facial and neck bruises were another matter. Even though they were now fainter, they could attract attention, so she tied one of Kate's scarves around her throat, drawing it high around her chin even though fearing it to be futile.

On the back of her bird sketches she wrote:

Dear Gran, I've gone to work and you're not to worry. I promise I'll be back tonight. Frenshaws bus is free to workers so no fare needed, but forgive me for borrowing your overall and second-best shawl.

Your loving Sarah.

She placed the note prominently in the middle of the table, with a quick thank you to her father for being fussy about her writing and grammar, then she flung Kate's second-best shawl around her and quietly left.

It was startling to hear her name shrieked the minute she boarded the bus.

'*Sarah! Lawks, if it ain't our Sarah!*'

The voice was unmistakable, as was the girl stamped-ing down the centre of the bus to hug her. At this early stage of the journey only a couple of other passengers were aboard besides Daisy, who seemed to live a nomad existence with that mother of hers, moving from village to village as the woman changed cohabita-tion with one man to another.

Together the girls were jolted on to the nearest pair of empty seats as the bus jerked forward, Daisy clinging on to Sarah's arm joyously, unaware that her friend had to brace herself to bear it.

'My, but its good t' see yer, Sarah luv! All sorts o' tales 've bin goin' around − that ye'd met with a'naccident or that blasted stepdad o' yours 'ad given ye wot-for for summat, an' a walloping from the likes of 'im would be enough to lay anybody out for days!'

'Only the accident is true, Daisy. I tripped and fell full length of the stairs when I was alone in the house, so what could I do but pick myself up and go to my Gran's? She made me stay till I got over it, an' very glad I were because I were in a bit of a mess. But I'm fine now.'

'Ye don't look it. Your eyes look as if they've bin a luvverly black.'

'Not as bad as that,' Sarah dodged. 'A bit purple, but my gran's a marvel with poultices and things.'

Daisy inspected her carefully. 'Should you reely cum back t' work?'

'I'd've gone dotty if not, Daisy, with nothing to do

but let my dear gran fuss over me when I was really as fit as a fiddle.'

But Daisy saw through the bravado. 'An' I s'pose its 'cos you're fit as a fiddle that you be wearing a scarf to 'ide the bruises?' The girl grinned affectionately. 'That'd be just like you, Sarah, but now *you* listen t'*me*. If Mr 'Obson sez ye're t'go 'ome, you do as 'e bids, but don't let on you be goin' back to your gran. Keep away from your reel 'ome, luv, 'cos that bastard Boswell's like a bear with a sore 'ead since Master Potter made Jack Lefever chief thrower above 'im.'

This was startling news to Sarah – pleasing, but alarming too, for nothing could be more guaranteed to enrage her stepfather than to be downgraded from a position he constantly bragged about. Even worse, to rank lower than a man much younger than himself and of whom he had always been patently jealous.

She asked when the change had happened.

'The day after you didn't turn up for work, but it'd nowt t' do with you, Sarah. Ev'ryone at t' potbank guessed 'twere because Boswell were found drunk by the wayside an' carted off to 'ospital. That'd be why you were alone in the 'ouse when ye fell down the stairs, an' it's a blessing you went to your gran an' stayed there. If I were you, I'd go back to 'er. Me mam sez it's a pity Boswell didn't conk out in the 'ospital (she useter know 'im well once upon a time). There'd 'ave bin no wreaths from any of us at Frenshaws if 'e'd kicked the bucket.'

Sarah fell silent, letting Daisy's chatter run on while her mind spun in further confusion, through which pity for her mother stirred. Mabel must be going through a bad time, which was probably why she had not arrived on Kate's doorstep, demanding to know whether her daughter was there. Perhaps she even hoped for it, glad to have her out of the way while Boswell was in a bad mood. At such times the pair of them were better left alone. But that brought back her own problem of where to go to save Kate from being evicted. The toothy lady had rightly pointed out that a girl with parents and a home should lawfully go to them.

The thought made her shudder. Sarah's shoebox of a room beneath the eaves was across the landing from theirs, and despite his size Joe Boswell could be as soft-footed as a panther when he chose to be. One night she had stirred in her sleep and sensed him leaning over her in the darkness. She had been twelve then, too frightened to cry out, and then his great hand had fondled her neck and he had laughed silently when he sensed her terror. His breath had spurted in hot, silent gusts on to her face until she twisted and buried it in the pillow. Then he had whispered in that hateful voice of his that crying out for her mam would be no use because once Mabel was asleep she was out like a light. Then, mercifully, he had gone, satisfied with a little provocative teasing which hinted at much more to come, and for the rest of the night she had lain taut and awake, praying God to keep him away.

When she had asked her mother, at breakfast next morning, if she could have a key to her room Mabel had looked at her in astonishment. 'A *key*? What on earth for? You got secrets or summat? You in with a nasty sneaky lot at that board school?' And Joe Boswell had added righteous disapproval, saying he'd call on the head teacher himself and not mince his words if he heard any more talk about wanting a lock on her door.

'Decent kids don't want to shut themselves away from decent parents like yours.'

Go back to that place of ugly memories? *Never. NEVER!*

But what alternative was there?

Daisy's excited news that Sarah Willcox was back spread quickly through the worksheds. Not yet showing any special talent for any particular aspect of clay-working, Daisy was rapidly becoming a useful runabout for all departments, and enjoying it. Spreading news was particularly enjoyable because it made her what she had never been in her life – the focus of attention.

'She's bin in a norrible accident – fell downstairs from top t' bottom an' looks summat awful, pore luv. She don't look fit t' be 'ere, but ye know wot Sarah's like – won't miss a day if she can 'elp it.'

Marie was the first person to whom Daisy broke the news. She travelled to work daily on the pillion of her brother's newly acquired motorbike and was dropped off by the entrance to the throwing shed, from where she went on to the slip shed which marked her first step up from her first year's basics. Immediately she wanted to know where Sarah was and Daisy called back as she danced away, 'In the turning shed, where else? She belongs there now.'

Her piping voice carried through the open doors of the nearby throwing shed from where the hum of a potter's wheel could already be heard. It didn't escape Jacques Le Fevre's ears as he moved on to the parking section for vehicles and he had no need to guess who was working that wheel. Joe Boswell resolutely arrived before the new chief thrower each morning, plainly determined to demonstrate who was the most conscientious. He was being the model worker these days, but failed to deceive Jacques, who smiled inwardly and wondered how long it would last.

Not long, apparently. Or not long enough. When Jacques returned Joe Boswell had left his wheel, a half-thrown pot abandoned.

'So you're back, Sarah me luv.'

The voice was low, threatening, and possessive, freezing her blood. She had neither heard nor sensed the panther tread coming up behind her. Through leaving the almshouse so early she was the first arrival in the turning shed, and alone. She had already started work on an upturned pot, painfully and slowly but resolutely, but now panic seized her as nauseous memory brought the horror of rape and violence and all-consuming physical revulsion rushing back. Shaking, she backed away, unaware that she still clutched a turning tool, its arrow point held out blindly before her. At that, the man bellowed with mirth. 'An' what d'you think a bloody scrap of a tool can do? Scratch me eyes out?' Mirth changed to low-voiced coaxing. 'Come on now, Sarah, ye can't pretend wi' me – not now we've fucked together and will again whenever I fancy. Tonight, for a start. I'll be taking ye home after work an' we'll go the way I choose, so don't try giving me the slip.'

Dear God, bring someone . . . bring the others . . . bring them quickly . . .

The prayer pounded through her numbed brain. She heard the clatter of metal hitting the bare floor and didn't realise the small metal tool had fallen from hands now completely nerveless. In the stunned recesses of her mind she was aware that she opened her mouth to cry out, but heard no sound. Only later was she to wonder whether Chief Turner Hobson walked in as she cried for help or whether she didn't cry out at all and he just happened to arrive at that moment, but suddenly he was there, blocking her stepfather's path and demanding to know why he was here.

'This isn't your workplace, Boswell. Get back to your own.'

Hobson expected aggression – instead he was met with bland affability. 'Why, Hobson, I'm sure ye'll agree I've every right to talk to my daughter, specially since she ain't been home for more 'n a week. I'll be back on the dot to take 'er safely there this evening. 'Tis a father's duty to look after his own.' With a smirk, the man sauntered out.

The chief turner had heard various reasons for Sarah's absence – that she was unwell, that she had met with an accident at home, that her grandmother was ill and, her mother being too busy to look after her, had sent Sarah instead. This last was hard to swallow since Mabel Boswell was rarely to be seen working on that neglected smallholding and the cottage looked equally neglected, besides which George Willcox's widow had become a slut since she married Boswell. So the accident at home seemed the most convincing and when he now saw fading bruises on Sarah's hands, he accepted it. He also noticed that she was wearing a long-sleeved overall instead of the usual wide-sleeved potter's slop, and a scarf inadequately covering her throat and chin. The scarf had partially slipped and as she stooped to pick up the tool it slipped further, revealing weals that told their own story. His kindly heart wrenched.

'My dear, you're not fit to be here. What made you come?'

She said with an attempt at a smile, 'I'm apprenticed, sir, and apprentices have to put in regular hours to get their regular training. I'm behind now, so naturally . . .'

He said no more, but the Master Potter's visit to the turning shed much later that morning was a surprise since it was not a normal inspection day. It consisted merely of a passing word with the chief turner and an odd one here and there with individual potters about items they were working on. Few noticed, except Hobson who was expecting it, that as he left he paused beside Sarah, and only she heard what he said because that was his intention.

'Don't be afraid of missing your place at the Design School. I've arranged for you to be interviewed as soon as you are well enough, and I'll check with your grandmother on that. Now put down that tool and go back to her.'

Surprise rendered her speechless, then she seized the first words that came into her head. 'But, sir, there's no workers' bus at this hour—'

'You won't need one.'

She stared up at him, filled with an urge to tell him about Kate's impending eviction and how she herself was the cause of it, but his normally calm face was looking down at her with an expresson she had never seen there before and could not read.

To hide it, he turned away, but with him went a heart-rending picture of a young and lovely face marred by brutality. And something more – fear. Her great dark eyes were full of it and instinct told him that it had been newly planted. There was no need to wonder when, and by whom. Hobson's visit to his office, the moment he arrived following a meeting of the Housing Board in Stoke, had been enough. Joe Boswell spelled menace to a girl who had not been out of his own thoughts since Kate Willcox's visit.

Eight

Cynthia Frenshaw flung open the double doors of her husband's study, stood poised with a hand on each carved knob, and declared, 'I don't believe it! Have you gone *mad*?'

'Not yet, my dear, though you often accuse me of being so.' Daniel's voice was amused and tolerant. 'What have I done now?'

'You must know perfectly well.' Cynthia closed both doors and leaned against them, head uptilted so that the lovely column of her throat was displayed to full advantage, even enhanced by the high cravat she wore with her riding habit of dark green velvet. The costume also displayed her slender waist, emphasised by a tightly fitting jacket, and drew subtle attention to long legs beneath sweeping riding skirts which moulded to her thighs as she walked. She carried the well designed ensemble with the magnificent ease of a beautiful body. Her husband still appreciated it, so she held her elegant pose, knowing how effective it was.

She often blessed her father for sending her to that exclusive Droitwich academy, where deportment and elocution were taught by the finest tutors. Mixing with girls from upper-crust society had helped too, and she had been careful to keep in touch with many of them.

'Good social contacts are always useful, so cultivate them,' he had urged, and she had never forgotten the advice. As for the rest – protection when it was needed, discretion and well-distributed money when silence was essential, and a cleverly contrived meeting with an eligible and financially sound man from the flourishing potteries when a desirable marriage seemed the ultimate achievement – she thanked him even more.

Strolling toward Daniel's fine Georgian desk set beneath high mullioned windows, Cynthia now used the grace of her movements to charm her husband as it unfailingly charmed his young brother. Bruce's admiration had been won at their first meeting. He had an unerring eye for feminine loveliness and it was not surprising that he should succumb to a sophisticated woman who was merely a few negligible years older than himself and just happened, rather tiresomely, to be his brother's wife. Bruce always liked to score over Daniel if he could, laughing up his sleeve in the way of younger brothers when outwitting their elders. *Dear* Bruce – what a lovable boy he was! In her present mood Cynthia could forgive him anything, but her husband – well, at this moment she was not so sure.

Perching on a corner of his desk, she leaned across and, with a flick of her gauntleted hand, closed the ledger he was engrossed in. He had been closeted in this panelled room for the entire afternoon, leaving his wife to her own devices which, delightfully and of course accidentally, had today included Bruce for a while. He had ridden half way across the park with her, until covert glances from estate workers indicated thoughts they had no right to think. She would remember those looks, *and* the identities of those guilty of them.

'At it again, Daniel?' she said now, tapping the leather-covered ledger. 'You deserve to lose that man Treadgold, always checking his work the way you do.'

'Double-checking is an arrangement he and I came to long ago. I value the work he does and he values my corroboration. That way, we avoid mistakes.'

'I should think you see quite enough of the potbank without bringing it home. I declare you are obsessed with the place.'

Secretly, she treasured these sessions when her husband shut himself away, though she betrayed no hint of it. They gave her more freedom than many a wife enjoyed, so who could blame her for making the most of them, riding at will about the countryside, going out with the hunt, socialising with moneyed newcomers to the neighbourhood, building up a circle of admirers, and winning applause for her involvement in public and charitable affairs? The diligence she applied to them was equalled only by her possessive pride in Dunmore Abbey.

This possessive pride now brought her here, exclaiming over what she had just seen out there in the park.

'I rode down to the gazebo by the lake to see how the workmen were getting on – a team I delegated to repair broken stonework, starting today. I expected to see them hard at it, but they haven't even begun. Not a single labourer was there! And where did I find them? Cleaning out the blacksmith's empty cottage for people who have absolutely no right to occupy it – old Kate Willcox and her granddaughter, of all people! I could scarcely believe my eyes! Naturally, I took the men to task while that awful old woman waited with her scrappy furniture stacked on one of our estate vehicles. And who gave her permission to use *that*, I'd like to know?'

'I sent it—' he began, but she swept on, unheeding.

'Both she and the girl had the nerve to speak in defence of the men until I silenced them, making it clear that workers who ignore my orders have to account for themselves. And so the men did. And what did I learn? That *you* are responsible. That *you* countermanded my orders and sent them to clean out an empty cottage which, let me remind you, can only be occupied by Dunmore workers, as with all the estate properties.'

'By tradition only. You make much of the interest you take in needy people and the help you give them, so the case of Kate and Sarah Willcox should interest you. It happens that they are both in need, Kate being evicted from her almshouse for sheltering her granddaughter following an accident, and Sarah in need of a safe and secure home. That's why I've wasted no time in moving them into the cottage made vacant when Foster's wife died and his son urged him to live with himself and his family on their farm at Crannock. Foster will do all our farrier work from there in future. And in my opinion cleaning out that cottage must be attended to before fussing about any ornamental work on the gazebo.'

Cynthia had learned from experience that when Daniel's voice became crisp and cool, as now, it could precede a demonstration of implacable will which it was wise to avoid. It was an effort to climb down, but she did so, using her own method of wile and guile. Leisurely putting aside her tall beaver hat and following it with her riding gloves, she leaned forward, took her husband's face between her hands and rubbed her soft cheek against it before placing her open-lipped mouth over his, slowly engulfing, sexually rousing. It was an unfailing ploy and one to which, at one time, he had never failed to respond, returning physical hunger for physical hunger. But now she realised her timing was bad, for although he did not reject her he gave her no responsive encouragement. Damn him, she thought, his mind is on other things again — that tiresome family pottery industry or (and the thought flashed through her brain like a warning light) that damn girl he's installing nearby. He's had a soft spot for her for a long time, so to hell with his sob-story about that old hag Kate being evicted from her almshouse! I don't believe a word of it.

With a practised swing of her legs, which never failed to catch a man's eye, she launched her graceful body from its elegant perch and strolled across the room, saying lightly, 'You're right, darling – this is neither the place nor the time for sexual dalliance. You see how well I read your signals? You have other things on your mind, and perhaps I read those too, but right now we'll concentrate on the fact that you've moved outsiders on to the estate without even consulting me. You know that's my exclusive territory and that I manage it well. I'm not the daughter of a successful industrialist for nothing. Everyone knows that since Arkwright's influence on the lace industry, Nottingham has become one of the most prosperous towns in the Midlands and my father one of its most important citizens. They'll be naming a street after him one of these days, just as they did for Arkwright.'

'All of which has nothing whatever to do with Dunmore's cottages and tenants. And the estate is not your "exclusive territory". I know you take a proprietorial interest in it, but it belongs to the family as a whole, not to an individual member – not to me, as head of it so I must currently take responsibility for it, or to Bruce as second in line, or to you as my wife, or to any children we may have.'

She made no response to that. The subject of children was one she preferred to avoid. There was plenty of time for that; plenty of time to contemplate the tiresome duty of ruining one's figure and having to work hard to restore it and then ruining it again as more breeding followed. And children had a way of growing up at an alarming pace, bearing visual testimony to a mother's equally advancing years. She had seen it happen all too often. A wife could be young and lovely until childbearing took its toll, then she grew stout and corsets became tighter and age more difficult to conceal.

Of course, it might never happen. She used the word 'might' from choice, jerking her mind away from the subject and from the echo of her father's voice saying, 'Marry him, my girl, and say nothing. He'll never hear of it from me and your mother will do as I tell her and keep her mouth shut. You'll be far away from Nottingham and its gossiping tongues, and that Glasgow doctor further away still. Besides, doctors can never betray secrets.'

Pulling herself back to the moment, she said lightly, 'Well, at least you won't be able to carry on with the young Willcox girl under her grandmother's watchful eye.' His quick frown made her realise she had overstepped the mark; she even had the grace to apologise. 'I'm sorry, Daniel. That *was* rather naughty of me. Bruce is the one to amuse himself with village wenches. I wonder if Annabel knows that.'

'Annabel?'

'She's in love with him. Has been ever since she reached her teens. He knows it, of course, and it amuses him, but she's too obsessed with the idea of becoming a porcelain painter for his liking. The dear boy might flirt with some of the pottery women, but if Annabel were fool enough to join their ranks he would never consider her seriously again. And your own taste has always been similarly fastidious, and thank God for that or you might not have married me.'

The words were spoken lightly, but she meant them. She was well aware of Daniel's pride in her and of his occasional disappointment when she didn't quite live up to it. Such standards were irksome at times, flattering at others, but no man should cherish too perfect a picture of his wife or he had only himself to blame if she found it difficult to live up to and slipped from grace now and then.

But guilt never touched Cynthia for long. Neither did disappointment. When, after the breathless rush of their marriage, she occasionally wondered why the sexual pace had slowed down more quickly than expected and, worse, why a gap had begun to widen between them, she would shrug it aside, blaming him, not herself. Daniel took his responsibilities too seriously and his obligations toward Dunmore and the family industry too personally, and that became boring. He should take life more light-heartedly, as Bruce did, and as she herself did up to a point – that point being her rights as mistress of Dunmore Abbey and her consequent social position. She was careful not to jeopardise that. She had also made it clear to Bruce. 'Enjoyment is one thing, recklessness another, and don't you forget it, my rascal.'

The pottery lords of Staffordshire were the social hierarchy, their wealth exceeding many of the landed gentry with their titles and their crumbling estates. To Cynthia, position ranked first in importance, marriage vows second, *affaires* third. After all, promises were easily broken and people in high society broke them all the time. They were now living in the roaring twenties, heralding a loosening of social standards and the beginning of more lax ones for those who could afford them. People wanted to forget; they wanted to *live*. After four vile years of death and disaster, who could blame them?

But here, in what Cynthia regarded as the Midlands backwoods, things moved more slowly. She had to be content with queening it at a local level and satisfying her yearning for London's sophistication by cultivating neighbours who kept houses there, or Londoners who came to their country estates to recover from what she imagined to be hectic social rounds before departing again to renew them.

Cynthia was resilient and philosophical. She had an established and enviable position here, and a highly presentable husband. It had been clever of dear Papa to get to know him, and cleverer still to foster such a profitable match. And despite the difference in their backgrounds – socially, not financially, for in her father's opinion and in hers the latter was an effective leveller – it *was* successful.

Although not as handsome as his younger brother, Daniel's irregular features were nonetheless striking. He had the strong, high-bridged nose which featured prominently in those impressive family portraits adorning the abbey's main staircase, and his rare smile held a warmth which drew people to him. He really was a most creditable husband, and the way in which he caught the eye when entering a crowded room always pleased her because people's glances then automatically passed to herself and remained there.

Only one thing marred their union – the fact that her husband had been brought up to what she considered sedate standards in a part of the country long ago influenced by Methodism. Not that the Frenshaws had been Methodists themselves, they had taken their place in the family pew of the local Protestant church for generations, and not that she could accuse Daniel of narrow-mindedness, quite the contrary. In many ways he was too tolerant, chatting with village folk as if they were on a par with himself and greeting older workers by first names, like friends. That was a familiarity she, as mistress of Dunmore, never indulged in. But standards here were very different from those of Nottingham, a city which, through its main industry, had inherited a certain French laxity. Cynthia had learned of it from her paternal grandmother, who had been prone to boast that her petite figure and tiny feet were proof of inherited French blood, and insisted on being called *Grandmère*. She was also chic, and knowledgeable about things dear Mamma would not even discuss, and if her sagacity was really French-inherited, it had certainly been useful when her granddaughter needed it most.

'There's a discreet man in Glasgow – I know him well and have recommended him often. In fact,' she had chuckled with a touch of pride, 'I myself found him useful once upon a time. Of course, like me, he is not young any more, which makes him more rich in experience *and* discretion . . .'

In Papa and *Grandmère* Cynthia had had two reliable allies. It was sad that the old lady had made a sudden exit from a life she enjoyed after imbibing too heavily of the cognac she enjoyed even more and, as a result, slipping off the pavement in Nottingham's Parliament Square straight beneath the wheels of an oncoming delivery van.

Suddenly Cynthia was anxious to appease her husband. Sitting there at his fine desk, wearing a smoking jacket of bronze satin which he often donned before changing for dinner, and surrounded by fine specimens of the antique furniture for which Dunmore Abbey was renowned, he looked the epitome of a dignified country gentleman, but who knew better than she that beneath his quiet exterior he could be fiery in passion and in temper?

Cynthia enjoyed variety in sex, but experiencing it with a gentlemanly Englishman had surprised her for he had exceeded expectations. As a lover, Daniel could be as good as the French whose sexual talents *Grandmère* had extolled, to poor Mamma's embarrassment and her granddaughter's titillation. The old lady had insisted that it was better the girl should know of such things than grow up in ignorance – so ignorance had become curiosity, and curiosity experience. The only irksome thing was being expected to confine it to one man. It became one of those marital restrictions Cynthia found hard to sustain.

Even so, appeasement now seemed both wise and desirable, so she let the petulant line of her mouth relax and her frown fade. Before going to change, she went back to him and rested her cheek on top of his head. He smelled of that new Pears shaving soap, and an eau-de-Cologne type of scent which was masculine and appealing. She kissed his brow and let her lips linger there.

'Darling, forgive me. You have every right to do whatever you like with the cottages, but I shall never understand why you feel so eternally responsible for that old woman.'

'Because she is seventy-five years old and bent through hardship. Because I owe her a debt I can never repay — she taught me more about pottery than I ever learned from my father. To him it was no more than an inherited family industry which had to yield consistently high profits. He had little concern for those who produced the goods. He wasn't a hard man, but he had been brought up to accept the division of human beings into liege and lesser folk, which meant workers who slaved for pittances and rarely lived beyond forty, and children exploited as child labour.'

Suppressing a yawn, for she had heard it all before, Cynthia said, 'And I suppose you're going to say that Kate Willcox was one of those children—'

'She was. And when she grew up she was beautiful. Through her, I discovered the wonder that can come out of a lump of dull clay. Through her, I longed to become Master of Frenshaws, but the kind of master it had never had before. I thought I was becoming that when the place robbed her of her greatest joy in life – her son. Because I had relied on a negligent foreman I shall never stop feeling that I shared the blame.'

'Oh, dear,' sighed Cynthia, 'we're back to that again, are we?' She swept impatiently to the door but he jumped up, seized her wrist and spun her round.

'I'm *damned* if you'll walk out like that! You'll hear me out, and when I've finished you will never again say an unkind word about Kate Willcox, or resent her living here at Dunmore.'

'In a cottage big enough for a married couple!'

'A couple, yes, this time including her grand-daughter, George Willcox's child.'

'You mean Mabel Boswell's brat. Oh, Daniel, don't be such a fool. You'll have that brassy creature around the place whenever she fancies, *and* that uncouth man of hers. I can just see them sauntering through the park as if they had every right to! And why take the girl away from them? Leave her with her own kind. She will never fit into a background like this, not even with our respectable tenant workers. As for her foul-mouthed grandmother, my mind boggles! What made you think of housing them here I won't even bother to ask. Another of your impulses, I suppose.' Cynthia stalked to the door, throwing over her shoulder, 'Be it on your own head, Daniel, but don't say I didn't warn you. As for expecting me to welcome such a pair, I shall do nothing of the sort. An apprentice brat and a rough potter woman!'

'Sarah Willcox is no longer an apprentice. She is to be enrolled as a full-time student at the Potteries School of Design – commonly known as the Design School. We send promising workers for such courses from time to time, and she is the latest.'

Surprise froze Cynthia's lovely features before they melted into laughter.

'How hilarious! Annabel Peterson and Mabel Boswell's brat as fellow students! You look surprised, darling. Don't tell me you haven't heard? Annabel's socialistic ideas have won her parents over and she's hotfoot for the same place. Your influence again, Daniel? All that persuasion you focused on Annabel during our supper party? As for the Willcox girl, don't you think you're extending charity too far this time? She and the old woman will surely take advantage of it. They'll never be off your back.' When his only reaction was one of amusement she flared, 'You've taken leave of your senses, or else you're just trying to frighten me.'

'Why should I? And how could I? You made a great display of offering shelter to people made homeless when the canals overflowed last winter. You even invited the local press to photograph them, with yourself in the foreground.'

'In the stable block, where they were housed – temporarily, let me remind you. Why not let your charity pair stay there until they can be moved back to Colney village?'

'Because I wouldn't treat them in such a way. There's a decent cottage here and they deserve it.' He finished impatiently, 'What possible reasons can you have for objecting?'

'Plenty. They won't appreciate it. They'll take liberties, making themselves at home wherever they fancy—'

'Not Kate. Not Sarah.'

'How do you know that?'

'Because they're two of a kind.'

'You seem to be very familiar with them. Even on first-name terms!'

A sudden instinct warned Cynthia to change her tone. She slid her arms over Daniel's shoulders again, her face close to his. 'You're teasing me, aren't you, darling? You're trying to shock me, just for fun, but though I know how indulgent you are with the pottery workers, I'm sure you'll be sensible and have second thoughts about this, so let's drop the little game.'

'It's no game. It's a situation you'll have to accept.'

'And what does that brassy Mabel Boswell have to say about her daughter leaving home? No – don't tell me! I don't want to know. I don't want to know *any*thing about this latest impulse of yours because there's plainly something more behind it.'

'There's nothing behind it but a desire to set the pair of them up in a comfortable place where they can live in peace. With a stepfather like Boswell, poor Sarah can have known little of that since her real father died.'

Ignoring the compassion in his voice, Cynthia said, 'But why the hurry?'

'Because at a meeting of the Housing Board I learned that Kate was being evicted from her almshouse.'

'*That* only happens when tenants prove to be undesirable—'

'Or, unjustly, when they shelter someone in need. I've made sure Sarah Willcox won't go back to the Boswell place. She's fifteen, too old for the authorities to insist on her being returned to a bad home when she can be housed with a close and caring relative in a good one. That's why I acted promptly. I took the girl home from the potbank to her grandmother and told them to prepare to move into the blacksmith's vacant cottage. I arranged everything. I hope you will welcome them and provide any extras they may need. They haven't enough to furnish the place and you do have a charitable reputation.'

Was that a sarcastic note she detected? The frank expression on his face belied it, but she answered defensively, 'I need no reminder of that. My only hope is that when they become firmly entrenched here you won't be putty in their hands.'

Amused, Daniel replied, 'My dear, the only time I've been putty in anyone's hands was when I first met you. But putty doesn't stay soft for ever. You'd do well to remember that.'

Nine

When Marie danced into the small living room of the Le Fevre home, bubbling with news, Jacques dragged himself unwillingly from a volume on Chinese ceramics borrowed from Burslem's public library.

'What did you say?' he murmured absently.

'That Sarah Willcox isn't coming back to Frenshaws! They're sending her to the Design School *full time*! Think of it! And she was so scared when the Master Potter caught us looking at her things.'

'What things?'

'Broken bits of china she'd been painting on. That was *days* ago! She'd done nothing wrong, but she was scared all the same. I could see it when he told her to take them along to his office, but afterwards her eyes were shining.'

Jacques could imagine it. Sarah Willcox's eyes were the first thing one noticed about her, big, dark, expressive. Whenever she pushed a load of wedged clay into the throwing shed he would see those eyes linger on the wheels, fascinated by the transformation of a lump of clay into a bowl or a vase or even some homely domestic article. Something ornamental held her attention particularly until that stepfather of hers shouted at her to get back to work, when she would beat a hasty retreat.

Although she put up a brave front, Jacques had always sensed her fear of the man and guessed how unhappy her home life must be. It also explained the withdrawn, shuttered look about her. He thought it tragic in one so young.

'We'd heard she might be going there two days a week, but *full time*!'

'It's splendid news,' said Jacques. 'I'm sorry I didn't see her when she said goodbye.'

'Oh, she didn't! Young Daisy came tearing in this morning, all agog. She'd had it from her mam, who'd had it from a farmer friend named Carter whose nosy old dad lives in one of them almshouses alongside Sarah's gran—'

'*Those* almshouses,' Jacques corrected automatically. He had become almost fanatical about correct English, but Marie wasn't listening.

'And there's more! Old Kate's moved out and taken Sarah with her and just *where* d'you think they've gone? To a cottage on the Master Potter's estate!' At her brother's surprise she nodded emphatically, her chestnut hair dancing, her face aglow. ''S true, Jacques. Every word. They say the old lady was kicked out for having Sarah living with her, but she was only nursing her after that accident—'

'What accident?'

'Haven't you heard? She fell full length down the stairs when she was alone at home. Luckily she managed to get to her gran's place an' stayed there, but judging by the look of her when she came back t'other day, she must've been badly hurt. Didn't you notice how awful she looked?'

'I'm afraid I didn't see her. I wish I had. I would have persuaded her to go home, or taken her when the dinner break came.'

'Oh, the Master Potter did that himself. People working in those sheds nearest to the garages actually saw him. He was driving and Sarah was in the passenger seat. And she hasn't come back to the potbank since.'

'Probably on his orders – to stay at home and get well until the Design School's new term starts.'

Marie nodded, but said thoughtfully, 'I can't help wondering what made him change his mind about her going there only part time.'

'Because he thinks she deserves it – why else? I'm glad for her.'

'Oh, *so* am I, but I do wonder what made the Master Potter change his mind.'

'He has the right.'

And the right to change his mind in other ways, such as upgrading a worker and downgrading his senior, Jacques reflected gratefully.

'Isn't Mam back yet?' Marie asked.

'*Maman*,' Jacques said automatically, his mind more occupied with gratitude because on a chief thrower's wages he was now able to contribute more to the household and so enable his mother to reduce the amount of home sewing she did for a local shirt-making factory. She should be back soon with her quota of work for the next week; also his father from the Burslem potbank where he worked as a mould-maker.

The Le Fevres were a small family occupying a two-bedroomed terrace cottage, the parents occupying the double room and Marie the single. Jacques slept down here on the sofa beneath the window — handy for his books on the sill and enabling him to read by candlelight after all were abed.

The cottage even had the luxury of a small bathroom and a patch of garden in which *Maman* grew vegetables. It was ridiculous to call her *Maman*, really, for she hadn't a strain of French blood in her veins and his father's was so watered down by now that it lingered only in their surname. Marie had once asked why they clung to French traditions.

'*I* think it's because we fancy ourselves as different,' she had said, at which she had received a sharp parental reproof. But she may be right, Jacques thought as he turned back to his book. By now we're as English as Sarah Willcox, though those dark looks of hers aren't typical and quite unlike that girl from Downley Court who looks and sounds real upper-class English . . .

Annabel Peterson had caught his eye in a different way from Sarah. He liked her mane of light brown hair which defied the control of hairpins, also her slim but softly rounded figure. He admired the air of confidence she carried with her. He wished he could meet her socially, but knew he never would. The social gulf was too wide. He had first noticed her at the Boxing Day Meet, which everyone turned out to see. He was then eighteen and had stood across the village square watching her father, then Master of Hounds, accepting the traditional stirrup cup from the landlord of the village inn, and there she had been, one of the field and mounted on a handsome grey. She had worn immaculate riding dress, seated side-saddle with skirts outspread, her hair coaxed into a chignon, her attractive face covered with a veil drawn tightly from her shining high hat. He had not known that it was the first time she had worn full riding dress instead of youthful jodhpurs and velvet jockey cap, or that she had been aware of his attention and been embarrassed yet pleased by it.

More recently, he had seen her shopping in a village store, looking appealing in a simple lawn frock. He had studied her appreciatively, again unaware that she was conscious of it.

Jacques was now twenty-six and girls had appealed to him strongly since early adolescence – and girls, according to Marie, were interested in him. She teased him about it. 'For the life of me I can't think what they see in you, brother!'

The Potteries School of Design was housed in an early Victorian building in the centre of Burslem. To Sarah, it was immense. To Annabel Peterson it was a place of cramped rooms and too many staircases. Her liking for space made her want to push down walls, open up passages, enlarge windows. 'Surely,' she whispered to the girl next to her, 'we'll work under proper studio skylights when we actually get down to painting!'

Sarah was almost too awed to answer, not merely by her surroundings but by her neighbour. She had never expected to meet Annabel Peterson in person. Until now she had been an enviable but distant figure far above her socially, their paths never likely to cross. Now she realised that all those rumours about the girl refusing a classier art training in London were apparently true, and since no pupil would be accepted in this local art school unless they had potential, her doubts about the Peterson girl dropped a notch or two, made easier by Annabel's friendly smile. To her own surprise Sarah found herself asking why she had wanted to come here.

'Why shouldn't I?' the girl asked frankly. 'I may not be a top-quality artist, but I mean to have a damn good try. I expect they'll chuck me out if I'm no good.'

'Chuck out the daughter of one of the patrons!' Sarah's incredulity overcame her shyness. 'I saw your father's name on that gold-lettered board in the entrance hall.'

'That was my grandfather, and if you think strings have been pulled because of those gold letters, you can think again.'

'I – I'm sorry—'

'I hope you're not, because if you are we certainly won't get along. So let's clear the decks and be honest, shall we? Yes, I *could* have tried for a place in London as everyone expected and – who knows? – I might even have got one, but I chose here not only because I thought I'd feel more at home but because I hope to get a local job at the end of it. After all, I'm a native of this place just as much as you or any of the others.'

'I didn't mean—'

'Of course you did and I don't hold it against you. Like everyone else, you're probably thinking I've pushed myself into a place intended for someone who can't afford to pay. I can almost hear it clicking in your mind.'

'You can *not!*'

Sarah's indignation overcame her shyness, and Annabel laughed. 'Don't worry – I expect antagonism. In fact, I've met a deal of it already, and I don't mean just from students. That stiff-necked Principal deigned to bend half an inch in recognition as we filed past him after assembly, but only with an effort and because he thought he should. And I suspect our tutor imagines he'll be indulging one of the idle rich, or what *he* believes must be idle, whereas I happen to come of jolly nice parents who are anything but idle and give work to people who need it and treat them well.'

'You don't *sound* full of revolutionary ideas.'

'So that's what you've heard, is it?' Annabel laughed. 'Well, I'm bursting with them. My father calls me a rebel and my mother indulges what she calls my "modern views"; convinced I'll grow out of them. Only this morning I was taken to task by a friend . . .'

Her voice faltered. Sarah saw a flush in her cheeks and guessed the friend was important to her.

With the switch in Annabel's concentration, conversation ceased and Sarah turned to her working area. Students sat at long tables divided into individual work spaces measuring four feet by four. Each student was responsible for keeping his or her area tidy and, stressed Clive Bellingham, the tutor, they were also responsible for tools and equipment. 'Lose or damage them at your peril,' he warned.

Sarah hoped he wouldn't notice her as an individual. Suddenly plunged into a total change in her life, she wanted nothing so much as anonymity, to be left alone to learn and study. In this new and unfamiliar world fellow students were noisy, free and easy, confident. Their fashionable slang was unfamiliar to her, their camaraderie bewildering. There was no hesitation in their getting acquainted with each other, no shyness, no waiting for the other person to speak first, no self-effacement, no self-consciousness. Had the class been entirely female she would have felt more at ease, so she was thankful for the friendliness of Annabel Peterson, who helped her to relax as no member of the opposite sex could now do.

Then she remembered Daniel Frenshaw and his kindness the day she had returned to the potbank and how astonished she had been to find him waiting for her when she left. 'Didn't I say you'd have no need of the workers' bus?' he had said lightly, and smiled, and driven her back to her grandmother without another word, there to rearrange their lives quietly and miraculously and with the minimum of fuss.

Sarah didn't know what she had expected an art tutor to be like, but certainly not like this one. His appearance was offbeat, his thatch of reddish hair rough, as if he had no time to bother with it, and the same applied to his clothes – crumpled shirt, tie askew, much-kneed corduroy trousers. Even the traditional artist's smock he wore hung haphazardly. Gran would no doubt call him 'arty'. She could almost hear her saying, 'Looks as if that young man's mind is allus on other things . . . too busy to think about 'imself.'

Bellingham's manner was brisk, his tongue quick, his tone well educated. After ticking his students' names at roll-call he then held up the register and said, 'Now I can put faces to this rogues' gallery and you'd better watch out because I never forget a face or a name.'

The class had been waiting in Room 21, standing around expectantly, when in he had marched and barked, 'Why the hell are you standing there like a bunch of lost sheep? Sit down, sit down – plenty of space – plenty of places – can't you see them?' And they had scattered like ants. Finding herself seated next to Annabel Peterson, Sarah had been overcome by shyness, scanned the room for another place but found none, and heard Bellingham's voice rap, 'You there – you with the black hair! Pay attention. No dreamers admitted here, girl.' There had been a few suppressed giggles and she had stammered an apology and the girl seated next to her had given her a sympathetic wink.

When break-time came Sarah followed her fellow students down a stone corridor to a room where a buxom woman was dispensing tea from a huge urn. One by one they picked up a mug as the woman's voice rang out, 'Milk's already in 'em, so git a move on, the lot o' ye!' The luxury of a tea-break impressed Sarah and when it came to her turn she held out a mug eagerly. The woman glanced at her and promptly looked again.

'Bless me soul if it ain't Joe Boswell's gal! Doan't tell me that skin flint be coughin' up fees fer ye!' Her raucous cackle filled the room and heads swivelled round. Red in the face, Sarah said, 'You've made a mistake. I am not and never have been related to Joe Boswell.'

'Aw, come off it! Yer ma married 'im second time round.'

'That doesn't mean we're related—' Sarah broke off, voice choking. She seized her mug and headed for a distant window seat, but her shaking hand spilled tea as she went. The encounter had unnerved her. It had thrust hideous reminder into a day which had started full of hope. Since that terrible night she had never been free of the memory, though she had resolutely tried to hide the fact from Gran and to banish it from her own mind – unsuccessfully in both instances.

'It'll all disappear with the scars and the bruises,' Kate had calmly announced one day after they moved to the blacksmith's cottage, reading her mind at a moment when Sarah was convinced that her silence was successfully hiding her continuing inner turmoil. 'Think I don't know wot you be goin' through, lass – the nightmares an' the dread of any man touching ye ever agin? Think I don't know ye have bad dreams an' wake terrified some nights? But heed me, luv – life'll take over an' one day ye'll live the way a woman was meant to live, with a man and with children born out of shared love, bodily and beautiful. The bruises on your face can scarce be seen now and the scars elsewhere are fading, just like I promised. Your memory will heal the same way – never forgetting, but remembering without fear and pain. An' life's taking over already, giving ye the chance to do the things ye've allus wanted an' wot your dear dad declared ye were meant for, so *that's* wot ye've gotta give your mind to now. There'll be no reminder of bad things at that art school.'

But she was wrong. It had come right at the start. A hideous reminder from the immediate and hideous past.

A hand reached out and took her mug. 'I'll carry that with mine while you go ahead and bag a place for us.' Annabel Peterson's voice gave no indication that she had heard anything or guessed that something was amiss.

Sarah reached the empty window seat feeling she had made an exhibition of herself and self-conscious because of it. The last thing she had expected to hear was Joe Boswell's name and, worse, to be linked with it. Since the horrifying rape she had been helped by Gran's determination to keep her occupied every moment of every day. This had been easy because of the hurried packing and the cleaning of the almshouse in accordance with the terms of tenancy: 'On vacating, whether voluntarily or by eviction, the occupant must leave all walls and floors cleaned, windows washed, doorsteps whitened, all neglect made good, in default of which due charges for damage will be levied and will fall due for payment on departure . . .'

Sarah had set to with a will, scrubbing and cleaning until her body ached yet nonetheless invigorated by this astonishing escape into a new life and a new world. Then she had helped Kate to wrap a few precious possessions ('so's them removal men don't wreck 'em!') but the removers were men from Dunmore Abbey, sent by Daniel Frenshaw. They had loaded Kate's goods carefully into one of the estate vehicles, all except a large cardboard box which the old lady had produced from beneath her bed and insisted on carrying herself.

Sarah's curiosity had been aroused. The box was similar to bandboxes used by modistes in Victorian and Edwardian days. This must date back to Kate's youth, she had reflected, and wondered what it contained and how long it had been hidden away, and why, but knew her grandmother well enough to refrain from asking. Nor was there time. The unbelievable move to the cottage in Dunmore Park was accomplished quickly, quietly, and with dignity. To the awe of watching neighbours, a car from the abbey had been sent to transport Kate to her new home, accompanied by her granddaughter.

But to Sarah there were unanswered questions. One

in particular. 'Why, Gran? Why should the Master Potter do so much for us?'

'Why shouldn't 'e? The place needs a tenant, so why not us? Take wot the good Lord offers an' ask no questions, that be *my* motto. Master Daniel's known me nigh on all his life so knows I'll make a good tenant and now, o' course, there be his interest in you. Shows wot good sense 'e's got, don't it?'

'But its all so – so *unexplained*.'

'Well, if it be explanations ye want, girl, ye won't get'em from me 'cos I know no more 'n you do, 'cept that Master Daniel's bin wanting to move me outa that place for a long time an' now 'e be kindly doin' so. As for wot's planned for *thee*, Sarah lass, 'tis plain enough. A good master potter knows talent when 'e sees it an' makes sure nobuddy else grabs it, so stop your silly questions an' look to the future. Don't forget wot your dear dad useter say – that one day ye'll git to the top. Well, now ye be at the foot an' ye'll start climbing.'

But one last question would not be silenced.

'He's not doing this out of any sort of pity, is he Gran? I wouldn't like to think that.'

'Pity! Bless ye, Master Daniel's nivver felt sorry for me, so why should 'e be sorry for thee? An' when were promising apprentices sent to the Design School just 'cos the boss felt sorry for 'em?' Kate had laughed at the idea.

'Even so, Gran, I've got to know something. Tell me and then I'll ask no more.' She took a deep breath. 'Does the Master Potter know about – about *me* and – what happened – 'cos if that's why he's done all this I couldn't bear it. Whenever I saw him I'd be too ashamed to look him in the face.'

'Well, for land's sakes, wotivver next! How the 'ell *could* 'e know? You an' me an' that bastard be the only folk in the world who know 'owt about it, an' that's the way it'll remain. Ye'll be askin' next if *I* told 'im! Don't ye go insulting me *that* way, Sarah Willcox!' Kate ruffled indignant feathers, silencing Sarah's doubts for ever.

Annabel's thoughts had been miles away when the tea-woman's voice drew attention to Sarah. In her mind she had been back with Bruce, listening to his protests.

'Chuck the whole idea, Annabel. You'll be a fish out of water and I dare say the fish will be as uncomfortable as you. The school was created for—'

'Working-class youth who might otherwise never have a chance to develop their talents, though the philanthropists who thought of the scheme didn't have their talents in mind, only their need to earn a living – and the potbank owners saw them as a good source of cheap labour.'

'Hey, hold on! You're not maligning the ancient name of Frenshaw, I hope?' Bruce spoke in jest, but Annabel considered the question.

'Possibly. After all, your family goes back a long way and you can't know how good or bad any of them were, any more than I can my own. We can only judge by the present generation, and Daniel is plainly one of the best pottery bosses in Staffordshire. All the same, there's a powerful need for industrial reform every-where. The Victorian revolution wasn't enough.'

Good-naturedly, Bruce told her to get off her hobby-horse. 'I've heard it all before, my pet, and there's not a thing either you or I can do about it, so don't give it another thought. Once you get over these socialist notions you'll see the sense of what I'm saying. So go to your working-class art school if you must, and get it out of your system. But don't imagine you'll be welcomed. When fellow students look at you askance, you'll soon quit.'

'You don't know me—'

'Not as much as I'd like to, and not in the way I'd like to . . .' His eyes sent a blatant message.

'Bruce Frenshaw, you're a flirt. Possibly worse. I suspect you've known plenty of females intimately.' When he laughed and said there was always room in his life for another, she cut the conversation short because from childhood he had been her hero and somehow she had never been able to replace him with anyone else.

But he had been right on one point. She had met with restraint on arrival here, as if an unseen barrier had been erected against her. Not until she had the luck to sit next to Sarah Willcox was she given a chance to talk to anyone, and not until the tutor started the roll-call and the girl answered to her name did she realise who she was. Prior to that Annabel had wondered why the girl looked familiar and concluded that she must have seen her around, but if so it had not been socially or she would have remembered a girl who looked interesting. Apart from the striking features, Annabel admired the well-shaped head poised on a neck which rose grace-fully from the collar of a spotless blouse.

Annabel was wearing a stylish frock made of expensive material and to an exclusive design. Now she realised her mistake. A blouse and skirt, plus lace-up boots which were so essentially a part of local working life, would not have marked her as different from the rest. Her expensive clothes did.

Fortunately, the smock provided for students covered most of Annabel's fashionable dress. At least in this I blend with the others, she had been thinking just before Sarah's name was called, cutting into her thoughts. So this was the girl people were talking about, the Frenshaw apprentice whom Daniel had taken under his wing.

'To Cynthia's displeasure,' Annabel's mother had said at breakfast only this morning. '"Another of Daniel's lame ducks," she said, and when I pointed out that many potbanks sent promising workers for additional training and that I thought it a good idea, she snapped that she was well aware of that but installing a former clay worker – "along with a mere apprentice" – in one of the estate cottages was really going too far. Sometimes Cynthia's snobbishness jars on me.'

'It's more than that. It's horrible. Like branding someone an outsider without even knowing who they are.'

A bell rang. The tea break was over. Together, the girls returned to their places. The first half of the morning had been spent listening to Clive Bellingham talking about the basic ingredients of glazes and the pigments used for painting on or beneath them, but nothing about their application.

'As you learn to mix both, you'll recognise the differences and the consistency to which each must be ground, and their suitability for application on glazed or unglazed ware. Decorative designs for pottery differ from the requirements of ordinary media.'

Sarah was not the only disappointed student. One

had even been bold enough to say, 'I thought we were going to be taught how to paint on porcelain, sir, not how to mix glazes.'

Bellingham had answered tersely, 'So you will, when you're ready, but there are necessary steps to take before that. If you lack the patience, quit now and seek some other kind of work.'

'And that's a flea in the ear,' whispered Annabel to Sarah, who whispered back that she was glad the ear wasn't hers. The easy communication which had sprung up between them surprised her, as had Annabel's tactful silence when they sat on the tea room window sill, a silence which seemed to say, 'Talk if you want a listener, Sarah. If you don't, I'll ask no questions . . .' But she must have heard Sarah's heated response to the garrulous tea-lady.

Realising that she should have ignored the woman's remark instead of drawing attention to it, Sarah resolutely turned her attention to the articles on her work space. A palette knife, a ceramic slab, and a series of small bowls containing a variety of powdered grits. She examined them one by one, touching them with an exploratory fingertip and taking her time until the tutor's voice arrested her.

'When Miss Willcox deigns to give us her attention, we will proceed.'

Her head jerked up. She blushed. Surreptitiously Annabel's foot touched hers and the encouragement helped, but the tutor's steely glance did not. With an effort, she apologised, but though his face relaxed she was convinced that catching this man's attention could only be a bad thing. She wanted no attention of any kind from any man, particularly sexual, the thought of which was now wholly repugnant.

The term was more than halfway through when Clive Bellingham began to wonder why the dark-eyed girl drew his attention so much. She was an unobtrusive member of the class. At first he had seen her as coltish and immature, but as the weeks passed he began to feel he was mistaken. There was a seriousness about her, a quiet intensity which seemed at odds with immaturity. He became convinced that something had made her withdraw into herself, and that intrigued him.

Another thing of interest was her work. He couldn't fault it, but always had the feeling that she was not giving the best of herself, even that the conventions of painting on porcelain were restricting her talent. Her marks were good, but always fell short of Annabel Peterson's even though she was dilligent, plainly anxious to do well, and skipped many a tea-break to redo something which dissatisfied her. Being a perfectionist himself, he appreciated that.

In contrast, that rich girl Annabel had a natural flair. There was nothing stilted about her work. She expressed herself with ease – that was the difference between the two of them. Sarah Willcox was *not* expressing herself. She was obeying rules and mastering techniques sufficiently well, but not as spontaneously as he wanted. However, he refused to write her off, not only because a pupil's failure would reflect adversely on his ability as a teacher but because he felt she had a talent yet to be discovered, and this became a challenge. In class and out of it she began to occupy his thoughts. He had to resist a temptation to concentrate on her more than on other students, and out of class he had to thrust aside a frequent reminder of her, a feeling that somewhere he had seen her before – which was impossible since he had never been in this part of England in his life.

In faraway Exeter, from where he hailed, he had read of this teaching vacancy in an arts journal and applied for it in the wild hope that it would offer the escape he sought. He had not expected success, but it had come, and when it occurred to him that perhaps his surname had helped he dismissed the idea. He never traded on the fact that his grandfather had been the Royal Academician, Joseph Bellingham.

He had seized this opportunity to get away from a part of the country which would remind him for ever of a woman whose memory accompanied him from that beautiful cathedral city to this stark industrial town. Carla Dupont had been French and frank. 'There has to be a beginning, a middle and an end to everything,' she had said. 'Nothing can go full circle and start again.'

The relationship was over and, for him, life in Exeter was replaced with life in Burslem, and now a virtually unschooled girl had latched herself on to his mind, troubling him with her shuttered face and elusive talent. He would take samples of her work back to his lodgings to study, but analysis eluded him. All he could feel certain about was that her artistic bent was not to be channelled into conventional design. He even began to wonder whether it would develop better in another sphere.

He wanted to talk to the girl, to get to know her, to find out if she had any specific goal, but she adhered strictly to the scholastic timetable, arriving and departing punctually, keeping herself to herself except for a growing companionship with the Peterson girl, and he could not delay her after class without attracting the attention and possible disapproval of the college authority. Fraternisation between staff and pupils was frowned on. He might logically explain an occasional post-class work session with a pupil who needed help, but not the series of meetings he felt to be essential if he were to discover Sarah Willcox's true talent. And even then he wondered how successfully he could penetrate her reserve. He also speculated on the cause of it, finally attributing it to a strict or strait-laced upbringing which would be a helluver barrier to break down.

Spring, summer and autumn terms ended. The year passed and end-of-term reports repeated the story – Annabel ahead, Sarah behind. Annabel was fulfilling herself. Sarah was not.

Sarah was sixteen when Clive made one final attempt. The idea came to him spontaneously on the day before the Christmas break. In class the atmosphere was charged with the usual sense of end-of-term freedom. There would be no serious work today. Exams were over and the school would close early; students would be allowed to work on whatever they pleased until the final bell rang. Instead, Bellingham challenged his class to produce an original design that differed strongly from the conventional.

'Sketch or draw or paint anything that comes without previous planning,' he said, distributing plentiful sheets of cartridge paper. 'Don't limit yourselves to ceramic design. Draw whatever you want to, spontaneously. Be adventurous. Let yourselves *go* . . .'

He didn't add that the results would tell him a lot about all of them, or that he would not be surprised if they automatically followed the channels he had been leading them along, or that he fully expected the results to yield some good designs involving the necessary combinations for repetitive reproduction on fine china or porcelain – or that in one way he would be gratified if they did because it would confirm that he was teaching them well. He merely left them to it, then gathered up their papers. His first glance proved that his expectations were justified, except in the case of Sarah Willcox.

To his gratification she had produced no less than six, all like lightning, all uninhibited, and all like nothing she had done before. There was not only spontaneity and life and movement in them, but depth and substance which belonged to another branch of ceramic art.

He took them back to his lodgings and sat before the fire and studied them. There were indications of animal and human forms waiting to emerge from shadow into reality. Excitement surged. *My God, I'm right about her . . . she's in the wrong field. She shouldn't be painting on porcelain, she should be modelling with it, creating ceramic sculptures . . . dancing limbs . . . leaping forms . . . vitality and life and movement and beauty. It's in the soul of her, repressed, hidden, craving escape.*

But what could he do about it? A teacher had to stick to a curriculum, especially when a pupil's employer had paid for the pupil to qualify in a specific field. Independent fee-paying students like Annabel Peterson could decide to study another subject if they wished, but master potters who sent apprentices to learn a particular aspect of their craft did so with the intention of employing them in that sphere and no other.

And it would be useless to appeal to the school's Principal, who would point out that Frenshaw had not sent the girl to study ceramic sculpture because his potbank didn't produce such a line. 'For over a century Frenshaws have been noted for their high quality domestic ware. They supply the finest dinner services to the finest houses in the country as well as abroad, also magnificent ornamental vases, but never have they produced figurines and ceramic sculptures. With established and well-proved selling lines no successful pottery lord wastes time on unpredictable new ones. Forget it, Bellingham.'

But he couldn't. He spent more and more time studying those expressive drawings of Sarah's, mesmerised and challenged by their quality until he began to feel that he was challenged by the girl herself.

That spurred him on. He realised he had to *do* something about it, but not until Christmas was almost upon him did he know what it was and decide to act.

Ten

The roar of an engine shattered the Sunday morning peace of Dunmore Park. It zoomed through the vast wrought-iron gates in total disregard for the early hour and the fact that people might be having a welcome lie-in after their week's labours. Others who, like the master and mistress of the abbey, traditionally attended Holy Communion in the parish church returned just in time to see a shabby two-seater racing to the opposite side of the lake. It pulled to a halt outside the blacksmith's cottage with a screech of brakes and a howl of agony from an engine which had plainly known better days.

'And who's the maniac driving that thing?' Cynthia commented as the rider flung his legs over the low-slung door. 'Don't tell me the Willcox girl has an admirer!'

As the Frenshaws' Daimler glided on toward the abbey she strained for a closer view. The young man appeared to be dragging a parcel of some sort from the side seat – heavy, from the effort it seemed to require. Not that she was really interested. Getting home after the tedium of a religious service held at what she considered an ungodly hour and attended, as far as she was concerned, merely because her social position demanded it, was of greater appeal.

Daniel said, 'Why not? She's growing up. She'll soon be starting her second year's art training.'

'Art? I thought she was learning to paint on porcelain.'

'And what is that but ceramic art?'

He said it tolerantly, but she sensed that half his mind was elsewhere. She even thought she detected a sidelong glance toward the blacksmith's cottage, but then he looked straight ahead again. Somehow she felt he knew the identity of the motorist and was withholding it. So he's in one of his inscrutable moods, she thought, and shrugged it off.

'This is for you,' said Clive Bellingham when Sarah opened the door. He indicated a large oilskin-wrapped parcel on the doorstep. 'Another to fetch,' he added over his shoulder as he headed back to the second-hand car he had bought in Stoke the day before.

Surprised and puzzled, Sarah stooped and prodded the parcel, convinced it couldn't contain what it appeared to contain, but only at the potbank had she seen packs like this. She was still examining it when Clive dumped the next.

'That's the lot,' he said cheerfully. 'Where can I put them? A shed perhaps?'

He was already across the doorstep, hoisting a pack shoulder high, when Kate called from an inner room, 'Who be visitin' at this Sabbath hour?'

But Sarah was too surprised to heed her. She was stammering, 'N-no, we haven't a shed – only an outside wash-house – and what's all this?'

'Now, what does it look like? You've seen clay packs all your life, haven't you?' Clive broke into laughter when Sarah called, 'It's my tutor, Gran! My *tutor*! But what he's come for goodness knows.'

'What does it look as if I've come for? Get the sleep out of your eyes, Sarah. Why should I deliver a load of clay except for a purpose? You've got to use it, girl. Make something out of it. Model with it. And soon.' So saying he strode ahead. 'I presume I'm heading for the back, and the wash-house?'

Kate met him at the kitchen door.

'No one goes into *my* wash-house! Out with you, young man. Sarah, lass, you didn't tell me anyone was coming. An' wots all this stuff?'

'Clay, Gran. Mr Bellingham says I have to work with it – and there's more on the front step – and there's no place to store it except . . .'

But Kate wasn't listening. Momentarily silenced, she was studying the visitor.

Sarah begged, 'Where can I keep it, Gran?' Then the enormity of what her tutor had demanded suddenly registered and made her spin round. 'Make something of it? *Model* with it? You know I can't do any such thing! I've never learned . . . never tried . . . never even thought of it!'

Clive deposited the first pack on the kitchen table. The room was small and well equipped, but only for kitchen work. He looked at the old lady sympathetically but determinedly, resolved to take no opposition. He had worked swiftly to get his way, which had not been as difficult as he had anticipated. Daniel Frenshaw had been co-operative and even offered a supply of clay. 'Take enough to keep her busy during the college break – a month, isn't it? – and then bring the results to me. Depending on them, we'll talk again.'

So here he was, faced with a disbelieving girl and an old woman who was studying him more closely than he felt was called for. He had heard that she was a garrulous soul, but at this moment she was silent, her eyes on his face and uncomfortably penetrating. She was obviously the kind of woman who could think a lot and hide it, but he took a liking to her. And, vaguely, something about her face puzzled him, as Sarah's had done when first they met.

Kate said abruptly, 'Ye've gotta do as you're told, Sarah. If your teacher says ye've t' do summat, that's wot ye've gotta do. There's an old dolly-tub outside. Won't matter if clay's stored in it 'cos the wrapping'll stop any rust getting in, and though the lid's seen better days it'll do well enough as a storage bin. An' we'll shove things round in the wash-house so's ye can use it. It'll be a bit of a squash but I've seen potters work in less space.' She turned to leave, but not before she had scrutinised Clive again. 'I'm afraid I didn't catch the name, sir.'

'Bellingham. Clive Bellingham.'

After a second's silence she said impassively, 'Well, that's nice enough,' and walked out of the kitchen.

After the clay was stored, Clive opened one of the packs. It contained red earthenware, and Sarah's face dropped.

'What did you expect?' he said. 'Porcelain? You won't be ready to model with that for quite a time. Meanwhile, this won't bite you.'

Her dark eyes looked at him scornfully.

'I know that. I've wedged enough of it in my time.'

'Then why are you scared?'

'Because I've never had the chance to watch anyone doing ceramic sculptures, let alone be taught. And I can't think what Mr Frenshaw will say if he finds out what you're up to. He's paid for me to study porcelain painting and I've got to master that because there'll be a job at the end of it.'

'Don't worry. He knows. How do you think I got hold of the clay?'

Struggling with disbelief, Sarah stammered, 'I – I didn't think. I was too surprised. Still am.'

'I knew you would be, but I had to act quickly. I don't want you wasting any more time in my class if you are better suited for another – as I believe you are. Those ad lib drawings of yours hinted where your real talent lies and I'm convinced I'm not wrong. Oh, I know you'd make a competent ceramic painter. You already handle a brush well and you've a good eye for colour – also design, but not the conventional kind. That's too flat for you. *Your* eye is for form and shape and depth and movement and all the qualities needed to bring a lump of clay to life.'

She said wildly, 'But Frenshaws don't market that sort of thing! Figurines and suchlike aren't one of their lines, so where and how am I to get a job even if I manage to do it? And where am I to learn? It's all very well to say I should study for something else, Mr Bellingham—'

'Clive.'

'—but who's going to pay the fees when Frenshaws refuse to – as they will, and who can blame them? And you know potbanks take on workers from families who've been with them for years, so who's going to employ an unknown modeller who's never worked in that line *any*where? And how d'you know the bosses at the art school will agree to switch me to another course anyway? They won't, Mr Bel—'

'Clive.'

'They *won't*, I tell you! Oh, my God, what've you been up to? The Master Potter's a kind man and I guess he let you have this clay just to humour you – or get rid of you. But you needn't think he'll give me a job if I can't be useful in some line of work Frenshaw produce. You've gone mad, Mr Bellingham—'

'Cli—'

'Stark, staring *mad*! I scarcely know how to handle clay, much less how to create anything from it.'

'Then find out. And you know more than you think. Your apprenticeship must have taught you how to wedge clay until it's in the right condition for use. And though I'm not a professional potter I do know that sculptures will blow up in a kiln unless they're hollow, so bowls and vases and tableware are easiest and safest to fire. Go to Stoke's museum and study the ceramic sculptures there. Look beneath the glass shelves displaying them above eye level and see the vent holes in their bases, put there—'

'*After* the sculptor scooped out the solid clay inside and then covered the base with a flat piece and punctured it to allow air to circulate during firing. I *know* all that!' she cried. 'My father told me when I was small. He read everything he could lay his hands on about pottery, but that doesn't mean I'll be any good at the job. Besides,' she choked, 'I've dreamed of being a paintress all my life.'

Clive put his hands on her shoulders and shook her

gently. 'You're scared, Sarah, but there's no need. I've a hunch about you and d'you know what it is? That you're courageous and talented but damned unsure of yourself. I wish I knew why.' His hands fell away because he felt her shrink from his touch. Her reaction surprised and troubled him because he knew he had not hurt her. He had not even gripped her, so the only other reason had to be that she found his touch distasteful – or was afraid. The first explanation was so unflattering, and so far outside his personal experience, that he seized on the second. She was shy and inexperienced, unacquainted with men.

His interest quickened. She was an odd creature to be sure, but what had made her so? A narrow country upbringing? Chapel-going on Sundays accompanied by warnings about what happened to 'bad' girls? If ever there was a diffident virgin, this girl was she.

He said briskly, 'You'll be interested to know that I went to see Daniel Frenshaw first. I showed him your paintings but concentrated on the basic drawings, pointing out the directions your imagination was taking – not that I needed to because he spotted them at once – and I told him point blank what I felt you should do and how far I thought you could go.'

Seeing she was still unconvinced, he added impatiently, 'Just because his potbank doesn't go in for ceramic sculptures *now* doesn't mean it won't someday! And listen to this – he wants to see what you do produce – it doesn't matter how rough or groping or amateurish or experimental. So now go and get down to it – create anything you want, follow any idea that comes into your head, and don't think Daniel Frenshaw's going to scorn them. He'll examine them critically, but not unsympathetically. So snap out of it, Sarah. Stop being afraid. And remember that if you fail you can still go back to porcelain painting, though which would you honestly prefer to be – a competent porcelain painter sure of a safe job, or a skilled ceramic modeller making a name for herself?'

It was a challenge and an alarming one but, fearful as she was, the moment Sarah touched the clay an excitement ran through her. She wrenched off a lump, then regretted it. Clay needed a wire cutter to leave the surface smooth. She rolled the discarded lump into a ball and set it aside, then dashed to the kitchen for Kate's old-fashioned cheese-cutter – two clothes pegs with a length of coarse wire between. What she really needed was the strong but smooth and supple kind with grip handles used by potters, but meanwhile this would have to do.

'And wot are ye doing with that?' Kate's voice demanded from the wash-house door.

'Don't be angry, Gran. I'll buy you a new one, soon as I can. There are modern cheese-cutters on the market now.'

'Don't want 'em. That cutter's served me well all these years so mind wot ye' do with it, lass. It seems to me that teacher o'yours should've brought some tools as well as clay since he seems intent on interfering with the Master Potter's scheme for ye.'

Sarah nodded toward a small pile of modelling tools. 'The only thing he forgot was a clay cutter. As for interfering with the Master Potter's plans, he isn't. Daniel Frenshaw knows all about it. And I'm only being tested, Gran. It probably won't come to anything because I've never tried to make something out of a lump of clay and doubt if I can.'

'Your dad wanted ye to become a paintress and always declared ye would be. So why should that young man take it into 'is mind to differ? 'E don't even come from these parts, I can tell.'

'What difference does that make?'

'It could make a big dif'rence when it comes to a knowledge of clay. This is clay country. That young man comes from the South, 'tis plain from the way'e talks.' She almost added that since Sarah had taken up with Annabel Peterson she was speaking less and less like folk in these parts, then remembered that Annabel came from these parts too, and so did Daniel Frenshaw, and somehow she liked to hear her grandchild echoing the way they spoke. Her dear son had also had an instinctive leaning toward 'eddicated' speech. Some of his fellow workers had pulled his leg about it, but how proud it had made her feel!

And she liked the friendship that had sprung up between Sarah and the young lady from Downley Court because it had done a lot to draw Sarah out of her shell. They travelled to and from the art school together, Annabel going out of her way to pick Sarah up at nearby crossroads in the second-hand Ford her parents had bought her – second-hand at her own insistence because she didn't want to look too well off compared with the rest of the students, most of whom travelled by tram or bus or walked, or used assorted vehicles of assorted ages and conditions. 'My old banger,' Annabel called it, feeling on a par with them and patting its bonnet with pride. Yes, she was a real nice girl, Annabel Peterson. Despite all she had, she wasn't spoilt.

Sarah's voice caught her attention. She was pointing out that a teacher had to know everything about clay and pottery-making to be able to teach ceramic painting. 'So I guess Clive Bellingham knows what he's talking about.'

Sarah surprised herself with her championship of the young man because only a short time ago she had been mustering her defences against him and feeling angry because he had left her in a state of bewilderment, parrying all her questions, brushing aside her protests. When she declared she had no notion of what to make or even how to begin he told her bluntly to try anything that moved and had life in it. 'Go down to the lake and study the wildlife there. And don't forget what I said about the exhibits in Stoke's museum. The sooner you go there, the better.'

And get there she would, she vowed after he had gone. It didn't matter that Dunmore Abbey was so far out. She would borrow one of the bicycles kept in an outhouse near the stables which Daniel Frenshaw had said were for the use of all on the estate, and she would time her journey to coincide with Joe Boswell's working hours at the potbank and thus avoid any encounter when passing the smallholding. It was the route Bruce Frenshaw had taken when giving her a lift on that long-ago morning. Better still, she could take a roundabout but longer route and avoid that stretch of road altogether.

Her mind was so occupied that she was scarcely heedful of Kate's presence, and even less so when a shape began to emerge from the clay in her hands, obliterating all other thought.

Kate fell silent, watching her granddaughter's fingers at work. The emerging shape seemed to suggest an animal of some kind, but when it became clumsy and unwieldy Sarah flung it down. 'What a *mess!*' she choked. 'I'll be no good at it, Gran. No good at all.'

'Ye certainly won't be if ye give up like that. Ye said just now that the Master Potter's behind all this—'

'Not "behind", only aware of it. Mr Bellingham took his idea to him and he wants to see what I produce.'

'Then you've got to, m' girl, so no more chucking things away in a temper. I've nivver thought o' ye doing anything dif'rent from painting, but wotever ye *do* go in for, ye'll get nowhere if ye don't believe in y'rself. That Bellingham young man must believe in ye a lot if 'e can win the Master Potter over, so now clear up that mess ye chucked away and we'll start shoving things around a bit to make more space for ye to work.' Her faded eyes misted. 'Your dear dad were right about ye, lass, and so were the Master Potter when 'e said your talent shouldn't be wasted, an' that young Mr Bellingham don't strike me as an idiot so mebbe the talent they've all spotted in ye is meant to take ye down a new road. Face up to the test, lass, an' find out. An' wot was all that I heard 'im saying about the Stoke-on-Trent Gallery – that ye should take a good look at things there?'

'I mean to, Gran, first chance I get.'

Everything was happening so fast. First the move to the

cottage and now this possible change in her future which excited and frightened her at the same time.

The move to the blacksmith's cottage had been like heaven pouring luxury into their laps – a *real* home with hot and cold water and a bathroom and indoor water closet, kitchen fitted with plenty of cupboards and a deep sink with draining-boards each side, and a cold larder in which food kept fresh and milk never soured. There were two bedrooms upstairs, one large and one small, and a living room which, to their minds, looked as good as a parlour when furnished with Gran's few things and a few more her ladyship from the abbey had generously sent over, including pictures of the park featuring herself riding side-saddle or seated beneath a tree looking pensive and beautiful. Sarah felt the pictures were meant to occupy pride of place in the best room, or maybe in the little square hall where everyone who called would see them, but Kate chose the kitchen instead.

'They'll do nicely above the cooking range,' she'd said, 'an' since 'er ladyship ain't likely to visit the kitchen even if she does do a duty call to welcome new tenants – which I doubt – I'll say they're hung in place of honour in me bedroom and 'ow proud I be to have 'em there.'

The back of the cottage was mainly a vegetable garden with a patch of lawn where they could sit in the sun. At the front, like other estate cottages, was a white entrance gate and a white fence surrounding a smaller garden with flowering shrubs and a path leading to a green front door. Part of the lake curved like an embracing arm round groups of workers' cottages, all with the same green and white colour scheme so that none looked better than another and the occupants felt socially equal. It was like a model village, Sarah thought, but without shops.

As for the bedrooms, Sarah had never dreamed of having one like she had now, compact and pretty and with such a view. From the lead-paned window she could see a wide span of Dunmore's sweeping acres, part of the curving lake and, beyond it, one of the abbey's towers. She was delighted that this was the one with the room at the top, the tower room which had caught her eye when she paused to gaze across the fields on her way to Gran's on her birthday night, and she wondered again what that room was like inside and why, unlike any other tower, it was surrounded by windows. On her birthday evening the setting sun had set them aflame; now she saw them every time she drew back her curtains, shadowy if the day was dull, alight when the sun shone, brilliant when the waters of the lake were ruffled in the wind and sent prisms of light dancing on the panes. What views that room must command at every hour of the day from every direction, and how wonderful it would be to see inside it!

Kate's bedroom overlooked the other arm of the lake, with orchards and woodlands spreading as far as the eye could see. Neither Sarah nor Kate had ever imagined themselves having such a home. Unexpected extras like thick rugs for the floors and carpet for the stairs and utensils for the modern kitchen range had presumably come from her ladyship at the abbey, though if they had Kate could take a good guess at who told her to send them. There was a Daniel Frenshaw touch behind all this.

And of course his wife wasn't 'her ladyship' – she was merely called that in a sarcastic sort of way behind her back by many of the cottagers who, surprisingly, didn't seem to like her very much though some curtsied dutifully when she passed. Not Pru from next door, however – *she* would incline her head and say good-morning if her ladyship acknowledged her, but bend the knee to anyone she would not.

Pru was the wife of Adam Bailey, brother of Constable Bailey, and the couple had been neighbourly from the start. Adam was a forester on the estate and Pru had been a schoolteacher before her marriage. They had two toddlers with number three plainly knocking on the door. Pru was round and beaming and liked everybody except her sister-in-law, Millie.

'I s'pose we'll have to put up with her at the abbey's New Year's Eve dance as usual. She'll doll herself up and think herself belle of the ball, but don't you let her patronise you, Sarah. Just because she's the district constable's wife, so they have a detached police house instead of a cottage in a row, doesn't rank her above folk the way she fancies. A pain in the ass is our Millie.'

Scarcely had Clive Bellingham departed that day when Pru rang the front doorbell.

'Just dropped in to see how you both are,' she said, 'and to remind you about the New Year's Eve do in the abbey. It's for everyone who lives on the estate so you're sure to be invited.'

'Everyone employed on it, don't ye mean?' said Kate. 'That don't include us, m' dear.'

'Well, I can't see either Mr Frenshaw or "her ladyship" leaving anybody out. She likes to queen it over an audience, if you know what I mean. The bigger the better.'

'Sounds as if you don't like 'er much,' remarked Kate.

Pru shrugged. 'I do and I don't. She can be graciousness itself if she feels so inclined and at the New Year's Eve party she'll play Lady Bountiful to a T – gifts for everyone, and the louder the applause the bigger her smiles and royal waves.' Lightly, she finished, 'You may be able to bring a partner if you want to, Sarah. How about that nice young man I saw driving off just now?'

Sarah hid a smile.

'Mr Bellingham, you mean. He's a tutor at the Design School – I'm at the other end of the scale. Tutors and pupils don't mix. *If* we're invited for New Year's Eve, Gran and I will enjoy looking on.'

'You'll do no such thing! You'll join our party, the pair of you. Tart yourself up to the eyebrows, Sarah, and knock 'em for six!'

Pru hugged her and was gone. From the garden next door came the sound of childish yells, followed by their mother's voice calling out lovingly as she bounced back to them. As Sarah closed the front door she had to squash the thought that if an invitation did come from the abbey, neither she nor Kate would be able to accept it because neither of them had dresses suitable for such an occasion, or the money to buy them. She consoled herself with the reflection that as non-workers on the estate they were unlikely to be included anyway, and went back to the wash-house and the lump of clay she had cast aside.

'Which would you rather be,' Clive Bellingham had

said, 'a competent porcelain painter or a skilled ceramic modeller making a name for herself?'

Making a name meant climbing to success, and success meant more than a safe, regularly paid, piece-work job. It meant real money, and things she and Kate would otherwise never have. More than all, it meant the wonder of creating beauty out of dull, drab earth and seeing it sparkle when it came out of the kilns, alive with colour, transformed, miraculous. And it meant the thrill of knowing that your own hands had created it.

First thing tomorrow I *am* off to that museum, Sarah vowed, and began to wedge the discarded clay until the texture was ready for use. The challenge had begun, and been accepted. The screech of a cockerel in the distance seemed to reach not only her ears, but her fingertips. Blindly, she began. A head, a beak, cox-comb, tail feathers . . . Dear God, it's a mess . . . it doesn't even *look* right . . .

But what would Dad have said? 'So start again, and stop your hands from shaking . . . You've all day ahead, no need to rush . . . work on the head alone . . . make a drawing of it, get the *feel* of it . . . try smaller pieces of clay laid on the skull and then on the body, mosaic-like, and see how that works out . . .'

But whoever saw a mosaic cockerel? What does that matter? Sarah chided herself. You're not painting a picture or making up a design. You're creating, you're modelling, you're sculpting something out of a lump of clay, you're bringing something to *life* and, dear God, it's exciting!

That night, for the first time since horror struck, no nightmares haunted her; no revival of male savagery plunging into her body and tearing her flesh while bombarding her mouth with a befouled tongue and reeking breath. That night, Sarah slept in peace.

Eleven

Cynthia Frenshaw was surprised and vaguely annoyed when Daniel returned from the potbank earlier than usual. She disliked being interrupted when busy at her elegant Edwardian desk, so she lifted her cheek briefly and carried on writing.

'You're home early,' she said, scarcely glancing up.

'Things ease off when all the Christmas stock is despatched – which, thank heaven, has been achieved well on time this year. What's that you're working on?'

'The usual Christmas list. It grows longer every year—'

'And of course the card you've chosen to send from us will eclipse all others,' he said indulgently.

'And why not? We have our social standing to consider.'

'And that depends on sending the most affluent greetings card you can find?' He sounded even more amused, but she ignored it and went on writing.

'I hope you're inviting your parents for Christmas?' he said.

'Oh, you know how hectic life is for Papa at this time of the year, with all that business entertaining he does. And Mamma would be like a fish out of water here, knowing no one.'

'She wouldn't be if you introduced her to people. I like your mother, Cynthia, and I don't like the way you neglect her.'

'I do nothing of the sort. She's a stay-at-home by nature and that's what she wants to be. She even dislikes playing hostess for Papa and when she tries she does it badly.'

'Because she is shy and has no encouragement from your father.'

'Because she is stupid and won't bother to learn.'

'So what does he do? Hire professional hostesses? I've heard of such things – *and* what their duties comprise.'

She detected impatience in his voice as he turned away, even a suggestion of sarcasm which she failed to understand. Whatever dear Papa did was no business of Daniel's. She went on writing as he poured himself a drink and settled into a chair. Without glancing round she knew it was a precious Sheraton upholstered in rose pink velvet (the soft furnishing scheme throughout the room) because he took only six steps to the right and the chair was that distance from the serpentine-fronted Sheraton sideboard on which she kept a silver tray of refreshments for friends who were privileged to visit this private sanctum.

She was meticulous about the positioning of every item of furniture in this room which she called her study, although she studied nothing but the social columns and magazines like *Vogue* and *Harper's Bazaar* for the latest fashions and *The Tatler* for high society's much publicised activities, in which she longed to participate. Involving herself in charitable correspondence bolstered her self-esteem, but was irksome. 'You should hire a social secretary for me,' she would frequently reproach Daniel, to which he invariably replied that he would willingly do so if her charitable work ever approached the amount she claimed.

Now she wished he would take his drink elsewhere; she hated being disturbed when absorbed in important things like Christmas lists and answering invitations.

'Since you've helped yourself to a drink, Daniel, you can do the same for me.'

'Sorry. I thought you were too busy.'

She heard the limp in his step as he went back to the sideboard and the thought struck her that it sounded less heavy than it used to. Was it actually improving? Perhaps all that exercising and walking he went in for was helping after all.

'Dry Martini, as usual?'

She nodded, and went on writing. He brought the drink over, placed it beside her and said, 'Do you really have to do that now? Can't it wait?'

She picked up the glass, sipped and at last looked up at him. A strand of her lovely blonde hair had become misplaced and lay fetchingly across her cheek. At one time he would have stooped and kissed it – now he merely admired it. It was a waste of time to try more than that when her mind was on things other than sex. He watched her brush the strand aside and toss her head back as she did so, a characteristic gesture. A society cartoonist would only need to sketch her uplifted hand and an outline of her head for her to be instantly recognised.

'You look tired, darling,' she said unexpectedly. 'Why don't you go and freshen up while I finish this?'

'When I've had my drink. What is that? The invitation list for the estate party?'

'Heavens, no. That's never altered – unless someone dies,' she finished with a laugh.

'Or is added to it.'

'No more staff have been taken on this year, so Bradley can deal with that.' Hannah Bradley had been housekeeper at the abbey for thirty years.

'Hasn't she enough to do? After all, she's getting on. And since you send out all other invitations person-ally—' He broke off, arrested by a thought. 'I hope you aren't forgetting that two more are to be added this year?'

'You don't mean the *Willcoxes*?'

'Of course I do.'

'But they're not estate workers.'

'They now live here like everybody else so they must be invited like everybody else. I won't have them left out.'

Slowly, Cynthia sipped her Martini. Slowly, she said, 'Now listen to me, Daniel. I've done enough for that couple at your behest. I've sent things for their cottage, the comforts you insisted on and even some of my own, such as pictures—'

'Of which we have a surplus, so none will be missed. You are generous enough when it comes to charities that exploit your name—' He bit the words off, remembering he had reminded her of that once before. He couldn't understand his wife's antagonism toward the Willcoxes and refused to give in to it.

'Where is the list?' he asked, and before she could answer he was skimming through a batch of papers beside her. The list was last of all. He added the

Willcoxes' names firmly at the end and walked away with it, saying as he went, 'I'll save both you and Hannah the trouble of dealing with this.'

Infuriated, she called after him, 'And that's another thing. I wish you'd stop calling old retainers by their first names. It's too familiar.'

'But traditional. As mistress of Dunmore I thought you prided yourself on tradition.'

The door closed behind him before she could answer.

Never had the old refectory hall looked more beautiful – but everybody said that every year. From the great rafters hung huge branches of holly and mistletoe, and log fires roared within deep stone hearths at each end of the room. The solid oak refectory table at which monks had once dined had been placed along one wall to leave space for dancing; it was laden with food temporarily covered with white damask and behind it waited hired serving staff. Candles shone from wall sconces and from candelabra on individual tables placed from the edge of the dance floor to the outer perimeter of the room. Giant pots of red poinsettia, that newly imported flowering plant now sold by the most expensive florists, added vivid splashes of colour.

Most splendid of all was the Christmas tree, which would remain until Twelfth Night. It had taken two of their strongest forest hands to fell it, convey it to the abbey, and finally erect it in the good-quality cedar tub she had ordered when she came here as a bride. That it had lasted so well was a tribute to her foresight. Her policy of holding the staff affair on New Year's Eve was equally sound – people always remembered it as the crowning event of the season and certain workers from the potbank, whom Daniel insisted on inviting, would be grateful for the addition to their two-day break and bless the Master Potter's wife for her generosity.

Like other manufactures, potbanks closed only for Christmas and Boxing days, and even during that time firings which had not reached their maximum temperature had to be checked periodically. She had even known Daniel to undertake that task himself so that his stokers could be released from duty. At such times Bruce had played host at the abbey in his stead, which pleased her.

But not tonight. Daniel had surprised her by announcing that since all orders had been despatched well on time this year, he had decided that unfinished work could wait, kept in condition by the usual storage methods. Well, at least he would be kept busy hosting the event, leaving her more free to dance with others – mainly with Bruce, she hoped, though that tiresome young woman, Annabel Peterson, would be there and he always seemed to spare time for her – out of courtesy, of course, though no doubt the girl imagined otherwise.

After a final inspection, and checking that the dance band from Burslem would be encouraged to give of its best through a good, but not too adequate supply of drinks, Cynthia hurried away to change. She had a new evening dress by Worth, that Englishman who was taking Paris by storm and was well named because he was worth every costly penny. Tonight, when guests admired it, she could truthfully say, 'Made in Paris, of course.' It was a ravishing affair, gold-sequined, backless and low in front, with the new knee-length skirt of which the staid disapproved. It showed off her shapely legs to perfection.

Before she went downstairs she pirouetted before her mirror, delighted by the way the spangled skirt swirled, revealing several inches of thigh as it rose and fell. It was perfect for dancing the charleston, twisting, kicking, leg-swinging. She would make sure the band played it a lot once the outdated numbers, for the benefit of the older generation, had been got out of the way – the polkas and valetas and military two-steps. Then on to the quicksteps and the foxtrots and the sambas and the rhumbas and the charlestons and the black-bottoms and the shimmies. Come to think of it, this dress could be even more effective in the shimmy. She practised briefly, shaking her body from shoulders to bottom and thanking God she'd been born in time for the roaring twenties.

A final glance in the mirror and a last adjustment of the sequined bandeau across her brow, a final touch of rouge and a further slash of bright red lipstick to prevent the brilliance of gold from eclipsing her colour, and she was satisfied.

'You'll do very well, my dear,' said her husband from the door.

Do? she thought. She wanted more than that.

'You will "do" too,' she answered, and was surprised when he laughed.

'Sorry. It was an understatement. "Beautiful" was the word I should have used. But you are well accustomed to hearing that and you will certainly hear it a lot tonight.' He gave her his arm and together they descended the abbey's wide stone stairs and took their places to greet the guests.

Later, when she had recovered from shock, Cynthia resolutely dismissed the cause of it. The fracas which followed some time later, at the table seating the local constable and his brother with their respective wives, was as nothing compared with it. That vulgar little scene even had its pleasing side because it focused on the Willcox girl and humiliated her – which served her right because it was she who was responsible for the initial shock which took place the moment she walked in, her hand beneath her grandmother's elbow and looking for all the world as if she were concerned only for the lame old woman and totally unconscious of herself.

She couldn't have been, of course. Not in a gown like that and looking the way she did. Her shining black hair hung loose over bare shoulders which rose from a gown of dazzling peacock-blue slipper satin, a costly affair designed by an artist to emphasise every line of a young and lovely body – small-waisted and slim-hipped, young breasts thrusting, long and shapely legs subtly suggested by a flowing skirt which clung delicately to her thighs as she walked.

Cynthia hissed in an aside to her husband, 'Where on *earth* did the Willcox girl get that dress from? Who bought it for her? *Someone* must have done!' But he didn't seem to hear. He was holding out his hand to Kate and greeting her warmly, then the same with Sarah, smiling that special smile of his when the sight of something particularly pleased him. My God, thought Cynthia, *he* bought it! Who else?

'I'm delighted you have come,' he was saying, and the old woman smiled and nodded in the way of old people when hard of hearing.

'I'd curtsy if I could, Master Danny, but me old bones won't bend much these days.' She said it with an echoing cackle. Inwardly, Cynthia shuddered, but betrayed no sign as she held out a cool hand and inclined her head graciously. Kate touched the hand and said politely, 'Ma'am, we appreciate the invitation,' almost as if she had rehearsed the words beforehand.

Then Sarah stood before her. Cynthia scarcely touched her fingertips but the girl seemed to expect no more. Her eyes were shining, her excitement genuine. Her face was lightly made up (applied by neighbourly Pru, though the abbey's hostess didn't guess that) and the youthful glow of her skin was beautiful. Cynthia had never seen her at such close quarters so she had never seen the quality of that young complexion, or the sweep of long lashes surrounding remarkable eyes, or the lovely curve of her lips when she smiled.

Envy sparked in Daniel's wife. Here was no gawky apprentice. Here was a creature on the threshold of womanhood. How old was she now? Sixteen? Seventeen? Old enough for Daniel to be attracted to her and buy her costly dresses? Cynthia did a swift calculation. Daniel was now in his thirties, but age differences were no barrier where sex was concerned.

The couple passed on, and as they did so Cynthia noticed a necklace round the old woman's throat. Her dress was obviously her Sunday best, like many another in this motley crowd, but whereas some workers had dolled them up with fake ostrich feathers and spangly beads, this old woman's necklet was of garnets in an antique setting. Cynthia recognised good jewellery when she saw it.

This time she made no comment because the

Petersons were next in line, Ruth clad in the latest fashion – an ankle-length, tube-style evening dress of eau-de-Nil net lined with matching satin, trailing loops of moire ribbon at the sleeveless shoulders and straight-edging the hemline. The colour set off her white hair beautifully. Charles was as immaculately tailored as ever and Annabel looked charming in a white chiffon dress slit to the waist at the back, the skirt consisting of rows of silk fringe terminating above the knees. It was a typical flapper dress and highly becoming.

Cynthia was forced to acknowledge that the girl was attractive, but was glad that Bruce preferred more mature women. And he didn't share Annabel's socialistic ideas or approve of her attendance at that art school where students were not of her class. A silly young thing was Annabel, and easy to dismiss.

Cynthia was turning to receive the next arrivals when Annabel cried, '*Sarah!*' and went racing to a table where the Willcoxes were seating themselves with two couples already there. All tables were unreserved, except the top one for the hosts and their personal friends, but this one wasn't so far away and Annabel's voice travelled clearly.

'How *great* to see you! Do come and join us – the parents will be delighted, I know. And, golly, you look *gorgeous!*'

Great heavens, thought Cynthia, can't she see the types the girl is with – the local constable and his flashy young wife (ostrich feathers in shrieking red) and one of the foresters and his wife, pregnant yet again? Annabel really should snap out of her silly all-are-equal ideas. As for inviting the Willcox girl to join the top table, she must know it's quite out of the question.

Mercifully, the Willcox girl did, for after returning Annabel's spontaneous embrace, she shook her head in smiling refusal.

All this time Cynthia continued to shake hands and exchange polite greetings, presenting her cheek to those with whom she mixed socially but not to others, and all the time watching for Bruce and wondering why he was so maddeningly late. Not that punctuality was one of his most reliable qualities, and she knew he wasn't keen on mixed affairs like this. 'Nor am I, darling,' she had said, 'but duty calls . . .' To which Bruce had said, 'Not *my* duty, but I'll put in an appearance to please you.'

And at last he did, taking his place at his brother's side and muttering something about being sorry he was late but traffic had made it the devil of a job to get back from the Leicester flat races. 'Too many charabancs on the road, laden with trippers . . .' Then he caught sight of Annabel in the distance and, to Cynthia's chagrin, said, 'This looks about the last of the line so you don't really need me, do you, Daniel?' and headed straight for the girl – except for a quick sidelong glance and an exclamation of, 'My! You'll certainly wow 'em tonight, Cynthia!'

At last the covers were off the food and the serving staff were getting busy. Waiters attended the top table, although Daniel couldn't see why they shouldn't queue up at the buffet like everyone else. 'This isn't a state occasion and we're not royalty.'

But his wife was in charge of things and knew exactly how they should be run, and the swift success of the evening proved her right. In no time at all there was that swinging atmosphere which made a party memorable.

Even some of the workers' rowdiness didn't matter. There were always a few who imbibed too freely – like that constable's wife. She became shrill in no time but it made no difference to her dancing, which she did well once the old-fashioned numbers were finished with. She danced the charleston so energetically that some of her cheap ostrich feathers were flying, and she was calling out to her sister-in-law to join in and let herself go, and that young woman was laughing and calling back, 'After the baby comes, I will. I don't want to bounce the little mite out of me!'

Bruce was momentarily without a partner. Cynthia was dancing with Charles Peterson and Annabel with a good-looking chap from the potbank – Le Fevre, the chief thrower who had replaced that lout Boswell. He was one of the personnel invited by Daniel tonight and Bruce had quickly observed that he and Annabel were dancing together almost constantly. That displeased him, though he had nothing against the man personally. They frequently came in contact at work because Le Fevre visited the export department every time a load from his shed was to be packed. He was meticulous about that, and tonight he had been equally meticulous about his appearance.

He was a nice chap, a cut above the rest, but what right had he to monopolise Annabel? Bruce noted, resentfully, that she was enjoying dancing with him so he seized the opportunity to cross to Sarah's table. He had asked Annabel if she knew who the girl in that gorgeous blue dress was, to which she had replied that she was her best friend, Sarah Willcox – a fellow art student.

'We began together and we've vowed to stay together when we qualify. Daniel urged me to study at the Potteries School of Design, which you were against, and I can't tell you how glad I am that I heeded him.'

Slightly peeved, he ignored that and said, 'She looks familiar somehow.'

He had been thinking that since he had first noticed the girl, convinced that he had met her some time, somewhere. What puzzled him was how he could have forgotten – she was lovely.

There was a white-haired old lady seated at the table, together with a plump young woman and a man who appeared to be her husband, as well as a man looking thoroughly uncomfortable because his partner was tipsy. She was tugging at his arm, urging him on to the floor, and her voice was as shrill as an empty tin can.

When Bruce bowed to Sarah and asked her to dance, a warm colour flooded her face. Her smile was surprised, and lovely. Then she said, 'I'm sorry – it's the charleston, isn't it? I'm afraid I don't know how to do it—'

'I do!' screeched the tipsy young woman, and was half out of her seat when her husband pulled her back.

Bruce took Sarah's hand. 'Then let me show you,' he said, leading her on to the floor, and the sound of his voice sent her memory winging back to a cold and windy morning when he had driven her to the Frenshaw potbank. His voice had stirred dreams – of speaking as he did, of living as he did, of becoming somebody. But he had dropped her prematurely and left her to go the rest of the way on foot. But for that she wouldn't have been faced with Joe Boswell and a threatening blow.

And now he didn't even recognise her.

He took her right hand, placed his other arm about her waist and said, 'Watch my feet and do as I do. The great thing about the charleston is that it can be danced on one spot so we can do it right here and avoid the crush on the floor.'

It was difficult at first, but soon she was twisting her feet and kicking her legs in time with his so he speeded it up until they were charlestoning like mad and she was laughing through sheer enjoyment. 'Faster!' he urged, and then dropped one arm, spun her away from him and twirled her back, her feet unfaltering. Other dancers stopped to watch and the old lady began clapping in time with the rhythm, beaming all over her face. Sarah's mane of shining hair was flying and her great eyes sparkled. Bruce smiled down into them and pulled her back to him swiftly, causing something to fly from her wrist and go sliding across the floor to the tipsy young woman's feet.

Sarah stumbled, stopped, grasped her wrist and cried, 'My bracelet! Oh, my bracelet!'

The tipsy girl's ostrich feathers shed more as she stooped and picked it up. There was a moment's silence as she looked at it, then screeched, 'My God, Charlie — d' you know what this is? It's the bracelet that was caught in Joe Boswell's clothes the night he were found by the wayside with his breeches down!'

Twelve

The quietness of Stoke-on-Trent's art gallery was a relief after the street noises outside. Here was peace. Here the question, which had been tormenting Sarah since New Year's Eve, was stilled, but no doubt it would stir again when she returned home and found Kate still unable, or unwilling, to answer it satisfactorily.

'Why did you tell me the bracelet dropped to the floor when I stumbled over your doorstep?'

"Cos it did. That tipsy young woman must've been talking about some other drunk yanked into her 'usband's police cell. No wonder the Master Potter suggested the poor chap should take 'er 'ome.'

'But there were the initials. Mine. She recognised them.'

'And wot did I say to that, m' dear?'

The sickening recollection of the moment eased a little with the recollection of Kate's instant action. Calmly, she had held out her hand for the bracelet and said, 'Thanks, Mrs Bailey. 'Twere my Christmas gift to Sarah so this be the first time she's wore it. I've no doubt ye've got one like it, seeing they're on sale every week at the Saturday market an' I can't see *thee* missing a bargain, fond of beads an' baubles the way y'are.'

It had been a valiant attempt to turn the tables, but it

failed. Millie Bailey had screeched, 'I don't believe it. Look at her – white as a sheet! Why should she look like that if it weren't true? Let *go* of me, Charlie.'

She had wrenched her arm from her husband's grasp and dangled the bracelet high before dropping it into Kate's hand. 'See those initials? S. W.'

'Plenty of those about,' Kate had retorted, but only she knew that the fingers she closed about the bracelet were tense. 'There be lots o' women with the same . . . Sybil Wright . . . Susan Walker . . . Stella Wain . . . an' plenty more, I dessay, so be careful wot ye hint, or ye could be up for slander from many another quarter.'

The incident had lasted only minutes, but an eternity to Sarah, struggling against a threatening faintness through which she was aware that Bruce Frenshaw had unobtrusively deserted her and Millie Bailey's tin can voice was rasping, 'I bet Joe Boswell didn't buy *that* gown for her favours. Wouldn't have enough dough. Must've been some other chap!' Sarah could still recall her shrill laughter as a red-faced Charlie Bailey dragged her away.

Then Pru's husband was saying, 'Thank God she's gone. Poor old Charlie – what a life she gives him!' and Pru was declaring it was the last time they would ever put up with her, and someone was taking Sarah by the hand and saying, 'I'm not much of a dancer with this dot-and-carry leg, but can manage a two-step without treading on your toes,' and Daniel Frenshaw was smiling down at her and leading her back on to the floor. His grasp of her hand was firm, his arm about her waist supportive. Sarah's faintness began to recede, but not her humiliation. For a while she avoided his eyes but when he said, 'Look at me, Sarah . . .' she heard something more than kindness in his voice and obeyed.

It was then that she saw him as if for the first time. As an apprentice she had seen him as a man socially far above her and much older. Now she saw him in a new way. Not handsome like his brother but more human, and by no means old. At close quarters his features were finer and stronger, more chiselled – features she wanted to sculpt when she was more experienced. At close quarters she also saw that his eyes were deep-set and observant, his mouth firm and, at this moment, gentle. She was conscious of his deep sensitivity, of his strength coupled with understanding and, gratefully, she relaxed and let her body move with his as if they were one.

When the dance ended he didn't escort her back to her table but retained her hand, waiting for the music to start again, and in those moments he admired her gown and said how lovely she looked in it. She answered truthfully, as she already had to others, 'My grand-mother made it for me. I mean she made it over for me. It was hers when she was young.' She was relieved to find her voice so steady when a short a time ago she had been bereft of it.

She expected the answer to surprise him as it had surprised others – some reactions had even been tinged with doubt – but all he said was that Kate must also have looked lovely in it, and then his arm encircled her waist again as the music swirled into a waltz. They danced in silence, and without reason her memory recalled the surprise she and Kate had shared when tonight's invitation arrived, and how the old lady had promptly ordered her to write a letter of acceptance ('in your best handwriting, mind') and then to go upstairs and fetch that box she'd kept under her bed in the almshouse and was now on the top shelf of her closet. 'The box I wouldn't let anybody handle when we moved, remember?'

And there, packed within layers of yellowing tissue paper and fragrant with herbs, had lain this gown of peacock-blue slipper satin, rich and beautiful and of such fine quality that time had not diminished it. Kate had lifted it out with pride and an ill-concealed emotion which she tried to overcome by saying brusquely, 'Ye didn't expect mothballs, did ye, Sarah? An old witch like me knows nature's way to preserve fine stuff like this.'

For a moment she had gazed on it as if it were some rediscovered treasure, then held it against Sarah and nodded with satisfaction. 'As I thought. I knew it would be right for ye someday.'

'But that isn't why you kept it.'

'Well, mebbe not. Once I useter dream o' wearing it agin but there y'are – chances don't allus come twice so ye've just gotta be grateful for the once, an' look back an' remember . . .' Her faded eyes had clouded, but she'd blinked them clear and said briskly, 'Now get outa that clay-splashed thing you're wearing and clean y'rself up afore trying this on. No granddaughter o' mine's going to a posh do at Dunmore Abbey wearing only her Sunday best.'

'But what about yourself, Gran?'

'Sunday best'll do me fine once I've added summat to it.' She then rummaged in the box and withdrew a flat morocco case with a gold catch. Opening it slowly, she revealed a necklet of garnets in a magnificent antique setting. This time tears brimmed in her faded eyes.

Sarah's arms were round her in a flash. 'Gran . . . dear Gran . . .'

The case snapped shut. Kate's voice snapped too. 'I thought I told ye to get outa that working frock, so get a move on, lass, get a move on. If I'm to alter this gown to fit ye proper, *I*'ve gotta get a move on too. Not that I think there'll be much t' do, from the shape an' size o' ye now.' Excitement appeared to replace her nostalgia, but Sarah sensed how strong that emotion was.

As Sarah shed the frock she now wore daily, working with clay in alternating moods of despair and elation and always fired with the desire to do more, the old lady's eyes ran over her and her head nodded approvingly. Her granddaughter's physical development from girlhood to young womanhood was beautiful to see.

'As I thought,' she said when Sarah stood before her in the lovely gown, 'there'll be nowt t' do but some darts to narrow the waist – I were older an' a mother into the bargain when I wore it – and the hemline'll need turning up a bit. Great gawky creature, I were.'

'I don't believe it. You must have been tall and beautiful and wore it like a queen. How did you come by such a gown when times were as hard as you've often said? It must have been very costly.'

After a barely perceptible hesitation Kate said, 'It were passed on to me,' and busied herself with lifting the gown over Sarah's head.

'And the garnets? Were they 'passed on' too?' Sarah's voice was muffled beneath the folds.

'Aye. Weren't I the lucky one?'

Emerging, Sarah said, 'If they'd been a gift I'd like it better.'

'And why, may I ask?'

'It would be a happier thing.'

'Well, that be an odd thing t' say.'

At that point in her recollections, the music had stopped and a break came in the dancing. Daniel Frenshaw had taken her back to her table and returned to a wife who ignored him as he sat down beside her.

Sitting here in the museum, her second visit since Clive Bellingham had brought the supply of clay and opened the doors to a new world for her, Sarah was resting her feet after more than three hours of studying ceramic treasures which whetted her creative appetite and fired her ambition, but now she recalled the questions she had asked her grandmother on returning home on New Year's Eve and Kate's noncommittal, almost evasive replies. Gran could be a sly old bird when she chose to be. And why not? Sarah thought. Everyone has a right to keep a secret. But mine is hideous and, please God, no one but Gran will ever know of it.

But Joe Boswell did. He was part of it and would for ever be. The thought sickened her. She prayed that time would purge her mind of the memory, but knew it never would. Since Millie Bailey's horrible reminder Sarah had concentrated every spare moment on working with clay, blotting out all other thought until her grandmother, or fatigue, made her stop. Then back would come black memory, refusing to let go. Only when Clive Bellingham unexpectedly arrived at the cottage one day after the New Year, demanding to see what she had produced, did the shadow lighten.

'I know I'm not your tutor now, but I do have a proprietorial interest deserving of reward . . .' He had smiled meaningfully as he said that, but she presumed he meant the reward of seeing what progress she had made.

Lakeside wildlife had been her first inspiration and when she finally produced a graceful replica of a mallard taking wing she experienced a wonderful sense of achievement. Clive was right – this was what she had to do, *wanted* to do. She had put the mallard aside for him to see, wondering when he would contact her. She supposed he would choose the moment in his own good time, so she had worked on and waited.

But since New Year's Eve unanswered questions had troubled her between working hours. Despite Kate's avowal that she had told the truth about finding her bracelet, the shock of Millie Bailey's reference to Joe Boswell's drunken body and a bracelet found on his clothes had sparked fear in her. She *had* been wearing it. It was on her wrist when she set off for home that night, aware that it was slightly big and therefore loose but not telling Gran because she hadn't wanted to spoil the old lady's pleasure.

Hard on these memories came others – that when she wakened next morning she found herself alone, and Gran had not returned until long after she had forced herself to do all that had to be done before she came back, carrying her old pewter milk can and saying she had just been along to the farm to have it filled.

But such a short errand could not have taken so long, even with her difficulty in walking. So where had she been and why, if the bracelet *had* fallen from Sarah's wrist on her panicked return, had Kate produced it from her coat pocket later instead of leaving it where Sarah would have seen it on waking?

It was time to arrest troublesome thoughts; troublesome memories, too, like Bruce Frenshaw's desertion when she had become the focus of that nasty scene. For some time the recollection had been hurtful, but work had driven it from her mind so that she now cared less. She only hoped Bruce would not hurt Annabel one day. Her friend's fondness for him was frequently self-evident.

Sarah was surprised to realise that she had spent three hours in this quiet gallery, studying and sketching fine ceramics. Now the museum's clock told her she had half an hour to spare before setting off for home, so she decided to make the most of it by visiting rooms devoted to paintings. Once there she was quickly enthralled. That human hands could have produced paintings so magnificent was awesome. She said as much to one of the gallery's attendants, who asked if she had yet seen those of the Staffordshire countryside.

'There's a whole room devoted to them, miss, and well worth seeing. Just go straight ahead. Makes me proud to be a Staffordshire man every time I look at 'em.'

She knew how he felt when she saw them. Staffordshire had been beautiful country before its landscape became scarred by smoking bottle ovens, but mercifully they were centred in one area and even then an artist's eye had seen beauty in this darkened span set amidst verdant fields and woods with the potteries in dramatic contrast. He had painted them as no other artist had ever seen them.

Sarah looked for the artist's name. The signature had been painted so unobtrusively on all the canvases that it was difficult to read; but the museum had rectified that by adding official identification on the frames. '*Joseph Bellingham, R.A. 1850–1909.*'

'I hope you are admiring my grandfather's works?'

Sarah spun round. Clive stood there, his copper hair tousled as usual, his clothes as casual as ever.

'I've been out to your home again. Your grandmother told me you'd come here, but since she said you'd left before noon I didn't think I'd be lucky enough to catch you. I thought you would have left before this.'

'I've been too absorbed.'

'In the ceramics, I hope.' He saw the sketch book under her arm and calmly reached out and took it. He was so long turning the pages that she was forced to point out that the museum was about to close. At that, he closed the book reluctantly.

'Fancy a cuppa?' he said. 'There's a tea-shop across the road. Let's try it.' So saying, he took her arm and led her out of the building and down the wide steps of the entrance. It was a cold day, with a threat of rain.

'I can't stay long. I want to get home before dusk.' She did not add that she planned to take the longer route back to the abbey to avoid passing the smallholding at a time when Joe Boswell might be returning from work.

Clive said cheerily, 'Don't worry. I'll run you there in my beat-up jalopy. It carried a load of clay without mishap, so it will surely carry you.'

'But not a bicycle as well.' She nodded toward the cycle stand provided by the Council, and saw his second-hand car parked nearby. It had been smartened with a spray of bright blue. He left it there, took her arm, and raced her across the road, traffic-dodging. Reaching the other side, he cast an approving glance over her.

'You've changed a lot since the day I first saw you,' he said. 'For the better, I might say. You're no longer the scared mouse, for one thing, and for another . . .'

'Another?' she echoed, but by then he was pushing open the tea-room door and looking round for a table.

'I want one where we can talk,' he said. 'The trouble with tea-rooms is that they're usually full of women yacketty-yacking sixteen to the dozen so you can't even hear yourself speak—'

'Don't insult my sex. We *don't* yacketty-yack!'

He laughed and propelled her to a table in a far corner. She had certainly come out of her shell; she would never have riposted like that at one time. He remembered the girl he had seen on her first day, tongue-tied, nervous. 'The sleeping virgin' was how he now thought of her and wondered what it would be like to awaken her.

'You said you wanted to talk,' she said after he had ordered. 'About what?'

'You, of course. I came back from Exeter last night and made your home my first port of call today. I wanted to see how you'd been getting on, how much more work you'd done. Your grandmother let me take a look.'

'And were you satisfied?'

'Yes.'

'I was hoping you'd say you were pleased.'

'I've got to be pleased to *be* satisfied. You've really

stuck at it, haven't you? More than I expected during a season of parties.'

'I went to one – New Year's Eve . . .' She paused for the arrival of tea and as she poured it she said, 'I didn't know your grandfather was a famous artist. You must be terribly proud of him.'

He admitted he was, even that, at one time, he had hoped to emulate him. 'But the Royal College of Art proved I never would. Geniuses like him rarely occur more than once in a family – the rest have to settle for what they do best. My father's interest has always been antiques. He has his own gallery in Exeter and it was there I became interested in ceramics.'

And there I first met Carla, he recalled silently, skirting over his recent visits to the Exeter haunts they had enjoyed together. She had come into his life after working for two years in her uncle's antiques shop in a Parisian suburb, taking an exchange job in his father's gallery to further her knowledge of British antiques and to improve her English. On both counts, and others, she was a quick learner.

But revisiting their old haunts had been a mistake. Without her, life seemed to have gone out of them and what few familiar faces there were left him discouraged. When they recognised him but couldn't recall his name he felt like someone from their forgotten past. Worst of all was finding that the terraced house in which he had shared rooms with Carla had been demolished along with its neighbours to give way to a block of flats. He had found himself hankering to be back at work even though his first sight of the Potteries had made him want to rush back to Exeter, but what finally made him return from this Christmas visit earlier than intended was a particular discovery he had made amongst some of his grandfather's paintings, stored and looked after by his father since Joseph's death.

'These should be exhibited,' he had declared. 'We should hold a retrospective of his works.' His father had dampened the idea by pointing out the cost and the amount of work involved, but now all that was forgotten in the enjoyment of talking with Sarah and wondering why he had never recognised her potential loveliness as well as her potential talent.

'So why did you go in for teaching?' she was asking, tossing her head to fling back her mane of black hair. It had become windswept during their dash across the road. As she pushed it behind her ears he noticed her hands, long and slender with sensitive fingers and nails filed short. This evidence that she had discovered the handicap of long fingernails in clay sculptoring and had dealt with it pleased him. It meant she was taking the work seriously.

He answered her question. 'My RCA training qualified me as a teacher, so here I am – and that's enough about me. The time has come to show your best pieces to Daniel Frenshaw. That was part of the bargain, remember.'

'And how do you propose to do it? Since I haven't even a hobbyist's kiln they're not even biscuit-fired, which means they could break in transit.'

'I'll choose those that are leather-hard and will be safe in Frenshaws loading trays. A few dents in leather-hard clay don't detract from good modelling in the raw because they can't hide the original concept. Frenshaw told me to contact him as soon as I had something to show him, and now, by gosh, I have! So first thing tomorrow I'll be at the potbank and the necessary transport will come from there. You didn't think I'd overlook important details, did you?'

He reached across the table and grasped her hand. 'Believe in me, girl. Trust me. I always back a winner.'

Neither of them realised the tea-room was closing until a waitress coughed discreetly and proffered the bill. To Sarah's dismay, she saw that it was already dusk and rain was falling. Kate would worry if she were home late; she also hated supper to be spoiled through waiting. That ruled out the longer route to avoid the smallholding, but if she rode hard she might still miss Boswell on his way home.

Clive watched her hurried departure with disappointment. He had been hoping to extend the evening into something more intimate because her physical appeal had been potent. Instead, all he got was a lovely smile as she thanked him for the tea, and a backward wave as she sped away. Only minutes before he had been marvelling over the change in her; the increased self-confidence and the more extrovert personality. That's what fulfilling one's creativity does to a person, he had thought. It pleased him to think that he was responsible.

Halfway through tea she had thanked him for changing her college course – 'If the Master Potter agrees when he's examined my stuff,' she had added, though surely she couldn't doubt that he would. The pieces she had made spoke for themselves and for how hard she had worked during the holiday, but when Clive commented on that she had burst out, 'But it wasn't work! Once started, I couldn't keep away from it. Poor Gran had little of my company but, bless her, she didn't mind. Sometimes she would squeeze into a corner of the wash-house and watch, quiet as a mouse – very unusual for her!' Sarah laughed.

There was a new vivacity in the girl, a vitality which made him aware of her physically. He felt a rapport between them which made him hope for much more. For the first time since returning from Exeter he forgot about Carla.

If increased rain had not slowed her down, Sarah would have passed the smallholding before Joe Boswell reached home and the dreaded encounter would not have happened.

Head down against a gathering storm, she kept her eyes focused on the road, measuring progress by familiar landmarks – the bus stop where Frenshaw workers were picked up, the turn-off leading to the Longton road down which Bruce Frenshaw had driven her on that long-ago morning, the immense wrought-iron gates to Annabel's stately home, where she herself was now so welcome, the tree behind which she had hidden on the morning of her fifteenth birthday . . . and after that nothing but uninhabited road until the smallholding.

Approaching that point, she braced herself for a burst of speed which was thwarted by a head-on wind, an increased deluge and the final obliteration of dusk by a darkness in which her cycle lamp cast an inadequate circle of light, wobbling and flickering until she feared it was failing completely. Then a lighted window outlined a familiar cottage gate and the open doors of a shed Joe Boswell used for stabling his horse. The man was locking up at that precise moment and at the sight of him fear lurched, but forced Sarah's legs to even greater effort.

Too late. He had seen her and recognised her despite the uncertain light. At once he was through the gate and planting himself in her path. When she tried to swerve past him he seized the handlebars, forcibly stopping her.

'Well, well, well – if it ain't my uppity stepdaughter! Coming to call on us at last, are ye? Or mebbe you're wantin' me to fuck ye again? I've bin expectin' it, biding my time . . .'

His coarse voice thrust through wind and rain. The sound of it and the sight of him repelled and terrified her. Driven by fear, she fought to wrench the handlebars away but was no match for him. The wind sent her drenched hair streaming back from her face and for a flicker of time the man paused. 'My, Sarah, but you're a beauty now, good enough for any man — but it's me that's going t' have ye agin' an' right now. To hell with the storm! We'll be snug an' dry in the shed, wi' plenty o' straw to lie on—'

She hit out at him blindly but he seized her wrist and began to drag her. Screaming, she clung desperately to the bicycle, whereupon he laughed. 'Save your breath, ye little fool. No one'll hear ye on a night like this, 'specially Mabel, snoring before the fire! Christ, lass, I'm going to make up for the days I perched ye afore me on that horse, soft an' close between my legs . . .'

With all the power in her lungs she screamed against the roar of wind and rain. Promptly, he clamped one hand over her mouth and seized her bodily with his free arm. She heard the bicycle crash to the ground at the precise moment that a sudden lull came in the wind's howling. She drove her teeth into his hand, hard and mercilessly so that he jerked away with a stream of oaths, and she screamed more powerfully the more he cursed her. In the wind's brief lull her yells echoed loud and long and a woman's voice suddenly shouted, 'That you out there, Joe? Wot's going on? Fell over summat or has that dratted horse kicked ye?' Sarah had a fleeting glimpse of Mabel within the porch, straining to see in the darkness, and in a flash she seized the bicycle and was off into the gathering night before her mother had a chance to recognise her. As her shaking legs managed to carry her away the echo of Boswell's voice cursing '*some blasted bitch on a bicycle* . . .' followed her on a renewed gust of wind.

It was more than fear that left her shaken. By the time she reached home she had learned one thing and was strengthened by it – that anger was the greatest weapon anyone could have against fear. It grew in her as she battled again with the wind and the rain, a blind anger against Boswell which, from now on, would be her greatest defence against hideous reminders of him. Was she to allow this man to threaten her peace of mind for *ever*? By the time she reached home rage was seething within her, but when Kate opened the cottage door she was careful to show no sign of it. On no account would her grandmother hear of tonight's encounter.

'My goodness, lass, you're drenched! Straight upstairs an' into a hot bath ye go, an' after that a good meal's ready an' waiting in t'oven.'

Sarah called thanks over her shoulder as she raced upstairs, anger still raging though resolutely hidden. It was implanted deeply and permanently, a ballast against fear of the man, equalled only by a desire to get even with him somehow, someday, no matter how long she had to wait.

Thirteen

A day or two later Joe Boswell stamped through the cottage door, slammed it behind him, and said to his wife, 'Heard the latest news about that daughter o' yours?'

'D'you expect me to?' Mabel crossed to the kitchen range to stir the pot of stew which she topped up daily. (No one could accuse *her* of not seeing there was a regular supply of nourishment for her man.) Returning to the armchair in which she slouched for most of the day and picking up the damp stub of a half-smoked cigarette, she added, 'Since she left Frenshaw's she's gone her own way – though I must admit she drops in regular on my birthday and afore Christmas.'

That fanned the resentment he'd been nursing since his recent encounter with the girl.

'She don't come when *I* be about. Why didn't ye tell me?'

'Didn't think you'd be interested. After all, you'd no fondness for the lass. So wot's this latest news about 'er an' how did ye come by it?'

'The Master Potter's spending more fees on different training for 'er – clever stuff the potbank's never gone in for before. Real favouritism *that* is. You know how word gets around – well, this time everyone's agog with it, an' more besides, thanks to that brat Daisy Wilkins who was an apprentice same time as Sarah and whose mam ain't no better 'n she should be.'

'And how d'you know *that*, may I ask? And wot d'you mean by "more besides"?'

'Daisy were bragging about her mam working at houses o' the gentry when big parties were on, an' how last New Year's Eve her mam were taken on for the dance at Dunmore Abbey, handing round trays o' champagne, an' she were standing close to the reception line when in walks that daughter o' yours wearin' an evenin' dress she could never've bought for 'erself. Knocked everyone back, it did. And knocked back *some*body for more than a tidy sum, from the sound of it.'

'Gossip,' sniffed Mabel, as if she never listened to it. 'That Wilkins woman's a born liar, anyway. And that New Year's Eve dance at the abbey is known to be for estate workers, which Sarah and her old gran are not.'

'They were there, anyway. That chap Lefever too. The Master Potter always invites one or two of his top workers.' Joe added in a resentful mutter, 'Should've been me, not that Frenchie,' whereupon Mabel looked wistful and Joe hoped t' God she wouldn't start whining about that when she'd had time to chew it over.

'That girl o'yours has got real uppity now she's in with the gentry,' he growled.

'The *gentry*? Our Sarah? Come off it, Joe. Living in a worker's cottage at the abbey don't mean she mixes with any but the neighbours. They were a lucky pair to get a cottage there an' I'd dear like to know how it came about. My guess is, Kate fixed it. First she gets that almshouse, an' next she's moved to the Dunmore estate! If I knew how she wangles it I wouldn't mind taking a leaf out of her book. This place is all work and no profit, though it could pay orlright if you'd lend a hand.'

'Or if *you* spent less time an' money on tarting yourself up.' Joe heeled off his muddy boots and kicked them across the kitchen. Mabel was becoming a real old whiner – hated living out here in the country, hankering for ever to be back in Burslem, and getting worse since he had been downgraded. If anyone had cause for complaint, it was he.

And now he was stuck in a rut serving beneath that Frenchie and hating it, while every other thrower heeded whatever the man said or did. Enough to make you sick, it was, and even more so when the Master Potter congratulated the bastard on the shed's increased efficiency. At the end of his first year the profits on Frenshaw's thrown ware were up substantially, due (so everyone declared) to those impressive Grecian urns that were selling to rich estates both at home and abroad. But Joe wouldn't acknowledge it. Instead, he reminded them that in the immediate years following the war there'd been a general boom in trade through-out the country and Lefever couldn't be praised for that.

'As for them newspapers now predicting a slump, they're talking up their arses.'

But no one seemed to pay much heed to his opinions these days. Mabel certainly didn't. Since that girl of hers left home she had been forever grouching, though there'd been nothing they could do to get her back. The authorities had made that plain enough since the girl was in the care of her grandmother and well housed, and now she was older there was even less hope. Mabel accused him of driving the girl away with his bullying. *Bullying*, when all he'd ever done was to get the hots for her! Not that Mabel suspected that, nor ever would. Not a soul in the world knew about the physical satisfaction he had craved, and finally seized.

But once wasn't enough, especially since his encounter with her on that wet night. He couldn't get over the change in her – the way she looked, the way she spoke, even an air of confidence about her despite her screams which, he had decided on later reflection, had had one intention only – to rouse Mabel – and in that she had succeeded, damn her. As for her air of defiant self-confidence, rumour had it that she'd gone on to greater things at that art school because the Master Potter had seen pieces she had modelled freehand, straight from the clay. No doubt such success had gone to her head.

Or was she so favoured because she was letting the man have his way with her? The thought made his gall rise.

'So wot's all this about Sarah and the gentry?' Mabel asked. He didn't mention his suspicions about the girl's whoring with the Master Potter because how the hell could he prove it? But it scared him nonetheless because having the man's ear that way could certainly mean she could cause trouble. So all he said was, 'She's well in with that Peterson girl from Downley Court.'

'I know that. They both go to that Design School an' I've seen 'em together.'

'Where?'

'Driving to Burslem. The Peterson girl's got a two-seater an' gives Sarah a lift. And why not? My daughter's as good as Annabel Peterson, an' don't you forget it.'

'Then why don't she come to see you regular, like, not just birthdays an' Christmas?'

There was only one reason that Mabel could see and she voiced it now, angrily. 'Mebbe because she don't wanta see *you*.'

That startled him. Surely to God Mabel hadn't got wind about that night, which he could only remember as a glorious haze of sexual savagery and satisfying brutality, but which he'd been confident no wench like his stepdaughter would dare tell anyone about. Now he had reason to fear otherwise and at a high and dangerous level, though he couldn't imagine a pottery lord like Daniel Frenshaw continuing to want a brat who'd been raped like a guttersnipe.

Mabel's voice jerked him back. 'And it's my guess she don't wanta see you because she never liked you. I always took your side, but it made no difference. I remember how she useter try to dodge riding to the potbank with you, though I never understood why.'

'That's all over,' he growled, 'an' a good thing; too. A mischief-making little bitch she were, spreading lies about me—'

'Lies! What lies?'

'That I useter strike her – me, wot never hurt a hair of her head! She even told that to the Master Potter an' got me downgraded. That's the sorta girl your daughter be. Ye should've brought her up better, so y' can't blame *me* if she don't give a damn for ye now.'

'Joe Boswell, I don't believe a word! Looking back, it seems t' me that trouble never started until I married you. Right from the start the kid feared you and, if you want the truth, I don't get in touch with 'er now for that reason. If she be happy the way she is, then let 'er be. As for wearing a fine ballgown, how d' ye know it weren't lent by the Peterson girl? Bet *she's* got loads.'

'Calm down, Mabel—'

But Mabel couldn't. Though she wouldn't admit it, she missed her daughter. Now she railed at her husband, 'This could've been a real home if *you'd* behaved nicer to her *and* pulled your weight with the smallholding.'

'The smallholding's yours, not mine. If ye'd have the sense to put it in my name, that'd be diff'rent. That's wot a wife should rightly do, specially one who don't know how to run the place. Women weren't meant to own property, so make it over to me or let it run to seed, take your pick, but stop laying blame at my door because your lass scarpered.'

'I reckon Frenshaws would have summat t' say if I tried to pass this property on to you or anybody else, since they settled it on me as a pension.'

'Frenshaws needn't know.'

'They'd find out, surely? I'd need a lawyer to do it, wouldn't I, since the thing was tied legally? So how could anything be hushed up?'

Mabel seemed to have calmed down a bit so Joe changed his tone from aggression to persuasion.

'There's no need to go to the same lawyer, Mabel luv, nor one anywhere near the Potteries. Liverpool's a centre for all sorts of goings-on and it ain't all that far to go. Dockside there is lined with pubs where all sorts o'folk can make all sorts o' contacts.'

'I wouldn't want anything crooked, Joe.'

In her voice, uncertainty vied with interest. It would

be a relief to hand over responsibility for this place. She disliked keeping poultry and pigs and all the mucky work that went with them, like when they had that cow Flossie. She'd been glad to sell the beast for a good deal less than they had paid for it, making the excuse that young Sarah was frightened of it, though at first she hadn't been. Mabel had never forgotten the way the kid had taken to crying at the sight of her.

As for the land work, the sewing and planting and hoeing and digging and all the other jobs that went with it, she couldn't for the life of her get the hang of it, and though folks told her it was easy to learn and all she had to do was ask some market gardener to take her on for a learning session (they were always glad of free help) she had lost interest after the failure of her first attempts. Man's work, as she saw it, was for husbands, so she had considered Joe to be heaven-sent, but that had proved to be right only in bed.

He was looking at her now with that come-on look, but for once she didn't respond.

'I can't see how you could run this place *and* work at the potbank, Joe. I know you don't have the position there that you useter, but you'd still have to work the same hours to get the same money.'

'Don't bank on that lasting. There's a slump coming, some say, in spite of the boom after the war. That didn't last, God knows.'

'You mean you're likely to be *out of work*, the finest thrower in Staffordshire? That's wot you've always called yourself, so surely the Master Potter wouldn't be so daft as to let you go?'

'He's bin daft enough to put that Frenchie above me, which speaks for itself, don't it?'

'But why did he? Ye've never told me.'

He dodged that.

'C'm' *on*, Mabel – face facts. Wot we need is security an' this smallholding can give it us providing I'm in charge. If you really can't put it in anybody else's name, then sell it. Nobuddy can stop ye doing that. It'll fetch a tidy sum an' set us up elsewhere in wotever way we fancy, an' don't forget that daughter o' yours ain't round our necks no more. It's just the two of us now. The sale of this place could set me up as a potter on my own – one-man potteries don't do so bad, y' know, working for themselves an' selling their wares direct an' taking all the profit.' He finished with a touch of impatience. 'Don't look so worried, luv. I can't think wot's the matter with ye lately. Y'useter ask my advice on everything.'

'But never on getting rid of property that belongs to me an' nobody else.'

She saw an ugly change in his expression and for the first time fear pricked her, followed by a startling question. *What would George advise?*

But George wasn't here. For the first time since she became enamoured of this man she thought of her first husband with longing.

Fourteen

At the precise time that the Boswells were enjoying their marital bickering, Daniel was riding through the Dunmore estates, taking careful stock of everything with an eye to a future which would astonish everyone in the pottery industry.

For a long time he had cherished an ambition – to build the potbank of his dreams set amidst healthy surroundings where Frenshaws' potters would breathe good, clean air and work in better conditions than the present ones. Now the war was over he was determined to fulfil that dream, and counted himself lucky that he was able to.

After a thorough survey of the miles beyond the abbey, he returned via the south side of the lake and turned east. He was just in time to see his brother heading for his own quarters. So Bruce had left the potbank before closure, which meant one of two things – that work in the export department had been completed early (which could be a bad sign, indicating a decline in overseas orders) or that he had left the staff to get on with the job while he himself knocked off – for what other reason than a social one? It had happened before.

Resolving to tackle his brother about failing to pull

equal weight with others, Daniel climbed the spiralling east staircase leading to the unused tower room. He was surprised that the door leading into the room should be locked, but for the purpose of surveying he had all necessary keys. Once inside, he was also surprised that the door leading from the room into the main body of the abbey was also locked, but was intelligent enough to guess why. His brother had taken double precautions against intrusion.

In one way that didn't surprise him; in another it did, for it barred Cynthia from easy access from within, confining her to outside entry at ground level, the whole of which formed Bruce's apartments. Daniel had no proof that his wife visited Bruce there, or indeed any proof of actual infidelity. All he had was the evidence of his eyes when seeing the pair together; Cynthia's unmistakable glow following sexual satisfaction, and the flimsy excuses with which she absented herself from home. A man needed more than that to free himself from a wife he no longer loved and who no longer loved him. Now, in the twenties, adultery was the most usual plea for divorce, though sexual deviations could also be cited but were diligently hushed up.

On the first of these grounds Daniel could not yet act because all he had was suspicion. Until recently, he had accepted the situation and found solace and forgetful-ness in work, but that was no longer enough. Since dancing with Sarah on New Year's Eve, feeling the closeness of her body and the depth of her distress, it was becoming impossible to deny the truth about his feelings for her. His outrage over her humiliation, and his swift desire to comfort and defend her, had dominated him that night.

The painful part was knowing that she saw him only as an employer who was also a benefactor – and a man much older than herself into the bargain.

Pulling himself back to the present, he reminded himself that he was here to inspect a room which he planned to utilise. He had been familiar with it in boyhood and it was ideal for the purpose he now had in mind. He jotted a list of things on which he would seek a surveyor's opinion and then, leaving both doors unlocked, climbed to the crenellated roof from where almost the entire span of Dunmore's estates could be viewed, only to find he was thwarted by a dusk which was beginning to obscure them. An early morning view would serve him better, but meanwhile he let his glance cover the near distance, spanning the area of grounds surrounding the abbey and the clusters of workers' houses beyond the lake. He could see the cottage now housing Kate and Sarah, and was glad he had at last achieved what he had wanted to do for a long time, but distressed by the thought of the events leading to its final accomplishment.

On two things he was determined – that never would Sarah learn that he knew about the rape, and that he would continue to campaign against Union rules which prevented him from sacking a man who was a capable worker despite being a bad character. He had started that one-man campaign the day Kate had arrived at his office and he would continue the fight until he won, no matter how long it took.

The air was growing chill up here on the abbey's roof, but he lingered awhile, gazing down on the lake. A dark shadow on the water's edge was the dilapidated old boat in which generations of Frenshaw children had learned to row. Now it was disused and, at Cynthia's decision, remained so.

'We can't risk the lives of estate children,' she had declared with unusual common sense. 'They'd be sure to take the boat out unsupervised, and if we tried to stop them there'd be protests from parents and we'd still be blamed if an accident happened. That could lead to a lot of expensive trouble and we don't want that.'

So there it lay at its moorings, permanently tied up, its duckboards likely to rot. 'That doesn't matter,' said Cynthia. 'We'll leave it where it is because it adds a picturesque touch.'

And how right she was, Daniel thought now as he looked down from high above. Even so, it would be wise to drag the boat ashore and have it examined. He made a mental note to suggest this to his wife, humouring her insistence on supervising outdoor matters.

But he would not yet tell her of the major scheme he had in mind because he knew she would be horrified.

Downstairs in his study was one of the objects that had finally persuaded him to take this giant step – the figure of a dancing fawn, one of Sarah Willcox's early attempts which he had kept for himself after showing the rest to the Head of Sculpture and Modelling at the Potteries School of Design, who immediately agreed to change her study course. The man's cool appraisal had drawn a verdict of 'distinct promise' and the rest of her attempts had been retained to enable her future tutor to estimate where her true bent lay. Whatever comes to her naturally, Daniel had wanted to say, but remained silent because an expert would surely see that for himself.

The dancing fawn now stood on his desk, a delicate creature with raised forelegs and curved back and poised head, executed with delight and sensitivity. She must have seen the creature in a clearing in Dunmore's forestland, and sketched it to aid her memory when modelling it. Did she still use the cottage's cramped wash-house, he wondered, or was it true that she cycled over to Downley Court sometimes and shared a garden summer house as a studio with Annabel? They would both fare even better when his plans reached fruition.

It was some time before Cynthia had noticed the fawn, which wasn't surprising since she rarely visited his study these days. She had picked it up idly, said, 'What is this supposed to be?' and touched the surface with a perfectly manicured finger. Inevitably, the unfettled and unglazed surface felt rough. 'A bit crude, isn't it?' she had said, adding that she supposed this sort of thing was all right if one happened to like it, but why keep something so amateurish on his desk?

He did not tell her that it was because Sarah Willcox had made it, and that having it there brought the girl closer to him. Suppressing a smile, he had touched on the only aspect his wife would appreciate – that the early works of talented and successful people fetched big prices eventually.

'Oh, in *that* case . . . but why not store it away until the time comes? If it does.'

Because then I couldn't look at it and think of her hands creating it. The answer was unspoken, heard only in his mind.

He had decided to wait until the national economy

hovered on the downward turn, which now seemed inevitable, before making his plans public. That way the fears of his employees would be assuaged. The family industry meant much to him and here, at Dunmore, he had the scope to save and expand it. It would mean an end to the ever-increasing maintenance costs of the ancient Longton Road site which Frenshaws had occupied since they established their first potbank, and which the Midland Canal Company had long coveted as a base midway between the Severn and the Mersey. Now he was ready to do business with them.

Like the great Josiah Wedgwood before him, Daniel intended to build his ideal potbank in a rural setting. Despite being further out, Dunmore was still within access of the heart of the Potteries. Existing outbuildings might well be utilised and more could be built. It would mean an end to the belching bottle ovens which far-seeing potbank owners were replacing with gas-fired industrial kilns, and Sarah Willcox would no longer be reminded of her father's terrible death every time she saw the fatal construction where it happened.

During her apprenticeship Daniel had often seen her turn away from the sight of that bottle oven when she crossed the potters' yard. It was an instinctive gesture, and told him much. The Midland Canal Company would clear the site for its own needs and the bottle ovens would be the first to go, so when she passed that way in the future there would be no painful reminder to cast a shadow over her lovely face.

He particularly looked forward to the inclusion of Sarah's talent and the skill of Annabel Peterson. It was hard to believe that both were now nearing graduation, or that so much time had passed since he had seen samples of Sarah's early modelling attempts and been impressed by their promise, now being splendidly developed. Since changing her course her talent had flourished, and she had blossomed with it. He found it hard to recall the shy, rather gauche apprentice she had once been, and though he prayed she was no longer haunted by her horrific experience with Boswell he knew that a sensitive person would never forget it.

Turning away from the twilight view, he glanced fleetingly toward the clusters of workers' homes. Beyond their lighted windows wives would be preparing evening meals, putting babies to bed or dealing with other household tasks, whereas beneath him, within the abbey walls, domestic activity would be humming in the servants' quarters while the mistress of the house – the day's menus having been approved by her that morning – would be making a leisurely toilet.

With a jolt, he was proved wrong. From a side entrance to the abbey, so far below that the view dwarfed her, Daniel saw the top of Cynthia's blonde head as it emerged. He watched her foreshortened figure as it ran along the wall below, hugging it as if for cover. A coat hung crookedly over her shoulders, as if thrown on impatiently, and her footsteps were so fleet that she was gone almost in a flash. He was too high above to hear the thud of a closing door, but in that area there was only one access through which she could have vanished so quickly – the main entrance of the east tower leading to his brother's apartments.

And despite the distance and the diminishing light, the eagerness of her flying feet was recognisable and significant.

He didn't wait to see if she emerged. He went back

to their own part of the abbey, where he came face to face with Hannah Bradley who gave the polite bob of the head so typical of her and said, 'Sir, the mistress asked me to let you know that she's been called to an emergency meeting of the Benevolent Society, which she can't avoid since she's president, so she had to leave early and you're not to worry about her getting back because she's driving herself. She also said not to wait dinner for her because the committee always gathers for a meal after a meeting.'

'In that case I'll have something in my study. Anything light will do. I have papers to pore over, so I hope Cook hasn't been preparing anything elaborate?'

'She asked what I thought you'd like, sir. I suggested melon *frappé* and a nice cheese soufflé to follow, knowing you're partial to both. And then some of Cook's profiteroles – I know you like them, too, sir.'

'With a glass of Côtes du Rhone, that will do very nicely,' he said, and thanked her and went on his way, wondering if the loyal soul believed as little of his wife's story as he did and if she had become as experienced as himself in turning a blind eye and a deaf ear. But for how much longer he was prepared to he did not dwell on.

After the meal he donned a comfortable old smoking jacket and settled down at his desk, the original plans of Dunmore Abbey spread out before him. Their ancient parchment was faded and slightly foxed with age, but he had touched up the main outlines so they were easy to follow. The abbey had been one of the largest in England before the containing walls had either been allowed to crumble or been demolished, the centre part eventually being restored by one of his Frenshaw ancestors and turned into the hereditary family home.

From the map of the abbey's exterior Daniel identified the original sites of glaziers' and carpenters' shops, of slaughterhouses where gamekeepers and, later, monks had hung up deer killed in the chase within its own parklands – killed not only for the exhilaration of the sport but also to feed the large number of occupants. Now such blood-letting activities no longer took place at Dunmore and the abbey itself was about two-thirds of its original size, but its vast acres were still there, standing idle for the most part but richly wooded and with ancient outbuildings suitable for restoration.

Materially, Daniel was fortunate and appreciated it. At the same time he wondered how many of his competitors were heeding the threat of miners' strikes and lock-outs which would deprive the Potteries of that most vital commodity, coal. How many were recalling the strikes of 1920 and 1921 that opened the doors to the present threatening depression, and how many regretted the financial support then handed out to miners' unions by the present Potters' Union, leaving little for clay workers when needed? And now here they were, in 1929, with the Wall Street crash hanging destructively over the world's economy and the 1930s looming ahead with wages in the Potteries forty per cent lower than they had been a decade before.

Daniel knew that the step he was taking was not only wise but inevitable. Cynthia would be aghast, of course. From her would come storms of protests, possibly supported by Bruce when he learned that he would no longer have a monopoly on the east wing and that two new workers would occupy the tower room with access via the main door which he considered his own exclusively.

It was late before Daniel flung himself on to the sofa in his study and prepared to sleep. The last thing he looked at was Sarah's delicate model of a dancing fawn.

'I've news!' Clive announced, seizing Sarah's arm so that liquid splashed from the cup she was carrying. Ahead, Annabel waited on the window seat she and Sarah still shared at tea-breaks. It had become their recognised spot which fellow students had learned to respect. After all, they were seniors now. And because their friendship had become so strong that they spent most of their leisure hours together they still adhered to the practice they had established that first day.

Clive's arrival was a surprise.

'To what do we owe this honour?' chaffed Annabel. 'Why not confer it on the hierarchy in the staffroom?'

'Because, as I said, I have news. Too important to wait.'

'Then tell us,' urged Sarah.

He took a deep breath and announced with pride, 'There's to be a retrospective exhibition of my grandfather's work in the art gallery at Stoke – exactly when I don't know because a helluva lot of work goes into preparing for such an exhibition.'

'You mean there are even more paintings of his than already hang there?'

'Considerably more. The idea is to represent his life's work – the best of it. They'll include his paintings of Staffordshire, of course, but he did a mass of other work, too.'

'Wonderful!' cried Sarah. 'Annabel, have you *seen* the Bellingham exhibits in Stoke-on-Trent's gallery?'

'Not since I was a kid and my parents took me, influenced by a school report which encouraged them to believe I might become an artist one day.'

'Which you have.'

'I mean a real one, not a ceramics painter.'

'That's art, too,' Clive reproved, assuming his stern-teacher voice. 'A highly specialised one, as is ceramic sculpture, so don't go underrating it. Do you know what I anticipate? That one day there'll be a combined exhibition of Peterson and Willcox ceramics. Meanwhile—'

'Meanwhile we're impatient to hear more about your grandfather's retrospective,' Sarah put in. 'Since the gallery has so many of his works already, how big is it likely to be?'

'That I can't say since I'm not actively involved, but the collection will certainly need considerably more space than the current display. My father is lending the best of what he personally owns, as well as sorting out a stack which had to be stored after Grandfather died. Experts are choosing the best and a panel from this end is joining them. The snag is that many may need cleaning and restoring after all these years. Then there'll be the business of packing and transport and the hanging committee's onerous job of choosing the best display sites, not to mention the cataloguing and publicising and everything else that goes into launching an important show.' Clive was zestful. 'I gather they're planning a big do – all the local bigwigs, etcetera.'

'They'd better make room for us!' declared Annabel.

'Since your people are among the bigwigs I can't see them being left out.'

'She meant *us*,' Sarah said, 'and I agree. Otherwise the pair of us will have to queue when the doors are opened to the public. Not that I think we shouldn't, but to even dream of attending a private viewing—'

'No need to dream. I'll fix it.' Clive didn't add that he had every intention of escorting Sarah himself.

'I hope some of the paintings will be for sale,' said Annabel. 'I'm sure my darling parents will want to own a Bellingham masterpiece since their darling daughter is a pupil of the artist's grandson.'

Sarah smiled. She loved Annabel's parents, who made her feel completely at home whenever she was there which, far from being less frequent, had become even more so since her and Annabel's art courses had separated.

Annabel cried 'Whoopee! There's going to be some excitement in this neck o' the woods at last!'

Kate's reaction to the news didn't match her granddaughter's, but that was hardly to be expected, thought Sarah, since art as a subject had never interested the old lady. She recalled Kate's reaction to the modernistic book Daniel Frenshaw had given her to study the day he had told her she was to train as a paintress, and Kate's dismissal of it as 'foreign', as if that explained its weirdness. Yet some of Annabel's most beautiful designs were now leaning toward fantasy.

'Well, m' dear,' said Kate now, 'an art exhibition sounds very impressive. I s'pose you'll be going?'

'Oh, Gran, we're *both* going!'

'Not me, luv. Wouldn't understand much of it.

Pictures of the countryside, yes, but not some of this freakish stuff folks seem to admire nowadays. I saw a picture t'other day in a magazine in the doctor's waiting room—'

'The doctor!' Sarah was startled. Kate swore that her herbal mixtures were better than any doctor's medicines. '*You*, visiting a doctor?'

'Don't worry, luv. 'Tweren't for me. Her ladyship from the abbey sends me on errands now an' then an' this was one.'

'Sends you on *errands*!' Sarah was aghast. The thought of a young and able-bodied woman despatching an elderly one on errands outraged her. 'I should have thought she could at least send one of her servants.'

'I dessay she does sometimes. Don't fret y'rsel', lass. She saw to it that I were driven, else how would I get there all the way from Dunmore? Not on *my* old pins. Felt quite grand, I did, sitting behind a chauffeur, though o' course she never sends the best motor for me and o' course the driver's any workman as can be spared, never the liveried gent. This time 'twere to collect some pills for Mrs Bradley's migraines – suffers from 'em a lot, the pore lamb tells me. In her free time she often drops in for a chat. Anyways, while I waited for the med'cine to be made up I took a peek at the classy magazines an' there was this picture of a naked body with an eye where the navel should be – I thought 'twere a joke. Laugh? I nearly split me sides! Call that art, I thought, but it were in a Lunnon exhibition an' people were gathered round gazing at it awed, like. Nay, luv, I don't think I'm the right person to go to an art show. You an' Annabel will understand it better 'n me.'

'Judging by Joseph Bellingham's paintings of Staffordshire, I don't expect it will be the kind of art you're thinking of, Gran. And I'm sure Clive will be disappointed if you refuse.'

Briefly, Kate was silent.

'That young tutor, y' mean?'

'You know I do. Who else?'

'See a lot of 'im, don't ye?'

'Yes.'

'In love with ye, is he?'

'I don't know.'

'Wot about thee?'

'You mean, how do I feel about him?'

'Aye.'

'I . . . like him very much.' Is it only 'like'? Sarah questioned herself, remembering moments which came like flashes between them, filling her with confusion and an unfamiliar excitement and fleeting sexual awareness. She thrust the memory aside because since that terrible experience with her stepfather the thought of having sexual intercourse with any man frightened her. 'You would like him too, Gran, if you'd get to know him, but you never take the chance to. Whenever he comes you're nice and polite but take yourself off, making excuses that you've jobs waiting in the kitchen when you know I've finished them all.'

'Well, young folk like t' be alone.'

'Gran, I suspect you avoid him.'

Kate picked up her knitting. 'For Pru's next,' she said. 'Y' know she's expecting agin? That'll be four, come summer.'

'Don't change the subject. Give me the truth. Do you dislike Clive? Do you really try to avoid him?'

'No to both. I like him well, but I'm not eddicated an' feel outa me depth with them as are.'

'You've never felt that way with the Master Potter.'

'That's diffrent. I've known 'im since he were a nipper.'

'Then give Clive a chance. Come to the exhibition with us. The invitation to the private viewing is for both of us. He's calling for us so we'll drive in state. And this exhibition of his grandfather's works means a lot to him.'

'Aye, Joseph Bellingham were famous, I know. But don't press me, luv. I'd be outa me depth. So let me stay by the fireside, thinking of ye having a wonderful time. I guess it'll be a grand dressing-up affair, so ye'll be wearing the blue gown agin. That'll make me happy. Ye don't know how much.'

But despite her words, Sarah was left with the feeling that there was more behind her grandmother's excuses than she could understand.

Fifteen

The event became the talk of the town, not merely because all the local dignitaries and the highest social names were there but because the press had a field day following it.

'There should be some governing body to control newspaper stories,' growled Annabel's father in his bluff way as he flung down the local paper at breakfast the next morning 'As it is, the blighters will milk the story for weeks if they can dig up a crumb or two to follow it.'

'It was Sarah I felt sorry for, having to face stares and whispers from people who are supposed to be well mannered. I could have *killed* them,' declared Annabel.

'You were not the only one, dear.' Her mother's voice was as serene as ever.

'So that makes three of us,' said Charles. 'I shan't forget Sarah's face when she looked up at the first portrait, full of startled recognition then bursting with pride. And there she stood, looking exactly like the picture, wearing an identical blue gown and her hair piled high just like her grandmother's and looking just as lovely. What a beauty Kate Willcox was in her youth! No wonder Joseph Bellingham painted her. I did hear whispers when I was a lad – that some artist from the south had come here to paint landscapes but also painted a portrait of a local beauty which he didn't show to anyone so, of course, no one believed it because no female member of the local aristocracy could claim the honour and nobody imagined a renowned artist would paint anyone less. As for the other portrait, there was never a whisper about that, but I should have expected people nowadays to be more broad-minded than some were last night.'

'Jealousy,' said Annabel. 'That always rouses spite. Personally, I thought that picture lovelier than the first. Clive told me both portraits had been stored since his grandfather's death. What a waste! He remembers seeing the blue-gown picture long ago when he was very small, but not the other. His father was bequeathed the care of them so he stored them in Joseph's studio. I wonder he wasn't tempted to display them in his antiques gallery – in their elaborate frames they would have blended well. I gather Joseph willed that they should never be sold, but he plainly put no ban on them being exhibited.'

'Well, I'm very glad they've been shown at last and I'm damn well going to let it be known.'

'Three cheers, Dad.'

'I endorse that,' said Ruth.

'Bless you both.' Charles pushed back his chair and apologised, in his old-world gentlemanly fashion, for leaving the breakfast table before them. 'I'm off to write to the local rag protesting that their salacious reporting only reveals their ignorance, and then to the *Morning Post* and *The Times*, urging them to send their best art critics to Stoke-on-Trent to view the exhibition.

That'll show these local hacks what good reportage really is.'

'And I must be off,' said Annabel. 'I've barely an hour before class.'

'You're picking up Sarah?' said her mother.

'At the crossroads, as always. We both hate to miss even a part of any session. It's Egyptian Design for me today and Life for Sarah. I shall tell her that the life study we saw last night was superb.'

'Having seen it for herself she'll hardly need to be told. And some of her work in the students' half-term display showed her own potential for ceramic life sculpture.'

'I know. Clive Bellingham was fit to burst because he spotted her potential first. I suspect he's in love with her. And now I really must be off . . .'

Annabel pushed back her chair, plonked an affectionate kiss on her mother's cheek and was off in her breezy fashion, thankful that she had successfully hidden from her parents the disappointment she still felt because Bruce had not turned up at the Joseph Bellingham private viewing, as promised. 'If *you're* going to be there, darling, wild horses won't keep me away even though art's not my cup of tea.' He had sounded as if he really meant it. That hurt.

Now she recalled that she had not been the only person without an expected partner. The absence of Daniel Frenshaw's wife had surprised everyone, for rarely did Cynthia Frenshaw miss any social event where she could shine.

And it was strange that Daniel had offered no explanation for her absence.

Sarah wakened early though she had gone to bed late. She felt languorous and possessed of an inner peace despite the disapproval which had filtered through to her from certain people in the gallery last night. On arriving, her eyes had immediately encountered the portrait of a woman in a shoulderless blue gown and it was as if the young Kate had leapt from her gilded frame to welcome her. The simple title, '*Kate*', was superfluous. A surge of surprise and delight and overwhelming pride had engulfed Sarah. She had stood still and gazed up at the portrait, displayed high on a wall where it caught visitors' eyes the moment they entered.

She had wished fervently that Kate had not refused to come. It would have been wonderful to walk down the long gallery with a handsome old lady who had been painted in her younger days by one of England's finest artists, walking head high with pride because the model was her own grandmother.

So absorbed had Sarah been in studying the picture of Kate wearing the blue gown that her glance had been held by it to the exclusion of others. Dear Gran, she had been thinking, were you too shy to come? Was that behind your excuses? Or were you afraid that people wouldn't believe you ever owned such a gown or had ever been so handsome? But the bone structure of your face is ageless. There was no reason for you to be afraid, but every reason for you to be proud, as I am.

So surprised and delighted had she been at the sight of her grandmother's portrait that she had been unaware of any other until Clive said, 'When we reach the next exhibit, ignore some people's comments. Those who know something about art, and many who don't, are full of admiration, and so they should be. Oddly enough, when I first met your grandmother I felt she was vaguely familiar, but I was a kid when I first saw the blue portrait in Grandfather Joseph's studio. Then when I was home last Christmas I came across it amongst others my father had stored, paintings Joseph refused ever to sell. I was startled because I knew then why your grandmother reminded me of someone, and I knew at once that the sitter couldn't possibly be anyone but Kate Willcox and that Joseph must have met her when he visited the Potteries. The second portrait was found by my father amongst another batch when the powers that be agreed to my suggestion for a retrospective and asked for more of his works.'

'So this exhibition was your idea?'

'And why not?' Clive had given a wry grin. 'I might as well make the most of a relationship that can give me a leg-up, so when my father said a retrospective would be too big a job to undertake I went straight to the bosses here and put up the idea. And am I glad I did!' His voice had tailed off as his eyes turned to a knot of people gathered round the adjoining exhibit. 'Your grandmother was certainly beautiful,' he had continued, 'and this next pose shows how unaware of it she was. Not a hint of self-consciousness.'

It was at that moment that Sarah heard murmured comments about nudity and brazenness. Until then excitement had made her unaware that her resemblance to the blue portrait had attracted attention and people clustering round the next one were now casting sidelong glances at her. She felt no embarrassment, only an aversion to some of their remarks, but she was glad when she saw Daniel Frenshaw coming toward her, smiling the smile to which she never failed to respond. What a friend the man had become! Whenever they met now it was on an equal footing, as real friends. During these growing-up months the social and professional division between them had become narrower and narrower until now it seemed non-existent.

Only his wife made Sarah feel socially unacceptable. It had first been evident when the woman had come across her sitting beside the lake at Dunmore, sketching. So intently had Sarah been concentrating on a group of ducklings, with the hen hovering watchfully near, that she had failed to hear the sound of Cynthia Frenshaw's high-stepping grey carrying her on one of her inspection rounds.

'And what are you doing on the wrong side of the lake, Sarah Willcox?'

Surprised and embarrassed, Sarah had faltered, 'Why – sketching, Mrs Frenshaw.'

'Ma'am.'

The tone was sharp, and so was Sarah's reaction. She controlled it by pausing before saying, 'I was unaware that any side of the lake was barred to me. Mr Frenshaw didn't mention it when he told me I could go wherever I wished and sketch whatever I wished *when*ever I wished – ma'am.'

The final word sounded like an afterthought and annoyance marred the mistress of the abbey's lovely face.

'I don't believe a word of it! Occupants of the workers' cottages are fully aware that they must never trespass beyond the bounds set for them. They have ample space for recreation – more than generous, in fact. It seems you decided to take liberties which I must warn you not to repeat. All matters relating to the estate come under my authority. Indulge your little hobby by all means, girl, but stay within your own area.'

The unwelcome episode had sprung into Sarah's mind as Daniel made his way toward her through the crowded art gallery. She found herself wondering if his wife had reported the incident and reproached him for laxity toward someone whom she regarded as one of the lower orders, but right now Daniel was holding out both hands to her and saying, 'You're as lovely as Kate was when young, and the portrait in blue is exactly as I remember her when I was small, though I never saw her in anything but a clay-splashed potter's slop with her hair scooped into a hideous mob cap . . .'

His hands encompassed hers. She felt suddenly breathless and couldn't understand why, or why her happiness soared. Then his voice clipped off and his hands withdrew as Clive's arm went round her waist and dragged her away. She had time only to smile back over her shoulder and see Daniel's own smile fade before she was confronted with a picture of a woman lying naked, with the title '*Kate nude*' in superfluous identification. It was a full-frontal portrait, Kate lying half-propped on one arm and looking straight at the artist with her frank and honest eyes, but something else shone from them – sheer happiness and a lack of self-consciousness because she was content for him to see her this way.

It was time to get up, to pad barefoot down to the kitchen as she always did, to brew the morning tea and take a cup to Gran, but even as she did so Sarah's thoughts were still in the art gallery and her emotions were still gripped by the memory of that picture of a woman in love. The memory was beautiful and stirring because it told her that Kate had once given her body to a man because she wanted to. She had found ecstasy with him. Her eyes had said so, with joy and no shame, even though by then she must have been the wife of another man and mother of his children. That picture had not been of a young and inexperienced girl, but of a woman sexually fulfilled. And deep inside her Sarah was convinced that the artist had been responsible for this rich fulfilment, a second blooming more beautiful than before.

Looking back now, Sarah realised that Kate's nude portrait had told her a vitally important thing – that sexual intercourse between a man and a woman could be beautiful if mutually desired and that her own experience had been vile because there had been only bestiality and cruelty in it, leaving a legacy of fear.

Automatically filling the kettle, lighting the gas and setting the tray left plenty of space in Sarah's mind to admit other recollections from last night, including the small celebration party Clive had held after the big event was over. He had been in a state of elation because, despite the remarks of a few ignorant critics, his grandfather's retrospective had surpassed any art exhibition held in these parts for a long time, and the gallery bosses had already intimated that it would not only be extended but very possibly toured afterwards. Other gallery authorities had attended and future bookings were ready to be discussed.

' "A feather in our cap" they called it, but really it's a feather in mine for pulling it off, so you can't blame me for being cock-a-hoop, can you, darling?' Clive had kissed Sarah soundly in front of everyone, elated and proud, and in his brief speech of welcome he had said, 'This is a treble celebration really – not only to drink to the exhibition's success but to my escape from depressing digs into a place of my own, and finally, though really this should come first, to drink to the memory of my grandfather who so brilliantly painted a woman he must have loved – and to her granddaughter, who would inspire him equally were he alive now. Luckily for me, *I* am.'

At that Clive had clinked his glass against hers and the guests had applauded and toasts had been drunk, followed by a noisy one to the pair of them. 'To Clive and Sarah!' The words had echoed around them and it was then that Sarah caught sight of Daniel Frenshaw on the outer edge of the crush. Their eyes met, and held, and somehow she felt there was a question in his, but when she looked back a moment later he had gone.

It had been a successful party and people had lingered until well past midnight. Throughout it Clive had scarcely left Sarah's side, touching her unobtrusively whenever he could and restraining her when people began to leave. 'You can't go,' he had murmured. 'I'm taking you home, remember.' With a meaningful smile he added softly, 'But not yet . . .'

In her enjoyment she was content to linger. It had been a wonderful evening and she didn't want it to end. Kate expected her home late and knew Clive would bring her safely. He had told the old lady so, assuring her that he would take good care of her granddaughter and she was not to worry. By now, Kate would be asleep. But when the last guest departed and

Sarah moved to follow, his restraining hand stopped her yet again. 'Stay,' he murmured. 'I want you to stay.'

'Do you know how late it is?' she laughed.

'Fully. And that's why I don't want you to go. I won't let you. I promise to deliver you to that cottage before dawn, so I won't be breaking my word to the tyrannical old lady. Until then, we can be happy together.'

She withdrew a little. 'My grandmother is not a tyrant.' She spoke defensively, not only against his joking belittlement of Kate but, had he known it, against the way in which he had referred to the home which was better than anything she or Kate had ever known, as '*that* cottage'. Had a faint disparagement really been there or was she being over-sensitive, imaginative?

With a laugh, he seized her. 'Come off it, Sarah. I was joking, but you must admit the old girl can be a real old battleaxe when she feels like it. Not that anyone looking at those portraits, particularly the second, could ever imagine her growing old that way.' His arms had tightened round her. His mouth had come down on hers, demanding but not savage, not cruel . . . tender and warm. She felt wanted because she was *herself*, someone to care about, and the feeling was good. She wanted it to stay that way, but as his tenderness increased to passion she shrank away instinctively.

'Good God, Sarah, what's the matter? You're not afraid, surely?'

'I – I'm just not ready for what I think you want—'

He laughed. 'My blessed little virgin, I'm not going to hurt you!'

'I know, but please – take me home.'

He sighed and said a little grudgingly, 'All right, but what are you afraid of? I'm falling in love with you; let me show you how much. And you can't remain a sleeping virgin for ever, you know.'

'Well, lass, let me hear all about it,' said Kate as Sarah banked up her pillows and wrapped a shawl about her. 'Ye must've come home pretty late 'cos I never heard ye come in.'

'Clive Bellingham gave a small celebration party in his flat afterwards.'

On that Kate neither made comment nor asked questions. 'A fine exhibition, were it, luv?'

'Wonderful. And something there thrilled me particularly.'

'And why?'

'I think you know why.' Sarah dropped a kiss on the old lady's forehead. 'What's more, I think I know why you declined the invitation. You were afraid your portraits would be there.'

Kate concentrated on her tea, relishing every drop. Every morning she called it her lifesaver and declared Sarah brewed a cuppa better than anyone. This morning she said nothing until she had drunk it, then she set the cup aside, drew her shawl closer around her, looked her granddaughter in the eye and said, 'Aye, so I were, even though I knew folks mightn't recognise me. But now, looking at you, I reckon they did.'

'And *I* was bursting with pride. Beautiful portraits of a beautiful woman – *my* grandmother.'

'*Portraits*, y' say. Meaning more than one. Well, there be no sense in pretending. Yes, that *is* wot I were afeared of – you an' everybody else learning the truth about me.' Kate's glance dropped, too embarrassed to meet her granddaughter's, and Sarah's arms went about the bony shoulders, half hugging her, half shaking her.

'You don't know how proud I was. The moment I walked in and saw you prominently displayed, wearing the blue gown—'

'*Our* gown now, Sarah. An' now ye know how I came by it. The artist bought it just to paint me in. "I see you in blue," he said. "Vivid blue to contrast with your jet hair, and a gown made exclusively for you . . ." He wanted to take me to a dress designer in Lunnon, of all places – *me*, a respectable married woman, mother o' five! 'Sides, I'd've felt like a fish out of water. But Joseph Bellingham weren't a man to take no for an answer. He even told me he'd supervise the gown's design 'cos he knew just wot I'd look best in, an' he'd got my measurements anyway. Well, that flabbergasted me till he said an artist knew how to calculate a model's proportions afore painting. He were right determined to get 'is own way, so off he went to a top Lunnon designer an' when the gown were delivered an' I put it on he were over the moon. Then came the garnet necklace even though, in the end, he decided not to use it – said me shoulders looked lovelier without it after all . . .'

Kate's eyes had become dreamy; even her voice seemed lost in the past. 'They must've cost a fortune, but Joseph Bellingham insisted I kept both even though he must've known I'd never get the chance t' wear eether agin. Nor did I, until the estate party, but I've treasured 'em, as ye know. Nor have I ever forgot the afternoons I slipped away to pose for him, making an excuse at the potbank that one of my childer were sick an' needed tending. That were a lie, o' course, 'cos the brood were a healthy lot. As for the evenings, I told the family I were working overtime at Frenshaws an' that explained the extra money I earned, which God knows we needed. 'Twere lack o' money that made me do it in the first place. The potteries were going through one o' their bad times, with hundreds out of work an' my husband one of 'em, but I never dreamed it would—'

'Grow into something bigger?' Sarah prompted gently.

To that, Kate said nothing. Sarah picked up the empty teacup and said, 'How about another, nice and fresh?' but the old lady stopped her before she reached the door.

'Y' say there was more than one picture . . .' Her voice was low, her glance downcast, her fingers plucked the bedcover.

'Yes, and even more beautiful. It was—'

'I know what it was.' The voice was bleak. 'He only painted two. And then he went.'

But something happened, thought Sarah. Something Kate had never told anyone about.

As she prepared breakfast, sounds from the adjoining garden distracted Sarah. Pru's children were at play, well wrapped up and rosy-cheeked, while the oldest, four-year-old Benjamin to whom any kind of barrier was a challenge, sat astride the dividing fence, yelling in frustration because one foot was trapped. She raced to rescue him and his rage promptly changed to beaming pride in his achievement, catching at her heart. She wanted to capture that chubby face just as it was – a whole series of chubby Benjamins to delight the world.

Whenever she could, from today on, she would watch him from her side of the garden fence, surreptitiously sketching, and then she would be off to her wash-house studio to choose the right clay and start working. She raced back indoors, the stimulation of the prospect urging her to get breakfast and household chores over and done with, only to be halted by an imperative knock on the front door.

To her surprise, Cynthia Frenshaw stood there. She wore riding clothes and the grey was loosely tethered to the front gate.

'Good morning,' she said in a tone of condescension, 'I have been knocking quite a while.'

'I'm sorry. I was at the back and my grandmother is not yet up. I take her breakfast in bed.'

'Then when she is up – and I hope it will be soon because my housekeeper is badly in need of her migraine pills – tell her I will send a car and driver as usual for her to collect them.'

The speed at which anger rose in Sarah astonished her.

'My grandmother is too old to be sent on errands. Why can't the driver collect them? Or why not send a servant? My grandmother isn't one – ma'am.'

With hauteur Cynthia Frenshaw said, 'A chauffeur must remain with his vehicle at all times, and the abbey staff are all occupied at this hour. But you would have no knowledge of such things, of course. To avoid delay, and out of compassion for my housekeeper's suffering, I called here personally—'

'Then why not collect the pills yourself – ma'am? I see you are equipped for riding.'

Fury dyed the woman's face. Her mouth opened on

a crushing retort and then promptly changed to an anticipatory smile as the hum of a high-powered car approached. It was Bruce Frenshaw's Lanchester and Daniel Frenshaw's wife spun round, her smile widening as she lifted a gloved hand to wave to her brother-in-law as he drove toward the main gates *en route* for the potbank. The quality of his smile in return was no more than friendly, whereas hers was self-betraying. Sarah closed the front door feeling that she had witnessed something she would be wise to forget.

Sixteen

Bruce said bluntly, 'It's time we had a talk, Cynthia.'

'About what?'

Her voice was drowsy and indifferent. In the aftermath of satiated sex, she felt in little mood for conversation.

'Us. Sooner or later the time must come to call it a day.' When her startled eyes looked back at him he said, 'You must have known it. Love affairs can't last for ever – especially one like ours.'

Now thoroughly awake, she said, 'I don't see why not. History is full of lifelong associations unblessed by the Church.'

'Name one.' When she couldn't, he laughed. 'Not much of an historian, are you? Nor I, if it comes to that, but neither of us can be fool enough to imagine that the end of our *affaire* isn't inevitable. The surprising thing is that it has lasted so long without Daniel suspecting. The only explanation is that you must serve him well in bed. With your lusty appetite that doesn't surprise me, though I don't like to think of it.'

'Jealous?' she teased.

'Guilty, more. After all, he *is* my brother. To be frank, I've often made up my mind to break with you, then failed.'

'And you'll fail again. As for feeling guilty, there's no need because Daniel sleeps with me less and less these days.' She didn't like to admit, because it was unflattering, that he had moved into another room without comment or explanation, his silence clearly indicating that it was final.

'That could mean he suspects. I know my brother. He's a man who hides his feelings, bides his time, then acts. He makes decisions and then takes you by surprise when he's thought them through thoroughly. He's a wise bloke and I respect him though we haven't a thing in common.'

'Except me,' she said in a coaxing tone which, after the physical exhaustion of the past hour, failed to entice him.

'You're overlooking one thing, Cynthia. When I marry, things will naturally end between us.'

'Sure of that? And who are you planning to marry?'

'Annabel, of course. Who else? "A man cannot marry his brother's wife." Ever read that page in the prayer book? I once browsed through it as a bored choirboy. And since divorce laws are so strict and mercilessly prolonged today, neither you nor I could tolerate their slow and relentless grind – nor you the social stigma. Imagine being refused entry into the Royal Enclosure at Ascot, the fate of all divorcees! The day may come when divorce is as easy and as commonplace in England as it is in America, but that's far off. Apart from all that, Annabel is part of my life. We were childhood sweethearts, as they call two kids who are inseparable, and there's never been any doubt in my mind about us marrying.'

'Does she know that?'

'I'm pretty sure so. It's one of those taken-for-granted things, approved of all round.'

'Then go ahead and marry her, darling. I won't mind. I won't be jealous. I can wait because I know it won't be long before you'll be wanting me again. Give her a couple of kids to keep her occupied and she'll be happy — that is, if you can lure her away from her current ambitions. Daniel declares she's highly talented and he's even planning to employ her when she's qualified. Your belief that she would quit that art school hasn't proved to be right, has it? She's plainly in her element with that mixed bunch of students, particularly the Willcox girl. She doesn't seem to recognise any social divisions. Do you really want such qualities in a wife?'

'Since New Year's Eve I've realised that I'll have to accept them if I hope to get her. She looked ravishing in that white dress and I had the devil of a job to get a dance with her, thanks to that French chap from the potbank—'

'He's very personable. I wouldn't have minded dancing with him myself, but he plainly thought he'd be overstepping the mark in asking the Master Potter's wife.'

'D'you think so?' A touch of amusement hovered on Bruce's lips. 'The truth was that he had eyes for no one but Annabel, and she certainly responded.' He added dismally, 'And *now* the truth is that after letting her down on the evening of the Bellingham exhibition I think I'll be damn lucky to get her. I'd promised to be there and *you* know why I wasn't. I felt a heel later.'

That irritated Cynthia. 'For heaven's sake, don't start talking about guilt again. From a rascal like you it's unconvincing, which is why I know you'll come back to me and continue to, Annabel or no Annabel, wife or no wife. And now be off with you, darling – I have things to do.'

Sliding off the bed, she walked naked to his bathroom, leaving him to dress and be on his way. She didn't see the resentful glance he threw after her.

'You always think of something to do when you've finished with me, don't you, Cynthia? What is it this time?'

While pulling on his clothes, he heard her answer above the rush of running water accompanied by the scent of her favourite bath salts. She made sure that his apartment contained all her vital necessities.

'If you have to ask that you can't have noticed what's going on outside,' she called beyond the open door. 'There seems to be some land measuring going on near the east paddock. If you don't know anything about it I suggest you take a look. Wait and I'll come with you. Men can frequently get answers where women fail.'

'Not women like you,' he laughed, 'and I've no time to wait. The export department needs my presence. And if anything *is* going on over there I dare say it's nothing more than some plan of Daniel's to improve the area – create more formal gardens, perhaps.'

'In which case he should have consulted me. The outdoor estate has always been my responsibility.'

Unofficially, he thought, quelling more irritation. Cynthia's self-assumed authority seemed to be increasing.

Fastening his collar stud and reaching for his tie, he called back dismissively, 'Well, it's probably nothing important – and now I'm off. There's a substantial export order being despatched today and if I'm not there to supervise it you can bet your bottom dollar Le Fevre will be because it consists of his best thrown ware. Orders of this size are less frequent than they were a while ago — to give the man his due, that isn't his fault. He produces finer work and runs the throwing shed better than his predecessor, and is almost fanatical about his goods being packed properly. But the post-war slump is begining to bite—'

'Don't *you* harp on that too! One hears enough about it these days.'

Cynthia cut off the conversation by slamming the bathroom door and Bruce departed, stung. Sometimes he wondered how it was that a solely physical attraction could bind two people who had little else in common. It was like wearing a strangulating collar he couldn't discard.

As he rode away he glanced toward the east paddock and, on an impulse, headed there. In his present mood it would be satisfying to prove Cynthia wrong about something, but what he saw proved she was not. A large area was being surveyed and measured.

So she was right, dammit. Something *was* going on, about which he knew nothing, and because he disliked her ability to crow over him, he resolved to find out what it was before she did. He would go straight to Daniel's office and ask him. It would be easy to concoct some satisfactory excuse for returning late from lunch.

In the event it was unnecessary. Daniel was on a routine tour of the sheds and had not yet reached his brother's. By the time he did, Bruce was well occupied. Seizing an opportune moment, and beneath the cover of industrial noise, he said, 'I'd like a word when you can spare the time, Daniel. Nothing to do with the potbank.'

'In that case, can't it wait until I'm home this evening?'

'Cynthia will be there, won't she?'

'And that will make a difference?'

'Well – I don't want her to be upset.'

'Why should she be?' Daniel gave one of his deep glances. 'What is it? Trouble? Haven't you learned how to handle it yet?'

'It's nothing of the sort.' Bruce tried not to appear affronted in the presence of his workers. 'I'm simply curious about what's going on beyond the east pad-dock.'

Daniel said lightly, 'Oh, that! Then by all means drop in after dinner tonight and I'll tell the two of you.'

On reaching home, Daniel said without preamble, 'I hope you've no engagements tonight, Cynthia, because I've something to talk about with you and Bruce. He's coming at nine.'

'That's rather soon after dinner at eight—'

'Since we no longer have leisurely tête-à-tête meals, we should get through it comfortably. Of course, if you've something planned for later, keep to it by all means. I can put Bruce in the picture alone, and since he owns his rightful share of the potbank that would be fairer.'

'Well, if it's anything to do with that place you certainly won't need me. If it concerned things here, that would be different.'

'It will eventually. In fact, I intend it to be soon.'

That made her uneasy, then wary. 'Then I'll join the

pair of you,' she said, and asked if it had anything to do with what was going on beyond the east paddock. 'I've seen men measuring the ground there. Why? What are you up to, Daniel?'

'Something a world-renowned potter did in the eighteenth century. Wouldn't you be proud to be the wife of another Josiah Wedgwood?'

She shrugged. 'You're renowned enough in the pottery world, exporting more than any of your competitors.'

'In top-quality domestic ware of fine china and porcelain, yes, but not yet creative or ornamental ware of Wedgwood's calibre.'

'And what has that to do with measuring the land here?'

'I propose to make good use of it – as you'll hear when Bruce joins us.'

Characteristically she shrugged again, indicating that it was really a matter of indifference and boring into the bargain, but adding that since she had nothing better to do this evening she would join them. She then steered the conversation to more interesting things – social events in London, Worth's latest Paris collection, the newest debutantes to be presented at Court and how splendid were the pictures of their carriages lining the Mall and the elegance of their Prince of Wales's feathers, then on to her father's increasing prominence on the financial pages, and finally the disappointment the Petersons must feel about Annabel's choice of career. 'Their hopes that she will marry Bruce must obviously be dashed.'

'How do you know they had such hopes?'

'Everyone knows it.'

'Perhaps everyone takes too much for granted.' Daniel closed the subject, whereupon she switched to a local press report on the Bellingham exhibition, a report which cast a slur on an elderly local woman who had been painted stark naked when younger, and the woman's lack of shame in allowing it to be shown when in her seventies. 'I gather they've identified her as old Kate Willcox. Hilarious, isn't it?'

Daniel's face tightened. 'No,' he said coldly. 'It is a wonderful painting of a beautiful woman in her prime. Whoever wrote that denigrating piece knows nothing about art and protests about it have been made by many, including myself for one and Charles Peterson for another. Charles has urged leading national newspapers to send their well-qualified art critics to view the exhibition, and since Joseph Bellingham was a Royal Academician of renown I have no doubt local bigotry will be put in its well-deserved place. By the way, it was a pity you didn't turn up for the private viewing. I won't ask why you didn't. I'll merely say that it would do you good to visit the exhibition before it closes because besides the nude painting there is a splendid one of Kate wearing the lovely nineteenth-century gown she passed on to her granddaughter – the blue one Sarah wore on New Year's Eve. I remember you speculating, cruelly, on who had bought it for her.'

Dinner was a silent meal from that moment.

When Bruce arrived they had coffee in the room the Frenshaw family had called the drawing room and which Cynthia insisted on calling the salon.

'So what do you have to tell us?' Bruce asked.

Before Daniel could reply Cynthia said, 'It's something to do with land adjoining the east paddock. He says he's going to put it to good use, like Josiah Wedgwood.'

'Wedgwood had to wait a long time before he could own anything approaching so much land as we have here,' her husband said. 'When he did, you know what he used it for. The Etruria Works at Barlaston are part of legend now. I'm resolved that Dunmore's will become the same.'

There was a stunned silence before Bruce gasped, 'You mean you're going to build pottery workshops *here*?'

'More than that. A wholly new Frenshaw potbank. Brick buildings instead of wooden sheds, well designed modern buildings far more accommodating than those we have used since our first potter ancestor set up his shed by the canal. This has been a dream of mine for years. I believe better accommodation will produce better work and do for the name of Frenshaw what the Etruria Works did for Wedgwood—'

Cynthia's voice cut in, sharp as jagged glass.

'I don't believe it! I *won't*! You couldn't be so insane! Scar such a place as this with filthy bottle ovens belching out filthy smoke? As for dirty pottery workers tramping all over our beautiful acres—'

'They won't. Areas for their recreation are already marked on the plans. The last piece now being measured will be the nearest to the abbey, and much of that is screened by trees. And what is offensive about human beings relaxing in distant fields? As for bottle ovens, there will be none.'

'No bottle ovens! Then how are we going to fire?'

The initial shock over, Bruce's voice now revealed interest.

'By newer methods, more up to date. Gas-fired kilns are proving successful and a hundred per cent cleaner. No smoke. No coal. No dust. Nothing to blacken the stokers or fill their lungs. That will be the greatest innovation. Others will be well-equipped workshops and good lighting – big windows, good ventilation and reliable heating in the worksheds. In conditions such as those, workers will be healthier and our output should double.'

Bruce said, 'But how are they going to get to and from this place? Dunmore is much further out in the country than the Longton road site. And what *of* that site? Frenshaws have used it since the potbank was set up and its situation on the canal gives direct access for the transport of goods—'

'And for their collection. Other potbanks will be glad to deliver their products there instead of sending by rail or road to north, south, east and west. That's why the Midland Canal Company has wanted to buy the site for a long time. It will double their trade. They've met my price and are willing to wait until we can vacate.'

Cynthia snapped, 'Which won't be for years, thank God. With all this talk about the depression and more and more businesses going under, how can you contemplate anything so crazy? It's worse than that, it's sacrilege! This beautiful abbey in its beautiful parkland is sacred, and you propose to overrun it with bricks and mortar and rough industrial workers. My mind boggles! The potbank should stay where it is, far away from us. What my father would say, I can't imagine.'

'I can,' Daniel said drily, then added, 'Do you know

exactly how many acres we have here? Over seven hundred, *excluding* the area occupied by the abbey and surrounding grounds and cottages. You should know that well enough since you have the freedom to ride over them at will.'

'Then put your buildings at the farthermost point, away from all proximity—'

'Where the cost of running gas to feed the kilns would be uneconomical. The abbey and existing cottages are already supplied with gas and I've checked that it can be connected to more buildings providing the distance isn't too great. That is why sitings have been carefully assessed. Moreover, they'll be concealed by natural forestry and therefore out of view of the abbey, so you've no cause for complaint on that score. And vast areas of land will remain untouched. Enough Staffordshire countryside has been polluted by industry. I have no intention of adding to it. In any case, there'll be no pollution with the end of bottle ovens.'

When she sulked, Daniel's patience ran out. 'You should have lived in earlier centuries, when families like Wedgwood's worked at home with bottle ovens in their back yards towering above their roofs. The Ivy House Works, The Brick House Works, even The Church House Works with house and garden and adjoining church smothered in perpetual smoke.'

Bruce said pacifically, 'But you do seem to be forgetting one thing. Dunmore is double the distance workers currently travel. How are they going to get here?'

'By the same method as now – buses provided by the potbank – and since the current vehicles are deteriorating badly they will have to be replaced anyway. And it isn't an extravagance – it's an investment Frenshaws can well afford. We may be temporarily hit by the slump, but we are rich enough to weather it. Everything has been settled and building starts within a month. I also intend to utilise the tower room because it is encircled by windows and equipped with worktops and cupboards and shelves. Remember them being installed so we could use the place as a hobbies room when we were boys? It will make an ideal working studio.'

'But it's part of the east wing!' Bruce protested.

'Which won't interfere with you since you occupy the ground floor. Beside the tower entrance door is your own inner front door near the foot of the spiral stairs, and in any case you won't be disturbed because not only will you be over in the main potbank buildings during working hours, but the tower room will be used for quieter work. Because of long disuse new heating installation will be needed as well as restoration of flooring and patches of wall where necessary, although surveyors' comments were that they knew how to build *and* insulate in those days. So it won't take long to put things right and then the creative workers I have in mind can move in.'

'By which I take it you mean the paintresses?'

'No. They and the men who produce decorative vases will occupy a newly designed building with big windows and roomy accommodation – there are more than fifty of them, remember, so it's important they be less crowded and enjoy better light and space. The tower room will be ideal for two new artists developing two new lines – designs never before used on our porcelain ware, and ceramic sculpture.'

When Cynthia's head jerked up, Daniel nodded.

'Yes – Annabel Peterson and Sarah Willcox. It seems no time since their training began, but it won't be long before they take their finals – Sarah later than Annabel because of her switch to sculpture, but the time gap will be caught up. I've kept a watching brief and seen the strides they've both made. Neither can fail to get high-grade diplomas and I'm not going to miss the chance of employing them. That's why I'm concentrating on the tower room first. They can start working there while new buildings are in progress and the rest of the potters will be transferred from the old site as workshops are completed.' Daniel paused, then added, 'You're very quiet, the pair of you. What are you thinking?'

Slowly and bitingly Cynthia said, 'That you've gone stark, staring, raving mad, throwing away money at a time like this. And that is what Papa will say, too.'

'Because the lace industry is badly hit. The financial pages confirm it.'

'Not my father's. He is shrewd enough to know how to cope with any so-called depression. I happen to know that trust companies and banks are investing more money in his business – he has told me so. That shows how successful he is. People like that wouldn't back him if *he* made bad moves.'

Bruce said unexpectedly, 'Well, the more I think of it, this move of Daniel's is a good one. And it isn't something Frenshaws can't afford. As I see it, it's an enterprise taken at the right moment. Builders, like other trades, are crying out for work. I'm with you, Daniel. All for it, in fact.'

Cynthia fumed silently, I'll bet you are, with the chance of seeing Annabel Peterson more frequently, waylaying her with careful planning. As for the Willcox girl – damn you, Daniel, you've planned this very carefully. D' you think I haven't guessed that you're in love with her, a girl almost half your age?

Seventeen

If there was one thing Jacques Le Fevre was not going to miss, it was the display of prize-winning students' work at the end of their training, though he was interested only in Annabel Peterson's, and if there was one thing he was not going to do it was to go straight from the potbank in his workaday clothes. He cut his midday break by half an hour to enable him to leave early and change into the well-tailored suit he kept for what his sister called state occasions. When she returned from the potbank at the normal time she eyed him with mock surprise.

'Well, don't we look smart!'

Marie's eyes were teasing, and even though he was intent on tying a new silk tie to perfection, he couldn't help noticing how pretty she had become in her growing-up years. Self-confident too. She had advanced from her apprenticeship to become a skilled glazer.

Things had gone well for the Le Fevres, and particularly for Jacques. He was now earning more than the man before him could have imagined, creating original works much valued by the Master Potter. Instead of being paid traditional piece-work rates with an extra emolument for his rank of chief thrower, he had become a high-salaried employee. The company's success had soared when his impressive Grecian urns caught the eye of the ceramic and art press, resulting in colour reproductions in leading art magazines accompanied by personal interviews with him. He was good looking and photographed well and was soon in demand as a fee-earning speaker and demonstrator at schools and colleges and craft training schools. Interviews on the wireless increased his personal renown and added to Frenshaws' reputation.

Marie declared that if only this new 'television-lens' camera, which a man called Logie Baird was reported to be developing, would really come along, her handsome brother would be seen as well as heard by the nation, and her spirit was not dampened by the scoffing of fellow-workers who declared that if 'that television thing' ever did come along only the rich would be able to afford it. 'In that case,' she retorted, 'the rich will be able to afford Frenshaws' finest goods, too.'

The potbank's workers were impressed by Jacques Le Fevre's success, with the exception of his brawny predecessor. Boswell could no longer brag about being 'the best thrower in the potteries'. He remained skilled but unimaginative, nursing a festering resentment of Le Fevre's popularity and success. He was now silent and morose when the man was around.

He also resented the rise in circumstances enjoyed by the 'Lefever' family as a whole. The father now headed the huge mould-making department which was the specialist section of the Burslem potbank where he worked. The man now drove there daily in a company motor which was one of the perks of his job, and his wife no longer did home-sewn shirt-making. Instead, she spent much of her time tending the garden surrounding the detached modern house they had moved into a year ago and, as a result, she looked a great deal younger now than Mabel, who did nothing but slouch around that neglected smallholding which she stubbornly refused to hand over to him (though he was still working on it). The Lefever house even had a double garage, accommodating not only the father's vehicle but his son's Morris Cowley, which was not a company perk. That meant Jacques Lefever earned enough to buy it for himself, damn him. Boswell smarted beneath the thought.

The Morris was the first car Jacques had ever owned, but not so fine as he intended to have one day. Meanwhile he dreamed of driving with Annabel Peterson in the passenger seat – this evening with luck, though he didn't bank on that because if her parents were at the students' display she would obviously travel home with them, and if they were not she would, of course, be driving her own two-seater.

The display of qualifying students' work was in the main hall of the Potteries School of Design, remaining open until nine to enable working parents and families to visit. Jacques hoped he would have the luck to meet Annabel, but his hope proved vain. Sarah, on the point of leaving with a red-haired young man, told him Annabel had gone home with her parents after their afternoon visit.

'*And* she's won top prize for original design!' Sarah was ecstatic. 'Not that I'm surprised, and I'm quite sure

Daniel Frenshaw won't be.' Jacques was faintly surprised at hearing the Master Potter referred to by name, like someone Sarah knew personally, then reminded himself that social manners were becoming less formal these days and he was glad of that. If it lessened the gulf between himself and Annabel it would give him hope.

'Her design is the chief exhibit,' Sarah raced on, 'and it's wonderful, isn't it, Clive? No wonder you're proud! You deserve to be.'

She introduced her companion as the college's tutor of porcelain painting and design, but Jacques paid more heed to the change in Sarah. She had bloomed. It was hard to recall the shy apprentice she had once been – the thin, rather gauche girl with the beautiful eyes for whom he had always felt an instinctive pity. He had to remind himself that she was now older, as he himself was, but somehow he felt that this man was responsible for the change in her. His last thought, before he made a beeline for Annabel's painting on the central stand, was that growing up and falling in love were inevitable things in life, and then he forgot everything in the enchantment of Annabel's beautiful design, inspired by Homer's *Odyssey* and showing Ulysses on his home voyage from Troy. It was intended for a large ceramic wall plaque, but excitement seized Jacques as he visualised it painted and even embossed on his Grecian urns.

That was what they needed now. He had learned very quickly that you couldn't sell one type of commodity for ever, popular though it might be. Rivals copied other people's best-selling lines so the art of maintaining a successful market was to increase its desirability by variety. And here was the very thing, something unique to add to his classical line, with the promise of more to follow . . . ancient Egyptian figures . . . Greek gods and goddesses of fable . . . the Arthurian legends . . . a whole world of myth and poetry to be illustrated and painted by Annabel's hand. Rival potbanks would be hard-pressed to find a decorator with her unique touch. The thought of working with her, discussing plans, growing nearer to each other in the process, set his pulses racing.

Through his absorption, a voice penetrated. It was the college porter calling nine o'clock and closing time. Jacques spun round and asked the man if the exhibits were for sale.

'Some may be, sir. I know the School Board allows it because sales encourage students, but ye'd have to ask. Something you fancy, is there?' Seeing the gentleman's eyes fixed on the top prize-winner, he added, 'Ah – yes. A work of art orlright. After ten years in this job a man gets kinda gut feelings, if ye know what I mean, sir.'

Jacques did, though his own feelings went much deeper than that, so deep that he wasted no time in waiting for tomorrow. Driving full speed to Downley Court, he fleetingly remembered that he should present his idea to the Master Potter first, then dismissed it because the man had never yet rejected any he put up.

He also thrust aside the thought that to arrive uninvited and unheralded on the doorstep of one of the leading county families might be considered a social gaffe. He didn't give a damn. He was determined to talk to Annabel without delay.

He drove through the huge gates, standing conveniently open, and along a seemingly endless drive until the great house came into view. The sight of it failed to intimidate him. He whirled round the wide gravelled expanse before the house, stopped at the porticoed entrance and mounted a flight of wide steps, refusing to anticipate failure. An impeccable butler told him that Mrs Peterson and her daughter were out, but the Master was at home and he would enquire—

Before the man could finish a genial male voice echoed from within. 'Don't keep whoever it is standing on the doorstep, Gibbs. Show 'em in, show 'em in . . .' and seconds later Jacques was face to face with Charles Peterson. There was an enquiry in the man's eyes, followed by instant recognition. 'Well, bless my soul, it's Le Fevre, isn't it? The chap my daughter spent New Year's Eve dancing with.' He held out his hand. 'Come in, my dear fellow, come in! Glad to see you. Glad to have your company. Wife and daughter deserted me for a concert in Stoke. Dull stuff, not for me. Topped up the decanter in my study, have you, Gibbs? 'Course you have, 'course you have,' he finished without waiting for a reply, and moments later Jacques was sitting in a deep armchair in a snug room, glass in hand, talking with ease to a most likeable man.

'So you're the chap who makes those damn great urns? Splendid stuff. You must see how grand they look on our terrace. Frenshaws have a winning line there, Daniel tells me. Very proud of 'em, he is. And rightly. By the way, I heard you on the wireless the other day. You came over well. Knew what you were talking about and made it interesting.'

Jacques thanked him and got to the point of his visit. 'I've seen your daughter's winning design—'

'That jolly Troy thing? Damn good, isn't it? I must

276

say my wife and I are proud of it, *and* of her. Having to eat our words, though!'

'Sir?'

'We were against her going to the local art school. Felt she might fare better elsewhere because that place was founded for local youngsters whose parents couldn't afford – well, to be blunt, we feared she wouldn't fit in, or would be resented, but she soon overcame all that. And she couldn't have done better, could she?'

Jacques admitted that that was his reason for calling. 'I'm hoping she will agree to her winning design being used on my Grecian line. I know the Master Potter wants her to work at Frenshaws and before any rival potbank grabs her Ulysses design—'

'*You* decided to.' Annabel's father laughed, but it was appreciative laughter. 'Put your mind at rest, young man. Daniel Frenshaw decided to employ her long ago, and told her as much, so I can't see her taking the design elsewhere. The idea of working at Frenshaws delighted her because that nice young friend of hers will be working there too. Besides, Daniel was the first to encourage Annabel to do what she passionately wanted to do – join the clay world. His wife was shocked, but more fool she, say I.'

Jacques departed on a cloud. First thing next morning he went to the Master Potter's office and told him what he had done, and why.

'I was so excited by her prize-winning work that I couldn't wait to talk to her about it, but was out of luck, except for her father's interest. Our Grecian line now needs a fresh touch before the market becomes overcrowded with copies. There's a hint of that already.'

'I know, but I've not yet seen any to match the quality of yours.'

'But with designs like her prize-winning one ornamenting our great urns in differing ways, they'll become a unique collection. Have you *seen* it, sir? Rival potters will be hard pressed to find anyone with her particular touch, and there's no end to classical fields she can draw upon to follow. I hope you'll agree, sir.'

Daniel smiled. 'I have yet to disagree with any idea of yours. And, yes, I have seen it – before you yourself did, actually, but I didn't have the wit to visualise its use in the way you have. She was thrilled when I said we wanted to buy the design for large wall placques and porcelain vases, and even to adapt on a smaller scale as a border design for table ware. But your idea tops all. Well done, Le Fevre. And I hope you'll be pleased to hear that your department is to have larger accommodation.'

'You mean a bigger shed? I admit I'll be glad of that.'

'Not a shed, and not your department alone. Nor on this site. I'll be making an announcement to the entire potbank first thing tomorrow morning – and with that,' Daniel finished with a smile, 'your curiosity must remain satisfied.'

Jacques was not the only person to notice a change in Sarah. Kate had already done so and was disturbed in an illogical way. She was proud of, and touched by, the girl's blossoming and, for a time, attributed it to the work Sarah found so fulfilling.

'It's so *lovely*, Gran – clay, I mean. The touch of it

278

and the feel of it and the smoothness and malleability, and the urge to create something from it, to bring it to life . . .' And she was doing that with ever-increasing success. Those heads she had modelled of little Ben – three in all – were so lifelike you almost expected him to open his mouth and chatter.

Yet Sarah had not been satisfied. When she promised Pru that she could have the models of her son as soon as she could get them biscuit-fired at art school, Kate had told her, later, that she was balmy. 'I should've thought they were good enough to win a prize!'

But Sarah's answer was, 'I've got to do better than that. I haven't yet caught the spirit of little Ben – he's so mercurial, if you know what I mean.'

Kate didn't, any more than she knew what malleability meant. The old lady thought with pride, Getting as clever as her father, she is, and the remembrance of George came back yet again and with it a disturbing fear which was increasing of late – that her granddaughter's blossoming was due to something more than her happiness at college or her love of the work she was doing there. And although she didn't want to contemplate it yet, Kate wondered if Sarah's blossoming was due to being in love.

Kate had not expected it to happen so soon. Despite conditions in her own early life, she was like any conventional mother of the twenties who wanted a daughter to retain her innocence until the right man came along. In Sarah's case the old lady's protective instinct was even more acute. To her, it was important that the horror of Sarah's early experience should be overcome by a man who would initiate her into the natural beauty of sex with tenderness and love, until he carried her to the peak of rapture she herself had only known after years of marriage to a dull but kindly husband.

But sometimes there was a price to pay for such rapture, and she had paid it – the price of desertion and pain. If Sarah's increasing beauty was really due to a man's love then the man could only be Clive Bellingham, who had become her constant and possessive companion. And there lay the root of Kate's fear.

The third person to observe Sarah's blossoming was Daniel. From the moment he had stood on the fringe at Clive Bellingham's party and seen his arm about Sarah's shoulders and heard the note of ownership in his voice when he toasted her, he had known what was likely to happen. She was radiant that evening and Daniel had found himself resenting the man's possessive air.

Bellingham's invitation to join 'a bit of a celebration at his place' was thrown to anyone within hearing as the big event had drawn to a close. Daniel had accepted it only because he hoped to get near enough to Sarah to talk to her. He had also hoped to take her home even though, from a window of the abbey, he had seen Bellingham drive into Dunmore Park and collect her from the cottage. At that moment he had not expected to be alone at the preview, but shortly before leaving Cynthia had announced that she would meet him there later because she had to look in on her bridge-playing friend Alicia. ('I *must* – she subscribes so generously to every charity I support that I couldn't refuse.') He had been neither surprised nor disappointed when she broke her promise, and guessed where and with whom she really was, his suspicion confirmed by his brother's noticeable absence. So he had joined the crush in Bellingham's new flat and heard the young man's significant toast and seen the possessiveness in his glance as he looked down at Sarah. Unable to bear it, he had left.

He had walked for a long time in the darkness, acknowledging the cause of his reaction and trying to come to terms with it. I am older than she . . . sixteen years . . . when she is twenty I'll be thirty-six . . . she sees me only as an employer . . . and I am married . . . and because of all these things I have no right to long for her . . .

He still regarded Sarah as innocent despite his knowledge of the rape she had experienced. What she had endured then was not seduction, but savagery at its worst. He still recalled the outrage he had felt after Kate's disclosure, and his overwhelming desire to wreak the worst possible punishment on the man. He had felt protective toward Sarah ever since, but now it was something deeper, but unattainable.

He made a further vow – that never would she learn that he loved her and wanted her, and would continue to love and want her in silence so long as his marriage lasted. Some day it must end, but when? And how? Divorce laws still prevailed from earlier years, ugly and prolonged and difficult. He could cite his brother as co-respondent in an infidelity case right now, had he undeniable evidence of Cynthia's adultery with him, but such evidence needed the avowed testimony of at least one witness – more often than not provided by hotel chambermaids these days, suitably bribed. On top of that, legal rulings and wranglings could drag on interminably before a decree nisi was granted, and even that could be set aside if any doubt could be produced by a clever legal mind.

So suspicion alone was not enough, and although he knew it was justified on the night of the Bellingham retrospective (confirmed when Cynthia's bridge-playing friend Alicia appeared there, and his brother did not) Daniel knew he could do nothing but continue living as he now did until breaking point came. He would at least be free then, but would Sarah? And could she love him even if she were?

He was thankful to have work and the development of a new potbank to fill his days, and he avoided Sarah by visiting Kate only when he knew the old lady was alone. He had kept up the habit of dropping in to see her every now and then, as in the old days, ostensibly to enquire about her welfare but really to listen to her voluble chatter about daily life and babysitting 'for Pru-next-door' and the joy of having home-grown 'vegies' and her own herbal bed and, at last, what he was really waiting for – news of Sarah.

'She be doing right well, as ye've probably heard since ye have a peg in that art school, Master Danny. And how she loves it! And the things she makes – high marks for all of 'em, which shows I bain't making all this up, don't it? Never can I stop her working away in that wash-house even when she gets home – and my thanks to ye, sir, for clearing out the old copper and other stuff to give her more space. She also does a lot with Annabel Peterson, over at that grand house – did ye know Miss Annabel uses a summerhouse as a studio? They spend a lot o' time in it, they two lasses. A nice young lady, Miss Annabel. She wouldn't like hearing me call her "Miss" – sez friends don't do it an' we're friends, aren't we? Bless the lass.'

But it wasn't Annabel he wanted to hear about, and on the day Jacques Le Fevre discussed the girl's Ulysses design Daniel called at the cottage when he knew Sarah would be absent, and told Kate of his plans for launching the new potbank and the use he visualised for the tower room.

'I've already promised you that when Sarah returns to Frenshaws she'll have no contact with Boswell. Using the tower room ensures it. As part of the abbey it will be away from the other buildings and Sarah and Annabel will work on their individual projects there. So have no fear, Kate – the promise I made will still be kept.'

'I know that, Master Danny, an' I bless ye for it.'

As he was leaving he said, 'Sarah has changed. She's grown up – and lovely. All the more reason to watch out for her. She is adult, but still vulnerable.'

When he had gone, Kate said to herself, 'If there be any man on earth I'd trust to care for her, it'd be thee, Daniel Frenshaw, wotever ye were, rich or poor, wed or unwed. 'Cos I've still cause to be anxious about my Sarah.'

Eighteen

The disadvantage of having a successful father, Cynthia mused petulantly, was that with increasing success he seemed to have less time for writing to the daughter who had come first in his life since her birth. Now phone calls had to suffice. She found them poor substitutes for the letters she used to receive, full of questions about her life and her happiness and then on to the repetitive recital of how proud he felt every time he read of her prominence in Staffordshire society.

'Here, in the East Midlands, socially successful people in other Midland parts are well known, so I make sure my daughter's name and her brilliant marriage get frequent mention. I have the ear of the local press. Dropping the right names is always useful, and you've climbed well.'

Nowadays there would be more about how much he would like to see her but could never take time off from the mills, which were flourishing. Shares were rising on the Stock Exchange since certain bankers and financial companies sought to invest, so why couldn't she come to see her old dad instead? Occasionally he lapsed into that commonplace term, though usually he stuck to the better class use of 'your affectionate Papa', especially after he moved into bigger and grander property and became another lord of the manor in picturesque Rutland, reasonably accessible for his lace mills in Nottingham and a speedy drive in one of his impressive cars.

She enjoyed visiting him, enjoyed being the daughter of the local lace tycoon, but had seen so little of him on her last visit that she had sought other company in his absence. And soon she didn't have to seek it. There were some attractive men in the Belvoir Hunt, but few compared with Bruce in sexual prowess when they shed their hunting pink and the rest of their clothes.

Gradually she had become aware that their initial eagerness to meet her because of her father's status had changed. Instead, they sought her when they knew he was safely in Nottingham and they did it as if they had only to crook their little fingers. 'You're a raving nympho, rich bitch,' one had said insultingly after bedding her. She was convincingly angry but inwardly alarmed. Creatures as coarse as that were the kind who boasted of sexual triumphs, and if her father heard even a whisper of how she passed the time in his absence he would not look upon it as he had looked upon that tiresome teenage episode – an innocent young girl taken advantage of. He would take it as a slur on his name because that mattered more to him since it had become prominent in the lace world.

She returned to Dunmore immediately.

'Dearest Papa, Daniel needs me. He put through a trunk call shortly after you left this morning – some problem on the estate which only I can deal with. It's been wonderful, being here with you, but my wifely duty commands . . .'

She left the note where he would see it immediately he entered the smoking room, his first port of call for a cigar and Scotch on reaching home each evening, then she ordered her car to be brought round, bade a cool farewell to Parker, the butler, spared a patronising nod for Mrs Grimmond, the knowing-eyed housekeeper, and drove away without a backward glance.

Some weeks later her father wrote,

I won't press you to plan another visit – I'll come to Dunmore instead. Incidentally, I gather you had no time to spare to drive over to Wollaton Park to see your mother . . .

(And who told him that? she thought furiously. Poker-faced Parker or Grim Grimmond?)

Even though we've lived apart for so long because of her inability to fit in with my lifestyle, I'm sure she would have liked to see her daughter again. Poor old Brenda, she always found it hard to adapt. I remember when Wollaton Park seemed Nottingham's social peak to her and she was so awed by the area that she feared she'd never fit in. Now she's got used to it she's quite content living there alone. One day I invited her over to see this place and she was overwhelmed. At least no one can say I don't do my duty by her and if she ever needs money (which she won't – I always see she's all right) she'll get a handsome price for that house. Wollaton Park is still considered classy by successful tradespeople, but not on a level with leading industrialists like your father.

Well, that's all I've time for now, Cyn. I think of you thriving and happy with a husband many women would give their eye teeth for. Isn't it time you gave him a son and heir? He'll worship the ground you walk on then, though I dare say he does already. How could any man fail to? I am well aware that the opposite sex pursues you, and I'm also well aware of your own partiality . . .

The first and last lines of that letter made her wonder whether any bragging from those local hunting types had reached his ears, or if his lynx-eyed domestic staff had dropped hints, but since neither question could be answered she dismissed them. That was her way of dealing with doubts and unpleasant thoughts.

Her father's letter had been written some time before Christmas, since when there had been silence from his end, relieved by phone calls which she herself had to make. Now she was contacting him less and less because the story was always the same – he'd had no time to get in touch because work demanded his attention day and night. 'That's the price of success, my girl,' he had said the last time they had spoken. 'That husband of yours was lucky enough to inherit it, so all he has to do is sit back and rake in the shekels.'

At that she told him about Daniel's expansion plans. 'Right here at Dunmore Abbey, Papa! And quite unnecessary since the old site by the canal was ideal and well away from the family estate. To bring it here, right on our doorstep, I consider bad taste and socially demeaning.'

'Well, the rich inherit the earth and can do what they like with it,' her father said bluntly. 'You should be glad of that, girl. Your husband couldn't undertake such a scheme at a time like this if he wasn't loaded.'

'But so are you, Papa. There's been news in the press about trust companies and bankers investing in Collard Lace Mills, which speaks for itself.'

'Additional backing is always useful,' he admitted, then changed his tack. 'So you keep an eye on the financial pages, do you? That's my girl. That's my Cyn.'

She disliked the abbreviation of her name, though sometimes she used it to amuse new male acquaintances and focus their attention. 'Call me Sin!' she would joke with arch insinuation, and share their laughter.

With less amusement she was now tolerating a longer than usual paternal silence. It was comforting to reflect that it was due to the demands of his flourishing mills and his financial genius. If having to forgo so much of his attention was part of the price she must pay for ultimately inheriting his fortune, she didn't mind in the least.

Clive chafed against every moment spent away from Sarah. He saw no reason why their meetings should be reduced just because her final exams were coming up. 'You're a glutton for work,' he grumbled good-naturedly, and when she pointed out that he was originally responsible for it, he could only agree wryly and say he regretted it.

'That's not true. You're delighted to have been proved right.' Her great dark eyes, lit by amusement, challenged him, forcing him to concede that what she said was true, but adding that had he known it would deprive him so often of what he wanted so much he wished he had thought twice. At that her hands stopped working, poised above the biggest ceramic model she had yet tackled. It was almost too big for the modelling stand, which was the only one she possessed at home, but this piece of work was so well balanced that he could tell how safely it could be revolved on the turntable. She was becoming amazingly skilled and he thought with pride, I *did* discover her. I *was* the first to realise where her true talent lay. That Master Potter at Frenshaws would have had her plying her trade as a porcelain painter, competent but not brilliant, so she has a lot to thank me for. He put his arms round her and kissed her possessively and, in so doing, dislodged the cover she had hastily put over her work when he arrived.

He had come to the cottage unannounced, entering by the single side path direct to her workshop, as she called it. He noticed that the place had not only been cleared but extended to provide more space. When he commented on that she said warmly, 'Thanks to Daniel Frenshaw, bless him. I can work on big things as well as smaller ones here, and take a break by cycling over to Annabel's when I want to do preliminary sketching. Mine aren't finished drawings, like her ceramic designs, but essentially basic, the kind ceramic sculptors work from, concentrating on bone structure and muscles and lights and shadows. Neither of us would give up sharing that summerhouse – we enjoy each other's company too much and spark creative ideas in each other.'

'And what are you working on now? It looks big and ambitious.' Glancing around, Clive saw no sign of any preliminary drawings and said, 'Don't tell me you're producing something from scratch, from memory? If so, it must be something, or someone, you're very familiar with.'

She nodded and said, 'Since I was young, yes.'

'There are practice studios at the college. Why don't you make use of them? Then I'd see more of you.'

'But they're available only for a couple of hours at the day's end. Here I can work for as long as I like, often until Gran packs me off to bed. I can also make an early morning start and accomplish something before going to classes.'

He said with a hint of petulance, 'I insist you leave *some* free time for me.'

'And don't I?' She was concerned. 'I see you as often as possible. Oh, Clive, you're not unhappy, are you? I'd be distressed if you were. I've believed you were as happy as I, and as busy. Since your grandfather's exhibition you've had a big promotion and I – well, look at the strides I've made since knowing you.'

'Since loving me,' he corrected. 'Face the truth, Sarah. Stop pretending you don't feel as I do and don't want what I want. D' you think I'm not aware of the way you fight it, though in the name of heaven I can't think why? At first you seemed frigid, and that baffled me because it only needs a glance to see you can't possibly be. When I've dared to kiss you I've sensed responses you've deliberately fought, as if they alarmed you. *Why*, in God's name? Love is a natural thing, a lovely thing. Trust me and I'll prove it to you.'

She listened to him in silence, her head bowed so that her long black hair fell like a curtain. He lifted it and saw that her face was flushed. He took her chin in one hand, lifted it so that the curtain of her hair fell away and, very gently, laid his lips on hers. At that, she trembled. He hoped it was from delight, but sensed otherwise. He said, 'My darling girl, whatever's the matter?'

The trembling was reflected in her voice as she answered, 'I'm afraid . . . I'm afraid . . .'

He gathered her close. He wanted to love her bodily right there and then, but instinct told him that this was not the moment. He had to lull her extraordinary reaction, which seemed stronger than the apprehension of some virgins he had known. He felt he would have to initiate her slowly and gently, with the world shut out, and the place for that was the privacy of his flat – not here in this crowded, stone-floored workshop with the old lady near at hand, likely to enter whenever she felt so inclined.

He continued holding Sarah. When she looked up and smiled, he said gently, 'I don't want to leave you, but I must because I won't run the risk of intruders. Next time we'll make it somewhere private. And soon. And you'll have no fears or regrets, I promise you. Trust me, Sarah.'

His goodbye kiss conveyed sincerity and kindness because he knew that was the right approach, for now.

When he had gone Sarah asked herself whether she was glad she had not told him that Kate was baby sitting next door, so there had been no likelihood of intrusion, but she also asked herself why she let the response she felt at his touch be quelled by fear and darkness from the past. She was mature enough now to know that she must not allow that hideous rape to destroy her future, and that the physical sensations Clive had begun to arouse in her were due to the natural ripening of her body – but she also knew that fear was interlaced with them like a black remnant of memory. Like any young woman, she felt the need to be loved and to bear children some day but, as yet, was unready for either. Even afraid. Whenever Clive's physical desire for her became too evident, she would instinctively withdraw. In her mind she questioned whether this was due to uncertainty about the genuineness of his feelings or uncertainty about her own.

That her liking for him had a special quality she was well aware. That she was always happy with him she was also well aware, but still her resistance persisted. And she knew it would continue until she no longer shrank from the thought of physical union with a man.

Surely I'll know when that moment comes, won't I, God? The question whispered in her mind and like a response from heaven she felt calmed, as if divine assurance was telling her to wait, to let life take over.

She heard the latch of the front gate lift and fall as her grandmother returned. Sarah was glad the old lady had not come home when Clive had been here because lately she had an uneasy feeling that Kate had some hidden attitude toward him which was beyond analysis.

Driving back to Burslem, Clive acknowledged to himself that he was glad the old woman had stayed indoors, unaware that he had been alone with her granddaughter in that place outside – hardly one in which to make love, crowded as it was with clay supplies and modelling equipment and a tiled floor with nothing to cushion it – but the truth was that he never felt completely at ease with Sarah's grandmother. Her faded eyes seemed to see everything, suspect everything, guess everything.

It wasn't that he disliked her, but all too often she made him feel that she was watching him, even summing him up. Deciding whether he was 'up to no good' with her granddaughter? The suspicion riled him. Whatever was to happen between himself and Sarah would be their concern and theirs alone. His father had never made him feel guilty about Carla and neither, had she lived, would his mother have done so because she had learned to accept the masculine Bellingham attitude to life.

Clive knew he had to make allowances for Sarah's background. He knew little about it but, obviously, it had been very different from his own. Fortunately none of it clung to her now and he respected the loyalty which bound her to an illiterate grandmother, but he himself could never feel on a mental level with the old woman – the difference between the educated and the uneducated, he decided, which was why he was surprised by Daniel Frenshaw's friendship with the woman. He hadn't been long in these parts before he heard of the Master Potter's liking for old Kate Willcox and of the personal interest he took in her, even to the extent of moving her and her granddaughter on to his estate.

And now, as he drove, Clive found himself wondering about Sarah's parentage. All he knew was that her father was dead and her mother had married again, but beyond that nothing. Neither was he sure that he really wanted to know much. Only Sarah mattered – she was intelligent, highly talented and lovely. Before parting from her this evening he had reached out to her, accidentally brushing against the big mound of clay she was working on, not paying much attention to it but remembering, now, how she had quickly covered it and how his brief glimpse had registered nothing but an impression of features not yet clearly defined.

So was it a portrait bust she was starting? If so, she must be forging ahead rapidly, for that was advanced work. He wondered who the sitter was, and why he should now recall that piece of unfinished sculpture. He had not been interested at the time, so it seemed odd to recall it now and to feel that the rough form was the basis for masculine features. It also seemed significant that she was working without even a preliminary sketch as a guide. Did that mean that the subject was a man she knew so intimately that she could recall every detail of his face without any reminder?

Jealousy stirred. He wondered if Sarah was reconstructing the man's face to keep beside her in tangible form for ever. The thought lingered with him, forcing him to waylay her when the college closed next day.

'We've got to talk,' he said, seizing her arm and heading for the nearest bar.

Sarah had never been in one. Pubs in the twenties were drinking places, serving no food, and the Victorian attitude to ladies who went in them still lingered here and there in these parts. And not without justification, she thought when she saw the number of loitering, unescorted women with a certain stamp about them. Clive saw them too and decided to take her elsewhere.

'I'd prefer a coffee,' she said outside, 'and I can't take too long about it because Gran hates her meals to be spoilt.' What a nuisance that old woman was, he thought yet again as he led Sarah to a respectable looking café. 'I also want to get home because I want to get on with something.'

'The thing you hastily covered yesterday?'

'I always cover my work promptly. Moist clay demands it – as you very well know.' She laughed up at him, her eyes teasing. 'So what do you want to talk about?' she asked after the coffee came.

'Us.' He reached across the table and halted the hand reaching for her cup. 'We can't go on like this, you know. I'm in love with you and I'm pretty damn sure you are with me. Come and share my flat. Live with me, Sarah. I want you with me all the time. Can't you understand that?'

She was taken aback. 'It – it isn't possible!'

'Why not?'

'I can't leave my grandmother alone.'

'With all those friends and neighbours around, I doubt she would be! And you could visit her every now and then. You're entitled to live your own life.'

'I'm doing that. The life I chose.'

'Sterile virginity. That's no life for you.'

Her face whitened.

'Good grief, I've hurt you! Forgive me – but it's true, isn't it? You've never been loved by a man, but you should be, need to be, and that man's me.'

She made no answer. She took a gulp of coffee, and then another, and a hint of colour came back to her face. She thought frantically, I've got to tell him . . . *got* to. And then, with bitter defiance, Why should I?

'Can't we just carry on as we are?' she said. 'We're good friends and see a lot of each other. Think of how often we meet after tutorials are over.'

'After which you're always in a hurry to get back to Dunmore—'

'Because it's a long way and I have to cycle to get there.'

'And I hate letting you. There'd be no need if we were together. I'm dead serious, Sarah. Give it some thought. Please.'

She forced a lightness into her voice. 'All right – here's the first thought. Where, in that flat of yours, would I work?'

'You wouldn't. You would use a practice studio at the art school, not for a brief hour when the day's over, but for a whole evening now and then. I'd fix it. I'm now well in with the powers that be and they know you're currently the star pupil in the ceramic modelling department.'

'An evening now and then wouldn't be enough. At the cottage I put in as many hours as I want. Gran understands. She knows how dedicated I am and how much it means to me to qualify highly, like Annabel. She only interferes when I forget all about time and have to be packed off to bed. She's wonderful, and she loves me as much as I love her. Besides, there's Daniel Frenshaw to think of, I want to qualify well for his sake.'

'I don't see why.'

'Then let me tell you. But for him I would never have gone to the Design School, never had a chance to become a ceramic modeller, and never have had a job waiting for me. But you know all that. You took a hand in it, too. *You* spotted where my real talent lay and I'll be eternally grateful for that. Don't change things, Clive. Let's continue as we are.' Without waiting for an answer she rushed on, 'And there's something you'd better know because you've got some wrong ideas about me.' She paused for the space of a breath. 'I am not a virgin.'

There, it was out. Something she had prayed only she and Kate would ever know about. And now Clive would ask questions – when, who was the man, and a dozen more things she would dodge. She pushed her coffee-cup aside and rose. His hand shot out, detaining her. And he was laughing. *Laughing!*

'Well, you could've fooled me, darling! In fact, you've done a mighty good job of it. What a blessed relief! Now I needn't feel guilty about wanting to seduce you because it's already been done and we can live together without a pang of conscience on either side.'

She shook off his hand and rose. 'I've already said no to that.' She was surprised by the calmness of her voice. When she moved to the door he dropped some money on the table and followed. Outside, he grasped her arm. 'I'm driving you home. You can leave that bike where it is and pick it up tomorrow. Annabel Peterson drives you in every morning except when her sessions differ from yours. See how much I know? I've also checked that her sessions are at the same time as yours tomorrow morning but not in the afternoon, so your bicycle will be ready and waiting for you.'

She glanced at her watch. It was later than she had thought and she had a great longing to be home, so she let him take her to the staff garaging quarters, his arm lightly about her waist. Even so, she had one stipulation to make – that he said no more about living together. He smiled, very sure of himself. 'No need, darling.

You'll give in, and I can wait. How about breaking the news to your grandmother tonight?'

Firmly, she forbade it and, indulgently, he conceded. After that they were silent until he broke it with an abrupt question.

'Who was he, Sarah?'

'No one you know, or ever will.'

Her tone was final and the silence became prolonged. They turned off the Longton road and a few miles further on Sarah suddenly called out to him to stop.

'Go back, please – as far as that cottage we've just passed.'

'What cottage – and why the hell—?' Clive reversed, even so.

Reaching the cottage gate, she sprang out and ran up a short path to a woman sitting on a half-broken bench within a rickety porch. What a God-awful place, Clive thought, staring at a wilderness of neglect, and what on earth is Sarah up to? He stayed where he was, watching her take hold of the woman's hands and stoop over her. A dreadful-looking woman, a wreck of a woman, scrawny as a starved cat. When Sarah beckoned him he climbed out of the car and joined her reluctantly. He heard her saying, 'Mam – it's me! Sarah. Don't you know me?'

The woman's stare was blank. Sarah choked back a sob. 'You're ill, Mam! Let me help you, let me *do* something! Are you alone? Is *he* here?'

A dim light of recognition showed in unhappy eyes. Her skin was pallid, her face lacklustre. She shook her head feebly. She tried to speak, and failed. She tried again and a hoarse whisper came out. 'Sarah? Sarah . . .?'

'Thank God, she knows me. Help me get her into the car, Clive. We've got to get her to a doctor – quickly!'

Clive had not expected the day to end like this, delivering a decrepit woman to a doctor's door and waiting while the creature was examined. He was all for leaving her there but Sarah went into the surgery with her so there he was, stuck in the waiting room idling his way through a pile of out-of-date magazines, then picking up an early edition of the evening paper which a previous patient had obviously thumbed through and tossed aside. Indifferently, he glanced at it. A headline screamed from the front page. WELL-KNOWN LACE MANUFACTURER ARRESTED FOR FRAUD. To pass the time he scanned the article, though he wasn't interested and had never heard of the man – a chap called Alfred Collard who had been passing faked share certificates and investment bonds to finance companies and bankers as security against substantial loans which now couldn't be repaid.

'Reminiscent of the Clemence Hatry case,' said the report, 'and likely to earn the same prolonged prison sentence . . .' The date for the Crown Court trial had yet to be announced; meanwhile, the man had been granted bail. Indifferently, Clive thought the fool would very likely skip bail and get away with it and that would be that. He tossed the paper aside and was thankful when Sarah emerged, but less thankful when she announced that an ambulance had been called and she would be going with her mother to the hospital.

Her *mother*? That dreadful-looking creature from that dreadful place? He supposed he should have realised it when Sarah called her by that Northern name 'Mam'.

'Will you follow and then take me home, Clive?'

'Of course. And you don't have to be grateful,' he said uncomfortably when she began to thank him. He supposed he should be touched by her concern but all he felt was shock tinged with a distaste he managed to conceal. He felt a twinge of guilt because of it, but more strong was a persistent thought. How would his people feel about him marrying a girl from a poverty-stricken background?

It was the first time he realised that the possibility of marrying Sarah had been at the back of his mind.

Nineteen

It was dark when they reached Sarah's home. He didn't want to go in because he was sure her grandmother would ask questions – where had they been, and why hadn't they told her they were going somewhere and would be late coming back, and had they eaten or not? The fussy, tiresome questions of old people for which he felt in no mood. And sure enough, the front door opened before he had a chance to kiss Sarah goodbye and make his getaway, which he very much wanted to do after the irksome delay and the disturbing cause of it. He had much to think about.

Kate called from the doorstep, 'Thought I 'eard ye drive up! Timed it well, m' dears – or I did. Supper's ready. Rabbit pie an' tatties.' She smiled that wide smile of hers and went ahead of them into the house, and because Sarah took it for granted that he was staying she followed, leaving him no choice but to do the same.

In a better light one glance at Sarah made the old lady say swiftly, 'Wot's the matter, luv? Ye look pale.' She cupped the girl's face in wrinkled hands and studied her in concern. For the first time Clive noticed how pale Sarah was. Now he wished he had stopped at an inn and bought her a brandy. Come to that, he could have done with one himself after that encounter and the shock of the woman's identity.

Mercifully, Kate produced a bottle from the living room sideboard and poured a tot. 'When ye've drunk this, Sarah, ye can tell me wot's upset ye. Sip it slowly, mind.' She hovered over the girl like a mother hen, but she didn't forget to pour a brandy for him too. 'It'll warm ye, young man. The night's a raw one.'

As she handed the glass to him there was a question in her eyes. There always seemed to be questions in her eyes and he wished he could down the drink quickly and get away. He'd prefer to knock up something to eat at the flat, or go round the corner to an Italian restaurant he was partial to. He'd been surprised to find a good continental eating place in a provincial working town. In Exeter, with its university and its cultured population and its loads of tourists of all nationalities, there had been plenty to choose from. In this part of the country he had expected nothing but homely fare such as he was being offered now. Pie 'n'tatties, whatever they were.

Guilt touched him again, but fleetingly. He knew he shouldn't be thinking this way when the old lady was being kind and hospitable. He looked at Sarah's lovely face, as lovely as her grandmother's had been in those portraits painted by his renowned grandfather, and found himself wondering if Joseph Bellingham had loved his model as he himself now loved her grand-daughter. Very possibly, for a time. Artists often fell in love with their models, even marrying them sometimes. Not that his grandfather would have ditched his very compatible wife for a rough potter woman. Clive remembered his elegant grandmother as vividly as he remembered his distinguished grandfather. And then he looked across at Sarah and saw the colour returning to her cheeks, restoring her loveliness like the sun shining on a flower, and back came his incredulity that she could be the daughter of that woman from that dreadful place. Surely he had misunderstood? There was a natural refinement in Sarah which could never have come from such a creature – or, if it came to that, from old Kate, who could be as coarse as they come when she felt like it, though he sometimes felt she exaggerated it deliberately.

But the picture which now flashed through his mind was of fading, brassily dyed streaks amongst grey hair badly in need of washing. He had found the sight, and the woman, repulsive.

The brandy must have loosened his thoughts, wandering in a way he didn't want them to. It made him feel disloyal to Sarah, but it also made him want to take her away from such a connection, to share her life without intrusion from people he would be ashamed to introduce to friends and relations. And I suppose that's a bloody snobbish attitude, he thought, but continued to feel that way because, after all, a man had to think of these things when contemplating marriage.

Kate's voice cut into his thoughts. 'Brandy suit ye all right, Mr Bellingham? It oughta – 'twere a gift from Master Danny for me birthday. An' if ye wonder who Master Danny be, 'tis Master Potter Frenshaw. I've called 'im Master Danny since 'e were a nipper, just as I were Katie to 'im.' She had set the food on the table after satisfying herself that Sarah was feeling better. 'Colour's back, m' luv. Ye look y'rself again, thank goodness. Later ye can tell me wot the matter were.

Now draw up, the pair o'ye, an' eat while it be hot. I'll bet neether of ye've bothered wi' food.'

Her voice was bland and unquestioning, but he had the feeling that she was thinking a lot. She was amiable throughout the meal, but all the time he felt that her shrewd eyes were assessing him and seeking answers to questions that worried her.

The food was good, so good that he was ashamed of his earlier desire to seek a better meal elsewhere. To atone, he complimented the old lady, whereupon she piled his plate high with a second helping, saying, 'As I thought – ye've not bothered to eat, the pair o'ye.' Sarah, lass, y' know I don't like ye going without food. Working the hours ye do now needs a good fuelling inside o'ye.' There was nothing but kindness in her eyes when she turned to Clive and continued, 'Don't think I'm blaming thee, Mr Bellingham, but next time ye make Sarah late home, stop an' see she eats summat, will ye? She works that hard – too hard, I sometimes think, but there be no stopping 'er. Just like her dear dad useter say – an' Master Danny too, as well ye know, else he wouldn't've put her through the Design School – my Sarah's got reel talent an', more than that, she loves wot she's doing now, fair lives for it. But I guess ye knows that too. An' now, if the pair o' ye be satisfied, we'll draw to the fire an' you, Sarah, can tell me wot brought ye home looking the way ye did. 'Tweren't tiredness, I could tell.'

But Sarah didn't move from the table. Clive's ill-concealed reaction to Mabel had left her incapable of pretence – she was in no mood for a friendly fireside chat. She said evenly, 'You'll be surprised to hear that my mother is in Longton Hospital. I saw her as Clive was driving me home, so we stopped and took her to a doctor, who called an ambulance. How long she'll have to remain in hospital I don't know, but very likely for some time. When she comes out, something will have to be done for her, Gran. We can't let her go back to that place. You should see it! A nightmare.' Sarah's voice shook. 'And so is she, poor soul.'

For the first time, Kate was lost for words. Then she gasped, 'Mabel! That woman who's never been ill in 'er life!'

'She is now. Advanced malnutrition, they said at the hospital. They also hinted at self-neglect and, judging by her clothes and the state she was in when I spotted her as we drove by, I should think that's a big part of it – like someone who no longer cares about herself or what happens to her. She was sitting in the dilapidated porch of that smallholding, staring into space, looking like a woman who had lost all hope.' Sarah could no longer control her voice. Her face crumpled; tears flowed unchecked. She cried, 'She *is* my mother, Gran!'

The old lady said gently, 'But not your responsibility, lass. She married that man. She's his responsibility now.'

'She *loved* me when I was a child. She was good to me—'

'Aye, when she were married to your father.' Kate turned to her guest. There was pride in her uplifted chin. 'My George were a good man, kind and loving and caring for 'is wife an' child. A natural born gentleman, the best of all my childer. I well remember 'im as a lad, forever with 'is nose in a library book, an' Preacher Latimer wanting to coach 'im for a scholarship to that grand school, Worksop . . .' Her voice trailed off, lost in the past.

Clive sat in embarrassed silence, longing to get away, but he couldn't just get up and express polite thanks for the meal and say an abrupt goodnight. He was also forestalled by Sarah declaring passionately, 'Dear Gran, never in my lifetime will I forget the smallest detail about my father. I loved him as you did – as we both do still. But he loved my mother when she was young and pretty and thoughtful and kind. It would distress him beyond words to see her now, *and* if I turned my back on her. I can't do it. She made a terrible mistake and she's suffered for it. The hospital doctor said that with prolonged rest and proper care and the right food she'll get well, and after their treatment she'll be sent to the County Recuperative Home in the countryside beyond Hanley until she's on her feet again. After that, we – I – must persuade her to leave that place, sell it and buy a flat or a terraced cottage in Burslem where she was once so happy.'

'An' d' you think that bastard will let 'er?'

'I think he'll do everything he can to stop her until it suits him. He may be trying to get his hands on that smallholding, persuading her to make it over to him, wearing her down until she agrees and *he* can then sell it and pocket the proceeds. Not that it would fetch much in its present state – to profit by it he would have to restore it to what it once was. Gran, I know this is a terrible thought but she looked like a woman who was deliberately being robbed of hope. And it's that man's doing. You and I both know how evil he is.'

Clive moved uncomfortably, clearing his throat slightly, deciding it was high time he went and hoping one or other of them would take the hint. He wanted to hear no more, pitiful as the story was. He was now thoroughly convinced that Sarah should move in with him. There were disturbing threads beneath this conversation which convinced him that she should move right away from here and live her own life. He pitied her, born as she had been into a social level he considered far beneath her. That wasn't her fault. No one could choose their background or parentage, but they could rise above it providing they had the sense to shed all connection with it, and that, he decided, was what he must make her do.

He became aware of Kate's eyes on him. He met them, and had the uncanny feeling that she knew exactly what he was thinking. She began to push her chair aside and he politely assisted her. Sarah gathered up dishes from the table and carried them out to the kitchen, saying over her shoulder that she would be back in a minute to say goodnight. There was a finality in her tone which troubled him.

While he waited awkwardly Kate seized the moment to say, 'Ye've never seen a photo of Sarah's father, have ye?' And before he could answer she had turned to the sideboard and opened a drawer and taken out a sepia photograph in an old-fashioned frame.

'We keeps it in there when the sideboard's needed for serving – other times it stands where we can see it all the time. Course, Sarah's father were a young man when this were taken . . .'

She handed the photograph to him and watched as he looked at it. The sudden stillness of his face didn't escape her.

'Aye,' she said softly, 'my George weren't a Willcox.

Born on the wrong side o' the blanket though 'e were, my son were a Bellingham an' no mistake.'

Sarah returned as Kate uttered the final words. She stood silently in the doorway, then cried, 'You've never told me! Why, Gran – *why*? Surely not through shame? I'll never believe that – you loved him too much. So was it because your generation would have called him a bastard and that would have hurt him, shamed him? No – don't stop me, Gran! You're a good and lovely woman and always have been, and my father was a fine man – and, dear God, he was brave! You've never heard how he died, have you, Clive? Then ask Daniel Frenshaw, who never looked down on him as I think you might have done. You were shocked when you met my mother, so I expect you'll be shocked to learn that my father was only a fire stoker. Do you really think I didn't know how you felt today? Well, I wonder how you feel now you know that you and I had the same grandfather?'

Twenty

Complacency had gone from Cynthia Frenshaw's elegant shoulders. Rigid with shock and rage, they had become those of a woman railing against fate, against cruelty (to herself), against humiliation, against embarrassment (how could she *ever* face people again?), and, more than all, against a father on whom she had depended all her life. She had believed him to be her ally; she had trusted him, admired him, boasted about him, and now he was branded as a fraud, his name shouted in condemnation from headlines and newspaper placards. The humiliation of it! The ghastly *shame*! My God, she vowed, I will never forgive him for doing this to me.

'Doesn't it occur to you to go to him?' said Daniel, after enduring days of her ranting. 'He will need you. Whatever he has done, he is still your father. Everyone will be deserting him. You can't too.'

'*Go* to him?' she screamed. 'Nothing would induce me! He's a liar and a cheat, telling me that big finance companies and bankers were bidding to invest in his damned mills when all the time he was borrowing money from them, swindling them with share certificates and investment bonds so well faked that they were undetected until the time came to call in the loans or seize the securities to cover them. *Now* I know why he's been increasingly silent. The *shame* of it! He's a criminal, and you expect me to rush to comfort him!'

'I think a daughter who loved her father would have some compassion. By now everyone will have deserted him — except your mother. I've always admired her acceptance of his neglect, not to mention your own. I am sorry for her — not you, living in security and comfort and now wallowing in self-pity. As for your father, he'll suffer for what he has done.'

'Not if his lawyers do their job properly. It's up to him to hire the best.'

'If he can raise the money. You do realise that bankruptcy is inevitable?'

That stunned her. 'Good God — then what becomes of my inheritance?'

'There won't be one. Everything he owns will have to go. If he is sentenced, and you must face the fact that he will be, there'll be nothing for himself when he is released. Hatry got fifteen years for similar fraudulence. I don't see how your father can expect less.'

'You callous bastard! At a time like this, in the midst of all my horror and grief, you don't give a thought for me!'

'Your horror, as you call it, isn't due to the shock about your father, but to fearing how it will affect you personally. Not your mother. Not anyone but yourself. As for grief, I see no real sign of it despite your floods of tears — merely anxiety about the reactions of so-called friends, the fear of being "dropped", of no longer queening it over local society, of pointing fingers and whispers behind hands, all of which only mark such friends as worthless. Meanwhile, you have a rich husband and a home you have always prided yourself on possessing, and you're determined that nothing shall rob you of either. My God, to think I once loved you and thought you the purest thing I'd ever met.'

He turned his back on her and headed for the potbank. It was unnecessary for the Master Potter to put in an appearance every Saturday, but the place was his refuge these days. He was also devoting increased time to it because his plans were forging ahead. The cheers of the workers had echoed beyond the walls of the potters' yard the day he had gathered them together and told them the news. The local papers had flaunted it in headlines the next day, but on the financial pages of the national press it was reduced to the level of a news paragraph in comparison with Alfred Collard's sensational arrest along with that of a colleague, head of a firm of fine printers with head offices in Nottingham's Wheeler Gate and substantial works off Arkright Street.

'He had to have a crony to produce the fakes,' Bruce had pointed out when the news broke, cheering Cynthia, but only temporarily. Her floods of tears were renewed when Bruce added that the forger would get off more lightly than her father since he had not been the inaugurator of the swindles.

Driving away now, Daniel was thankful to be leaving the atmosphere in his home. Reaching Downley Court, he turned through the gates and found Annabel and Sarah in the summerhouse. The Design School closed on Saturdays and although Annabel was now in Daniel's employment as a porcelain painter and the pottery world worked a full six days a week, he knew that she planned many of her designs here before finishing them off in the overcrowded paintresses' shed where the women had received the arrival of a rich man's daughter with a certain resentment.

'Give it time,' he had told her. 'Once they know you they'll accept you, besides which we'll all be working in better conditions at Dunmore pretty soon.'

He didn't mention that, to raise the women's self-esteem which, for centuries, had been downgraded by the term 'paintresses' – as if they were inferior to men who decorated ceramics – he was changing that term to 'decorators', applying it to both sexes, and if the pottery world raised surprised eyebrows he knew it would soon follow suit.

He saw now that Annabel was engrossed in a Crusaders' design which, she told him, Jacques already planned to use on a new and impressive style of Eastern vase. 'It will be ideal,' Daniel said.

'And we'll follow it up with stories of the Holy Grail to entice people to collect the series. Jacques is brilliant with marketing ideas. I'm terribly excited and so is he, but I do wish we had closer contact. The throwing shed at the potbank is so far away.'

'It won't be when the new one is ready. I'm off now to collect him, along with Hobson and the other foremen, taking them to Dunmore to see the progress of the new buildings. They're in for pleasant surprises, I can tell you. And I also want to show you and Sarah the room being prepared for the pair of you, a room with wonderful light. I thought you would both like to work together.'

He turned to Sarah then. She looked pale and rather tired, he thought. 'Have you been working too hard?' he asked. 'Kate tells me she has the devil of a job to make you stop.' She smiled and went back to her drawing, which he saw was of a child's head. A pile of sketches lay nearby. 'May I?' he asked, and picked them up. They were studies of a small boy from differing angles and with varying expressions. Laughing, mischievous, wistful, tearful, questioning, sleepy . . .

They touched Daniel's heart.

'I hope you're planning to produce models of these for your diploma submission?' he said. She nodded, and because he was sensitive to all her moods he could feel an undercurrent of unhappiness in her and was concerned.

'She's already produced one at home,' Annabel put in, 'but she gave it to the little boy's mother, to Kate's dismay because she thought it wonderful. I thought the same, but Sarah's not easily satisfied.'

'It was only a practice one,' Sarah explained. 'These are going to be a series of six, and a hundred per cent better. I'm determined on that. I want that diploma more than I want anything in life.'

It was said simply, but it was a declaration delivered with an underlying passion that didn't escape Daniel. (More than anything in *life*? he thought. More than your young lover – if he is your lover? If not yet, I'm sure he intends to be . . .)

He thrust the thought aside because it awakened mixed feelings – sympathy and understanding mixed with a disturbing envy, but also hope because, if true, it could be the first step in overcoming Sarah's terrible memories, but his personal disappointment was dominant. He had not wanted Clive Bellingham to be the man to show Sarah how beautiful sex could be.

Daniel said briskly, 'I am confident you'll get your

diploma, Sarah, and in the highly unlikely event that you don't I still want you to work for me. If I can't have you to create the first Frenshaw sculptures then I'll have no one. When you see the tower room waiting for you at the abbey, you'll have no self-doubt, I'm sure.'

Gratitude showed in her dark eyes, but he knew that whatever was troubling her was still there. Then suddenly she burst out, 'Did you say the *tower* room? I remember once gazing across the fields and wondering what lay behind all those windows. The setting sun was shining on them and I thought it a magic tower and longed to see inside.'

'And so you shall this very day, the pair of you. I've ordered one of the larger company vans to convey others from the canal site to Dunmore because a car wouldn't be big enough to hold everyone. I'm on my way there to see they're all aboard.' (And how Cynthia will abominate the sight of a commercial vehicle parked near the abbey, with the Frenshaw trade name writ large on it!) 'I'll give a blast of the horn outside the gates when I come back to pick you both up.'

'We'll be ready and waiting,' Annabel declared. She was excited not only for herself but for Sarah, who seemed unusually quiet today. Annabel had asked no questions, but only the other evening she had seen her friend driving out of Longton with Clive Bellingham, and though in the dusk she had been unable to see Sarah closely, she had caught a clear view of Clive at the wheel, staring at the road ahead. It wasn't essential that they should have been talking to each other, she had thought later, but why had he been looking so tense? She wondered now if something had gone wrong between them and if that was responsible for Sarah's uncommunicative air this morning, also the impression of inner unhappiness which, she sensed, Daniel had detected too.

Annabel was glad when the sound of a horn summoned them.

While Jacques Le Fevre, together with Hobson and the other foremen, followed the route to the new site indicated by the Master Potter, Daniel took Sarah and Annabel to the east wing, entering the tower by the main door at ground level, passing the inner one leading into Bruce's apartments, then climbing the stone spiral staircase. On the threshold of the tower room both girls stood still, surveying a big, round area brilliantly lit by encircling windows and commanding panoramic views of Dunmore's spreading acres. There was an air of stability in this centuries-old place, coupled with a calming and serene beauty. Sarah felt the inner turmoil, which had been with her since Saturday's events, slowly quieten.

'It's wonderful!' cried Annabel. 'By golly, Sarah, just look at the size of this room – and the worktops, and the cupboards, and the shelves, and loads of slatted ones for drying your pieces before firing – and adjustable easels for design work – and this marvellous, marvellous light!' She flung her arms round Daniel and hugged him.

He laughed. 'Then it's been worth waiting for?'

'I'll say!'

'And you, Sarah?'

She was starry-eyed, speechless, but her expression

said it all. If only briefly her depression was eased. Then she said breathlessly, 'I don't know how to thank you.'

'You don't have to. I just want both of you to work in an atmosphere you'll enjoy.' He couldn't say that what he particularly looked forward to was knowing that she would be here in the abbey for long spells, closer than she was in the cottage on the other side of the lake. He could not pinpoint the moment when he had fallen in love with her, but he did know that he loved her more than he had loved any woman before, and he no longer reminded himself of the gap in their ages for there seemed none when they were together – which was always too briefly but, hopefully, would increase in the days to come.

He would also have the enjoyment of coming up here to see her at work and watch its development. Clive Bellingham's diagnosis of the right field for her had been brilliant, but he thrust reminders of that young man aside.

He said briskly, 'Weekly supplies of materials will be brought up for you. Similarly, all heavy goods will be carried down. You'll be able to phone direct to any department in the main buildings – that's being installed this week. This other door leads into the abbey so don't be startled if I sometimes come in that way. My brother occupies the ground floor but you needn't worry about disturbing him or him disturbing you. The stone walls and floors are thick, shutting out sound. Warm and serviceable floor covering for this room will be fitted before you move in. Only within the abbey have oak floors replaced stone and the walls panelled to make it more home-like.'

Home-like? he thought. Once it was, but no longer.

He said pragmatically, 'Now I'll leave you two to look around, unless you'd like to see the new buildings as far as they've got? Hobson and Le Fevre and the others are over there now.'

Sarah longed to stay. In this high, round room she felt near the skies, which faced her whichever way she turned. The moments when she had gazed at this tower across distant fields, awed and enchanted and wishing she could see inside, came back to her – and now she was actually here, capturing a dream. Slowly, she turned in a complete circle, unaware that Daniel was watching her until she finished up facing him. His eyes remained on her, and he was smiling. She had never noticed the curve of his mouth before, the gentleness of it, and the kindness, and the warmth, and something else she could not define but which someone more sophisticated would have recognised as the sensuousness of love.

The sound of Annabel's voice echoed from the stairs, accompanied by her flying feet. 'Come on, come *on*! I'm dying to see Jacques' new quarters . . .' Then a pause and a break in her eager descent. 'I hope they're not too far away because I need to consult with him frequently. Come *on*, you two!'

Daniel called back, 'They're only a brief walk beyond the east paddock, close to the abbey side of the lake – handy for both of you.'

'You've thought of everything!' Annabel shouted, and her racing footsteps went on.

Reluctantly, Sarah moved toward the stairs. She wanted to linger in this tower room. She wished she could work on the models of young Ben here, but it was a strict rule that a free choice item to be submitted for a student's final diploma had to be produced at the

Design School in the course of normal work, along with stipulated examination pieces. Preliminary drawings and plans for the free choice item could be executed as part of homework, but had to be approved by a student's tutor when completed. This morning they had not been going well, and now Sarah wanted to rush back to the summerhouse to retrieve them. She was convinced that in this room they would come to life.

Daniel sensed her hesitation. 'What is it, Sarah? Are you wanting to stay awhile?'

'More than that!' All hint of her earlier depression had gone. There was a zest about her now. 'To tell the truth, I was struggling with important sketches in the summerhouse this morning, sketches which have to be approved by the college before my free choice piece can be included in my final diploma exams. But here – in this room – I know I could produce them well.'

'Then come back this afternoon. You'll be disturbed by no one, but in such an unlikely event you can truthfully say that you're here at my invitation. And encouragement,' he added with a smile.

He held out his hand to help her down the twisting stairs. She had no need of it, but accepted it nonetheless, withdrawing only when they reached the foot. Outside, Annabel was almost dancing with impatience. Flinging her arms round Sarah, she whirled her into a jig, crying, 'Isn't it marvellous? Perfectly, perfectly *marvellous!*'

It was a couple of hours before the group had toured the layout of the new potbank, lingering in half-erected buildings and in ancient ones which had been there since the abbey had been built and were now skilfully modernised.

Jacques was excited and impressed by the new throwing quarters – brick-built and, like the rest, spaciously designed. They were also only a short walk from the tower via the east paddock and across a rustic bridge spanning a stream, then along a path skirting the west side of the lake, so contact was easy. 'Wedgwood's Etruria Works had nothing on this,' Annabel enthused. 'Aren't you thrilled, Jacques?' She slipped her arm through his. '*I* am. You deserve it so much.'

Her head accidentally brushed his shoulder and his hand touched her hair. Sarah saw it and felt their happiness and was pleased for them. She wanted Jacques to replace Bruce Frenshaw in her friend's affections because she herself recalled incidents revealing unlikeable aspects of Bruce's character – his quick desertion to avoid becoming involved in an embarrassing scene on that memorable New Year's Eve, and his premature rejection of a lowly apprentice from his splendid Lanchester rather than be seen arriving with her at the potbank.

These pinpricks returned now, but more sharply, reviving the uneasiness Clive had left her with – his ill-concealed reluctance, not only to enter Mabel's shoddy place but his shock on learning her identity and his unwillingness to continue to the hospital from the doctor's surgery. 'Did we really have to go there?' he had said later. 'Couldn't we have left it to the ambulance men to take her?' And throughout supper, she had sensed his desire to be gone, even more so later when faced with Kate's news. Courtesy had made her accompany him to the door, but she had been longing to be alone with Kate, to hear more about her father and his childhood and growing-up years. Memories of him wrung her heart. In the night she had wept for him. That he had been illegitimate did not matter, but all that he had been denied and tragically suffered did.

She had wept quietly, so Kate should not hear.

When Sarah set out her drawing equipment in the tower room early in the afternoon following Daniel Frenshaw's suggestion, and set Kate's alarm clock for three-thirty to give her time to get home and change before going to the hospital to see her mother, the ambience of the place claimed her. As if inspired, she covered sheet after sheet of cartridge paper with pictures of young Ben, so lifelike that in her mind she could almost feel the smoothly textured clay which she would use to form the roundness of his cheeks and the chubbiness of his chin and the pertness of his childish nose. Studies of his sturdy limbs then followed automatically, for although she had planned to produce only close-ups of his head, she had a feeling that eventually she would produce lively statues of his romping young body.

Confidence replaced yesterday's uncertainty; she became lost to time and the world. Even the distant thud of a door failed to disturb her, neither did the sound of footsteps far below until their echo became sharp, and rising, and then swift and staccato as they entered the room and stopped dead.

'What the devil are *you* doing here? And how dare you use this room?'

It was Cynthia Frenshaw, looking elegantly dishabille in a casual dress which, partially buttoned up, looked as if it had been thrown on in a hurry, confident that she would meet no one. Her usually immaculate hair was ruffled and badly smudged lipstick had made a mess of her mouth. Not until later did Sarah remember these things, and ponder on them. Right now she was conscious only of frustration because this startling entry had caused her to jerk, making the charcoal she was using slither heavily across her drawing, ruining it.

'Didn't you hear me, Sarah Willcox?' Cynthia stood with casually folded arms, hiding the unbuttoned gap.

'I'm here at your husband's invitation. As for what I am doing . . .' Sarah held out a handful of sketches. 'You can see for yourself, Mrs Frenshaw.'

No 'ma'am', and no apology. Carefully plucked eyebrows rose. The tall, slim figure swept to the door leading into the private quarters of the abbey, but before closing it behind her, Cynthia Frenshaw looked back.

'I don't believe a word of it. My husband would make no such concession to an outsider.'

The door closed sharply behind her.

Twenty-One

Because her final exams were drawing near, Sarah had to turn her back on the sculpture she was producing secretly at home and which had aroused Clive's passing curiosity. She found it hard to keep it under covers and to content herself with regular check-ups on its condition. The remarkable thing was that Kate never asked what the covers concealed, although she took a lively interest in everything else Sarah worked on, from the early exercises set in class and practised at home, to the lively animals she made for Pru's children – inevitably broken if they managed to lay their eager hands on them before Sarah could get them biscuit-fired at the Design School, and that always meant waiting until there was a spare corner in one of the kilns.

But now the oncoming diploma exams obsessed her. As soon as the last bell rang for the day, she would cover her classwork and leave by a rear entrance to avoid any chance encounter with Clive. She had found a convenient spot in which to leave her bicycle so she could be off and away without hindrance. It was also far from the official bicycle storage for students, where he might possibly look for her. The time would come when she would be ready to talk to him again, but for the present there was nothing to say. She was sure he felt the same.

There she was wrong.

'At last I've spotted where you hide your bike,' his voice said behind her as she stacked textbooks into the saddlebag one day. 'Cunning place, this, well away from all the rest, but not intended for students.'

'I leave it here to avoid delay.'

'Or to avoid me.'

'Are you surprised?'

'No. Disappointed. I've been wanting to see you. I hurt you, I know, but it was impossible to hide how I felt.'

'I know how you felt – embarrassed and shocked. Not because your grandfather turns out to have been mine illegitimately, though that's bad enough from the "respectable" point of view, I suppose, but because of my mother and my background and my upbringing, all so inferior to your own.'

'Sarah – please—'

She gave him a compassionate glance. 'Don't feel contrite, Clive. I still don't like the way you felt but I do understand it because never in your life have you been poor, or mixed with people who were.'

'But you've risen above it. I admire you for that.'

'Oh, thank you,' she murmured. Although she knew the patronage in his voice was unintentional, it jarred, but the gentle irony of her tone was lost on him.

He said confidently, 'So now you must move in with me. Reject your past completely.'

She gasped. 'You mean turn my back on my people? My grandmother? My mother? I can't believe I'm hearing this.'

She put a foot on the bicycle pedal. He tried to waylay her and a momentary flash of memory winged back to a wet night and Joe Boswell doing the same thing. She said quietly, 'Don't delay me, Clive. I'm going home.'

'I want you in mine. I insist that you move in.'

He uses that word 'insist' too often, she thought, but answered lightly, 'Wouldn't a situation like that be bordering on something like incest? Or does the wrong side of the blanket and skipping a generation make it acceptable?'

'Don't be ridiculous. Even first cousins marry.'

'But we are not first cousins and marriage isn't what you have in mind. What you're asking me to do is out of the question because nothing could make me turn my back on my grandmother, whom I love, or my mother, whom I pity. When she married again I longed to get away. At that time I was too young to be able to, but eventually I did. That's all in the past and I am well content with the present.'

He gave a resigned shrug. 'A short while ago you suggested we should carry on as we were. Good friends, I suppose you meant. If you still want that, I'll have to accept it, I suppose. For the time being,' he finished under his breath.

'It will mean accepting everything else – all that embarrasses you but is part of my life. You probably think it strange that a man as rich and as cultured as Daniel Frenshaw is the closest friend Kate and I have and that he doesn't mind her illiteracy and her background. That's because he likes her for the woman she *is*. A man such as he would never have treated her the way Joseph Bellingham did – using her and then discarding her along with a beautiful gown and a rare necklace, neither of which he was interested in keeping. They were nothing but stage props to him. Believe me, I would never wear that gown again but for the fact that Kate loves to see me in it.'

He answered impatiently, 'All this has nothing to do with *us*!'

But Daniel has everything to do with it, particularly with me . . .

The thought halted her. When had she begun to be aware of Daniel as more than a respected employer? She could point to no exact moment because the change had been imperceptible, its roots deepening.

She said sincerely, 'Clive, you know I appreciate all you've done for me, discovering where my ability lay and encouraging me and helping me and believing in me. I'll never forget any of it and one day, I swear, I'll achieve all you predicted for me and I hope you'll be proud. But let's face facts – we met at what was a crossroads for me and a crossroads for you. We've been important to each other but the story ends there because there'd be no happiness in moving on to a situation which satisfied one of us and not the other.'

He had no answer. This wasn't the shy, immature, ignorant girl he had first met. Ruefully, he watched her cycle away. Just before she was out of sight she turned and waved. It's over, she thought with a touch of sadness mixed equally with gladness.

He waved in return. I'll get her back, he decided, confident as ever.

As she turned through Dunmore Abbey's open gates Sarah was forced to draw aside to allow an arriving taxi to pass. She caught a brief glimpse of a woman passenger but felt no curiosity until, dismounting at the cottage, she saw the vehicle drive on round the lake and up the distant approach to the abbey. So a neighbour's cottage was not its destination, as she had assumed, although the estate workers didn't normally drive around in taxis. At the same time she thought how agog with curiosity Kate would be. Her grandmother took a lively interest in the activities of her neighbours, but the peak of her week was taking tea in the housekeeper's sitting room at the abbey, and reciprocating on the woman's free day. They were now firm friends, Kate respecting Hannah Bradley because she never discussed her employers and Hannah respecting Kate because she never asked questions about them.

Even at this distance Sarah had a view of the sweeping approach to the abbey and the taxi stopping at the wide front steps. Across the span of water she also saw a figure climb out. It was discernible as that of a stout, middle-aged woman who had some difficulty in descending and who then turned as if waiting for someone to follow. After a minute, a young girl emerged slowly. Even at this distance she seemed unwilling. In the same way she mounted the abbey's steps behind the woman, who looked over her shoulder once or twice, seemingly urging her on.

Sarah turned and wheeled her bicycle to the rear of the cottage. Before going indoors she went to the wash-house and looked at her abandoned model. Her fingers itched to continue working on it, but she resisted. Tomorrow would be the first of three examination days. She had the technical side to swot up tonight because it would be the subject of the first day's examination paper – questions on varied clays and their individual constituents, on the appropriate degrees of thickness and weight for modelling with earthenware, terracotta, china, stoneware and porcelain, on the avoidance of 'undercutting' on models intended for mould-casting so that the mould could be finally removed without dragging away projecting pieces of the work and ruining it, and finally on the correct firing temperatures for varied types of clay.

The second morning would be an oral examination dealing with the chemical ingredients for a number of glazes, their mixing and application, and the student's personal choice of suitably blended oxides for colouring a range of unglazed articles placed before them. And the third day would be most crucial of all – the examination of ceramic models the student had produced in class, some being of set subjects and others of the student's own design. From these, the finest work would be chosen for display in the building's main hall, as Annabel's had been and as Sarah prayed her portrait models of young Ben would be.

Kate was in a quandary. Determined not to bother Sarah at a time like this, she kept her disturbing news to herself. Mabel and her problems would just have to wait. To Sarah's gratitude, familiar as she was with her grandmother's attitude to her daughter-in-law since her marriage to Boswell, Kate made a point of visiting Mabel in hospital whenever Sarah was unable to, but now Mabel had been moved to the recuperative place beyond Hanley, too far for Sarah to visit in between working and studying, and beyond the physical ability of Kate to travel alone. But today Annabel had arrived unexpectedly and driven the old lady to and from the convalescent home – so typical of the lass, Kate thought gratefully. And today Mabel had felt well enough to talk and Kate was uncharacteristically silent all the way home.

The problem Kate was now keeping to herself was worrying. She wished she could talk it over with someone, but the only person she felt able to confide in was the Master Potter and he was tied up with the final stages of the new potbank. The place was almost ready for occupation, some of the potters already installed in completed buildings, so Kate had not seen him for some time.

She had never yet gone knocking on the abbey's doors. Her visits to tea with Hannah Bradley were made through the staff door and she was missing the times when Daniel Frenshaw dropped in at the cottage to see her. And what with this financial scandal involving his father-in-law, God knew, the poor man had enough on his plate without listening to Mabel Boswell's problems. I'll bet Cynthia Frenshaw's putting 'im through hell, Kate thought, though it was hard to imagine a man like Daniel tolerating that indefinitely, despite his patience and compassion.

The pity was that he'd put up with that wife of his for so long, Kate mused. Since coming to live on the Dunmore estate she had heard whispers about Cynthia Frenshaw's partiality for her brother-in-law, and his for her, but because she hated to think of Daniel Frenshaw being hurt in any way, Kate had closed her ears to such gossip. Nevertheless, she sensed that things were very wrong in that marriage. One day a breaking point must come and Daniel's iron will would snap, and the sooner that happened the better.

Hannah Bradley showed the guests into the room her mistress called the salon, but which the master still called the drawing room, as his family had always done. 'Quite incorrectly,' Hannah had heard his wife say to him one day. 'Drawing room is an abbreviation of "withdrawing room", absurdly Victorian and quite out of date. All the right people have salons today.'

Her husband had answered in amusement, 'Then I belong to the wrong people.'

That had made Hannah smile, the family history of the Frenshaws being well known in these parts, but she wondered, not for the first time, what sort of a background her mistress had really come from. That it was one of wealth (or had been before the recent news) was well known because Cynthia Frenshaw was the kind of woman to broadcast it, but that neither impressed nor endeared her to the housekeeper.

Today Hannah's curiosity was aroused. The unexpected caller seemed very nice – a homely woman in good but undistinguished clothes, grey hair which had never seen one of these 'permanent' waves but was coiled into a neat bun at the back of her head and anchored with giant hairpins, a kindly smile to which one easily responded and an obvious fondness for the child accompanying her. Though unexpected callers were usually shown into the smaller reception room at the rear of the main hall, and only then if they produced satisfactory credentials (the mistress was fastidious about that), Hannah's attention was alerted when she saw 'Mrs Alfred J. Collard' on the visitor's card and guessed at once who she was. As for the young girl accompanying her, a fleeting glance revealed an unmistakable resemblance to the mistress. A niece, perhaps. Undoubtedly a relative.

So the salon it was, with tea and biscuits served in the correct manner. At least Mad*ame* would be able to find no fault with that (as a bride the master's wife had insisted on the French pronunciation the day she arrived). As an afterthought Hannah added some fancy cakes which she knew a child would enjoy. She smiled when the little girl's eyes lit up.

Half an hour later the housekeeper met the master of the house on his return from the potbank and told him that Mrs Collard was waiting in the drawing room.

Daniel was surprised, but pleased. Although Collard was a common enough name, he took it for granted that this Mrs Collard was Brenda, his mother-in-law. At the elaborate wedding Alfred Collard had given his daughter, Daniel had met a mass of people unknown to him and remembered none of them except Cynthia's mother. He had scarcely grasped all their names and couldn't sort out relatives from friends, except his own. Cynthia had never invited her relatives to Dunmore (because some were still loom workers and ill fitted for her new social scale?) and, worse, she was always unwilling to invite her mother. If her father's arrest had made Cynthia think of her at last, perhaps some good was actually coming out of it.

'And she has a little girl with her, sir.'

'A little girl?' he echoed, puzzled. He knew of no little girl in the Collard family.

'About twelve or so, I should think, sir.'

'And my wife? I take it she's with them?'

'Madame isn't yet back from shopping in Leicester.' It was bound to be Leicester, Daniel thought, Stoke and Burslem lacking the really fashionable shops she insisted on dealing with. 'She said I could expect her around teatime, sir, so no doubt she'll be here any minute now.'

The sound of his brisk footsteps and the way in which he flung the door open, wide and welcoming, brought a smile to Brenda Collard's face. She had not seen her son-in-law for years, but she remembered him well and liked him as much as, at one time, she had pitied him. That had been when her husband's covert matchmaking had succeeded and she had looked on, hoping and praying the marriage would not be the tragedy she feared.

'Brenda – I refuse to call you mother-in-law – how good to see you!' A minimum of strides brought him to her side, his hands grasped hers and he stooped and kissed her on both cheeks. His welcome was warm and genuine. She was thankful for that and prayed it would not change when he heard why she had come. She watched him turn to the child with a questioning glance, his fine-hewn face lighting up with the smile which always drew young people to him.

'Aren't you going to introduce me, Brenda?' For the little girl his smile widened, became almost conspiratorial, as if saying, We'll do what grown-ups expect us to do, shall we – be ever so polite even though that means ever so stuffy when what we really want to do is just say hello and start getting to know each other? But the girl had stood up with well-drilled good manners, held out her hand and said, parrot fashion, 'How do you do, sir? My name is Margaret. May I ask yours?'

He was taken aback. Such stilted speech in a child was unnatural and surely the result of training rather than instinct. Even her careful enunciation was unnatural in one so young. It sounded as if she had been taught to speak by some mechanical tutorage. Where did she go to school? he wondered. He also wondered how far he could question his mother-in-law, whose eyes, when on the child, displayed a deep affection. So absorbed had he been in talking to the little girl that he had taken in no details of her looks other than the blondeness and the prettiness of her.

The sound of his wife's voice echoed from the hall, calling imperatively, 'Bradley! Where *are* you, Bradley? Tea at once, for God's sake. Leicester was crowded and I'm exhausted.'

As always, Daniel wished she would not call loyal Hannah by her surname as if she were a menial instead of one of the family, as she had become after years of devoted service. Then Cynthia stood in the doorway, looking as elegant as ever and laden with *modistes'* boxes and bags bearing names of leading fashion houses. He was thinking how quickly a good shopping spree always overcame her bad moods when she stood still abruptly, staring at her mother, aghast.

'*Mamma!*'

The parcels slid to the floor.

'Hello, Cynthia. I'm glad to see you looking so well.'

Cynthia's glance went to the child, enquiringly and then dismissively because she plainly didn't know her, then returned to her mother. She said without warmth, 'I wasn't expecting you, Mamma. Why didn't you let me know you were coming?'

Her mother answered calmly, 'There wasn't time.

The home gave us little notice. They won't keep Margaret any longer because your father can't pay any further fees.'

It was the first time Daniel had ever seen his wife's face blanch. Against whitened cheeks the rouge she used so subtly stood out in bright patches, like a painted Japanese doll. He had a sudden conviction that the two women shared a knowledge of something concealed from himself, and a dawning and incredible comprehension stirred when he looked closely at the little girl. At first he refused to believe the enormity of this comprehension, but the evidence of his eyes compelled him to.

He saw his mother-in-law take the little girl's hand and hold it protectively. He watched Cynthia's eyes swivel to the child and away again, as if denying what she saw.

Brenda spoke again. 'What else could I do, Cynthia? Where else can she go? Everything is being sold. My house and I are safe because when we parted Alfred put it in my name, together with a fund to cover maintenance permanently and gilt investments sufficient to give me a safe income – he has always done his duty by me that way. But you are rich, and Margaret's mother. It is time you took care of her.'

The girl cried, *'No! NO! Don't leave me – not with her! Oh, please, Granny, not with HER!'*

'Hush, my darling – you will be happy here and go to a normal school with other children, I'm sure. You will like that.'

'But I don't know her and I don't like her and I can tell she doesn't like me so please – *please* – don't leave me! I don't care about leaving the home. I know they helped me but I was only happy when you came to see me – someone who belonged to me. When other girls asked if I had a mother I said no and I didn't need one because my granny loved me and that was why she came every Saturday and never missed. So take me back with you now – let me live with you, *please!*'

Compassion cut through Daniel's scorching anger. He sat down beside the child and said gently, 'Margaret, I have an idea. Tell me how you like it.' He put a comforting hand on her shoulder. 'You and your grandmother can both stay here until whatever it is is sorted out.' He turned to Brenda. 'Will you agree to that?'

The woman nodded, scarcely able to speak. The anxiety in her eyes and the strain in her face had plainly been implanted long ago.

He turned back to the little girl 'There's plenty of room here, and lots of things to do. How old are you?'

Stifling a sob she said, 'Twelve.'

'Do you ride?'

Wiping her eyes with the back of her hand, she hiccuped, 'A – a bicycle—'

'I was thinking of a pony. How d' you fancy that?'

A glimmer of interest came to her eyes. They were the same amazing blue as her mother's, her hair the identical colour, the same forehead, and a strong similarity in the chin and nose. He realised that he should have seen the resemblance at first glance.

Pity for this unwanted child possessed him. Outrage against his wife's deception was equally strong, but he would handle that later. This child had been born well before Cynthia married him and well had the secret been kept. The recollection of their wedding night came back to him, and her convincing pretence that this was her first sexual experience. 'You will be gentle, won't you?' she had whispered tremulously as he drew her naked body to his. 'All – this – is new to me . . .' And she had put on such a wonderful act, even shrinking slightly as if apprehensive of what was to come and wincing when he began to penetrate her, even contracting her vaginal muscles to make entry less easy and so create an illusion of virginity, a practice as old as time amongst brides of races whose religion demanded virginity as a prerequisite of marriage and who, unwisely, had been disobedient before it; even, when necessary, procuring small quantities of blood with which to stain bed sheets which had to be presented to rabbi or priest for blessing the next morning.

Who had put her wise to such things? Her scheming and knowledgeable old *grandmère*? Had the old woman recognised the idealism in him and his besotted belief that his bride-to-be was the epitome of purity, and told her granddaughter how to avoid disillusioning him? 'An experienced man can tell whether his bride is a virgin or not, especially if she has had a child. You know the demands of convention these days, so don't jeopardise your marriage from the start, *chérie*.'

Fortunately, the blessing of wedlock sheets had not applied in their case and he, passion-driven, trusting and adoring, had accepted the illusion Cynthia created and had taken her body with infinite kindness. He was ecstatic when she climaxed and cried out how wonderful it was, more marvellous than she had ever dreamed of – 'I've wondered so often what it would be like!' – and in his delirium he had believed her.

Now the memory spun through his mind like a wind laying bare the bleak truth – she had fooled him, cheated him, and continued to cheat him about something more cruel than her wedding-night deception and her later infidelities. But he considered this poor child the greater victim.

When he and Cynthia were alone he would have questions to ask. Who connived with her to discard the child and to remain silent for ever? Who else but her father, with her sad mother subdued into silence? All this stormed through Daniel's brain as fast as lightning splitting the sky. He looked at Cynthia now and said with a calmness he did not feel, 'Ring for Hannah and ask her to prepare two rooms right away – unless, Margaret, you'd rather share one with your grandmother? Alone in a strange room in a house as big as this might perhaps be a little frightening.'

The little girl nodded vigorously and Daniel stood up, withdrawing his reassuring hand from her shoulder. She then clung to her grandmother, turning her back on the woman who frightened her.

But Cynthia made for the door, her littered purchases forgotten. They would be picked up later and delivered to her room. All she wanted now was to get there, but Daniel stopped her. 'I asked you to ring for Hannah. I think the yellow room would be the most pleasant and comfortable for your mother and daughter. It is spacious and has a beautiful view.' He turned back to Brenda and the child. 'I want you to make yourselves at home here, and remember,' he added as Cynthia jabbed a furious finger on the bell, 'you are welcome to stay until matters can be settled happily for the pair of you. You've brought things with you?'

'An overnight bag for myself and clothes for Margaret. We came by train from Nottingham to Stoke, changed there for Burslem, then by bus to Longton and a taxi from there because there didn't seem to be any other way—' Brenda broke off, aware that Margaret was looking at her with desperate appeal. An overnight bag for her grandmother but more for herself held an alarming implication. In an attempt to calm her fears Brenda said lightly, 'I don't need much, darling. I've worn this suit for years and there's still a lot of life in it!'

But the child's anxiety was not lost on Daniel. He said reassuringly, 'Hannah will be along soon to look after the pair of you. She'll see that you're comfortable and happy and make you welcome, too.'

His departing smile for them was kind as he took hold of his wife's elbow and led her from the room. Cynthia felt the firmness of his grip and knew there was no escaping him. In some far corner of her memory she heard an echo of Bruce's voice saying something about his brother's ability to tolerate situations until he had investigated them thoroughly and was ready to act, then to do so decisively and swiftly. 'Don't underrate my brother.' Wasn't that what he had added?

Cynthia steeled herself.

'So who was the father?' Daniel put the question in the casual tone of someone discussing an item of gossip.

He sprawled at ease in her favourite armchair in her private sanctum. The room was nearer than his study upstairs and he had no time to waste. He sat with his long legs out-thrust, his body relaxed. The chair was the one upholstered in pink velvet which she always

337

wished he would avoid when dropping in after a day at the dusty potbank. She knew his office was kept spotlessly clean and free from clay dust, and that when touring the worksheds he donned the protective covering worn by all potters – thereby looking very much on a par with them. At least dear Papa had walked amongst the looms immaculately tailored and markedly distinguished in comparison with his workers, every inch the boss.

She was clutching wildly at any thought to delay answering her husband's question which, despite its note of indifference, failed to mask an impending inquisition.

Stalling for time, she helped herself to a cigarette, inserting it into a foot-long silver holder which her shallow mind registered as being far too short to be fashionable now. Tapering holders of twice the length, some elaborately ornamented, were currently affected, even by some young offshoots of the royal family and their satellite groups of raffish friends who constituted 'the bright young things' of today's so-called Society and could be seen after late theatre hours in places like the Arts Club off Leicester Square. Cynthia wished she could belong to them. Her mind swung from one thing to another, like a drifting balloon and as empty, but she could not escape from her husband's persistence.

'I asked who the father was.'

Cynthia exhaled smoke slowly then inhaled deeply, summoning only a shrug in answer. Her best defence was boredom, but Daniel's expression told her clearly that he saw through it so she had better drop that guise.

Cornered, she said, 'Frankly, I can't remember,' and took another drag on her cigarette.

'You can't *remember*? A man makes you pregnant and you can't remember who he was?'

'I was young. Very young. We all were. It was my birthday party, and Papa indulged me. I could invite anyone I wanted and Mam – Mamma – and he would clear out and let us have the house to ourselves. Mamma was shocked and of course objected, but she was always a wet blanket. Young people were demanding more freedom and going about it in their own way, and who could blame them when shreds of Victorianism still clung to many parents? Edwardianism in the case of mine, which was merciful since the King had established the Edwardian Set with all their luscious scandals and everyone who could afford to aped them – and on a lesser scale if they couldn't. So my father had enjoyed himself when he was young and saw no reason why I shouldn't. 'You're too strait-laced,' he told my mother, and I thought how right he was. So freedom I certainly had, especially that night when invited friends brought along others I'd never even heard of. And all brought bottles – bottle parties were becoming fashionable then among adults so why not those in their teens? Actually it started off as a pyjama party, though I admit I'd hidden that from my parents. You must remember pyjama parties – newspapers like the *Daily Sketch* and the *Daily Mirror* reported the wild goings-on of fashionable debutantes and the wealthy young gangs of 'Debs' Delights' with whom they painted Mayfair red, so why shouldn't we? You didn't have to live in London to enjoy yourself and Nottingham's always been a lively place.

'Everyone had to turn up wearing nothing but pyjamas and then the fun began, swopping tops and pants and then ripping them off each other—' another shrug '—so you can imagine what happened next. They called it experimenting, which really meant "See how many partners you can do it with". I didn't even get some of the names – you know how it was.'

'I can imagine.' His tone was dry, even tinged with something she couldn't define and somehow didn't want to. 'And that is why you don't know who the father was and why you got rid of the child.'

'I tried to do it naturally at first—'

'You mean aborting, a do-it-yourself job?'

She shut her ears to the tone of his voice. 'I mean in ways members of the gang told me about, but all failed. So I had to endure the whole beastly business and my parents had to put up with it. Papa was great, but Mamma, well, you can imagine – all tears and reproaches and protests when he said the child should be put out for adoption. At that, she declared she couldn't bear the thought of a baby being given away, but when it was born something was found to be wrong with its hearing – deafness was detected very early – and my father did a very sensible thing. He found a home for babies with birth defects—'

'A place with qualified medical staff and proper facilities, legally registered, I hope?'

'Oh, yes. I thought it splendid of Papa to think of that. He left everything to them and told me not to give it another thought. It was all over. I was to put it behind me. I was young and would marry well and no one need ever know. He's taken care of everything ever since.'

'Except to bother with the child, as your mother has mercifully done. For you, that was the end of the story

340

and I was the dupe you "married well". What a bloody selfish bitch you are! And what a cheat. I wonder how you feel now you discover your child's deafness was cured and that she would have been no inconvenience in your life?'

'Of course she would have been an inconvenience! I was far too young to be a mother.'

'You are not too young now, but you still don't want her. Fortunately for her, your mother does. Poor Brenda – overpowered by a domineering husband on whom she was financially dependent and an unscrupulous daughter without a conscience. I expect she will be able to tell me how the child's hearing difficulty was overcome – detected at such an early age, I know it can be cured by a variety of methods. I take it little Margaret remained at that home and it was there Brenda has been visiting her ever since. I also take it that Brenda chose the child's name and no doubt saw that she was baptised.'

All this time Cynthia had been inhaling deeply. Now she exhaled a cloud of smoke, stubbed out her cigarette, and snapped, 'How the hell should *I* know? I had nothing to do with any of it and I'm not staying here to face an inquisition.'

'You'll stay until I've finished. Your mother brought the poor child here because of your father's inability to meet any more fees. I gather he's been paying them all these years, still hushing up the fact that his much-admired daughter had an illegitimate child he considered retarded.'

'He could afford to, so why not?'

'That's not the point. As I see it, he must have done it partly to save your face and partly his own. The pair of you obviously thought the child's affliction would be permanent and result in an inability to speak. Deaf and dumb, they'd call it. If a child can't hear sounds it can't hear speech or learn how to utter words until eventually it becomes a lifetime's handicap – and tiresome, even an embarrassment, for people lacking a heart. Your father would have hated it to be known that a man as successful as he had a daughter who had produced what callous people like you would call an abnormal child, and illegitimate into the bargain. I'm sure he dismissed anything his wife might have said to the contrary. The pair of you have always considered Brenda to be stupid. No doubt for that reason she hid the fact that she visited Margaret regularly so the child would know she belonged to *someone*. And now the people paid to look after her send her back to those who should be doing so – and that means you.'

'Me! *I* can't look after her! I don't know what to do with children, never wanted them—'

'I learned that long ago. But now you're face to face with motherhood and we'll see how you cope.'

'We will *not*! I don't want the child, nor she me, thank God. My mother can look after her.'

'You can afford to more easily than she. I made a handsome settlement on you when we married, an independent income and some sound investments. You will support Margaret on that because its your damned duty to and you can well afford it. If you refuse, and your mother takes over, you will still be responsible for your daughter legally. I shall see that my lawyers also make a claim on you for financial responsibility toward your mother for her care of your child.'

Cynthia mouthed incoherently, then raged, '*My*

342

God, what a bastard you are! Do you imagine I'll stay in this place one minute more to be dictated to by you and trapped by a brat who means nothing to me, *nothing*?'

'The choice is yours.'

'Then I choose to leave. I'll live my own life, go my own way, and not a penny I own will be spent on anyone but myself.'

'That means I'll be able to divorce you for desertion instead of adultery. Whichever is quicker will suit me. And as a matter of interest you won't be entitled to alimony in either case. Having ample means of your own, that shouldn't worry you. Adultery cases, by the way, can take infernally long to settle these days, even when the co-respondent is one's own brother and evidence has been rife on one's doorstep.'

She tried to make her laughter incredulous – instead, it revealed panic. 'Cite your own brother! Drag the precious name of Frenshaw through the mud! I can see you doing *that*!'

'You will, if necessary. Desertion would simply be another option. Which I choose depends on you, but I *will* choose one or the other. There is nothing so dead as a dead love, and that's what mine became a long time ago.'

He could almost see wheels in her brain spinning like cogs in a machine. Rapid calculation showed in her eyes. Give up her position as chatelaine of Dunmore Abbey? Why should she? When her father's case was finished and done with, it would be forgotten like yesterday's news and friends would reappear, the social round would be renewed and she would be reinstated as if nothing had happened to isolate her for a while.

People who were generous to charities were always sought after. As for the child, *if* she was forced to keep her she could be passed off as the child of a previous marriage. ('Didn't you know I'd been married before? Oh, my dear, I was very young then, too young for it to work out, and now her father's abandoned her, or gone off with another woman or something, I naturally can't turn my back on the poor kid . . .')

Confidence began to creep back. Cynthia prided herself on being able to handle any situation, so let Daniel make any threat he liked about suing for divorce, or claim that evidence of adultery had been rife on his doorstep. Rubbish! She and Bruce had never been caught in the act and in cases of adultery eye-witness evidence was required by law in the absence of signed confessions. No one was going to persuade her to provide *that*, and she knew Bruce wouldn't be fool enough either. Besides, she could cast a few aspersions of her own . . .

'And what of that insolent Willcox girl you've given a home to? Whenever we meet she's too confident by half – shows no deference to me despite the fact that I am mistress of Dunmore Abbey and refuses to address me properly. She even makes herself at home in the tower room, claiming it's with your permission. I didn't believe her, but now I wonder – do you meet up there, the pair of you? A damned uncomfortable place for an assignation, I should have thought.'

'You are right. I would treat Sarah Willcox with more consideration than to try to seduce her in a room equipped as a workroom for herself and Annabel.'

Cynthia yawned, and rose. 'I must change for dinner. I expect I'll get through it somehow, though my mother's company is always so damned boring.' She sauntered out of the room in her usual graceful way.

Twenty-Two

Two events marked a stepping stone in the lives of Annabel and Sarah. The first was the final removal of the Frenshaw potbank to its new location in Dunmore Park, and the second was Sarah's graduation from student to qualified ceramic modeller.

'*Fully* qualified, and that means sculpturing too,' Annabel told her parents during their usual breakfast chat before she hurried off to work on the day the last pantechnicon left the canal banks and the destruction of the ancient bottle ovens began. The thought that Sarah would soon be working alongside her was stimulating. There had been few shared hours in the summerhouse during the last weeks of Sarah's studentship – she had either remained behind to complete curriculum work after the days' sessions ended, or borrowed volumes on varied techniques from the library to study at home. Sarah had isolated herself and Annabel wondered how Clive Bellingham felt about it. She had not seen them together during these past intensive days, but the thought of any possible rift never entered her head. He might even be responsible for Sarah's incessant work, urging her on because he had 'discovered' her and was determined to justify it. Not that Sarah's enthusiasm needed any urging, but there had been something possessive in his attitude to her for a long time.

The upheaval from canalside to Dunmore's fine new buildings was exciting, but at this precise moment Annabel was full of Sarah's success.

'You'll see why this afternoon,' she told her parents. 'Don't forget we're going to the exhibition of qualifying students' work. I haven't seen Sarah's final model of what she calls her "children" though she did some of the preliminary sketches right here so I've an idea of what to expect. When Daniel saw them he urged her to turn them into her big test piece – pieces, I should say, since she was planning half a dozen. He'll be delighted that his protégée has won the highest marks in her field.'

'As you did in your own category,' Charles Peterson reminded his daughter proudly.

'That's why I'm over the moon! We'll be working side by side, on a par, two professionals in that gorgeous tower studio. Sarah and I have marched in step since the first day we met and we'll be doing so again. *Golly*, it's exciting!' And off Annabel went in a whirl of happiness, feeling that Sarah must surely be feeling the same way despite the renewed anxiety she was enduring over her mother. She had kept that anxiety to herself for days then suddenly burst out, 'I've got to tell someone or *bust*!' And out it had come.

'Gran's been keeping it to herself, but I felt something was wrong and finally she admitted it. It's about my mother, of course.'

Annabel had been in Sarah's confidence about Mabel Boswell's illness and had continued to help by taking Kate to visit the woman whenever she could if Sarah was unable to. So Annabel had been the first to see anxiety on the old lady's face when she emerged from the hospital one evening, but after Kate's assurance that Mabel Boswell was 'doing nicely, thank you, m' dear,' Annabel had asked no more questions. Then a few days later the news came pouring from Sarah on a tide she couldn't hold back. She had never hidden her loathing of Joe Boswell, or her wish that her mother could get away from him, start afresh, be free.

'As soon as she's fit enough to go home, we — Gran and I — are determined to make her leave that man. Our idea was that she should sell the smallholding and buy a place for herself on the proceeds — a good distance away, such as Burslem which she's always missed. And now she really wants to go back to where she has old friends and be happy. Joe Boswell would then have to find somewhere to live within reach of his work, and she'd be rid of him. He's not likely to be taken on by any other potbank at his age, and he's no longer "the finest thrower in the potteries", as he used to brag, so he'll hang on to his job at Frenshaws to the end. If she could be out of his reach, I know my mother would become herself again and the hideous years would be gone. The hospital has almost revived the woman she used to be. She's even helping other patients, like reading to those with bad eyesight and cutting up food for arthritic people who can't do it for themselves. She loves helping and the nurses as well as the patients appreciate it. But what will happen when she's finally discharged, I dread to think.'

'Why? What can happen?'

'Nothing of what we planned! Gran got the truth out of her. Boswell had been nagging her to sign the place over to him, promising to run it properly, and she gave in when she became too weary to resist. And all he has done has been to let it go to rack and ruin until it's practically worthless, but whatever money it could fetch would now be his. She's trapped. That's why she lost heart and neglected herself and endured his bullying until she became ill. If only someone would bump that man off!'

Unfortunately, men like that never get bumped off, thought Annabel as she prepared for work. Jacques was picking her up and she couldn't help wishing that Marie, fond as she was of her, was not travelling with them because every moment spent with Jacques seemed to be increasingly enjoyable. Even important. This bewildered her, because whenever she saw Bruce he would revive some of his old attraction by talking about the past and the things they had done together and even what the future could hold – 'Remember the time we pricked our thumbs and pressed them together to seal a lifelong bond between us?' – and though she laughed it away by reminding him that they had been kids then, he had said, 'Kids grow up but promises remain . . .' To that she had had no answer, but she had felt tentacles from the past reaching out to claim her, and strands of affection still binding them.

Marie had begged a lift. 'I've a heavy box of items I don't want the removers to pack, and they're too heavy for me to carry on the workers' bus.'

'All right, just this once, but none of your non-stop chatter,' her brother had chaffed. 'It can't be switched off like the wireless, alas.'

This morning Marie's lively glance observed a parcel

Annabel was carrying. It was wrapped in tissue paper and decorated with a bow of red ribbon to which a small card was attached. Someday someone should design fancy gift paper, she thought — tissue paper was too flimsy. 'That looks interesting,' she piped. 'Is it a present?'

Annabel admitted it was. 'And I suppose you want to know who it's for.' She laughed.

'We-ell — I didn't ask.'

'Curiosity will kill you like the proverbial cat one of these days,' said her brother.

'Since a cat has nine lives, I've plenty of time,' Marie retorted, at which Annabel laughed again and told her the gift was a tobacco jar.

'Made by you?'

'No. One of Frenshaws' stock lines.'

'Annabel isn't a potter,' Jacques reminded his sister. 'She's a skilled porcelain decorator.'

'But I did decorate it myself,' Annabel said, 'and just to save you further questions, it's for a childhood playmate of mine. We've remembered each other's birthdays since we were kids when we were taught to take presents to birthday parties. We still keep up the custom through habit.'

Annabel hoped Bruce would like it, though she had no idea whether he smoked a pipe or only cigarettes. At least her design of galloping racehorses should appeal to him.

She intended to leave it at the door of his apartment before going up to the tower room, but in the event she forgot. She put it aside to deliver later, then set to work on the first of a series of wall plaques ordered by one of London's West End stores. Instantly absorbed, she was startled when the door leading directly from the abbey opened to admit a young girl who stopped on the threshold and said calmly, 'I beg your pardon. Last time I came here the room was empty, so I thought I would be alone.'

She was blonde, pretty and almost unnaturally polite. Not 'I'm sorry,' or just a casual 'Sorry!' but a precise 'I beg your pardon.'

'Are you wanting to be alone?'

'I don't really mind. My name is Margaret. May I ask yours?'

'There's no law against it.' Annabel expected the child to smile, even laugh, but the solemn face just looked at her, waiting. Annabel laid aside her brush, wiped her right hand and held it out, matching formality with formality, secretly amused by such adult courtesy in a child.

'I'm Annabel.'

'Have you no surname? Mine is Collard.'

That's interesting, thought Annabel. She must be a relative of Cynthia's, Collard being her maiden name – a niece, perhaps, judging by the child's age which must be around twelve or so. Annabel had not seen Daniel's wife since Alfred Collard had been arrested, then released on bail while awaiting Crown Court trial. Until then, as usual in such cases, his liberty was restricted and his passport withdrawn. She wondered if some relations had come to give Cynthia their company and support, though with a husband like Daniel she could surely have none better.

'*Don't* you have a surname?' the child repeated.

'Sorry – it's Peterson.'

'So you are Annabel Peterson.'

'That's right. A friend of Daniel Frenshaw, as are my parents. Very long-standing friends, in fact.'

The little girl's eyes brightened. 'I like Daniel, but I don't like my mother and she doesn't like me. I'm glad we are only staying here. I think it's a beautiful place, but I would rather go back with my grandmother. Have you met her?'

Startled, Annabel could only say, 'Not yet—'

'Then I will introduce you.'

(What adult tones the child used and who taught her to speak so carefully and precisely? More than precise – stilted, like someone who had had to learn a new language.)

Margaret continued, 'I like this room. I found it the day after we came. There is lots to explore in this abbey, it is so huge. Bigger than the home I grew up in. Here I can find hiding places where nobody would think of looking for me – like this room. It is lovely. All big windows, and you can see for miles and miles.'

'Then you must come again. You can stay now, so long as you let me get on with my work.'

'You mean you want me to be quiet?'

'Not exactly, but you mustn't mind if I don't hear you. I get absorbed, you see.'

'*I* couldn't hear at all once upon a time. I was tiny then. But after surgical treatment when I was old enough to have it I was cured and the home took care of me. I went to special classes to learn how to talk. It took a long time but now I hear everything and speak well, don't you think?'

'Very well indeed.'

'May I sit up there while I keep quiet?' She indicated a worktop space and climbed on to it without waiting, but she couldn't keep silent. 'The lake looks huge from up here, but it isn't. Daniel told me it is very deep and I must keep away from it, but I would very much like to sail in that boat . . .'

'I shouldn't try. It doesn't look too safe.'

'Daniel warned me about that, too.'

'Good,' said Annabel absently, and turned back to her easel. With almost unnatural obedience Margaret became silent, but after gazing outside for some time she announced abruptly, 'My mother's husband owns *all* this.'

Her mother's husband? Since Daniel owned 'all this' her mother's husband could only be he, and her mother no one but Cynthia. So the child was not a niece. Annabel clamped down on her curiosity, but couldn't suppress surprise. To be the mother of a child of this age Cynthia must have been married before, when extremely young. That was logical and shouldn't arouse a feeling of concern for Daniel, but the feeling persisted. Why had Cynthia kept quiet about it, or either of them for that matter? She turned back to her work and Margaret said no more, but when Annabel reached a convenient point in the elaborate lotus design she was painting, she called a halt.

'How'd you like to go to the potters' canteen way over there beyond the trees?' she said. 'You can have orange juice or anything else you fancy.'

When no reply came she was surprised to find that young Margaret Collard had gone. Did she walk on tiptoe or have I been so totally absorbed that I didn't even hear?

Annabel cleaned her hands with turpentine, scrubbed them and removed any lingering smell with hand cream. Glancing at her watch, she saw it was lunchtime, and it was then that she saw Bruce's forgotten present and decided to take it down to him before joining Jacques in the comfortable canteen provided for workers.

She picked up the parcel and descended the spiral stairs. Her conversation with the little girl still lingered in her memory; so did her curiosity, though she knew there was no cause for it. Neither was it any business of hers if Cynthia Frenshaw had been married a long time ago and told no one about it. Daniel must have known and to them it was in the past, so to the past she must relegate her curiosity.

There was no need to knock on Bruce's door for it was slightly ajar, as if he had pushed it behind him when returning for lunch but failed to shut it. It swung open at her touch, revealing a hall with double doors at the far end. She called, but no one answered. Presuming he must be over in the main potting buildings, she decided to leave his birthday present on a hall table. Her hand was poised when she heard sounds beyond the double doors. So someone *was* here. Automatically, she opened the doors and looked straight across a room at two naked figures on a couch.

One was Cynthia with her legs apart and Bruce between them, reaching the climax of their desire.

Not until later did Annabel realise she had dropped the gift in her haste to get away. Not even the sounds of shattering china penetrated her shock.

Twenty-Three

The charm of Sarah's exhibit was the surprise of it. Instead of a group of individual children's heads, as Annabel expected since she knew Sarah had been working on several, they were modelled on a slope, like a cluster of cherubs climbing a hill to heaven, some looking up, some down, some over their shoulders, some sideways, as if watching their companions to see who would get there first – except for one at the foot, following the rest with pleading eyes as if fearful that he might be left behind, but in some subtle way all the other cherubs gave the impression that they were ready to give him a hand and that the suggestion of tears behind his wistfulness would soon disappear.

Apart from the originality of the work's presentation, Annabel had never seen such lifelike facial expressions created from clay. She was enchanted and so, she saw, was Daniel, standing in quiet contemplation. Alone, his guard was down and revealed something she had never observed in him before – a suggestion of loneliness which, in so vital a man, was surprising. He had always seemed so self-reliant, a man on whom every employee of the Frenshaw potbank and every estate worker at Dunmore Abbey depended, and who shouldered responsibility for their welfare not only because it was part of his inherited duty, but because he cared about people – except one, that man Boswell. Daniel had once confessed to her father that he would have got rid of him years ago but for union laws which shackled him.

On closer scrutiny Annabel now saw something different from loneliness in Daniel's face, a gentleness which was plainly due to the appeal of 'Sarah's children'. Promptly she recalled young Margaret Collard and her startling news that Cynthia Frenshaw was her mother and Daniel 'her mother's husband' – not her stepfather, which an average child would normally call a second father. Plainly, a secret had been kept for years. Margaret bore her mother's maiden name, not because she was the child of a relative in the Collard family but because she was Cynthia's.

Annabel could not forget the scene she had stumbled on yesterday. To witness something no other eyes should see had shocked her, and in the startling moment when she had seen their entwined bodies she had known instinctively that it was an accustomed practice between them and that casual sex was a familiar thing to Cynthia, long practised, part of her life, and would always be.

In the same instant Annabel's lifelong trust of Bruce had undergone a change. She had always made excuses for his flirtatiousness and for the fact that he had very likely sown what her parents' generation called 'wild oats', meaning a few peccadilloes which mattered little, but the real depth of yesterday's shock was that one brother should be capable of cheating another in such a way. Her affection for him withered.

Annabel told no one about what she had seen,

although in the immediate aftermath she had felt a need to. When she had joined Jacques at the canteen he had taken one look at her and asked what was wrong, and she had said 'Nothing, nothing' so swiftly that he was unconvinced.

'Tell me,' he had urged.

But how could she baldly announce that she had just seen Daniel's wife having passionate sexual intercourse with his brother? The words wouldn't come, but she had reached for Jacques' hand beneath the table and he had said calmly, 'I can wait. Just remember I'm the one you can pour your heart out to.'

Now, seeing Daniel absorbed in Sarah's work, Annabel wasn't surprised that he was alone. It was well known that his wife never accompanied him to artistic events at any level unless celebrities were to be there. Art was no more her cup of tea than it was Bruce's.

Thrusting aside all thought of her childhood sweetheart, she went in search of Sarah. The place was as crowded as on the day when her own design had dominated, but eventually she spotted her friend in the centre of a group, on the fringe of which was Clive Bellingham. He looked impatient, but also stubborn – as if he had been waiting to speak to Sarah for a long time and intended to go on waiting. Then Annabel forgot him when she saw Kate Willcox, her white head held high, unabashed pride on her face and in her eyes. She was with the friendly neighbour she always referred to as 'Pru–next-door', and the two eldest of the young woman's four children, one of whom was Benny. 'Just look at yourself!' his heavily pregnant mother was urging him as Annabel drew level. 'I'll bet you're going to be famous!'

'Not like that,' scoffed Benny. 'All – all—'

'Angelic—'

'Soppy,' he retorted.

His mother laughed and turned to Kate. 'Did I tell you I'm having another? Well, I guess you can tell anyway! I dare say folk think it's awful. "What, *another*?" I can hear them saying it, but I don't give a damn. I adore kids.'

''Course I know you're expecting – see you every day, don't I? Motherhood suits ye well, luv, but don't go overdoing things. 'Twere good of your hubby to let ye use his estate van, an' mighty kind of ye to bring me, but should ye really be driving? Now the clocks've gone back we'd best leave soon so's you can get home afore dusk sets in.'

Pru laughed. 'Don't worry, Kate. I'm not due for another six weeks and, who knows, it may be more than that. I've gone beyond time before.'

Clive had been trying to catch Sarah's eye since the display opened at four, but she was constantly surrounded, mainly by fellow students. Once or twice he lost patience and strolled away, hoping she would notice that he wasn't competing for a chance to talk to her, but whenever he returned there she was, still surrounded and enjoying herself.

He also noticed that Daniel Frenshaw hovered in the offing, looking at other exhibits and talking with members of the Design School board, but always returning to Sarah's orbit. Plainly, he had no intention of leaving yet and that led to a conviction that the man was waiting to take her home. Clive's determination sparked immediately. He had been cheated once today and didn't mean to be again.

Earlier, on an impulse, he had driven to Dunmore to bring Sarah here, only to learn that the Petersons' car had already collected her. He'd had the news from her grandmother, departing at that moment in a forester's estate van with a young woman and a couple of kids.

It might have been disappointment or defiance which made him stride down the side path to Sarah's wash-house, or it might have been unsatisfied curiosity. Whatever the impulse, he didn't regret it, for he had found out something he had not even suspected and which had brought him here in a more than disgruntled mood. So I'll damned well wait, he vowed now, and I'll face her with what I know. When he saw Daniel Frenshaw moving toward her again he deliberately forestalled the man, taking hold of Sarah's arm and pulling her away. 'I've waited long enough,' he snapped.

Taken by surprise, Sarah retorted, 'You want me to be rude to people who are kind enough to congratulate me and wish me luck?'

His hold on her arm remained even when they reached a more private spot, when he stunned her by blurting, '*Now* I know who you lost your virginity to.'

Her face was suddenly still. It even paled a little, so he knew he had hit the mark. He waited, feeling triumphant.

She said at last, 'You can't know. Nobody has ever known, or ever will.' Her voice was low and shaking. Sick remembrance of Boswell's savage attack surged from corners of her memory she had believed to be blocked out.

'You *can't* know,' she repeated. 'No one ever has.'

'Well, everyone will once that piece of work you've covered up in that workshop of yours is finished. You won't be able to hide it then.'

That silenced her again, but not for the reason he imagined. She was hearing the truculence in his voice and looking at its reflection in his face, and vying with her anger was an overpowering desire to laugh. Laughter won and continued irrepressibly until she became aware of amused onlookers wondering what the joke was about.

He said uncomfortably, 'Stop it, for heaven's sake!'

Her laughter subsided. 'So you've been snooping, have you, Clive? When? And what right have you?'

'I've a right to be interested in everything you do, but I acted on impulse. There I was, standing at your cottage gate after your grandmother told me the Petersons' car had collected you, and then she drove off herself with that young woman from next door, leaving me standing and—'

'Feeling rejected?'

'And why not? I don't really know why I took it into my head to go to your workshop, except that I've been curious about that work you keep covered and annoyed because you would never show it to me. I once caught a glimpse which suggested a masculine subject, but you covered it quickly. I notice you've done a little more to it since then.'

'Very little. I've not had time.'

'Well, *I've* had time to get curious, and rightly, it seems. I recognised the basic form of Daniel Frenshaw's features today and guessed at once what he meant to you. You wouldn't have been working in secret otherwise, cherishing it as something precious. *He* was your lover, wasn't he? *He* seduced you. That's why you're wanting to keep his face beside you for ever.'

Her face quivered with laughter again. 'Do you imagine, do you *really* imagine that a man in Daniel Frenshaw's position would fall in love with someone in mine? The idea's so ridiculous I can't help laughing. Socially, he and I are poles apart. He's been kind and helpful, but to him I'm only an apprentice who'll be worth employing now I've got my diploma. Besides, he's married and his wife happens to be beautiful.' Her amusement faded. 'However, you're right on one thing – it is, or I hope it will be, a replica of him, and because I want it to be a good one I don't mind how long it takes or how much work I put into it. I'm trying to model his clear-cut features because they are interesting and splendid to reproduce. But on another count you are wrong – I don't intend to keep it. If it's good enough I want to see it displayed prominently at the entrance to the new Frenshaw potbank – a portrait bust of its Master Potter. And finally there's something else you're wrong about. Apart from the fact that Daniel Frenshaw was not and is never likely to be my lover, he would never have seduced a young girl in the way that I was. I was raped when I was fifteen and a virgin. It was violent and brutal. You are the first person I have ever told about it, except my grandmother, and you are the last. And if you even so much as hint about it to anyone, I shall never in my life forgive you.'

He stammered, 'Sarah – I didn't know – never suspected. Forgive me – please – I beg you to.'

'I suppose I will, in time.'

She walked away, straight to Daniel Frenshaw who still waited where Clive had last seen him, a little apart from everyone.

'I'm proud of you,' Daniel said, and she coloured with pleasure as she looked up into the face of which she now knew every curve and angle and line. Concerned, she saw strain in his face. 'You're tired,' she said, then sensed that the strain was due to something more than fatigue. 'Something is worrying you—'

'Just something rather trying. Something unexpected. I only wish it had happened years ago, but I shall cope. Meanwhile, I have the pleasure of seeing you achieve all I hoped for. You poured your heart into that group of children.'

Clive Bellingham's irrepressible voice interrupted. 'Sorry to butt in, but don't forget I'm the chap who spotted her talent and I'm bursting with pride because of it.' His normal personality had returned. 'I haven't even congratulated her yet.' He kissed her on both cheeks, as if reclaiming a right. None of this passed unnoticed by Daniel.

Clive raced on, 'Let me tell you why and where this model of hers is so clever. She's made it ideal for casting. Minimum undercutting means reproductions can be made in piece-moulds without damaging the smallest part of the original model or dragging off any projecting bits. I estimate that a good mould-maker could do the job in a maximum of six pieces.' He turned to Daniel with a slightly apologetic smile which was plainly meant to be tactful. 'Don't think I'm trying to teach, but I know Frenshaws aren't exactly experts in casting because they don't produce figurines and suchlike, so don't have a modelling department.'

'They have one now,' Daniel said pleasantly. 'Modelling and casting departments have been set up in the new Dunmore premises. You must visit them some time – you may well be impressed. And Jacques Le Fevre's father is relinquishing his job as head of a casting department in Burslem to take the same position with Frenshaws because ours is more up to date. If Sarah is willing to sell her original to us, as Annabel did with hers (the copyrights in design remain the artists') Sarah's group of cherubs will go into production without delay.'

'Then you'll have a winning line. It will boost the Frenshaw name.'

'Sarah's too. As with Annabel, all her work will bear her name. The Annabel Peterson designs have already been launched, the same with Jacques Le Fevre's productions. As for boosting the Frenshaw name, it has been well known for many years but we'll no longer be trading under it exclusively. It will underline the name of Dunmore Abbey Ceramics, each boosting the other.'

Clive was impressed but tried to hide it. Inwardly he felt a bleak touch because he saw Sarah going beyond his reach. Their earlier encounter had done nothing to advance things and he was anxious to repair the rift. Instead, he found himself floundering. To cover it he burst out, 'I haven't yet congratulated you, Sarah, but you must know how much I do. I'm hellishly proud of you, in fact.' Still floundering, he turned to Frenshaw and quipped, 'She's quite a rags-to-riches story, isn't she?'

There was coldness in Daniel Frenshaw's answering

glance. To Sarah he said, 'I saw your grandmother leaving with your nice young neighbour a minute or so ago and I've let the Petersons know I'm taking you home. We'll probably overtake Kate and her party. I must say goodnight to a few people and then, if you're ready . . . ?'

He left Sarah and Clive alone. She wished he had not. Watching his tall figure walk away, she noticed that his limp was more pronounced and was concerned because she had learned, from secret observation, that it worsened when he was tired. She wondered what the trying and unexpected thing he had referred to actually was, and guessed it was the cause of his fatigue and the strain he was unable to hide.

Beside her, Clive said, 'Sorry, Sarah – I shouldn't have made that rags-to-riches remark.'

'I agree. It was cruel, but let's forget it.'

'Can you?'

'I already have.'

'*And* how close we were and could be again – have you forgotten that?'

'I haven't forgotten our friendship, if that's what you mean. It was never more than that, though I know you wanted it to be. I'll always be grateful to you for channelling me into the right work, but I've already told you that. Now I'm going to make a suggestion which may surprise you, but I think you'll realise it's a good one. Find your Carla again. You've never told me much about her, but I think she was important in your life. Go in search of her. You once mentioned that she came to your father's gallery from her uncle's antiques shop in Paris, so why don't you make a start there? I wonder if you realise how often you've mentioned her? I think you hoped I'd be her substitute.'

Pru and her passengers were halfway home when unexpected birth pains began. *They can't be – they can't be – I'm not due for another six weeks!* Gritting her teeth, she drove on, thankful that the children, banked on cushions in the back, were tired enough to be quiet and that Kate was dozing in the passenger seat beside her. She began to time the pains by the face of her luminous wristwatch. Dammit, it was true – every twenty minutes from the first sharp back pain. Don't panic, she told herself. They can go on like this for ages. We'll be home in plenty of time. She thrust aside the recollection of her second child's birth, which had come in a mighty rush. That was unusual and not likely to happen again. She put her foot hard on the accelerator but this estate vehicle was of necessity not high-powered. But the interval between pains became narrower.

The reflection of headlights in the driving mirror dazzled her momentarily. She put up her hand to cut them off and was thankful when the driver behind dipped them, and it was then that a quicker and more devastating pain shot through her, causing her body to jerk and the wheel to spin and the estate van to swerve on to the verge and topple sideways into a ditch. She heard her children's cries and Ben shouting 'Mam! Mam!' as they slid downward and stopped, half overturned. The jolt pitched her on top of Kate. There was a cry from the old lady, and then silence.

In a daze Pru struggled to pull herself up, groping for the door handle above her and gasping as she did so, 'Forgive me, Kate! I hope – I haven't – hurt you—' and from the old lady came a reassuring sound, a sort of breathless grunt.

The door handle was beyond Pru's reach. She managed to say, 'It's all right, kids, we'll get out. Hold on to each other.' Pain lulled for a moment and then came back more fiercely and through the mist of it she heard the following car stop, then pelting feet and voices and the door above her being hauled open to the sky, then a man's arms were reaching down to her and a girl's voice was calling, *'Gran – GRAN!'* Then she heard her own name, but the pains now clutched fiercely and without pause and Pru knew that the child was already close to birth.

To Sarah, waiting beside Kate seemed an eternity after Daniel had rescued Pru and she herself had helped the children to climb to safety and they had all been transferred to Daniel's car. He had returned quickly to Kate, throwing a car rug to Sarah and then carefully extricating the old lady from her trap in the lower side of the vehicle below the steering-wheel. She had borne everything stoically, dazed but conscious. Daniel had put his jacket about her shoulders and lain her gently on the rug Sarah had spread on the ground and now wrapped around her. Then, squatting on the verge, she half lifted her grandmother into her lap and cradled her like a child.

'Kate – are you badly hurt?' Daniel's anxiety sounded in his voice. 'Pru's in labour and I must rush her—'

Kate's thin hand lifted, weakly, dismissing him. She even managed a feeble shake of the head. 'I'll be back for you as quickly as possible,' Daniel threw over his shoulder as he raced away. Then the world was silent until Kate opened her eyes and, with a shadow of her lovely smile, tried to whisper something Sarah could not hear. She bent over the old lady and kissed her, wrapped the rug even closer about her and went on cradling her, rocking her more gently than a child. Kate's eyes never left her face and occasionally she summoned the semblance of a smile, but gradually the eyes became dim and the smile grew weaker. Then her lips moved uncertainly, feebly, and Sarah had to lean close to hear her whisper, 'I'm . . . proud o' ye, lass . . . that proud . . .' Then the voice died and the eyes no longer saw her.

Alone on this isolated stretch of country road, Sarah and her grandmother waited for Daniel's return. Although it seemed an eternity, it was mercifully quick. He called as he hurried across the verge, 'I reached the maternity hospital just in time and an emergency unit's coming to examine Kate—' Then he reached Sarah and saw her face, frozen in grief. He dropped to his knees and cupped it within his hands and laid his check against hers, and only then did her tears erupt.

Carefully he lifted the old lady from her lap, carried her to the car, laid her on the long seat at the back and covered her, then reached again for Sarah and held her close. In silence she clung to him. She felt the power and safety of his body and wanted only to merge into it. His arms pressed her closer and his lips covered hers, not solely in comfort, and she knew in that moment what it was like to want to give herself to a man and that it would be beautiful to do so. And from an unknown distance Kate's voice called to her. *I told you, didn't I, Sarah? I told you you'd know what it would be like*

to love a man and want to be part of him. Beautiful, I said —
remember?'

Twenty-Four

The loss of Kate Willcox shocked everyone inside and outside the abbey. Tenants crowded to her funeral and the potbank closed for the day to enable workers who had known her over the years to attend. The only absent one was Joe Boswell, but his wife was there, looking far from well. Returning to the smallholding because she had nowhere else to go, or the means to, seemed to have undermined the hospital's good work. She looked tired and tragically resigned. When Sarah came and sat beside her and took hold of her hand, she smiled in mute gratitude, but they had no words for each other. In time, thought Sarah, I'll work out what to do for her, but knew in her heart that so long as Boswell lived she could do nothing.

The following day a note awaited Daniel in his study.

'You once said that a daughter should have compassion for a parent who errs and suffers for it, and you were right. Papa has always been there when I needed him, so I should have been there when he needed me. There is little I can do now, but at least I can be a comfort to him as his trial approaches.'

No more. No indication of how long she had gone for. No message to her mother and, of course, no mention of her child. He crumpled the paper and tossed it into a waste basket, feeling grateful for even a brief respite from the constant clashing between Cynthia and her daughter, and Brenda's unsuccessful attempts to reconcile the pair of them. He felt sorry for Brenda, who had wanted nothing from life but the happiness of motherhood and the nice middle-class life of her neighbours. She was awed by the world of Dunmore Abbey, impressed by its beauty and its setting, grateful for the welcome Daniel gave her, but out of her element. Above all, she had a strong sense of maternal duty and could not understand her own daughter's lack of it. She really believed that the hostility between Cynthia and young Margaret could not last.

'It's like a mother who doesn't immediately respond to a baby,' she had said one day, pleading on her daughter's behalf. 'She can be afraid of handling it, afraid of hurting it, but the feeling passes. I'm afraid it's something I just can't understand, but I'm sure that's why Cynthia agreed to let her baby go, believing she really would be better off without her, and doubly so in view of the special care she needed. Since then, alas, Cynthia has had no experience with children, so naturally she was shocked when I arrived with Margaret. I blame myself for not preparing her and I'm sure the two of them will get on better when they really know each other.'

'And if they don't?'

'Oh, dear – do you really think that possible? That distresses me because I did think Cynthia would take to the child when she saw her. Margaret is so pretty and she does need a mother's love.'

'Which she has found with you, but will never find with my wife.'

To hear himself utter the words had surprised him, but they were true. A solution to the problem would have to be found, but at this moment all he wanted to do was sit back, close his eyes and recall the moment when he and Sarah had clung together in shock and grief and something deeper, so much deeper that he had thought of it time and again. He did so now, discarding his wife's note and reaching across his desk to pick up Sarah's early model of a dancing fawn. He often looked at it and sometimes placed it near at hand when he settled in his favourite armchair for an evening drink. It was the only thing he possessed of her.

He handled it now, feeling the crude texture which failed to hide the delicacy of movement in the tiny creature's high-stepping limbs and the enjoyment which had gone into its creation, and then his memory went back to a long-ago moment in the turner's shed at the old canalside place, and a cardboard box containing fragments of discarded pots on which she had experimented, revealing evidence of latent talent. The memory touched him. She had been tense with anxiety, expecting a reprimand; though he had not understood why. Relief when none came had spread across her young face. The picture came to him vividly, along with another near the entrance gates when she had faced up to Joe Boswell's threatening fist, despite her ill-concealed loathing of the man and her clamped-down fear.

And then she had walked away across the potters' yard and he had seen the grace of her coltish young figure and become aware of her approaching woman-hood. She had been gauche and shy and poorly dressed, but she had walked with pride. His eyes had followed her out of sight, that lasting impression of her remaining in his mind. And now she had matured and had responded to his manhood in the midst of her grief, and in that moment he knew that the hideous memories which he had feared were to haunt her for ever had been eliminated in that silent, passionate and mutual confirmation of love.

Later, going downstairs for dinner, he met Brenda in the hall. She said anxiously, 'Cynthia has gone to see her father—'

'I know. She left a note. When did she leave?'

'After the telephone call. Almost immediately. I don't know who was ringing, but it was early afternoon. She packed at once and Margaret helped to carry her bags down. That was a hopeful sign, I thought – that she didn't call for a servant but wanted her child.'

(Or because a servant might ask where she was bound for or, if it were Hannah, display surprise because her mistress had not summoned her to pack her clothes or left any special instructions for while she was away . . .)

'Did she say when she would be back?'

'There was scarcely time, she left so hurriedly.'

'And an incoming call, you say – not one she made herself?'

'Well, I heard it ringing here in the hall and thought I'd better answer it and take a message, and right at that moment she came in from the garden and picked it up so, of course, I didn't linger.'

So she'd left in a hurry, following a phone call which might, or might not, have had some influence on her departure. He now felt that to visit her father had not been her own idea, as her note implied. There could have been some pre-arranging. There was certainly no indication of how long she had gone for, only that she apparently needed more baggage than for a weekend. He recalled dismissing her hysterical vow to leave for ever if she were to be 'trapped by a brat who meant nothing to her', but she had calmed down after that and made no further threats – or any effort to smooth troubled waters of her own making. He had endured this disrupted life with mixed feelings of frustration and anger, combined with sympathy for Margaret and his mother-in-law. And now he was praying that wherever Cynthia had gone, she would remain there.

At dinner that evening Margaret chattered like a magpie released from a cage. She had visited the potters 'over there across the bridge' and was full of the fascination of watching them, especially the men spinning pots out of wet clay on whirling wheels, not one of them telling her to run away as her mother did whenever she intruded. 'But there's one man I don't like. He's big and smiles at me in a nasty sort of way, but he did let me have a try. He even guided my hands—'

Daniel said quickly, 'And how did he do that? And what was he like?'

'He leaned behind me and put his arms over my shoulders, and I must say I didn't like that because he was so close and smelly and his prickly chin pressed my cheek, and I hated it when he squeezed me in front—'

'Squeezed you in front!' gasped Brenda. 'Where?'

Margaret touched the buds of her potential breasts. 'I pushed him away, of course, and the nice man in charge — the chief thrower, I think he's called — came straight across, shouting at him to get back to his wheel and threatening to report him to the Master Potter, but the man only laughed. The man in charge then asked if I was all right and I said of course, and I washed the mud off my hands and walked out. The chief thrower followed and said he'd see me safely as far as the bridge, but that wasn't necessary because I know my way just about everywhere now. He was kind, but I could see he was angry underneath.'

Aghast, Brenda turned to Daniel, but his expression was so tight with anger that she knew he shared her feelings. All he said was, 'Don't worry, Brenda, I can guess who the man was and I shall deal with him first thing tomorrow. It will give me the greatest satisfaction to do so.'

Later, when Margaret had gone to bed, Brenda asked if it was really safe for Margaret to visit the workshops.

'More than safe. Potters are honest, hard-working, decent folk, but sometimes there's a rotten apple in a barrel, which has to be dealt with.' He refilled her wine glass and continued, 'Now we must talk about Margaret's future and face facts. She is happy here only because you are with her. If you leave her to her mother, it will be a mistake. She needs you, she trusts you and she loves you. Facing facts again, when Cynthia returns the situation will be as bad as it has been all along — impossible and, for the child, unbearable. She needs a normal home life. She would get it only with you.'

'But I'm her grandmother. For that reason I doubt if

374

I'm the right person – a generation too old. It's a mother she needs.'

Daniel smiled. 'I'd like you to meet someone named Sarah Willcox. She was brought up almost entirely by her grandmother, following the death of her father and her mother's remarriage. She had a wretched life until her grandmother rescued her from it. Now she's the loveliest and most well-adjusted young woman one could meet.' He added tactfully, 'If caring for Cynthia's child would be a problem financially . . . ?'

Brenda shook her head. 'It wouldn't. My husband may be something worse than a rogue but he has always provided for me. I have a house in a very good neighbourhood and the means to run it. If I choose to sell, it will fetch a high price, so I'm hanging on to it because I know Alfred will be unable to do anything more for me. It may even prove to be a matter of what I can do for him when he is released. What the verdict will be seems plain. Don't think I haven't been considering the whole situation carefully. I am still his wife and he is still my husband and – who knows? – prison may change him. It has been known, I believe. As for Cynthia, I realise that what you say about her is true – she would make a poor mother. One last thing – Margaret is not your responsibility so no offers of financial help, please.'

'You wouldn't be able to refuse if I made a transfer to cover Margaret's care from the income Cynthia receives from me. But that is my concern and it depends on what transpires.'

Brenda said with surprising calm, 'You mean, if she comes back. For your sake, Daniel, I hope she doesn't. For Margaret's sake, and my own because I love the child, I will gladly take care of her. And she has the same surname as myself, which makes it convenient because it confirms our relationship. Every child has to have a birth certificate and in the absence of a father, of course, the mother's surname is registered instead. It is kinder than telling her that her mother didn't even know who he was. And now I'm off to bed. We'll leave tomorrow – it's time we went.' At the door, she turned. 'You're a nice man, Daniel. A fine man. I'm sorry I didn't give you a wife worthy of you.'

'She was the wife I chose, and I loved her at the time. *I* am only sorry you didn't have a daughter worthy of yourself.'

Before he went to bed he went up to the tower room and gazed down on the lake and the cluster of workers' cottages beyond. A light burned in the cottage where Pru and her family lived. Five children now – quite a family, he thought, not without a twinge of envy. She had come home from the maternity hospital with a girl this time.

His eyes then turned automatically to the cottage next door. A light filtered along the side passage. He had seen it frequently since Kate's death and guessed that Sarah filled in solitary hours there, working on something which, the old lady had once told him, was secret. ('But you know me, Master Danny – can't resist taking a peep 'cos I'm that proud of everything she does. And wait until ye see wot this is. Just wait!')

Like a destructive interruption, Kate's words were replaced by some of his wife's. 'Of course, the girl must move out now her grandmother's dead. I'm taking on an additional gardener and that cottage will do for him.'

'Sarah will live there for as long as she wishes. I want her to and as a Frenshaw employee she will be entitled to. You know perfectly well that she and Annabel will be working together in the tower room.'

'Oh – Annabel.' Cynthia had dismissed the name quickly. 'Anyway, I'm sure the Willcox girl will move of her own accord. With money in her pocket she's sure to start hankering for something better. Can you imagine any girl being content alone in a country cottage? She'll be after some eligible young potter, you can bet on it.'

Daniel left the tower room, depressed by the prospect of Cynthia's return. She valued her position as chatelaine of Dunmore Abbey too much to surrender it. She wouldn't risk giving him grounds for divorce; she would return from visiting her father and their sterile life would continue. But life was opening up for Sarah and he must accept it. And he must not allow himself to think about that moment when they had been physically close. He reminded himself that she had been in a state of shock and desperately in need of comfort and help. He had no right to want more.

As for his wife's sudden departure, it could be no more than a whim and her desire to see her father no more than an excuse to escape from the disruptive presence of her mother and the child she refused to accept. He thought ironically that Cynthia would be cold comfort for a man faced with imprisonment and bankruptcy.

On that thought he opened the drawing-room door and came face to face with Bruce, awaiting him.

Twenty-Five

'You know why I'm here, of course,' his brother said calmly. 'Annabel will have told you by now and there's no sense in denial. Cynthia's run away because she's a coward and a snob and can't face the comedown of ceasing to be "lady of the manor". She wouldn't mind divorce as long as you were the guilty party and she could claim handsome alimony. Anyway, after Annabel burst in on us that day she knew the game was up. I saw her as she was driving off this morning and she hurled at me, "Don't imagine your blessed Annabel won't have told Daniel all about it," and off she went, shouting that I was a bloody fool for not making sure the door was locked.'

After the surprise of hearing Annabel's name and the implication attached to it, Daniel studied his brother. Bruce looked suave and self-confident, expensively tailored, unflappable. The suspicion that he was here to make a clean breast of things because he was guilt-ridden was difficult to accept.

'Annabel?' Daniel said quietly. 'What about Annabel?'

'She walked right in and caught us in the act. Don't say she didn't tell you! If she hadn't dropped this . . .' Bruce indicated a bundle beside him, wrapped in torn tissue paper '. . . we wouldn't have heard her, but the breakage came like a crash at a damned inconvenient moment. Shock when you're climaxing isn't a pleasant experience – it destroyed more than her birthday gift.' He spread out the tissue paper, exposing broken pieces of china. He picked up a small card. 'Her greeting, bless her. We've exchanged birthday presents since we were kids – no more than a friendly habit, but I've liked it.' He read the card aloud. "Many happies, for the sake of auld lang syne – your old playmate, Annabel." Bruce sighed. 'I've always taken it for granted that we'd marry eventually, but I suppose that's off now, like everything else. Anyway, it's plain that she and Le Fevre are serious about each other.' He gave an uneasy laugh. 'Am I talking too much?'

'Not enough. Why are you here – to make a clean breast of things in an attempt to clear your conscience, or to get some kind of an oar in first?'

Bruce shrugged. 'I'd no choice. Annabel burst in on us at the worst possible moment, so you have an infallible witness. We didn't hear her come in, but she did and she saw us, so that was that. The game was up. All you needed was evidence of adultery, and Annabel could provide it. It seemed obvious that she'd go straight to you.'

'She didn't. She wouldn't. Not Annabel. Not because she'd take the coward's way out of anything unpleasant by avoiding involvement, but because our family friendship goes back a long way and she wouldn't want to hurt me by exposing something she imagined I knew nothing about. Neither would I drag her as a witness into any squalid court case.'

'I must say you don't seem very concerned.'

'I'm not. I'm relieved. Even grateful. For a long time I've craved release from a marriage that is no longer a marriage, and I now have no qualms about naming my brother as co-respondent since you've confessed without a pang of conscience. There's a convenient way round the situation which should expedite the end without involving anyone else. It will be to our mutual advantage if you take part in it. In fact, I intend that you shall.' There was an undercurrent beneath Daniel's words which began to disturb Bruce. 'You will agree to sign a written statement in the presence of lawyers, admitting your relationship with my wife and any other indisputable details legally required, then you can leave Dunmore and set yourself up elsewhere – in another job.'

'But I've a share in the potbank!'

'Which you are entitled to keep, but with no active participation. I'll be glad to be rid of you. You've never pulled your weight and the new set-up can't afford to carry dead wood.'

'But that department I ran was so damn *boring*!'

'Anything to do with pottery is boring to you, which is why there was no other niche for you to fill. Even so, coming from a long line of established potters, *some* knowledge of it must have rubbed off on you, and at least you know which products are good and which are not. All this is leading to a way of getting rid of you and, if you are sensible, helping you to restart elsewhere. I don't entirely blame you for having an affair with my wife because, knowing her as I do, I'm aware that the seduction wouldn't have been wholly on your part.'

Bruce shifted a little. His expression was wary, his eyes alert.

Daniel continued, 'Frenshaws may seem to be taking risks at a time when other potbanks are cutting back, but I believe that the time to expand is when building contractors are in need of work and free to undertake it, so that's one reason why I relaunched. And I'm not stopping there. I'm aiming for bigger production and wider markets, including lines we've never produced before – for a start, Jacques Le Fevre's splendid creations and Annabel's unique designs for spectacular wall plaques that can also be adapted for decoration on Le Fevre's finest pieces. And now, Sarah Willcox's ceramic sculptures.'

'Sarah *Willcox*? Isn't she the daughter of the fire stoker who was killed?'

'She is. She is also the girl you slighted at a memorable New Year's Eve party.'

'Well, for heaven's sake, she was involved in that awful scene! *And* she was only an apprentice.'

'Even an apprentice shouldn't be slighted. If you saw her now you wouldn't dare. She's a fine modeller and a promising sculptor and she's starting with us tomorrow. Wait until you see her prize-winning group of children.'

'A single group? That means only a one-off.'

'On the contrary, it's so skilfully crafted it can be cast successfully. It has tenderness and tremendous appeal. Displayed in any gallery or shop window it would stop people in their tracks. And that's what I'm leading up to. We're going to promote the work of our three fine artists. Le Fevre's name is already known through arts-and-crafts magazines, also wireless broadcasts and lectures in galleries and schools. We're going to broaden the horizons for all of them.'

'That's all very fine for *them*, and I dare say for you, but what about me? Apart from my rightful share in the family industry, which can't be taken away from me, I need a salary too, but I gather you're kicking me out.'

'Call it that if you wish. You've tried my patience long enough. The present situation is the culmination. It isn't from any sense of brotherly duty that I'm going to help you at a time when it would be tactful for you leave of your own accord. It's a practical solution for many things and it's been growing in my mind for some time. You can listen, and then make up your mind.'

Bruce listened.

'Many of our rivals have run successful showrooms in London, selling high-quality but conventional domestic and ornamental chinaware, of which sales dropped badly after the post-war boom and its subsequent slump. Now the country's in an even worse recession. Some firms are already quitting their quality show-rooms, which means we should have a good choice. Display Le Fevre's work and Annabel's work and Sarah's forthcoming work in moneyed areas – and they still exist despite the country's wavering economy – then work like hell, and Dunmore Abbey Ceramics will be well launched. The name will have greater snob appeal than the Frenshaw potbank. I'll look for a showroom in Bond Street or Knightsbridge or Regent Street. And that's where you come in. You're gregari-ous, you get on with people, though you'd have to learn to do the same with all types – you do that at racecourses, don't you? – so you should get the new start you need.'

Bruce looked almost humbled. 'You're being very generous,' he said.

'I'm not. I mentioned working like hell and that's what you'll have to do. If you don't, you'll be squandering your personal investment. Don't imagine Frenshaws will finance this scheme totally. Your participation will rely on a personal share in it. We're both free to cash any part of our Frenshaw holdings at any time. I've sunk a lot of mine into the present expansion. This is the time for you to do the same and invest in the London end. The beneficial side will be a salary based on a fair share of profits so it will be up to you to boost sales, and stocks of Frenshaw goods will be supplied free of trade charges since it's a family venture. The reverse side is that you'll have to compete with others whom we will also supply – Harrods, Liberty, Harvey Nichols, Waring & Gillow and other carefully selected stores. The choice is yours. Think it over.'

To escape to London. To be one's own boss. To be at the heart of things, not a cog in a wheel and buried in the country. To have no time in which to be bored. To have a challenge. A fight. A goal. Bruce welcomed it, and said so.

'Then we'll set the wheels in motion at once. And when Cynthia returns from visiting her father she'll find you gone.'

Bruce stared. 'Visiting her *father*? She can't be. Didn't you know? It was on the wireless news tonight – he's jumped bail and is believed to have fled the country. A porter at a private air club adjoining that small airport at Croydon recognised his picture today and said he'd seen a gentleman rather like him a couple of days ago, boarding one of those inexpensive cross-channel flights for businessmen run from the private set-up. That was after enquiries had drawn nothing but blanks at main airports. Alfred Collard will be well into France by now – and anywhere beyond, most likely. A man who can get forged documents can lay his hands on forged passports easily enough. No, Daniel, your erring wife is probably erring elsewhere. She had a pile of bags. She's run away, I tell you.'

The summons to the Master Potter's office took Joe Boswell by surprise. It came the moment he clocked in. With his usual cocksureness he smirked in the direction of the man who, he still believed, had ousted him. There could be only one reason for this summons – promotion. He was going to be reinstated and how would the blasted Lefever feel about *that*? Be damned to all those fancy jobs the man was turning out – the Master Potter was at last realising that nothing could compare with the good, old-fashioned pots his former chief thrower had produced.

He was convinced that this summons meant a climbdown by the boss. He relished the thought, also that he deserved it because day after day, week after week, year after year the great Joe Boswell had produced the good conventional stuff people were accustomed to. So now he sneered in Le Fevre's direction. *Now* we'll see who's the better man for the job, *now* we'll see justice done, said his bloodshot eyes, but the Frenchie didn't seem to notice. He was intent on another big job, another fancy sort of piece which nutty members of today's buying public seemed to like but would soon grow tired of. Whoever would want those gigantic things in their gardens? Only million-aires, to stand on terraces or like sentinels beside flights of entrance steps, and millionaires were becoming fewer these days. Even some of the pottery lords in this heartland of the industry were cutting down on production costs and Frenshaws would have to do the same. Surely to God the Master Potter must be realising this, after all his splashing out on new headquarters equalled only by the greats, like Wedgwood?

Mentally licking his lips, because he knew what was coming and couldn't wait to hear it, Joe Boswell cast one last satisfied glance in Jacques Le Fevre's direction, then went to meet the Master Potter.

The new office was more impressive than the one at the old place, but the Master Potter's desk was still the one handed down from generation to generation of Frenshaws – carved mahogany, immense, leather-top-ped, multi-drawered, produced by some skilled crafts-man from the past. With all this lavish spending, thought Boswell, you'd've thought Daniel Frenshaw would've bought one o' them modern desks, all shiny chrome, typical of the twenties and now the thirties. People were mad about that sorta thing nowadays, showing off their money, posh-like.

As before, the floor was covered with hard-glazed Frenshaw tiles ornamented with traditional designs, and very impressive they were, Boswell had to admit. And all the old mahogany cupboards were there, and shelves of files with the same bindings which had lasted for years, and more shelves to accommodate others of recent years, and fine glass-fronted cabinets displaying a much bigger range of Frenshaw products. And the room was twice as big, with a recessed area in which that old black crow still sat scratching at his ledgers. Why couldn't the bugger have had an office to himself, getting him out of the way?

Boswell's storehouse of resentments still included those moments when the Master Potter had insulted him in front of that beak-nosed old bird, downgrading and humiliating him when he had done nothing to deserve it.

Well, he thought with relish, now the moment's come. He'll be eating his words and that damned Frenchie, for all his cock-a-hoop ideas, will be back under my thumb, and the bookkeeper with his high celluloid collar will stop looking at me over his spectacles in that nasty way of his, and the finest thrower in the potteries will be top dog again. And there'll be drinks all round at the old pub where the potters used to gather in the good old days at canalside.

'The Master Potter has not yet arrived,' the crow announced without so much as a 'good morning'.

'That so? Seems he's forgot my appointment.'

'The Master Potter never forgets an appointment and is rarely late. You are early.'

Boswell shrugged. 'I can wait,' he said, and sank his gross body into a deep leather armchair. It was new – not chrome, but damned comfortable. He saw the bookkeeper's disapproving glance, and enjoyed it. He also enjoyed it when the Master Potter walked in and saw him seated there. The man's face was expressionless, but Boswell sensed, rather than saw, his disapproval. What did the man expect – that he should wait to be invited to take a seat? Bugger that, thought Boswell. The pressure of a hip flask boosted his confidence. He carried it regularly now, despite Mabel's perpetual protests. Stupid bitch. He wished that convalescent place had kept her for ever – but no matter, the smallholding was now his and he could kick her out if he chose.

The Master Potter gave him no greeting.

'I see you've made yourself at home, Boswell. You'll be glad of that comfortable seat when you've heard what I have to say.' Turning to the creaky old book-keeper, he said, with the courtesy of one gentleman to another, 'Would you care to take a break, Treadgold? I know you enjoy the canteen's coffee, as I do. Take your time, though I'll have finished with Boswell shortly.'

Good, thought Joe. That means he don't want the man to hear him climb down to me.

When they were alone Daniel Frenshaw said, 'I can see from your face that you think you know why I've sent for you. Let me tell you, you are wrong. I have sent for you to sack you, as I have wanted to do for years.'

Shock was like a hammer on Boswell's brain. He felt the blood rush to his head and his face drain of colour (or as much as its permanent florid hue would allow). He swallowed, he stared, he mouthed incoherently; he felt the walls recede and come rushing back. He groped for his flask with fingers that wouldn't function.

'Mr Treadgold will give you the normal wages in lieu of notice before you go. Don't come back to this office for them. He will deliver them to you in the throwers' shed, by which time you will have cleared your workspace and packed any personal belongings. You are also entitled to know the reason for your dismissal. Insolence and aggression toward fellow workers are only part of it. There is also insobriety and unreliability and, very recently, physical familiarity with a minor which could be classed as sexual. I am also aware, and have been since it happened, of your violent rape of your stepdaughter when she was a young apprentice. You want to speak? Don't try. You will hear me out and then leave this potbank and never set foot in it again.'

'That blasted Sarah! Couldn't keep 'er mouth shut, eh?'

'On the contrary, she has never been aware that I know of it, and you'd get nowhere if you went around trying to spread the story and denying it now. Everyone would believe you were making it up because normally something so vile would have been heard of at the time. Her grandmother and I protected her from that. But your fondling of a twelve-year-old girl yesterday was witnessed by fellow-workers and dealt with promptly by the chief thrower, so there'll be no chance of denial when I report the incident to the union to show them the undesirable type of man you are and name it as just one of my reasons for dismissing you.'

Boswell lumbered to his feet, shouting thickly, 'You can't do it, d' ye hear me? You can only sack a man for bad workmanship – "inferior", the union calls it – an' my work ain't that.'

'It is now. The current thrown ware coming from this potbank is vastly superior to anything you ever produced. You are no longer "the finest thrower in the potteries", as you like to boast. Your senses are too often fuddled and you've learned nothing since Le

388

Fevre took over, but the rest of the men have. They're all way ahead of you.'

'I'll go to the union an' claim unfair dismissal!'

'Go ahead. You won't have a leg to stand on but I'm willing to take on the union single-handed if need be.'

'They won't believe your lies! Child offences! You bastard, I'll deny 'em all!'

'As I've made plain, I'll have no hesitation in reporting the way in which you laid your hands on that young girl because the chief thrower and your fellow workers all saw it and were equally disgusted. There isn't a man among them who won't testify against you because most of them have children of their own. For your stepdaughter's sake I will never reveal what happened years ago, but don't forget that I have known about it all along. I'll allow no traumatic memories to be revived for her. She has a career ahead of her and a talent that will make her name. Moreover, she is adult and self-confident and she has gone out of your life. The next thing to do is to make sure you go out of her unhappy mother's.'

At that, Boswell's bravado returned. 'And what's that gotta do with you? No one can come between man and wife. Only a husband can kick her out. But Mabel's no wife now. She's a mess an' the sooner she goes back to that hospital the better. And she can stay there until kingdom come if they'll have 'er.'

'While *you* occupy the property Frenshaws gave her when George Willcox was killed? It is hers by right.'

A wide, gleeful, vicious grin spread across Joe Boswell's face.

'Not now it ain't. 'Tis mine. She made it over to me.'

'I have heard about that.'

'So she's whined, 'as she? A real whiner, that's wot she is. She don't appreciate the good turn I did 'er by taking over that smallholding—'

'And letting it go to rack and ruin.'

'That don't matter. It'll fetch some sorta price—'

'Which you intend to pocket.'

'It's mine now, so I be entitled.'

'You got it by coercion. We'll see what the law will make of that.'

Boswell didn't know what the word meant but, as on a similar occasion, got the gist of it. He fell silent, but he seethed inside. The world was a bloody awful place, no fairness in it. But this man couldn't frighten him. No one could frighten him! He stumbled out of the swank office and walked unseeingly toward the distant belt of trees which marked the boundary between the new potbank and the private area of the abbey and its parklands. He took a good swill from his hip flask and thought, smouldering, To hell wi' the lot of 'em! To hell with the Master Potter an' his lady wife, lording it over everyone, living like royalty, saying wot we can do an' wot we can't, where we can go an' where we can't, "keep out of 'ere and keep out o' there, you ain't good enough t' mix wi' the likes of us!" Oh, ain't I? I'll damn well show 'em.'

So on Boswell stumbled, heading toward the bridge which marked the great divide, while Daniel remained at his desk, thankful he had at last done what he had wanted to do since Kate told him about Sarah's savage rape.

When Sarah had climbed the spiralling stairs to the

tower room this morning, it had been like climbing to heaven. Today she would be a craftswoman on a par with those whom she had once thought far above her. She was excited beyond measure, happier than she had ever been, predominantly because she would be working for Daniel. She would be within reach of him, perhaps see him daily. From the windows of the tower room she might even see him leaving the west door of the abbey and walking along the lakeside to the distant bridge leading to the new pottery area in its beautiful woodland setting. Visitors and tourists were known to flock to what was regarded as the Wedgwood kingdom; the day would come when they would flock here. Pride in being part of Dunmore Abbey Ceramics filled her.

Because Annabel had further to travel than her own short walk, Sarah expected the tower room to be empty. Instead, Daniel was waiting for her.

'I've come to tell you how glad I am to have you here.' He didn't draw near. He stood with his back to the sunlit windows, silhouetted, broad-shouldered, tall, lounging against a worktop with his wounded leg crossed casually over the other and lightly resting on it – like an unimportant branch of a strong tree tiresomely damaged by a storm but in no way depleted in power.

She was unable to conceal her pleasure but at the same time unable to think of anything impersonal to say. Here they were employer and employee, no more, but she was conscious of greater intensity of feeling than Clive could ever have aroused. Those early stirrings of emotion as their friendship had ripened had been no more than a young awakening, but in the silence of the tower room something far stronger communicated between herself and her employer. It was in the head and the heart and the mind, from where the well spring of love came and from which lasting physical desire grew. It had been there when they clung together in the shadow of grief on a deserted country road, and it was with them now.

He said, 'I must get along to the office, my first task there being something to relish – getting rid of a rotten apple I've been wanting to throw out for a long time. Now I'm determined on it. But I didn't come here to tell you that, only to see you, to make sure you are here. I can't pretend any longer, though perhaps I should, being so much older . . .'

'Gaps in ages grow smaller as the years pass,' she answered.

He took a step toward her, then halted. This was not the time to say what was in his mind, and at any moment they would be interrupted by Annabel's arrival. He turned to the staircase door. 'Now I must go and start the working day with that job I so relish . . .' He spoke with satisfaction, but when he looked back at her she saw more than that in his eyes. There was promise and there was joy, and when the door shut behind him both remained.

At the high windows of the tower room she waited until she saw him reappear below and go on his way. He wore tweeds and a roll-top sweater and thick leather Oxfords. His dark hair ruffled, lifting in the wind, and she remembered seeing early silver threads at the temples and longing to touch them. One day, please, God, let me do more than that . . .

Before Daniel disappeared he turned and looked upward, his face toward her, his hand uplifted, and then he was gone and the door leading from the interior of the abbey opened. Startled, she saw a young girl standing there. She was fair-haired and pretty and there was a disturbing resemblance which Sarah couldn't quite place.

'Hello,' said Sarah, 'and who are you?'

'Margaret. I came to see Annabel.'

'She'll be here soon. We'll be working together from now on.'

'Then you must be Sarah. She has told me about you.'

Then I wish she'd told me about you, thought Sarah as she held out her hand. There was something about this precisely spoken child which made her feel that formality was expected.

'Annabel hasn't told me your surname.'

'Willcox. And yours?'

'Collard. My mother is Daniel Frenshaw's wife.'

Collard. Frenshaw. Sarah couldn't align the two names without realising that this young girl bore her mother's maiden name. She felt she had stumbled on some tangle she ought not to know about, though really it was plain enough and common enough. She suddenly felt shut out from a corner of Daniel's life.

Annabel's feet came racing up the spiral stairs at the precise moment that Sarah was wishing they would. She was uncertain what to say next to this young girl who seemed to pronounce her words so carefully. To bridge the moment Sarah busied herself with a modelling stand and tools, then opened a brand new storage bin and thrust in her hands. It contained porcelain clay of beautiful quality, smooth and perfectly wedged so that no air bubbles remained, so malleable it would be a joy to use. The familiar excitement which accompanied an urge to create took hold of her.

'So you beat me to it,' panted Annabel, bursting in. 'I made an early start, hoping to be here to greet you.' (*I'm glad you weren't . . . so glad you weren't!* The words sang in Sarah's mind.) Then Annabel seized her and forced her into a jig, bubbling with excitement until young Margaret piped, 'Why are you dancing without saying hello to me, Annabel?'

Annabel jerked to a halt. 'Oh – hello there, Margaret. Sorry, I didn't see you! It's just that I've been longing for the day when Sarah joined me.'

'But you have had me.'

Annabel threw Sarah a glance which said, 'Oh, dear, now I've upset her' . . . but took no notice and prepared for work.

'And you won't have me after today,' Margaret added with further reproach. 'My grandmother and I are leaving this afternoon.' Her mood suddenly changed to one of anticipation. 'And we are not even going by train! Daniel is having us driven all the way, so she won't get tired.'

'That's typical of him,' Annabel said as she fixed prestretched watercolour paper on to one of her biggest drawing boards.

'So I've time to go and and say goodbye to Daisy,' Margaret went on. 'She is nice though she does speak very badly, but she can't help that. She is poor and didn't have speech therapy, like I did. My grandfather paid for all that when he put me in the special home. When the matron told me years later she said how generous it was of him, but a nurse told me it was the least he could do since he never bothered to visit me

and it was included for the speech-handicapped anyway.' Margaret's mercurial mind flashed away again.
'Can you *imagine* – poor Daisy was a potter's apprentice
when she was little older than I am, and now all she
does is odd jobs about the place, but she says she
doesn't mind because she's no good at anything else.'

Sarah cried, 'Daisy! D'you mean Daisy Wilkins? I
knew her well and I'd love to see her. Wait while I get
this clay off my hands and I'll come with you.'

'I'll go ahead. I know the way. And I have to hurry.'
The door to the spiral stairs closed behind her.

'If you're wondering who she is,' said Annabel, 'she's
Cynthia Frenshaw's daughter.'

I should have seen it, Sarah thought, recalling the
vaguely puzzling resemblance.

'I didn't know she'd been married before.'

'It seems she wasn't and that's why she has Cynthia's
maiden name. That's all I know, except that I'm glad
Cynthia has gone and I hope she doesn't come back. I
think it's about time Daniel had some happiness in his
life.'

Sarah's heart stumbled. Her thoughts had been with
Daisy, who had once been badly in need of help and
still seemed to be. If a potter's skills were beyond her,
other clay skills might not be. Her small hands might be
well adapted to ceramic flower-making, petal by petal.
I'll teach her and then show the results to Daniel, she
was thinking just as Annabel's words snapped the
thread.

Gone? Daniel's wife *gone*?

They worked in silence until Annabel glanced at her
watch and said, 'Time for coffee! Let's go. It's great stuff
over at the canteen.' Wiping her hands on a turpentine

rag, she finished, 'I expect we'll meet young Margaret on her way back now.'

And by now Daniel would have completed the task which he had anticipated with such undisguised satisfaction. Sarah wondered what it was, and how soon she would be lucky enough to see him again. She cherished the thought that he had waited for her in the tower room.

'Ready?' asked Annabel, holding ajar the door to the spiral stairs. Sarah was scrubbing the last traces of clay from her hands, her back to the window. Now she dried them, turned round and reached across the wide worktop to pick up her purse. Then she froze and in a strangled voice cried, *'Boswell! Dear God, what is he doing down there with that child?'*

When Boswell left the Master Potter's office he walked blindly, enraged, swearing vengeance, ready to wreak it on the first person he met. Cursing the whole Frenshaw clan to hell, he struck out toward the forbidden territory surrounding the abbey. 'The Holy Land!' he yelled, uncaring who heard him. 'The damned Holy Land where the likes 'o me must fear to tread! But *I* ain't afeared of any blasted Frenshaw an', by God, I'll prove it!'

From the worksheds he stormed across the east paddock allotted to the workers for recreation and made for the bridge over the stream that marked the forbidden boundary. He relished the echo of his stamping feet on the solid boards, defiance in every step, fury in every heartbeat, hatred in every heaving breath. And then he saw the lake, and the boat moored at its edge, and the figure of a young girl walking ahead of him, blonde hair down her back and the body of a young sylph, and he remembered the feel of her budding breasts beneath his fingers and exultation welled up in him. Carefully, he stepped from the bridge on to soft grass, avoiding the hard path so that his footsteps were unheard.

He caught up with her just as she was approaching the moored boat. It was floating a foot or two from the lake's edge. With an out-thrust foot he pulled it closer, grabbed her from behind and held fast. When her screams pierced the air he laughed and whispered in her ear, 'Come for a sail, little lass . . . just the two of us . . .'

The boat rocked uncertainly but his strong leg anchored it. Still clutching her he stooped and released the mooring rope, then had to strain harder to hold the vessel because she fought like a tiger, striving to claw at his face, kicking wildly and helplessly. He revelled in it. The more she screamed, the louder his laughter. 'You'll enjoy it, little lass – I'll not let ye go overboard – ye'll be safe in my lap!' Her screams now mingled with terrified sobbing and his laughter bellowed, so loud that his ears were full of it, blocking out the sound of racing feet and a young woman's voice shouting, *'Let go of her – you swine!'* Then other feet pounded on the hardcore and arms reached for his victim at the exact moment that blows struck the back of his head and neck and shoulders so that his arms went limp, releasing her, and his foot on land toppled toward his other. Collapsing into the boat he had a flashing glimpse of Sarah Willcox, her face ablaze with hatred as she poised a hunk of timber to strike again while the Peterson girl clutched the child. Then through his stupefied brain came the sound of breaking planks as the boat drifted to the centre of the lake . . . broke up . . . and sank.

The mighty Joe Boswell could not swim.

Twenty-Six

It was a few weeks since Mabel Boswell had inherited 'all of which her husband died possessed' and found herself once more the owner of what had rightfully been her property in the first place. Apart from that, the man had left nothing but that old nag stabled in a stinking shed which he had never made any attempt to clean up.

Unfortunately, she had also inherited the mess in which he had left the land which he had sworn would flourish in his hands. Bad as it was, she was thankful to get it back, though she faced the fact that no one in their right mind would consider buying it now, any more than anyone would buy the dilapidated cottage. 'Best demolish it and get rid of the land,' a neighbour had advised in mournful tones. 'At least ye'd get *summat* for that.' It was the sort of advice old Kate Willcox would have handed out in the days when she was not the friend she turned out to be later, visiting her regularly in hospital and never referring to Joe Boswell or even murmuring 'I told you so.'

But as for selling the smallholding, Mabel could see with half an eye that she would be lucky to get the price of a song for it. Sitting in the rotting porch one day she faced facts. The land needed more than tilling and replanting; it needed extensive uprooting, and surgery for fruit trees that no longer bore, and every other mortal thing she could think of, the least of which was putting the cottage in order and making it presentable so that it would at least catch the eye at first glance. As for selling it, Mabel hadn't the faintest idea of how to go about it, though she longed to.

So I'd best find out, she decided, common sense at last taking over. Looking facts in the face now spurred her into action. I'm ashamed for Sarah to see this place, she thought, and immediately recalled her daughter's efforts to restore order to the living room, the last time she had come, and her own half-hearted protest that it was a waste of time, whereupon Sarah had sparked, 'Nothing is a waste of time if you want it badly enough and I can't believe you don't!' And, with that, left her to it. She also left a batch of fresh cleaning materials and a present of some pricey shampoo.

It was the shampoo that really began Mabel's journey back to a normal life. Convinced that she was only using it to please Sarah, she felt a surprising sense of well-being afterwards, when she beheld a transformation in her mirror – a head of shining white hair. Clean and shoulder-length, with a slight wave in it, it looked almost like that new page-boy bob featured on the covers of women's magazines she saw on the stands but never bought. She was about to brush it when she saw that the hairbrush was clogged with a mixture of brittle red hairs mixed with dirty grey. They must have been there for ages because Joe had denied her money for hair dye a long time ago.

The sight made her shudder. Like everything else in the place, that hairbrush needed a thorough cleaning, and her thoughts went back to the small home in Burslem in which she and George Willcox had lived and loved. Hard up though they were, she had kept it spick and span, the windows washed, the curtains crisp and clean, the floors spotless, and their clothes well cared for.

Spurred on by shame, she tied a scarf over her hair and set to work. It took all of three days to clean the house and when she had dealt with the inside she began on the outside. The first job to tackle was the dilapidated porch. To that she took an axe lying discarded on a heap of rubbish at the back of Joe Boswell's shed. Stroke by stroke and blow by blow she attacked the crumbling timbers. Not until the job was done did she notice that she had left the shed doors open and that his old nag had wandered off as if he knew the man he had served had gone too, for the beast would never have dared to roam had Joe been there. If it comes back, Mabel decided, I'll tie a rope round its neck and lead it to the Saturday market and see if I can find a home for it.

She was tired but exhilarated when her campaign was finished. Pieces of furniture which Joe had smashed or damaged in periodic rages were piled on the heap of rotten porch timbers. Now to get rid of that foul shed, she thought. She was standing by the open doors, wondering how and where to start on it, when a truck halted in the lane and a couple of men descended. 'Want to get rid of all this?' the first one said. 'We'll do the clearing first and then come back and get on with the other jobs.'

She stared. They were workmen and seemed honest

enough but, all the same, a woman on her own had to be careful . . .

'What other jobs?' she asked suspiciously.

'Clearing the land, then giving it a good going over with a hand plough – same as we do every season on patches of Dunmore Park. It's plain ye can't do it on your own, lady. Some other blokes'll be along to do the house decorating soon as ye say when. No use putting something up for sale without it looking at its best, is it?'

'How do you know – and what – and who is behind all this?'

The first man shrugged. 'We takes our orders an' asks no questions, lady. It's the sorta thing the boss often does – if he hears of someone needing practical help, he sees they get it. An' your daughter works for 'im at the new pottery premises, don't she, so maybe he heard through her.'

The men had loaded half the rubbish when Sarah arrived. She propped a bicycle by the gate and called, 'I've brought lunch for both of us!' Mabel noticed that she no longer called the midday meal "dinner", the way working folk did. But a lot about Sarah was different from the old days. She didn't even speak the same, which made Mabel feel proud in an odd sort of way. Dear George would have liked it, too.

Sarah took one look at her mother's shining hair. 'It's beautiful, Mam' – the old term put Mabel at ease again – 'I wish Dad could see you now.'

'Aging and white-haired? Would he recognise me, d' ye think?'

More easily than he would have done a while ago, Sarah wanted to say, but answered, 'He would be aging and white haired as well, don't forget. And now let's eat. Pru packed this for us. Five children and a husband to look after, and she stopped to pack this when she heard where I was going! Life will be easier in the bigger forester's house the Master Potter is moving them into. By the way, she sends an invitation to the christening on Sunday week. And what d' you think the baby's to be called? Kate. Pru loved the old lady.'

'But wasn't it her fault that Kate was—'

'No. It was not. Time and babies come when they're ready, I told her when I saw she was blaming herself, and Gran wouldn't have had it otherwise. Now let's go indoors and eat and then I've something to tell you—' Sarah stopped dead where the old porch had been, and again inside, but all she said was, 'My goodness, you've been busy. You must feel great after it.'

Mabel admitted that she did feel pretty good and asked if it was true that the Master Potter had sent those men along, and how had he known she needed help? 'Was it through you, Sarah? Do you really know him well enough to ask a favour of him?'

'I'd no need to ask. He drove past here yesterday and saw the signs and guessed what was going on. First thing this morning he asked if you were planning to move and I said I certainly hoped so but, never having sold property, I doubted whether you knew how to go about it, and that brings me to what I came to tell you. An estate agent from Burslem will be coming to see you and everything will be put in hand – including finding you a place there. You've always wanted to go back, haven't you?'

Mabel nodded, too overcome to speak. When her daughter's hand reached across the table she grasped it, and the tears she had not shed for Boswell flowed in gratitude now.

From a balcony of a luxury hotel set high in El Laquito, Cartagena's rich area of skyscrapers and casinos and epicurean restaurants, Cynthia Frenshaw viewed the old walled city and, beyond it, the fine residential district of La Manga where, from tomorrow, she would live as the wife of Dom Pedro Felipe de Barajas in one of the area's most magnificent mansions. Complacency was back on her elegant shoulders. Inwardly, she purred.

Her journey to this place of emerald millionaires had started from the moment she had received the telephone call for which she had waited so impatiently, confirming that her bank accounts and all personal investments had been transferred from Stoke-on-Trent to a leading bank in Panama in accordance with her instructions, thereby speeding her departure from the dull respectability of Midlands England and the unpleasant prospect of being the guilty party in a divorce case from which she could not fail to emerge the loser.

Relief and optimism had accompanied her on the Queen Mary to New York – five days of first class luxury travel across the Atlantic, making the most of every moment and every useful contact. She had been on the high seas for three days when her father had made a less comfortable journey from some one-eyed airport outside London, about which she knew nothing until listening to a daily international news bulletin broadcast aboard. She thanked God that her excuse of wanting to visit him had been so well timed, exactly when dear Mamma's company was boring her to death and that child nothing but a nuisance and an embarrassment. Even more importantly, it enabled her to get away before Annabel Peterson provided the eyewitness evidence (which she undoubtedly would, the bitch) that would defeat all hope of alimony from a divorce case she now could not hope to win.

Later, in New York, she had picked up a copy of *The Times* and read further details of her father's escape. She wished him luck, wherever he was. It was through him that she had first heard of the Caribbean port of Cartagena and its legacy of piracy and plunder and accumulated wealth. 'It's one of the places to head for these days – one of the richest sources of emeralds,' he had said. The other was Brazil. Would he head there? 'A man can hide in the Brazilian mountains or in the rabbit warren of Rio, a place rich in financial pickings.' She remembered his words now and wondered which he would choose.

That was the last thought Cynthia spared for the life she had left behind, for Cartagena was proving all she hoped for, though it had taken her more time than expected to reach here. She had dallied for a year in New York, but without success, for the competition was too great in a place where elegant women were the rule rather than the exception. But Cartagena, thank God, proved to be her El Dorado. A woman as blonde as herself and as good-looking as herself and as well dressed as herself caught the eye in a city of dark beauties. She was also poised and self-confident and (when she chose to be) dignified. She looked unattainable and took care to remain so until she settled on the right target.

Dom Pedro Felipe de Barajas caught her eye in one of Cartagena's leading casinos. He looked, and was, aristocratic. His ancestry could be traced back to the family after whom the once impregnable Castillo de San Felipe de Barajas on the summit of the San Lazaro hill had been named. Cynthia had done her homework before responding to the glances he focused on her night after night in the casino.

She was waiting for him now. Latin Americans seemed to have little sense of time. She supposed she would have to get used to their *mañana, mañana* approach to life, though when it came to making money here in Cartagena the wealthy ones didn't let the grass grow under their feet. And that, thank God, included Pedro.

Idly, she picked up a discarded newspaper. It was English and somewhat out of date, but the first thing that caught her eye was a front page photograph of a bridal group on the steps of London's Caxton Hall following the civic wedding of 'the pottery lord, Daniel Frenshaw, and his young bride, formerly Sarah Willcox, the talented ceramic artist who sculptured the portrait bust of her husband which stands at the entrance to the impressive headquarters of the family's century-old industry.'

My God, she's done it, thought Cynthia. An uneducated apprentice from the pottery sheds who would have been lucky to become a working potter's wife, finishing up by marrying the boss – and a pottery lord at that! Grudgingly, she had to admit that the girl looked striking in what was obviously a Schiaparelli model. She wore it superbly. Why did I stick to Worth? Cynthia thought sourly before scanning a picture of wedding guests, some of whom she recognised – the Petersons and their daughter, who was standing hand in hand with a good looking man whom she was startled to recognise as the one with a French name whom she had rather fancied herself at a long-ago New Year's Eve party in the abbey. She also recognised that tutor from the Design School whose grandfather had turned out to be a famous artist. His arm was thrown possessively round the shoulders of a sophisticated young woman quite unknown to her.

She read on.

> Daniel Frenshaw is the hereditary heir to Dunmore Abbey and the family pottery industry, now known as the Dunmore Abbey Ceramics company which rivals Wedgwood and other big names in the Potteries. Dunmore products are exceeding demands in the company's Bond Street showrooms and their exports are increasing worldwide.

And when did they open London showrooms? *I* knew nothing about them, Cynthia thought, remembering how she had longed to be part of the London scene. With a husband's flourishing business represented in the heart of the West End, a London home at a fashionable address would surely have been inevitable, despite Daniel's affection for the place of his birth.

Petulantly, she tossed the newspaper aside but when she saw Pedro coming toward her she brightened. He wasn't as striking as Daniel, being rather swarthy and somewhat shorter and might even become portly if she didn't keep an eye on his diet, but when he smiled his teeth flashed and his dark eyes glowed. And tomorrow she would be his wife, living with him in that La Manga mansion. How could a pottery lord compare with an emerald millionaire?

Pedro's eyes were glowing now and she responded until she saw he was not alone. A group of Latin-American children stood behind him, looking for all the world as if they were shyly waiting to be presented. Nephews and nieces, no doubt. He was unwed and therefore without children – and would remain so; on that she was resolved.

With a flourish, he presented them. 'My *niños*,' he said proudly. 'Their mother died in childbirth, alas, but tomorrow, my lovely Cynthia, we will marry and have more babies, you and I, yes?'

No! she wanted to scream. The complacency vanished from her elegant shoulders. She no longer purred. Her every feline instinct was to bare her teeth and hiss. Instead, she turned tail and headed for Reception to book the earliest possible departure to Rio. In her handbag she had a small sheaf of cards acquired on board the Queen Mary. One had been pressed into her hand by a Brazilian gentleman whose Rio address sounded impressive. He had looked affluent and his spending had matched. Slightly aging ... but he seemed like a good start.